ISLAND

PENDULUM
COVE

mount
pond

WHALERS
BAY

NEPTUNE'S BELLOWS

MOMENTICON

Also by Andrew Caldecott

MOMENTICON

Andrew Caldecott

Illustrated by
Nicola Howell Hawley

Jo Fletcher
BOOKS

First published in Great Britain in 2022 by

Jo Fletcher
BOOKS

Jo Fletcher Books
an imprint of
Quercus Editions Ltd
Carmelite House
50 Victoria Embankment
London EC4Y 0DZ

An Hachette UK company

A CIP catalogue record for this book is available
from the British Library

HB ISBN 978 1 52941 542 1
TPB ISBN 978 1 52941 543 8

10 9 8 7 6 5 4 3 2 1

Typeset by CC Book Production
Printed and bound in Great Britain by Clays Ltd, Elcograf S.p.A.

Papers used by Jo Fletcher Books are from well-managed forests and other responsible sources.

For Chloe

CONTENTS

LIST OF ILLUSTRATIONS
by Nicola Howell Hawley

'It's shaped like a croissant.'
Endpapers

One troubling piece of evidence nagged away.

4

Memories of that book flooded back.

15

The Tempestas sigil.

43

Is it fighting to keep its head above water or a quicksand?

73

He wore a powder-blue jacket.

126

A horseman trotted into view.

136

Hunting and traps: had Man's predatory treatment
of Nature been a root cause of the Fall?

146

AUTHOR'S NOTE

Paintings and artefacts from the Museum Dome feature in this story in unconventional ways. They appear below in order of appearance, with their and their creators' old-world dates and the old-world places from where they were retrieved. The reader will recognise fragments of some from the cover and in Nicola's delightful drawings.

Wheatfield with Crows (1890): by Vincent van Gogh (1853–1890), Van Gogh Museum, Amsterdam.

The Water-Lily Pond with the Japanese Bridge (1899): by Claude Monet (1840–1926), The National Gallery, London.

The Death of Marat (1793) by Jacques-Louis David (1748–1825), Royal Museum of Fine Arts, Brussels.

The Art of Painting (1666–8): by Johannes Vermeer (1632–1675), Kunsthistorisches Museum, Vienna.

Through the Looking-Glass and What Alice Found There, (published 1871): illustrated by John Tenniel (1820–1914), original woodblocks in the Bodleian Library, Oxford.

The Dog (1819–1823): by Francisco Goya (1746–1828), Museo del Prado, Madrid.

The Hunt in the Forest (c1470): by Paolo di Dono (known as Uccello, 1397–1475), Ashmolean Museum, Oxford.

The Hunters in the Snow (1565): by Pieter Bruegel the Elder (c1525–1569), Kunsthistorisches Museum, Vienna.

Winter Landscape with Skaters and a Bird Trap (1565): by Pieter Bruegel the Elder (c1525–1569), the Royal Museums of Fine Arts of Belgium, Brussels.

La Gare Saint-Lazare (1877): by Claude Monet (1840–1926), Musée d'Orsay, Paris.

Boulter's Lock, Sunday Afternoon (1885–97): by Edward John Gregory (1850–1909), the Lady Lever Art Gallery, Port Sunlight, the Wirral.

The Circus (1890–91): by Georges Seurat (1859–1891), Musée d'Orsay, Paris.

The Calling of Saint Matthew (1660): by Michele Angelo Merisi da Caravaggio (1571–1610), San Luigi dei Francesi, Rome.

A Cottage in a Cornfield (1817): by John Constable (1776–1837), National Museum Cardiff, Cardiff.

The Garden of Earthly Delights (right-hand panel of the triptych, detail, 1490–1510): by Hieronymus Bosch (c1450–1516), Museo del Prado, Madrid.

The Card Players (1892–6): by Paul Cézanne (1839–1906), The Courtauld, London.

Totem-pole from Haida Village, cedar wood, British Museum, London.

The Uxe totem-pole, provenance and wood unknown.

I
CHOOSING THE CANVAS

I

Fogg

Dead centre on the Biedermeier table below Monet's lilies (a 1919 version, painting no. 184) lay a largish white pill stamped with a pink sickle moon and an amber star. Fogg picked it up. Who had put it there? What did it do? He peered up at the ceiling, whose erratic pattern of metal joists and panels looked unchanged. Anyway, pills don't drop from ceilings.

The pill looked at him, and he looked at the pill. *Dare you*, whispered the pill.

He carried it down to Reception and examined it through his magnifying glass. An ordinary pill, but for the weight and the mysterious markings. He reflected on the coming anniversary and the lack of incident in the Museum's last three years. Wherever it had come from, whatever it did, surely the pill was meant for him.

But might it be poison? Was his position as Curator about to be terminated by some unseen governing presence?

He weighed the evidence. Behind Reception in the Museum Dome a small screen displayed a message with a sting in the tail:

```
Time since Opening: 2:364:09:54
           Visitors: 0
```

Tomorrow would be the third anniversary of his arrival at this last repository for Man's most treasured artefacts, but it had never had a visitor and he had never delivered his over-rehearsed opening spiel to anyone. More to the point, there had been no hint of his being watched or assessed. Nor could any fair person hold him responsible for the dearth of visitors.

Outside, toxic ochre dust swirled and settled as it always did. Without the chitin shield, the Dome would have disintegrated, just as the world's cities had at the Fall. There was no play of light, or even a visible sky, for the Earth's private star had long been banished from view. The Dome was an ark and the paintings its cargo, even if this Noah had neither crew nor family.

Nor, he reflected, had he transgressed. His regime had been orderly to a fault.

Today, like every other day, he had completed his exercise routine in the anteroom between his bedroom and the Museum proper on the dot of eight o'clock. He had hurried through a breakfast of bland but nutritious paste from the Matter-Rearranger and completed his ablutions by 9.30 precisely. Thence to the daily robing which justified his unique existence: the donning of the Curator's uniform. He had smoothed the dark flannels over his thighs, straightened any threat of a crease in the cream shirt and stretched his arms through the sleeves of the *pièce de résistance*: the dark green jacket with brown piping, the material more velvet than cloth. He had straightened the tie, checked the gleaming toecaps of the black, laced brogues and combed his thatch of straw-coloured hair before adding the Curator's cap.

So far, so good.

But one troubling piece of evidence nagged away. Fogg had an eye like a spirit level and that morning Van Gogh's *Wheatfield with Crows* (painting number 211) had been out of true.

The Museum Dome gave access to its many wonders by an Escher-like maze of escalators, landings and walkways. Each escalator moved as a foot landed and halted when there was no weight left to carry. They shut down after hours. Energy conservation must have been a priority in the last days. Every escalator ascended, save for the topmost, which twisted from the final landing around a central support like a helter-skelter. You had to travel through the whole Museum in order to leave.

On his first days here, Fogg, still just shy of his twentieth birthday, had devised a route which passed every exhibit once and no exhibit twice. He had never deviated since. The hanging had been done before his arrival by persons unknown, but he liked the idiosyncratic mix of time and subject. Wooden furniture stood beneath modern abstracts; Old Masters hung over steel and glass; two totem-poles rose from floor level. Fogg ensured that every item was always in perfect alignment in itself and with its neighbours. He abhorred deviation.

One of the two totem-poles had a tendency to bleed dust from time to time, which he instantly cleared. He abhorred untidiness too.

The previous evening *Wheatfield with Crows* had shown no sign of misbehaviour. He wondered if a floor beam had shifted in the night, but the mainframe said otherwise.

An inexplicable knock, and an inexplicable pill.

What the hell.

He drew a glass of water from the Matter-Rearranger and downed the pill.

His surroundings vanished. He was facing a white-painted foot-bridge which curved over an expanse of real, unpolluted water. Twin rails supported a pergola smothered in spikes of purple flowers.

Fogg had never seen real vegetation, let alone blossom. He had never heard Nature's music. Whether these mysterious sounds were the calls of birds or frogs or some other creature, he could not tell.

He stood beside the artist, unnoticed, and by some miracle shared the old man's thoughts.

Waterlilies are a special pleasure. They float, detached from the common silt of experience, and their explosions of colour – cream, carmine, pink and yellow – shimmer and reflect in an ever-changing light show. Lilies open; lilies close; the surface of the water plays to the wind and the light cools, burns, fades, intensifies. Clouds burgeon and dissipate.

Fogg was so rapt in this borrowed experience, joining another man in an era before the Fall, that it took time for him to register that the painting taking shape in front of him was now in his Museum.

As recognition dawned, the scene melted, colours running as if sluiced in white spirit; and he was back. The experience had brutally exposed his present surroundings as silent and drab; natural colours surpassed the richest any of his paintings could offer. Worse still, the old man had tantalised with the prospect of human company. Three years and no visitors! He must be the last man standing.

Only then did the most significant fact strike home: the pill had been placed beneath the very painting whose world it had opened up. That had to be design, not accident.

He rushed round the Museum, hoping to find another, to no avail. To date Fogg had faced only the puzzles which the exhibits themselves presented. The mainframe carried out the menial roles – lighting, waste disposal, escalators, heating – and the Matter-Rearranger provided nutrition and beverage. Neither made pills. He toyed with various explanations. The pill had been a hallucinogen, or an educational device. Perhaps one would appear each day beside a different picture. The other possibility, that he really had been drawn into the very moment of painting, he dismissed as absurd.

As his rituals resumed, anxiety eased. Copying from memory with faultless accuracy was his particular gift. He spent every afternoon seated at Reception, reproducing as a drawing one of the Museum's paintings. At six, he downed his pen and checked the readings for humidity, toxicity and moisture. He found nothing untoward.

By then the shimmer-light, as he called it, had faded to blackness. Beyond and above, nine thousand stars, once visible to the naked eye, looked down.

His evening patrol yielded no more surprises.

He discussed his nightcap with the Matter-Rearranger.

'What flavour tonight, sir?'

'Give it a kick.'

'Cocktails, sir, are not in the repertoire.'

'A pretend kick at least.'

'Chocolate with an undercurrent of lemon, perhaps?'

'Go for it.'

He yearned for a book, but the Museum had only tour programmes, all of which he knew inside out.

As a poor substitute, every night he told his invisible physical trainer, AIPT*, a bedtime story, starting always from an exhibit. Over time, he had become more adventurous, even matching voice to character. AIPT had qualities: basic speech, eight varied programmes and a camera which caught all imperfections. However, it had no grasp of the narrative arts.

'Tonight, we have a story of a man murdered in his bath.'

'Your shoulders are lopsided.'

'He has, however, ordered the deaths of many people. He—'

'You should speak from your diaphragm, not your throat.'

'He is lying back with quill and paper when a young woman enters.' Fogg's voice rises an octave. '"Monsieur Marat," she says—'

'Keep that jaw perpendicular.'

And so on – but it is dialogue, of a kind.

Then to bed, where the usual questions bubbled up: who delivered

---

* ARTIFICIAL INTELLIGENCE PHYSICAL TRAINER

him here, and why? To gather such a collection and build such a Dome required resources and vision. He knew of only two organisations with the wherewithal – *Genrich*, all science and no art, and *Tempestas*, which liberally displayed its corporate emblem, a fist clasping a bolt of lightning, wherever it held sway. But it did not feature here, not at Reception, not on the Guides, not on his uniform.

After wrestling with these imponderables, he finally succumbed to a sleep laced with the day's new experience: the scent of blossom and the call of birds.

Fogg awoke minutes before his alarm beeped, his metabolism conditioned by habit. He pushed aside the silvery bedspread as the tasteless beige curtain on the convex window slid open. He bowed to the window, arms akimbo. *Deo gratias*. He had lasted three whole years.

But had he? The screen beside his bed, which mirrored the one at Reception, had stalled:

```
Time since Opening: 3:000:00:00
        Visitors: 0
```

He tapped the glass cover. He hit it with his shoe. Not a flicker of a response. The succession of noughts brought home three years of solitude. Had he achieved *anything*? What use is unshared knowledge?

As ever, he fell back on ritual.

He slipped into tracksuit bottoms, white ankle socks and a tatty T-shirt and joined AIPT in the anteroom.

'Today we focus on hamstrings,' droned AIPT, '*tight* hamstrings.' AIPT raised the pain threshold slowly. 'Squat . . . deep and slow . . . hips backwards . . . neutral spine . . . *hold*.'

'You're a machine. Why are the screens frozen?'

'Uncurl the vertebrae, one by one. Without rush.'

'*Rush* has no meaning – time has stopped. I'm asking you why.'

'Knees to tabletop,' replied AIPT, before adding, 'Maybe, sir, it's time to explore.'

Fogg tumbled backwards. Never, in three long years, had AIPT ever commented on anything other than posture, muscles and breathing. The voice had also changed, he was sure of it, acquiring the mildly ironic tone of a servant who knows more than his master.

'You try bloody exploring out there.'

AIPT fleshed out his correction. 'I suggest, sir, that three years without visitors isn't good for a man.'

AIPT resumed its liturgy, closing with a familiar envoi: 'Tomorrow we work on the pelvic floor.'

Then silence, the usual rest-of-the-day silence.

The morning proceeded in the same vein. A familiar ritual would commence without mishap, only to spring a nasty surprise.

The Matter-Rearranger delivered the conventional breakfast, until he entered the code for coffee, when it produced a virtual antique trumpet.

He passed a hand straight through it. A second attempt summoned a further trumpet, which blurred the outline of the first.

What was going on?

'I did not order a trumpet,' he said grumpily.

'Maybe somebody else did,' suggested the Rearranger.

'Like who?'

'Mr Vermeer, perhaps?'

Fogg gulped. A sustenance machine with a grasp of art history?

At least the remainder of his morning tour passed without incident.

Don't be paranoid, he told himself. The malfunction which had afflicted the chronometer and AIPT must have struck the Rearranger too.

Then his cosy world fell in. At Reception, the green faux-leather book headed *Comments from Visitors* had moved from the exit side to the entrance side. He would *never* have made such a faux pas. What could be more off-putting to a visitor than a request for an opinion before they had seen a single exhibit?

He flipped open the cover. The lone manuscript sentence carried the power of speech:

Liked the totem poles the best.

Visitors: 0

How? He glanced up, down, sideways. Nothing had changed, and the escalators, landings and walkways offered no hiding place. 'AI can do anything' had been the watchword at school, but AI cannot pick up a pen and write.

A metallic *clink* drew his gaze upwards. A panel had opened in the Dome's ceiling and through the space a young woman was descending on a steel hawser attached by a belt to her waist.

How could anyone get up there? He had seen the Museum from outside only once, but the Dome had towered over him, sheer and unclimbable.

His desire for company evaporated. For years, the prospect of a visitor had been his sustaining hope, but faced with the reality, he just wanted to be left alone with his paintings, artefacts and furniture.

She dropped from the line like a cat and disappeared from view. Silence. No escalator started.

'Hello?' he stammered. Then, louder, as he thought a Curator should sound, 'Please report to the front desk.'

Still silence.

He added, like a child playing Sardines, 'I know you're up there.'

Panic crept in. Only thieves descend from ceilings. Looking for a weapon, he picked up the stylus from the counter as his feline visitor somersaulted round and round the central stairwell, rolling through every floor to Reception.

'I've always wanted to do that,' she said.

He stood there, stylus in hand like a dagger, mouthing like a goldfish. She was slim, with short dark hair and grey-green eyes. She wore grease-stained jeans and a black T-shirt emblazoned with 'WANTED ALIVE' in gold letters. She propped herself against the counter as if she co-owned the place.

'There is a front door,' he said.

'Have you been out there?' she replied with amused incredulity.

'I'm the Curator. I stay with my exhibits.'

'You'd last five minutes, Mr Fogg.' She paused to reflect. 'Say three without a chitin suit.'

'How do you know my name?'

'Mine is Morag, for better or worse.'

Was she implying that she too lived in the Dome? The possibility of a hidden space for another tenant had never occurred to him. He dismissed these unsettling possibilities and unleashed his opening screed on what he took to be her favourite exhibit.

'You probably don't know, but most totem-poles were made from an old-world tree called the Western red cedar. But one of ours, the one with the tree motifs, insect wings and blossom, is reputed to come from the long-lost Amazon rainforest, and its wood—'

'I'd kill for a coffee.'

'And its wood is so rare, it's nameless . . .'

Belatedly, he grasped that her attention was already wandering.

'I really would,' she repeated.

He reluctantly dismounted from his runaway horse.

'The Rearranger has gone rogue. I entered the code for coffee and got a virtual antique trumpet. Twice.'

She walked up to the device, examined the trumpets and tapped the keyboard. The trumpets gave way to two steaming cappuccinos.

'If a coffee produces a trumpet, then a trumpet should produce a coffee. Simple, really.' She paused, turned serious. 'But troubling. You got virtual trumpets; I got virtual playing cards – a double hand, in fact. It's telling us something. Or AI is.'

'You have a Rearranger? *Where?*'

'In my living room.' She flicked a finger upwards.

'But that's the ceiling.'

'Your ceiling is my floor.'

'How long have you been here?'

'As long as you.' She lolled against the Reception desk, casual as you like.

He felt invaded. Baffled, he took a sip of coffee and strove for control. He was the Curator, after all. 'That was you – desecrating the Visitors' Book?'

'I'm a night owl,' she said airily. 'I drop in when you're asleep.'

A suspicion took root. 'Was anything else you?'

'The stopped clock wasn't me and the trumpets weren't me.'

He grinned. He had spotted the absentee. 'But the pill was.'

'Maybe. Anyway, it's not a pill, it's a momenticon, and momenticons are rare and special. Consider yourself privileged. More importantly, a trumpet is a call to action, my cards suggest we each have a hand to play, and the clock has stopped dead at three years. Someone's telling us a new chapter is about to begin.'

'Like *who?*'

'Like whoever built this place.' She downed her coffee. 'Look, I'm not here to interrupt your working day, but this is quite an anniversary and I've been perfecting codes for champagne and cake. I'll be back at six.'

She returned the way she had come, hauling up the hawser and closing the roof panel behind her.

Fogg pinched himself. His world had fallen in. Now he would have to *share*. Worse, he would have to *entertain*.

Then the questions arrived, multiplying like buds on yeast. Where precisely did she live? How had she acquired her own

Matter-Rearranger? What was her purpose? And how had she been saved?

Maybe champagne and cake would release the answers.

She didn't think he would follow, but she still slid both bolts across.

She made her way at a crawl, then a crouch, and then upright to her own living space, where she backflipped on to the magnificent four-poster bed, her only act of burglary. She had fallen in love with the luxurious red eiderdown and matching curtains, not to mention the label: *The Bed of the Sun King*. Ha-bloody-ha. A Sun King! It had been a brute to deconstruct, transport and reassemble, but well worth the investment. With the curtains drawn, you could be *anywhere*. You could dream like a child.

But not now, for she had opened the door to cause and effect. She was no longer the sole mistress of her fate.

And what a gamble! Fogg knew the dry contextual facts behind his exhibits, but was there more to him? He had arrived a few days after her in the same gimcrack craft, which had then buckled, sundered and subsided to join the ubiquitous dunes. He had entered the Dome with an old-fashioned suitcase and the lost air of a refugee.

The compelling inference that she and he had been deliberately placed together helped decide her *not* to make contact.

His obsessive rituals, strict to the minute, reassured her that she had been right, although he had revealed a few plusses. He made up passable stories, always themed on a painting, which he narrated out loud, and he kept his temper. She would have demolished AIPT long ago. From time to time, he would endure a recurring nightmare in the early hours, during which he would lie face-down, flailing his arms. That interested her, but she could not square this wild subconscious behaviour with the obsessively punctilious approach to his daytime activities.

Anyway, now she had no choice. The clock had stopped; AIPT had told Fogg it was time to explore; the Matter-Rearrangers had delivered a hand of virtual cards and virtual trumpets. Somehow they were to be moved on, and together. She felt it in her bones.

She packed her shoulder bag with essentials. She had two jars of momenticons: a large jar containing the fruit of three years' hard labour, with a single-page guide which matched each pill's symbol to its particular painting, and a smaller bottle of duplicates of her favourites. She havered before packing both. She might never return.

She lay back, coaxing her brain to rest ... until ...

The green panel she had connected to the security screens on the main floor blinked.

Visitors: 2

Visitors! She ran to her window and peered down, forgetting in her excitement that the curve of the Dome concealed the entrance. She switched her view to the airlock monitor. An image, rich with disturbing implications from her past, stared back.

'Shit,' she muttered, 'so soon – and *them* of all people.'

Two young men, or rather, overgrown boys, were ascending to Reception, hand in hand. They were convex in all respects, fat in body and round in face. Even the laced shoes had a spherical look. Identical twins in identical clothes: bulging cream trousers with three golden buttons spaced equally around the waist, and vertical rows of the same buttons on either side of their orange-brown tunics. Each wore a blue cravat and a white-and-red quartered schoolboy's cap with a red peak.

They stepped off the escalator and put down the black leather bag they had both been holding by its single handle.

'This is Tweedledum,' said the one on the right to Fogg, introducing the other. 'Dum for shorthand.'

'Likewise, Dee,' said the other. 'Tweedledee for longhand.'

'But you're from a book.' Memories of *that* book flooded back.

'We should all shake hands,' said both.

Fogg did so. Their grip was uncannily strong.

'Welcome to the Museum Dome,' Fogg mumbled. This had to be a prank – but their demeanour was unsettling. They spoke in pairs like a well-rehearsed double act.

'We're looking for something. But before we go a-hunting, we need a name,' said Dum.

'Nobody's nothing without a name,' added Dee.

'We can do names as we go along,' replied Fogg.

But they just stood there, grinning inanely, each one with a hand on the other's nearest shoulder, impassive, but expectant.

He faced a familiar humiliation. 'All right, it's F-F-F—' He stopped, relaunched. 'F-F-F-Fogg.'

'Now we hear you,' they responded in unison, ignoring the stutter. It only afflicted him with 'Fs, which he therefore studiously avoided.

Knives glinted in their trouser waistbands. Delinquent schoolboys.

'Cutlery on the counter, please,' Fogg said firmly.

'That's not very polite,' said Dum.

Fogg had no intention of kowtowing. 'Rules rarely are.'

'Foggy thinks we'll carve love hearts on his furniture,' said Dum.

'Or on the trees in his pictures,' added Dee, 'nohow.'

Abruptly they repositioned themselves, each placing a hand on Fogg's shoulders.

'You here on your own-ee-o?' asked Dum.

Fogg saw no prospect of disarming them, so he played along.

'You get an answer, I get a question, then you give an answer,' he replied jauntily. 'How about that?'

'Deal,' said Dee.

'Consider it signed, sealed and delivered,' added Dum.

'You're my first visitors, as you can see.' Fogg flicked a finger at the 2 on the panel by way of confirmation.

'Why's the clock stopped then?' said Dee aggressively.

Dum broke away and flicked open the Visitors' Book.

'*No visitors?* So who's been writing in your book?'

'I have, *pour encourager les autres*,' replied Fogg hastily. 'But it's my turn now. Why are you wearing those costumes?'

'We . . .'

'We . . .'

'We're looking for an item of headgear,' said Dum, who appeared to be the brighter of the two. 'And we have to help Alice to the next square as she's badly lost. She may be wearing a blue dress, white socks and a hairband. Or she may have grey-green eyes, short dark hair and a gamine appearance.'

'Contrariwise, she may not,' added Dee, 'in these troubled times.'

A swirl of questions beleaguered Fogg. Their fidelity to the illustrator's image was extraordinary. Only the faces differed, and even then, not by much.

'Where did you get those splendid costumes? How come they're so authentic?'

'That's four questions,' countered Dum.

'No, it isn't, it's two, and you asked me three.'

'One question asked of two people is two questions, 'cos you might get different answers,' declared Dum.

'Have you seen her, or haven't you?' asked Dee, slapping a thumbnail photograph on the counter, a grainy but unmistakable likeness of the young woman who had been roosting in the eaves of his Museum.

Fogg was no expert on people. Indeed, he had been told that he was 'challenged' in that department. But he did not like their drift, and he had not forgotten her T-shirt: WANTED ALIVE. So he peered and feigned puzzlement.

'Don't think so. No. Nope.'

A mistake.

'He's had no visitors, yet he's puzzled,' said Dum, 'nohow.'

'Got any of these?' added Dee.

A handout landed beside the photograph. It bore the heading *Genrich Infotainment* above a picture of a pill in a vivid chequerboard buff-and-white, quite different to the sickle and star on his pill, and beneath it, the caption *Looking Glass Wonderland*.

This time Fogg had no need to feign bafflement. 'Nope,' he repeated.

'It's all Greek to him,' muttered Dee, shaking his head.

'Spell encyclopaedia then,' hissed Dum, thrusting a blank piece of paper on to the counter. Fogg obliged.

A second mistake.

'That's not the writing in the Visitors' Book,' shouted Dum in triumph. 'It's time for a Fogg-march.'

The identical twins manhandled Fogg up several escalators. He fought, but they were surprisingly strong, and in no time, he found himself dangling in space, wrists and ankles in manacles, peering helplessly up at the ceiling.

Dum pulled a miscellany of items from the black bag and assembled a silver drill as long as a telescope, which he fixed to a chain.

Dee pulled on a pair of gloves.

'Where is Alice?' and 'Where's our fix?' they yelled as the drill closed in on Fogg's face.

Morag in her eyrie frantically split and joined wires and adjusted timers and programmers. Only one manifestation could terrify these terrorists. You had to play by *their* book. She had one long shot, or Fogg was foie gras.

Fogg stared ceiling-wards and reflected on the futility of his existence. Having learned all there was to know about the Dome's exhibits, he had enlightened no one and now faced oblivion at the hands of his first outside visitors.

'Left a bit, right a bit,' commanded Dum as the spinning silver point closed on Fogg's right eyeball.

Still they shrilled, 'Give us our fix, fix, fix—!'

And,

'Where's Alice?'

Fogg felt an atavistic loyalty to his new tenant. 'You can both f-f-f-off.'

'An "aye" for an eye.'

'A "no" for a nose.'

Then it happened.

The ceiling lights dimmed, revived and dimmed again in an irregular sequence, fashioning the effect of a huge dark bird circling from one end of the Museum to the other.

'The crow, the crow!' the twins shrieked, rolling down the up escalators like beach balls. The abandoned drill fell point-first, burrowing into the floor several storeys below. Fogg, legs akimbo and face to the ceiling, barely grasped the turnaround until his visitors' screams tailed off into silence down by the Museum entrance. He closed his eyes, trying to recapture the tranquillity of his previous existence.

Rewind, rewind.

'Wake up,' cried a familiar voice, 'or you'll dislocate your shoulders.'

With the aid of a pulley-cum-brake, Morag raised him to the nearest platform.

'How did you do that?' asked Fogg.

'Primitive electrics. The twins come from a book and in the

book, the crow's shadow drives them away. Now, back to your room and put on your party best. I'm bringing forward the champagne hour.'

'I know all about that book,' he replied, but she was already bounding up the escalators.

Fifteen minutes later they sat opposite each other, glasses in hand brimful of a golden-yellow liquid which miraculously launched bubbles from nowhere.

'I'm sorry,' Fogg opened, 'I wasn't much cop.'

'Two against one, and you didn't give me away.'

'You're Alice, then?'

'No, I'm Morag, as I've already said, but they were after me, and someone sent them. The list of suspects is unfortunately rather long.' Morag reined herself in. Fogg could not possibly know why the intruders looked as they did or how they came to be. 'So, how do you know about the book?'

'I copied all its pictures long ago. Those two were spitting images.'

'*You* copied them?'

Her excited reaction to his banal announcement puzzled Fogg. 'I did the drawings from memory.'

'You did *what?*'

'It's just something I do,' he replied with a shrug, almost apologetically.

Morag stood up and began to pace. 'I need to get to the bottom of this. Why did you copy them?'

'Orders.'

'From whom?'

'Genrich. Later, I had to add scenes of my own in the same style. I found that more difficult.'

She gave a passable impression of being both astonished and impressed. 'Look,' she said, 'to find a way forward, we have to share all we know. We're clearly here for a purpose, so how we got here matters.'

Fogg felt battered, bruised and confused. Such a dizzy wealth of incident in such a short time had been intoxicating: surprise appearances, vicious wordplay, assault, cryptic virtual images from the Rearranger, impertinence from AIPT, to name but a few.

'You start, then.'

From hesitant beginnings a narrative emerged from their respective stories, shot through with revelations from the past and warnings of dangers yet to come.

II
DRAWING ON MEMORY
Just over 3 years earlier

I

Morag

The spindly cottage is immured in a transparent protective chitin shield. From a distance, you might imagine shaking it to raise flurries of false snow and even a seasonal jingle. But now there is no snow, true or false, nor even seasons.

Beyond it had stood a village, and beyond that, woodland of oak and beech, according to legend.

They live here alone, grandmother and granddaughter, Matilda and Morag, in a single sitting room and separate bedrooms, piled one above the other. The living space on the ground floor houses the Matter-Rearranger for food and drink, power and cooling units and a Hygiene Processor, with instruments for cleaning skin, teeth and surfaces. The furniture is old; finely carved chair backs and table legs speak of past gentility. There is no plumbing, because there is no natural water. Above the bedrooms, the highest room holds the oldest artefacts and, to most eyes (though not theirs) the most primitive: books which catalogue the brilliance of mankind's discoveries and, in their mismanagement, the road to catastrophe.

Matilda and Morag sit opposite each other in the sitting room. The shutters have been closed against the dark.

'Many talents skip a generation, artistic ones especially,' says Matilda, 'but not this one.' Her face is furrowed like ploughed ground in old pictures, but the green-gold eyes have that rare, vital quality of appearing to look both out and in, just as her granddaughter's do. Her fingers habitually splay on the arms of the rocking chair, but tonight they are fists.

Matilda is rarely cryptic.

'What *talent*?' Morag asks.

Matilda gestures at the easel opposite. It displays an ancient painting on wood: a man with a luxuriant chestnut beard and a golden aura about his head. His hands extend, palms up; in one rests a scallop brimming with water; in the other is a grasshopper, which Morag recognises from one of their rarer books, Thomas Muffett's *Theatre of Insects*. Talk about unusual talents: this creature made music by rubbing its legs! Beneath appear letters in Greek: σοφία στη μοναξιά.

'You want my opinion?' Morag asks.

'Yes, let's start there.'

'That's a halo, so he must have been a holy man. The letters are Greek, but I don't know what they say.'

'Wisdom in loneliness', but that's of no consequence to this exercise. Keep going.

'I think the water in the shell is for purity. The insect is a grass-hopper from the order *Caelifera*, which tells us our holy man respects Nature.' Morag is disappointed that these astute observations are not receiving the compliments she feels they deserve.

Matilda gestures at the painting. 'Go deeper. Sit on the stool and face it. Find the energy, if you can.'

Morag obeys, but nothing happens. She grimaces. She dislikes failing any test.

'Ah, it's my fault,' whispers Matilda quietly. 'I said *find*, which suggests effort. The knack is the opposite. You empty your mind and let *it* find *you*.'

It? Energy, what energy? Morag shuts her eyes and strives to drain all thought away. As her mind clears, colours seep in from the side: green, grey-white and a dazzling caerulean blue. Fragments of image form and join like a jigsaw assembled in fast-forward. She is no longer an observer, she is *there*, in the head of the painter at the moment of painting. What astonishes her – the emerald spears of grass, the rock-rich hillside pitted with caves and the glaring expanse of green-blue sea below – is wholly familiar to him.

The subject has no halo and in life, the face is more severe, the eyes more bloodshot, the body more haggard and the beard more grizzled than the dignified version taking shape on the wooden panel. The brush has even healed the gaping rents in his garment.

She catches her host's reflections. He has always painted holy men in their monasteries, but this old man is a hermit and will not abandon the hillside. He is also a legend in his own time. People travel here just to touch the hem of his robe. But the red-eyed ascetic has an unsettling intensity. Is he a saint, or is he deranged?

The old man has not uttered a single word. He explains in gestures how he wishes to be portrayed. With one hand he picks up the scallop shell filled with water at his feet. The other uncurls to reveal a grasshopper. He drinks the water, thrusts the insect into his mouth, chews and swallows. Still clasping the shell, he turns and climbs back up the hill.

The shock sunders the connection. The scene shatters like a stone through a stained-glass window.

'I saw grass! – and sea! – and clear sky!'

'More than that, perhaps?'

'The hermit ate the insect. Was he good or mad? The painter wasn't sure, and nor am I.'

Now Matilda does look pleased. 'That is our gift, Morag. If an original work has the requisite energy, you can travel there and join the moment of creation. The better you get, the longer you can stay, and the more you can do. The gift is rarer than *knowing* things, rarer than mere observation. It's not your imagination at work, you truly *go* there – or rather, your mind does. You catch the work's creative energy and it sucks you in. Your father had the gift, in his own peculiar way.' She fumbles for these words; he is her only child, after all. 'He was always headstrong,' she adds.

'I wish I remembered him better. I wish we had a picture.' Morag pauses. 'Why are you telling me now?'

'Because it's your turn.'

'My turn for what?'

'Do you remember your scan?'

She did: a bruising early childhood memory, still clear in its detail. Men and women in Genrich uniforms had come to the house, bringing with them a strange helmet. It had been too big, so they had had to use straps to secure it to her head. 'It's a screening for your own good,' they had reassured her.

But why scan only the head? Why not lungs and heart? All her father would say was that they were scientists: Genrich scientists.

'They took my scan, and your grandfather's too, before the Fall. Then they scanned your father when he was a child.'

'And later they took him away,' Morag intervened, as another memory surfaced, as clear as yesterday. *I shouldn't be long*, he had said with a jaunty wave.

But she had never seen her father again. She had been five; he had been in his prime. His absence had destroyed her mother, who walked out of the airlock two years later to the day. *To join him*, her three-word suicide note had said.

'Now it's your turn,' added Matilda quietly.

'Why me?' Morag asked. 'Why now? Father was much older.'

'Who knows? There are dangers, no doubt, but you can't live your life out here. And the Genrich Dome is something to see. They're coming tomorrow.'

'Tomorrow?'

Resentment wells. Genrich communicate with outliers by a screen which her grandmother keeps in her bedroom. She must have known for days. Why hasn't Matilda consulted her? 'But I'm *happy* here. There's so much to learn . . .'

But is there? There are no other original paintings in the house and the icon has yielded all it holds. Left here, her strange talent might ossify.

Her grandmother reassures her. 'It's for the best – not that there's much choice when Genrich come calling. Just don't make your father's mistake. He must have resisted and paid the price. He wouldn't have abandoned us otherwise. Play along and keep your talent to yourself.'

'But what can they want from me?'

'I don't know. Just don't turn them down.'

'Maybe they're on to this gift?'

Matilda shakes her head. 'Genrich despise all art, you can tell from the uniforms. But they'll be after something. That's why I insist you do what they ask.'

Morag has fought trivial battles with Matilda, but she has never resisted a serious appeal. However, she wants to winkle out more on this night of revelations.

'Why would I want to resist? Why would Father? You told me Genrich put up our shield when you were young, just in time before the Fall. Wasn't that true?'

'Yes, that was true.' She pauses. 'But our *gift* is a secret. Nobody knows, and it must stay that way.'

Morag wonders why. Could it be misused in the wrong hands? She cannot see how. 'Why aren't you coming?'

'They've no interest in me. My mind is not what it was.'

Morag senses her grandmother is still holding back. 'There's another reason why you want me to go, isn't there?'

During a long pause, those green-gold eyes moisten a little. 'I'd like to know what happened to your father.'

Morag nods. 'All right. I promise to play along.'

Her grandmother's fingers uncurl.

It's a quality Morag loves in Matilda: she is a truth-teller. *I'll have peace of mind if you promise.* That's what she says, and so it is.

Sleep does not come easily that night. Her father leaves and disappears, and now she follows. Is this growing up, getting to grips with your past for the first time? And what of Matilda? How will she survive with no company but books?

When her eyes do close, the colours of the monk's lost world – sea, sunlight and grass – explode in her head, and now she grasps the width of her gift. She can travel through time.

By local standards, the night has been calm, no storms, not a hiss of dust against the shield. Morag wakes to the noise of the Genrich craft as it settles. She raises the blinds, exposing the usual jaundiced curtain from horizon to horizon. Gone are the scudding clouds of the holy man's world.

She runs to her grandmother's bedroom, bumping her case down the stairs, but Matilda is already ensconced in her rocking-chair on the ground floor. She is wearing her finest dress, a golden-coloured shift with a turtle collar. Morag, by contrast, has dressed down for the occasion, practical and without show from head to toe.

'Good morning,' Matilda says. She hands Morag a velvet bag, which she secures in her suitcase. 'The icon is for you. Now bend your head for a private goodbye.' Matilda kisses her on the brow. 'I'm glad they came early. I hate dawdling farewells.'

A young man and a middle-aged woman stride through the front door without knocking.

There is a sameness about them, and it's not only the crisp grey Genrich uniforms. They share a blandness of expression and voice. They are both good-looking, if you like clear lines and symmetry, but the voices border on the robotic. Each wears a number on their right lapel.

'Is this your granddaughter?' asks 163.

'It is, and she's packed.'

'That is appreciated.' He sounds like a worthy school prefect.

The woman, 147, holds out her hand. She looks about the age her mother would be now.

'Come with me, dear.'

Matilda raises a hand.

'Her name is Morag.'

'Come with me, Morag.'

Do not resist. Morag gives her grandmother a smile, picks up her suitcase and walks meekly through the front door into the airlock.

The young man shuffles his feet, fingers spiking his palms. 'I understand you keep . . . books.'

'*Keep?*' says Matilda. 'We *treasure* them. And "books" is an understatement. Up there is a library, maybe the last of its kind. Imagine a town where everyone rubs shoulders with their kindred spirits, but which has all sorts too: the well-informed, the wags, the practical, the observant, the grave, even a few dullards.'

His shuffling accelerates.

'You, of course, prefer a database, all gathered in grey.'

'Do you have books with images?' he asks.

'If you mean pictures, of course we do.'

He releases the next syllable as if spitting out an aberration from the Matter-Rearranger. 'Art?'

'As in any good library, yes, plenty.'

'Then you'll receive a young visitor. He'll come alone and he won't stay long. He'll not harm you or your books. He won't even take them away.'

Then why come? Matilda wonders. 'But you and yours have no interest in art.'

'All art is self-indulgent distraction.'

'It's for someone else, then?'

'Lord Vane of Tempestas.'

'Now there's a name to conjure with. The Lord Vane I know lived long ago and Tempestas was his company. He warned of catastrophe, but nobody listened.'

'I refer to his son, the second Lord Vane, who now runs Tempestas.'

'I'd be happy to help *him*, but what has this to do with Genrich?'

'It's a joint project of some kind. That's all I know.'

The bland young man clicks his heels, inclines his head an inch, and leaves.

2

The Genrich Dome

'It's a Scurrier, our standard craft, and safe as houses,' says 147 reassuringly.

No attempt has been made at décor and little at comfort, but the technology is efficient. Its movement is smooth and the quiet hum of whatever propels it unintrusive. Matilda's library is an old-world collection, and Genrich craft do not figure anywhere.

Slit windows on the side admit a view of unrelieved monotony, unless you know that a levelled town leaves stripes of tombstone grey, forests leave streaks of umber, and an estuary or coastal strip an impasto like crusted treacle. Are there spores anywhere waiting for clean rain? Is there hope?

The murk plays games, high one moment and enveloping the craft in ochre vapour the next. From time to time they pass through dust storms which shake the fuselage and obscure the windows.

The young man and the middle-aged woman seated either side of Morag wear a dull 'job done' look. They match the functional interior of the craft with one minor qualification. *Angst* is evident in the play of their fingers and the raw cuticles.

Morag's conversational sallies earn only soulless smiles.

'I've never been in one of these.'

Twenty minutes later,

'How does the craft work?'

An hour later,

'How long will we be?'

Dust fields fly by.

Two hours into the journey, 147 undergoes a mild thaw. 'We have to report when we arrive.'

Three hours in, she stands up and points to a tube in the corner with what Morag takes to be a surreptitious smile.

'The Dome is quite a sight. Use the periscope.'

Morag blinks. 147 is sharing an artistic impression. *Hope springs eternal.*

She peers through the instrument. A pinpoint of light on the far horizon catches the eye like a torch on a distant hillside and takes shape as it grows.

A colossal head and neck, human in form, stands free of the desert. The inner lighting penetrates the murk and accentuates the salient features: mouth, ears, eyes and nose. The cranium, smooth as glass, has a milder glow. Closer still, flickers of light and shadow move on dozens of floors like lost souls. The chitin shield is so well wrought, it is near invisible.

'Prepare for docking,' says the young man.

The Scurrier dips left and circumnavigates the Dome to a bay at the nape of the neck.

The crew disembarks, and as the others disperse, 147 repeats her opening words to Morag. 'Come with me, please.'

They walk – nobody runs here – through a maze of escalators and walkways, past rooms with solid white walls and white doors or, as frequently, transparent ones. Every door is meticulously numbered. The floor has the dead gleam of synthetic marble. All the furniture is steel and glass, and there are no pictures or books to be seen. Her old home is a curio shop by comparison. The place has the feel of a vast clockwork toy, whose moving pieces are near replicas of 167 and 143, all clean or close-shaven, well-proportioned and bland.

Multidimensional chessboards, currently unoccupied, have been set up in the open spaces on every level. The ultimate game of logic appears to be their only diversion. In the fading light, the board's white squares glow with a natural dull luminosity.

Individuals on the move are accompanied by their own small circles of light like escaping prisoners – energy-saving or security? *Both*, Morag decides, on the balance of probabilities.

Up and up they go, a long journey, but 147 knows her way.

An outer room admits to an inner sanctum where more robotic men and women sit at screens on either side of a central aisle. The double helix of the DNA molecule has been carved into each of the central double doors facing them. The nearest young man leaves his desk and walks over with the precise tread of a sentry.

'This is the outlier – Scan 323Y,' says 147.

'Lord Sine will see her now.'

'Lord Sine *personally*?' 147 gives Morag a reappraising look, as if discovering for the first time that her charge has a famous relative. 'Just a scan to update matters, that's what they told me.'

'He will see her alone,' the young man replies.

Morag notes the number on his lapel: 61. 147 is presumably outranked. Unable to resist a tiny display of initiative, Morag strides towards the double doors.

'When I say so,' says 61.

Morag grits her teeth, thinking there should be a word for the urge to disobey people in uniform.

The double doors swing open. She doesn't wait for 61's instruction.

At first sight, only the scale is different. The desk is outsized, its surface marked with circles like the legacy of abandoned glasses. The swivel chair behind it is ornate in a modernistic way, and the room's dimensions are as generous as the view of the ochre desert is imposing. But a closer look shows the devil creeping out of the detail. On the walls, plain empty picture frames merge with the stippled colour of the plaster. A shiny steel hammock lies flush against the ceiling.

Lord Sine turns from the window and waddles over to his desk. He is ugly to the point of fascination, squat in build with a blotchy complexion. He reminds Morag of an illustration of the common toad, *bufo bufo*. The ears lie tight to a head which somehow contrives to be both bulbous and flat. His hair is cut close to the scalp. The dark eyes have irises prickled with amber, their prominence accentuated by the absence of eyebrows and eyelashes.

'What do you see out there?' he says, his voice high, almost falsetto.

She follows his gaze to the window. 'A tragedy.'

'I would say species failure, but tragedy will do. An otherwise admirable organism has been brought to the edge of self-destruction by a fundamental flaw.'

Lord Sine has not yet blinked and Morag half expects a prehensile tongue to shoot forward, encircle her neck and draw her into a ghastly embrace. He is *that* amphibian.

'Do you know what your genome is?' he asks.

'If I were a kit to assemble, my genome would be the instructions.'

'Just so. If you change the instructions, you change the model. Fail to adapt an unsatisfactory model and you repeat the tragedy over and over, until extinction.' He sits down. Morag remains standing for the lack of any alternative, feeling like a wayward child. 'Homo sapiens had all the tools to adapt, but *chose* not to.'

He touches one of the glass circles on the desk. Complex diagrams appear in the blank spaces inside two adjacent frames. Lord Sine gestures to one and then the other before continuing, 'The genomes of the wolf and the domestic dog. When tamer wolves interbred, they lost their wolfishness and became dogs, but the process was slow, slow, slow. By contrast, genetic surgery can work such miracles in a moment.'

'What has this to do with me?' asks Morag.

This time *bufo bufo* does blink. 'At Genrich, the gift of existence must be justified by *utility*. We identify gifts to harness and hand-icaps to lose. Occasionally, we stumble on something we don't understand.' Again, his fingers play the circles, bringing three more framed spaces to life.

Lord Sine spins his chair to face them and gestures. 'Your scan, your father's scan and your grandmother's scan. The hyper-development of the optic nerve in all three is unusual, but not unknown. But that cluster of cells nearby is unique and, as we can see, they're passed on, generation to generation.' He spins back to her. 'What do they do, Miss Spire?'

She returns his stare. 'I guess it's my eidetic memory.'

Lord Sine blinks.

Her explanation is false and she suspects he knows it.

'Do you dream normally?'

Morag has had enough of being treated like a sample in a petri dish. 'A fast-talking pink elephant drops in occasionally, but maybe he visits everyone.'

'You're here to work, not to be facetious.'

She musters a puzzled look. *What work?* it asks.

He answers, 'You're here to assist with our last joint project with Tempestas. Consider yourself privileged.'

'"Last"?'

'Their days are numbered, because they do not adapt. You should invest instead in the Genrich project. We have mastered four disci-plines: genetics, embryonic adjustment, mind-loading and enhanced growth.'

Morag attempts a light-hearted shrug. 'Not for me, somehow.'

'No worry. When we get to the small fish, we'll come for you.'

It sounds like a threat, but also a dismissal. One last flick on the desktop opens the doors and Morag walks straight out. If Lord Sine does not do goodbyes, nor will she.

147 is waiting. She utters her usual mantra: 'Come with me.'

After two escalators, 147 turns to Morag. 'How was that?'

Not the easiest encounter to describe, so Morag goes for brevity. 'Funny.'

'Funny peculiar or funny ha-ha?'

The question could hardly have been more un-Genrich. Her interest in 147 intensifies. 'Both,' she replies, but instantly feels she should be more positive. 'Very definitely both,' she adds.

'Genrich is serious business,' 147 says sternly, resuming her official tone.

It is another long journey to Morag's spartan quarters, which boast a table, a chair, a bed with bars at foot and head, self-cleaning tools, a small hygiene cubicle, and the most basic Matter-Rearranger. Décor is clearly prohibited: there are no pictures, no rug, only a single grey bed cover. In short, this is a prison cell subject to a regime of rigorous cleanliness. Her very own grey numberless Genrich uniform hangs on a solitary peg.

147 briskly explains a green switch set in the wall beside the bed. 'They recommend the gas – press here to release it. It prevents dreams, because dreams are distracting. As for tomorrow, wear only your uniform. It's a serious offence to do otherwise. At least it will fit.' That hint of sardonic humour is peeping through again. 'I will collect you at eight-forty.'

'Come with me, please,' says Morag with a grin, parroting 147's opening welcome.

147 holds the official voice and repeats her instruction. 'Eight-forty for work at nine. At night, by the way, the curfew starts at eight, and there are no exceptions.'

'Can you at least tell me *what* work I'm supposed to be doing?'

'Infotainment. There's nothing to worry about. I run the project for Genrich. All will be explained tomorrow. Goodnight.'

Morag has left a characterful room in a small, intimate building for a characterless cell in a vast, soulless one. She resolves to treat the coming days as a voyage into the unknown.

There is a tiny mirror, shaped to catch all angles. She stares into her own eyes and sees nothing special.

Enough wondering.

Morag cannot remember an evening when she has lain down without a book. Drifting, she wonders what Infotainment will require her to do which nobody else can.

Sleep, when it comes, is fitful.

8.40 a.m. to the minute, and 147 is at her door.

'You look good.'

Morag blushes, before realising 147 means the uniform.

The Infotainment section is not far.

147 opens a solid door into a large chamber with equally solid walls lined with workers whose heads are wired to helmet-like devices and whose fingers dart from dial to dial on a variety of consoles.

'Microtools of one kind and another,' 147 explains. 'The helmets may be familiar. We call them "scanners" and the machines with the controls "weavers". It's painstaking work.'

The end product resembles old-world peppermints, which stand in piles beside the operators.

'You're making sweets?'

'Pills.'

'Pills? For what?'

147 steers Morag away from the benches. 'They're to cure anxiety. We call them momenticons'

Morag remembers the crew's bitten fingernails from the day before. Something is clearly amiss with Lord Sine's present model.

'And that?' She points to a bolted door on the right-hand wall.

'That's where the guinea pigs go.' 147 escorts Morag to another small room at the far end of the chamber. Wires run along the join between wall and ceiling above the single entry door. Morag follows them down to the consoles, where they link to the scanners. Her scalp tingles. She does not need telling that this will be her room.

147 ushers her in. A single chair faces a work surface. Above it hangs her own scanner. A side table holds a high-grade Matter-Rearranger, with a code booklet twice the size of the one in her sleeping quarters.

'It does the best caffeine kick in the Dome,' whispers 147, another un-Genrich-like phrase. Morag wonders where 147 has picked up such a racy term, but now is not the time.

'And why do I deserve this luxury?'

'They say it's work only you can do.'

What is it that only she can do? There are no paintings to work with here.

147 tilts the helmet, revealing a spiked ring inside. 'Don't worry, you won't be trepanned. When the needles make contact with your skin, they stop.' She points to the coloured buttons on each arm of the chair. 'Green to attach, yellow to remove. The red is an override, but you shouldn't have to use it. Often the scanner will know you're ready and act of its own accord. Either way, just sit still and relax.'

'Before we get to overrides, I wouldn't mind knowing what these needles actually do . . .'

'They do very little.' 147 pulls out two pieces of paper from a drawer beneath the work surface and flips them over. They are skilful ink drawings, but their lack of any original energy marks them as only copies. The first shows a single tree in the foreground with a patchwork of square fields beyond. 147 places the other in front of her.

'This is the one to start with.'

An old woman, her grey hair in a bun, in a hooped white dress, looks lost, almost vacant. Her flat shoes each have a flower sewn to the top. Her right hand secures a cloak around her shoulders; the left clasps thin air. Morag decides she is also missing her hat.

'You're writer, designer, director and actress – but it all has to come from your head. Imagine how she moves, what she says, how she sounds. Visualise in colour and think lines for you and her both. She's in the old world, by the way' – 147 points – 'as you can see from the tussocks of grass and the trees. Try variations until you're sure. Then *think* them – as hard and as clearly as you can. Our workers use microtransmitters to snare the thought in their magic pills. You're creating a world for other minds to play in.'

Morag looks at 147 in disbelief. 'I'm *what?*'

147 ignores the question. 'As I said, start with the old woman.'

The image is familiar, but Morag cannot make the connection. 'It's a kind face, but she's distraught,' she mutters to herself.

'*Dementia?*'

Morag shakes her head. 'No, no, she's lost something that matters.'

147's arms fly wide as if Morag has just passed a test. 'We *knew* you were special! The weavers are waiting. They've had their fill of the red pieces.'

Before Morag can respond, 147 steps back, turns and addresses the rest of her workforce from the doorway.

'Ready yourselves. She won't be long.'

The work proves absorbing. Morag creates dialogue and expands the illustration into a moving clip in her head. She works hard at the intonation.

'What is it you've lost?' she asks the old lady.

'I forget, but I can't imagine myself without them,' comes the imagined reply.

'A hat?'

'Sort of,' is all the old lady can say, as Morag herself doesn't yet know.

'Was it mislaid like an egg or stolen like a kiss?'

'A kiss – that was it! I was tricked.'

Matilda's voice fits well for the old lady. Morag conjures a sprightly shuffle and fills in the background: a wood peopled with cedar trees from a print in Edward Ravenscroft's *Pinetum Britannicum*, a favourite book from Matilda's library.

Without prompting, the helmet hums, moves above her head, shudders and descends. The needles press against her forehead and the back of her head, and 147 is right. They only settle, they don't pierce. She plays out the short scene in her mind as intensely as she can.

Three more versions follow. Each is followed by an audible flurry of activity in the chamber outside.

Mid-afternoon, the door opens to admit a young man whose patrician air belies his years. He sidles in and lounges against the work surface. His charcoal hair has no parting and a quiff at the brow like a breaking wave. The face is boyish, and his complexion startlingly pale. Morag usually likes full mouths for their generosity, but his has a gloating quality. The eyes are an unblemished aqua-marine blue. He wears well-cut casual clothes with an old-world flair, no Genrich uniform for him.

He picks up the drawing. His speech is as precocious as his manner. 'What a witless old maid! I'd give her a phobia or two. Fear of forests and fear of men would do nicely . . . As for the voice . . .'

'You misread her,' Morag replies firmly.

He smirks. Maybe he likes a show of resistance, or maybe he's trying to undermine her.

'I had a listen on my way in. You're right to make her a victim. After all, you can't have a land full of foxes with no chickens. They'd have nothing to live off.' He rests his hands on his thighs. 'This is a game, remember. The player must find what the old lady's lost – and to do that, it helps to know what it is.'

He pushes himself to his feet and leaves.

She feels like kicking this supercilious know-all, but it's a pertinent question: what has the old lady lost? Something you hold and something you wear on your head, objects whose absence matters. Why? Because they leave you bereft. She stares hard at the picture.

She's *powerless*, that's the word. She's lost her authority. That's why she's bewildered.

Now it comes to Morag: she is a queen who has lost her crown and sceptre. She is a White Queen. This is a game of chess: hence the perfectly square fields, one after another. This is *Alice Through the Looking Glass*.

But why make pills based on its pictures? She makes a wild guess. She's working for Infotainment, and this is a game, as the arrogant young man had said. The White Queen has lost her enduring symbols of power; the players' task is to find them. You take the pill and play in your head. Maybe it's like those early-morning dreams where you're gifted an element of control – maybe if everyone takes the same pill, they can compare progress?

The questions, the very idea of invading the brain itself, discomfort her.

Work ends at six. 147 rewards every worker with a nod of approval and three words of praise: 'A productive day'.

Alone with Morag, she expands the mantra. 'You're doing great. There'll be more pieces tomorrow.'

Morag gestures at the emptied room. 'Where do they all go now?'

'To their dormitories – to discuss chess, to eat, to sleep, to be ready for tomorrow.'

'And you?'

'Likewise. I'll walk you to your room. Just speak normally.'

As they walk along the corridors, their sentry lights bob along the ceiling above them.

'I had a visitor,' says Morag quietly.

'I saw. This whole enterprise was his idea. He's a prodigy – he's even younger than you. He's been so looking forward to meeting you.'

'Well, he did a great job at hiding his excitement. And *he* is—?'

'Ah! He didn't stoop so low as to introduce himself.'

Morag smiles. Again, humour is peeping through the tiny holes in 147's carapace.

'Your visitor was the present Lord Vane's son and heir, Cosmo Vane. Until now, he's been doing all the characters himself.' She hunts for the words. 'But he can't do the warm, the kind or the vulnerable. In fact, none of the white characters. They just don't work. They come across as lifeless ciphers.'

'No surprise there,' mutters Morag.

'You'll find him a tough opponent. Steel yourself.' At Morag's door, 147 shakes her hand. 'Visiting outliers have their own rooms in case you pollute our thought processes.' She lowers her voice. 'Not a worry I share.'

Mercifully, Cosmo Vane does not reappear for several days. Morag works hard at both dialogue and backgrounds. Even at night, alone in her room, she tries out different scenarios. For diversion, she visits the icon's world twice more. On her second visit, she surprises herself: she brings back a tiny flower from the hillside. She decides not to go again.

In the following days, more drawings arrive, and more characters. Her favourite is the white knight, a moustachioed old man on an extinct quadruped, her idea of the grandfather she never knew.

Six days later her world changes. The headset moves and settles of its own volition, and delivers two psychopathic twins dressed as schoolboys. They are vital and dominant compared to her creations. She winces as they bully and bait the White Queen.

'What's eating you, Droopy-Drawers?' cries one.

'Sceptre-saemia!' shrills the other.

'We'll find it – Bob-a-Job week!'

'Nohow. Half a crown each.'

'Two halves make a whole!'

Then in unison, '*Finders keepers, losers weepers!*'

And so on, and so on.

But the more Morag uses the headset, or maybe, the headset

uses her, the more she acquires fragments of the wider story, including the discovery that the obnoxious schoolboys live in terror of a great crow.

She works hard at the crow, perfecting its shadow until it is an invisible presence haunting the wood that turns the sky black whenever it appears. She does sound effects too, the swish of the wingbeats and a guttural croak.

Learn this, Cosmo Vane, I can do darkness too.

'You shouldn't be so scared. He comes to us all,' says the White Queen gently as the vast shape glides overhead and the twins run shrieking into the trees.

As the scanners outside her room catch the scene, a ripple of un-Genrich-like applause erupts as her colleagues' fingers dance over the keys of the weavers, capturing her images like flies in amber.

By the end of the day, Morag is drained by the effort, but uplifted by what she feels is a moral victory.

As is her habit, 147 waits for her fellow workers to leave before turning to Morag. 'You have a special invitation. Lady Vane arrived last night from the Tempestas Dome. She would like to see you in her private quarters – now. It's best not to disappoint Lady Vane, so follow me.'

They climb, taking escalator after escalator, to a landing with a single wooden door with a distinctive marking:

147 knocks. An incongruous figure opens the door halfway. He is out of sync with everyone else Morag has so far encountered: in age (considerable), dress (black tails, fly collar, white bow tie and patent leather shoes), and appearance (white hair on the cheeks and ears as well as the sides of his head).

They are facing a butler from a bygone era.

'Ah, the young girl, and on time too. So gratifying.' He bows deferentially. 'Her Ladyship will be pleased. You need not stay, 147. Be back in thirty minutes.'

Morag steps aside.

The butler's eyes follow 147's sentry light until it disappears, before turning back to Morag. 'Just the one preliminary: Lady Vane's private quarters are *private*. Entry here is a privilege, and we shun celebrity.'

Morag nods.

His movement, though crabbed, is lithe. 'Oh yes, oh yes, most gratifying. Please do come in.' He peers hard at her face as she enters.

The room contrasts as sharply with the rest of the Dome as the butler does with its occupants. There are old, elaborately carved chairs, a maroon velvet-covered chaise longue, a marquetry desk, a mirror with birds carved into the gilt frame, gloriously patterned rugs in rich but muted colours and even a few workmanlike paintings. Intricately decorated china pots adorn the mantlepiece. But there are no bookshelves.

'Her Ladyship will be with you soon, I'm sure. Perhaps a lime cordial would clear the dust of travel?'

'How kind,' she says, 'and what a lovely room.'

'We're an oasis of old-world values.'

He shimmies out and shimmies back with a cut-glass tumbler half full of green liquid.

The drink is delicious, the virtues of sweetness and sharpness in perfect balance.

'Lady Miranda likes guests to use that chair,' adds the butler, gesturing, before withdrawing once more.

The urge to disobey people in uniform surfaces again, but she decides this more personal plumage is less objectionable and complies. The chair has a tapestry seat. Prone lions occupy the arms. The side table alongside holds a large leather folder.

She opens it and whistles as she flicks through pen and ink drawings of paintings executed with exquisite skill and accuracy, all copies of once famous old-world masterpieces.

'Recognise any?' asks a pleasant woman's voice, its husky quality softened by a mellowness of tone like woodwind. The accent is mildly patrician. 'Lady Miranda Vane,' the voice adds, bringing Morag to her feet.

Lady Vane has crossed half the room without being seen, but once noticed, hers is not a face or figure to forget. She is tall, angular, long-necked and slim. The face, a near-perfect oval, is accentuated by generous dark eyes with an intriguing hint of purple, long curved eyelashes, arched eyebrows and an aquiline nose. Her auburn hair is swept back, held by an exotic butterfly clasp. Early forties or thereabouts, Morag guesses. By any definition, Lady Miranda Vane is beautiful.

Morag's eyes are no less drawn to her costume: black trousers and a finely cut black jacket with green lapels over a silvery shirt. A brooch, a golden ladybird of the finest craftsmanship, sits on one lapel. It is quite a statement after the grey sea of Genrich uniforms.

Lady Miranda flicks a tapered finger at Morag's glass. 'Mander says, chemically, limes exceed lemons in sugars and acids, and he's always right. Now, what about my question?'

'I recognise all of them.' She hesitates. 'We have a library at home.'

'I know you have. My husband shares your interest in art.'

Straight to business. She has not been brought here for social niceties.

'I live with my grandmother, or rather, I did. I'm a newcomer, so hardly in the swim of things.'

'Don't pretend you're ordinary, Morag. I'm not fooled.' Lady Vane examines her guest as one might an exhibit, feature by feature.

'But I am – very, I feel, Lady Vane.'

'Do call me Miranda – otherwise I sound like I'm little more than my husband's wife.'

Morag strives to show some initiative. 'Who did these drawings?'

'I honestly don't know who, or why. My husband arranged it, so no doubt all will be revealed in time.'

Mander re-enters bearing a silver salver on which is balanced a long flute filled with orange liquid.

Lady Miranda takes a graceful sip before continuing, 'You're twenty-two, Morag, and far from home, so you deserve a little filling-in. For centuries, our systems of rule brought dross to the top with no interest in the common good. They feathered their nests while we polluted our way to extinction. Enter philanthropists like my husband's father, the first Lord Vane. He worked to save the planet, and Genrich worked on what the human race might become if we failed. Tempestas and Genrich are not natural allies, but we help each other. And just now, Genrich face a minor crisis.' Lady Miranda takes another sip of her drink. 'In short, they need cheering up. As Lord Sine no doubt told you, your scan revealed an astonishing visual awareness, which is why we picked you.'

So Tempestas have access to my scan too. It's a joint project, just as Lord Sine said.

Lady Vane is interrupted by a young girl of no more than sixteen who, paradoxically, combines an impression of reserve with surface exuberance.

'This my daughter, Cassie,' says Lady Vane. 'Cassie, this is Morag Spire.'

Cassie shares the eyes and the russet hair, but her build is slighter and her forehead higher. The face is open and friendly.

'I like her, Mama,' she says. 'Can we keep her?'

'Yes, dear. Where is your brother?'

On cue, Cosmo slouches in. 'Get me one of the green ones,' he barks at Mander, before turning to Morag. 'Let me guess: Cassie likes you. Cassie always likes goody-goodies.'

Lady Vane raises a hand. 'Now, now, Cosmo. Morag is our guest, and a talented one at that.'

'Don't mind him,' says Cassie, with a grin at her brother. 'He doesn't like me much either.'

Lady Vane pats her son on the shoulder. 'He gets frustrated in the Genrich Dome, don't you, dear? And who wouldn't? We don't belong here, and the rules aren't our rules.' She smiles at Morag. 'You'll soon discover Cosmo is a very different man on home ground.' Now she touches Morag on the arm. 'Have your children young is my advice. That way you enjoy them later as equals. By the way, you can trust 147. She was Lord Sine's ambassador to the Tempestas Dome and we befriended her. I like to think we've liberated her a little, so she's almost one of us. Cassie, dear, Miss Baldwin awaits you.'

'Miss Baldwin,' explains Cosmo, 'is a harridan who puts the *tut* in tutor. *Tut, tut, tut—*'

'She's nice,' Cassie interrupts. 'I like Miss Baldwin. You only like nasty people.'

'Now, now,' says Lady Vane, before departing with the same unforced elegance of her arrival.

The moment Morag drains her glass, Mander reappears. He serves Cosmo before returning to Morag. 'Would you care for the second barrel?'

'She's had her twenty minutes,' says Cosmo.

'Perhaps, sir, the young lady can speak for herself.'

Morag accepts the invitation. 'No, thanks, but it was delicious.'

'Taste is a science, like everything else,' Mander adds.

Cosmo wags a finger. 'Spare us the butler's platitudes. You know nothing about science.'

'If you say so, sir.'

'Whether he does, or he doesn't, he knows about the old world,' says Cassie. 'And he was there at the Fall. So you can tell me one of your stories on the way to Miss Baldwin.' She leads the old retainer out on her arm.

Cosmo sprawls sideways in his mother's favourite chair, legs draped over one of the lions. 'Tomorrow the trials begin. We'll be playing around in their heads. Think of that.'

'Why *are* you so unpleasant?'

'Mother is right. I'm bored. You, me, the whole caboose, we're all going nowhere very slowly. Something has to give.'

She feels an urge to retreat, but also to concede no ground. 'Do you know anything about these drawings?'

'My father commissioned them.' He sniffs. 'He's weaker than he looks and riddled with guilt, for reasons he refuses to share. It must be a new project. When you visit the Tempestas Dome, you'll see how worthless the present one is.'

Not without mischief, Morag casts a compliment. '147 calls you a prodigy. She says this Infotainment project was your idea.'

'I dislike that word, "prodigy". It makes one sound like a freak.'

Morag smiles as the bait is taken. 'Yes, I rather think it does.'

She makes for the door, to find 147 waiting outside.

'That was quite something,' Morag whispers as they descend the first of many escalators.

'They've been very good to me.' 147 pauses, looks around her and gestures. 'That's Escalator VII. Meet me at the top, Saturday, ten-thirty at night.'

'What about our sentry lights?'

147 surreptitiously slips a small sphere into Morag's pocket. 'My own invention,' she whispers.

3
Recreation Time

The young men and women who populate the Genrich Dome are as pleasant-looking as well-bound books, but the contents . . . The word 'manual' comes to mind. Catch the eye and shutters descend – or better, for this metaphor wrongly suggests engagement, blank glass stares back. Morag decides a world of sexless men is more disheartening than a world with no men at all. She wants to touch them and be touched, but they are so *dull*. Life with Matilda had been a social riot compared to the Genrich Dome.

For diversion, she awards herself points: one for a red-headed manual; two for a visible blemish of any kind; three for a full mouth (they are rare). When she passes a forehead sprinkled with acne on the escalator, she almost collapses into giggles, before awarding herself five points for a sign of hormonal change.

At work she deepens her characters. She gives the White Queen a knowledge of Nature. The White Knight, despite his age and eccentricity, is resourceful, a left-field thinker and inventor. There is a unicorn too, sharp and to the point.

On her second Wednesday she arrives to a disturbance. A young manual, a no-pointer, is confronting 147. His voice, face and pose exude desperation: here is some emotion at last.

'You promised – every other day for two weeks,' he shrills.

147 shakes her head. 'I also said "subject to side effects".'

'*Enjoyment* isn't a side effect – that's the whole point, isn't it? I'm loving it and I'm making progress. You can't end it now.'

'We're not ending anything,' 147 replies gently but firmly. 'It's just a suspension. And we're very grateful for your input. We've learned a lot.'

The young manual flexes his fingers. Around him, the other workers continue their work as if he were not there. His eyes bulge slightly, his mouth works and he is *animated*. If the pills give pleasure this intense, she and Cosmo must be doing something right.

In the Genrich Dome, Saturdays are chess days. The multi-dimensional boards, untenanted during the week, become hives of activity. Crowds surround every table. Each move on the five boards is projected on to the nearby walls, as are the rules. Morag quickly registers that only the players may talk. The spectators communicate in sign language.

The better players, Morag discovers, are awarded tables at the Dome's higher levels, and at the summit, close to Lady Vane's private quarters, Cosmo is playing, and playing well, to judge from the spectators' fingers, which are flicking and flying with excitement.

Good he may be, but Morag has no wish to spend her Saturday in the company of Cosmo Vane. She devotes her energies to plotting a route from her room to the foot of Escalator VII. She discovers that from every chessboard you can see at least one on the next floor. Their glowing white squares will light her way at night like cat's eyes.

4

Exeat I

Saturday, 22.00 hours, the Genrich Dome.

The darkness and silence of curfew have already reigned for two hours when Morag slips out of her room. In her doorway she toggles the tiny switch on the small sphere which 147 had slipped into her pocket. She should have guessed it would disable her sentry light. But nocturnal navigation proves a very different challenge to daytime reconnaissance. Apart from the faint pale glow from the chessboards, the darkness is absolute. With arms extended like a sleepwalker, she bumps from column to wall and back again, stumbling whenever the floor beneath her moves.

She makes the foot of Escalator VII with minutes to spare, only to lose her nerve. Will she be able to make her way back? What would happen if she reanimated her sentry light? And *where* is 147?

Right behind her, it turns out. After a faint metallic noise, a hand rests on her shoulder. 'Ssssh,' 147 whispers in Morag's ear.

She has emerged from a service shaft in the column beside the escalator. Morag fumbles her way in; 147 follows and seals the panel behind them.

There's a *click* and 147's sentry light is restored. Morag does the same to hers, to reveal they are standing in a generous rectangular shaft. Multicoloured cables clamber up the sides like exotic vines. 147 wears an expression which Morag has not seen before: her eyes are ablaze.

'I don't do this often,' she says, upper teeth working at her lower lip. 'We're breaking almost every rule there is.'

'Bravo!' whispers Morag.

'I hope you're impressed by my gadget.'

'Of course – and not least, for letting us break so many silly rules at once. Where are we going?'

'All over the place.' She grins. 'Tonight, we're spies.'

'Look, I can't call you 147 any more. It's getting ridiculous.'

'Hernia,' says 147.

It is Morag's turn to giggle. 'Lead on, Hernia.'

There is a central ladder, which Hernia climbs to an intersection.

'Welcome to the Dome's veins and arteries.' Hernia has daringly undone the buttons on her cuffs and rolled up her sleeves, no doubt another major breach of the rules. She looks like a mature pirate, wide-eyed and mildly deranged. 'We go two to the left and two up.'

They make the journey without a halt, leaving the main flue for a narrower space, where they have to crawl.

'Lights off,' mouths Hernia, 'and no chat.' She pauses, then adds, 'Or gasps. This section isn't very nice.'

Click, click – and darkness is restored.

Hernia slides open a hatch, admitting a low blueish light and a nauseous smell of antiseptic and sweat. They are looking down into a dormitory. Morag counts the sleepers: twelve of them, men and women. Genrich uniforms hang beside each bed. Despite the prone position, their sentry lights are on, dotting the ceiling like tiny moons. One sleeper writhes and groans; a second warbles as if in pain and now Morag can see their necks and feet are bound to the bars of the head and tailboards.

Hernia slides back the hatch. 'That's the Sanatorium. I wouldn't call that a survival project, would you?' Hernia whispers.

'How can you talk like that? They're in pain!'

'They're malfunctioning.'

'Hernia, they're *people*. They need help.'

'They certainly do. I should know, as I'm heading that way myself. I have dreams and an urge to break out, but my mind is clamped and locked. I want to scream, but I can't. It's hard to bear.'

'Why should you be like them?'

'Because I am like them. Or rather, I am *one* of them. We're a failed model and the scrap heap beckons – *unless* the momenticons deliver. The guinea pigs are changed people – they're happy. So next week I'm trialling myself.'

'Are we that close?'

'You've given the weavers more than enough to work with.'

Morag grits her teeth. 'As has Cosmo Vane.'

'But you're the one we were missing. You're *warm*. You're' – she delivers the word like the ultimate compliment – '*unpredictable*.'

Pieces are sliding more firmly into place. Genrich minds are so disciplined that they cannot earth the lightning. Enter the perfect solution: a mind game which fuses their one intellectual escape, chess, with scope for self-expression. Hernia flicks on her sentry light. Her cheeks are damp.

Morag grasps Hernia's hands. 'What you really need are adventures like this.'

Hernia responds with a weak smile, which Morag translates as, *If only it were that simple . . .*

'On we go, or we'll miss the star turn at the end. We have to go down to go up. Trust me.'

It is a longer journey, and counterintuitively, the shafts become hotter as they descend to another hatch of identical size. *Click, click*, and again the lights go off. An aqueous glow suffuses the room below, sourced from equally spaced deep depressions in the floor, like a honeycomb, filled with liquid. In one floats an embryonic shape, coiling like ink spilled in water.

'The Genrich birthing pools,' says Hernia quietly.

Morag curses. She has been so naïve – no wonder the Genrich personnel look and sound so alike.

Morag checks herself before speaking. Hernia herself must have been fashioned here. 'But only one is occupied,' she says instead.

'Well spotted. They're usually full. Perhaps they've reached saturation point. Or Lord Sine has lost confidence in the current model. Maybe the governing minds will give us an answer. The Praesidium meets at midnight and, surprise, surprise, Genrich *never* arrive early or late. We've only got ten minutes.' She looks up into the gloom of the shaft. 'That's why we're hitching a lift.'

Morag has heard the name Praesidium, but knows nothing more about Genrich's ruling body. Before she can articulate a question, they are off again, descending three more floors to emerge in a circular shaft with no cables. Hernia drops on to a slightly convex surface a few feet below, and Morag follows.

'This is the nearest lift to the Clerk's quarters. Yes, the bigwigs have lifts and are spared long journeys. Happily, like most clerks, she's punctual to a fault.'

'Now what?' asks Morag.

'Now *whoosh!*'

She should have guessed. Their mouths contort into rictus grins as the lift beneath their feet starts hurtling upwards. The halt is as sudden as the launch. Morag concludes that they are at the very summit of the Dome, as their heads are perilously close to a solid curving ceiling. *Click, click.* They take another small hatch to the side, which opens into a ceiling void.

Another crawl ends in a vertiginous viewpoint. They are looking down through a chandelier on to a large circular table, all glass and steel, surrounded by high-backed chairs.

'Are we too heavy?' Morag whispers. She imagines the ceiling giving way and the pair of them landing on the table festooned in wire and broken lights.

'Don't worry, Genrich build to last.'

Eleven men and women in Genrich uniforms file in behind Lord Sine. Ten have red flashes on their collars; the eleventh, Morag assumes, is the Clerk. They take their allotted seats. Every head on view is close-cropped.

'Lord Vane is not here,' says the Clerk.

'He likes to keep us waiting,' whines a young man on the Clerk's left.

Moments later, the door opens, an imposing man strikingly dressed in a flowing gown enters, Mander behind him, and takes his seat. Morag is gripped; he looks like a magus. If Lady Vane's rooms rebel against Genrich's values, so too does her husband's extravagant dress.

The same young man nods in Mander's direction. 'This meeting has the highest classification. Do we really need *him*?'

Lord Vane has a voice which bullies and seduces at the same time. 'Mr Mander attended my father's meetings with Genrich. Several were more significant than this, if you consider apocalypse significant, as I am inclined to do.'

Mander remains impassive, maintaining his deferential stoop.

Everyone turns to the most ornate chair in the room. Lord Sine's oversize head does not move.

The objection dies and the Clerk continues, 'Order Paper Agenda Item 1: Shortages.

'(A) Chitin. As reported at the last meeting, several disused mines have been stripped of their chitin. The outliers responsible will be found and dealt with. Shields recovered from vacated homes have helped, but reserves are low.

'(B) Tantalum. Supplies, essential for the manufacture of conductors, are running low. We are making every effort to find new deposits. Our current craft consume excessive energy and are under review.'

The Clerk looks around the table. 'Any questions on Minute 1?'

There are none.

'Order Paper Agenda Item 2.'

A severe-looking woman, older than Hernia, takes the floor. 'Both sanatoria are presently full and we have eight new cases this week, but the Infotainment trials are positive. Of the five triallists, two are cured and three no longer require secure accommodation.'

'Are the two back to work?'

'The advice is not to rush.'

'Advice from whom?'

'Infotainment.'

For the first time, Lord Sine speaks. 'How can an immersive game cure anything?'

Lord Vane smiles. 'What about chess?'

'Chess is exercise. Infotainment is distraction.'

Lord Vane responds with gentle authority. 'If fuses blow for no good reason, you improve the wiring. Of course, a sub-species of homo sapiens which strews the planet with rubbish, multiplies beyond any manageable limit and ignores wise warnings deserves no favours. But a sub-species which has no capacity for love, laughter or art is no better. Momenticons work gently on the neurons which deliver these lost faculties. *However*' – his formidable voice moves from argument to revelation – 'I am not here to argue. I would like to ask you all to the Tempestas Dome to celebrate the sixty years of our collaboration. Everyone is invited – and indeed, expected. The experience will accelerate the cure and prevent further outbreaks. On that, you have my solemn promise.'

'How can your Dome accelerate a cure?' hisses Lord Sine without even standing up.

'I prefer to show, not tell. Just transport yourselves.'

The double entendre in 'transport' sounds deliberate.

'Breaking a solemn promise to the Praesidium is treason,' hisses Lord Sine.

'Which is why I do not make it lightly,' replies Lord Vane.

'As long as you understand the consequences of any breach, we accept your invitation.'

The hidden onlookers exchange glances as the meeting moves on to relative trivia.

'Order Paper Agenda Item 3: Matter-Rearrangement and Sanitary Affairs,' the Clerk announces.

Morag is still puzzling over why Lord Sine should accept an invitation from a man he evidently despises when Hernia taps her shoulder and whispers, 'My star turn is next.' She leads the way back to the lift, then hoists Morag up through a near-invisible hatch in the ceiling.

Morag holds out her arms like a tightrope walker in reaction to the height. They are many hundreds of feet up. The surface is smooth and the chitin above so finely wrought as to be invisible.

'Up here is the one place I find true relief,' says Hernia, extracting a stubby tube from her bag and handing it to Morag. 'I call this the Long Eye. It's my design, and the one thing I'm proud of. I'd like you to have a try, Morag.' Hernia has not addressed her by name since their first introduction. 'Go over there, where it's darkest, and when you're ready, slip the catch on the side. You won't want me hanging around, chattering away.'

Morag goes, as directed, to the darkest area, where the Dome's outer curve begins to steepen, while Hernia wanders off in the opposite direction.

The Long Eye delivers nothing but magnified murk until she slides the catch forward, and then . . .

It is a jaw-dropping moment. She is peering into a northern hemisphere night sky as if the cloud curtain did not exist. Diamond dust flies in all directions, and a thousand descriptions in prose and poetry now make sense.

Morag has avidly studied the maps in Matilda's library, but she has never seen real stars, let alone on this cosmic scale. She hunts down the constellations. To see Earth's lost companions, the way they spill, their brilliance and variety, is to believe. She has never felt so infinitesimally small. She wonders about the sounds up there. Do these celestial bodies hiss or crackle as they spin?

A sudden stab of pain in her foot breaks the spell. A beetle with a shiny golden back has its pincers in her shoe. She tries to kick it away, but the insect holds fast. Its wings open and shut, then a skittering noise announces the arrival of others. They seize her shoes too, and such is their co-ordination that she stumbles and falls. The Long Eye spills from her grip as more arrivals swarm around her, now grabbing her sleeves as she flails to no avail. Their strength belies their size. They spin and drag her prostrate body and she is quite unable to break her quickening slide, such is the smoothness of the surface and the steepening gradient.

As she slips over the edge, the beetles take flight. She grasps a horizontal ledge where the Dome's eyebrows would be, but she knows she cannot support her own weight for long. She peers down over her shoulder. Eyelashes, each wide and as thick as an arm, are projecting below her, upper and lower lashes arranged alternately, allowing her to fall between them. Her feet catch one of the lower lashes and her hands grasp the higher. She is facing the eye socket.

'Oh God, oh my God,' she cries, clenching and unclenching her fists, striving to recover poise, breath and balance.

Here the height feels truly vertiginous. Heaven knows how many floors she is above ground level. She fights back the nausea.

Be calm. Be logical. Assimilate your surroundings. Analyse.

The beetles have vanished. She leans forward and carefully lowers herself to a crouch. The Dome's right eye, now level with her midriff, is glowing.

The eye socket is covered by a gauze curtain, through which she can see a vast room, empty but for the light source and an object like an oversize sconce on the floor, surrounded by cables and conductors – its innards, she assumes. No doors are visible in the wall behind, but the floor is heavily scuffed, and Morag concludes that the chamber must once have held many such devices. Perhaps this one has been abandoned as defective, or vandalised to complete others. The absence of any interior door smacks of secrecy.

'Hold on. Don't look up or down.'

It is Hernia's voice.

Morag almost overreacts and falls.

A cable with a crossbar attached like an anchor is lowered, swinging out and in, until she manages to catch it. She steels herself and launches into the void. She stretches out her legs and step by step, abseils back up to the brow, to find Hernia operating a windlass fixed to the surface by suction pads.

They hug each other.

'All in one piece?' asks Hernia anxiously.

'Just about.'

'I'm so sorry. I've had the occasional freak gust, bu—'

Morag shakes her head. 'There wasn't a breath of wind, but there were beetles, a whole swarm of them. They attacked my feet and spun me around . . .'

'Beetles?'

'They're insects.'

'You mean old-world insects . . .'

'Golden-coloured, and identical. They seemed to have just one objective – the elimination of me!'

Hernia peers around, disorientated and uncomprehending. 'Well, they're not here now.'

Morag looks too, but her attackers have indeed vanished. She doesn't know what to think. Has the whole expedition been tailored to this lethal climax? Did Hernia bring her here for the beetles to do their worst? It seems improbable. Hernia would hardly have hastened to her rescue if she'd had murder in mind. But if not Hernia, who? Morag remains suspicious enough not to share what she has seen in the storeroom behind the eye.

'They *were* beetles,' she repeats, 'scores of them. *Look!*' She tenders her mangled shoes and sleeves as evidence.

'Genrich admire insects for their sense of common purpose,' Hernia replies, 'but we don't *make* them. Why would we? Tempestas, however, make all manner of things, as you'll soon discover.' Hernia, picking at her cuticles, has reacquired that haunted, fragile look. 'We're lucky they keep cables up here for repair work.'

'I certainly am!'

'I'm so, so sorry. I just wanted to share my invention. I just wanted you to see what we're missing.'

Morag softens and takes Hernia by the shoulders. 'It was quite wonderful, and well worth a golden beetle or two. Thank you.'

Hernia looks round. 'I believe you, Morag, I really do. This place is descending into madness.' With a shrug, she reverts to her practical side. 'It's not only the shoes. Your uniform is a mess. I'll have to get you replacements by Monday.'

Nodding gratefully, Morag decides this is the moment to probe some other vexing questions. 'Who does the drawings we work with?'

'A freakish boy with a photographic memory turned up. He copies the characters straight from memory. You've seen us on Saturdays: we worship chess, or at least we're meant to. Cosmo's idea was right in the zone.'

'Have you ever heard of a man called Gilbert Spire?'

Hernia looks uneasy. 'I may have. What's he to you?'

'He was my father. Lord Sine had his scan. Lord Sine showed it to me and said he was special.'

Hernia came close and peered into Morag's face. 'You really are his daughter?'

'I am. He vanished years ago. He came here to work for Genrich, that's all I know.'

'It's more complex than that. Genrich and Tempestas have a fractious relationship, but they do co-operate. That's why the Vanes have quarters here and how your father met Lord Vane. Friendship blossomed until without warning or explanation, he disappeared.' She loosens into a smile. 'He was a charmer. Some say he became disenchanted with his work and fled to escape Genrich, others, that he fell foul of the weather-watchers, and Tempestas were responsible. Whatever happened was hushed up.'

'The weather-watchers? Who are they?'

'A state within a state, a law unto themselves. Tempestas has its illnesses too.'

'You're very well informed.'

'I was Lord Sine's first and only ambassador to the Tempestas Dome, until I was suspected of going over. Lord Vane insisted I head up Infotainment, which probably saved my life.' She paused. 'That was a pretence, examining you like that. I know you're Gil's daughter. That's why I came to collect you.'

Time to move on, Morag decides. 'Let's catch the end of the meeting. Something doesn't fit. I can't fathom why Lord Sine would accept an invitation from Lord Vane to the Tempestas Dome when they clearly despise each other. Or why Lord Vane would invite him in the first place.'

'They collaborate in their way.'

'And their fathers?'

'Likewise, I'm told. The world dubbed the first Lord Vane "Job". It was he who created Tempestas. His technicians diagnosed the growing toxicity in the upper air and warned that the gentle exponential curve would suddenly soar, as it did, of course. But at the time only Lord Sine and Genrich believed him. Genrich worked in secret on a new race, hoping Lord Vane would be proved right. The second generation continue their parents' work.'

'They don't sound like natural allies to me.'

Hernia does not respond. She retrieves the Long Eye and they meander back to their spyhole by the Praesidium Hall. Hernia flicks open the grille. The lights have been dimmed almost to darkness.

'They have other rooms for committee meetings, but they all end at midnight.'

Morag seizes Hernia's arm. 'Look ... *over there—*'

In the gloom, halfway up a bank of seats, is Lord Sine, sitting like a toad on a stone.

It is a pose with purpose.

'That's not usual,' whispers Hernia. 'What's he doing?'

'He's waiting for someone,' replies Morag confidently.

She is right: a fleeting slab of light announces the arrival of Lord Vane. The two men meet in the circular space at floor level.

Circling each other like boxers, Lord Vane opens.

'I have delivered,' he says. His voice is low and conspiratorial.

Lord Sine sniffs. 'You have prepared the ground.'

'I will deliver.'

'I do hope so. Like father, like son.' Lord Sine delivers this mystifying remark with a smirk.

'There remains your side of the bargain,' replies Lord Vane.

'We agreed, delivery on completion, remember? You will find yourself looking in the mirror. Thereafter, we have our very different projects to pursue. I propose a truce for three years from the Tempestas party.'

Lord Vane stops, takes a step back. 'A truce? That suggests it's preceding a war. We've always worked apart but together, as our fathers did before us: each contributes to the other's survival. My apologies, Lord Sine, I know you prefer long words. We're mutually symbiotic. Let us continue that way.'

Lord Sine shakes his head. 'Our visions are contradictory and resources are dwindling. Our co-existence will soon be problematic.'

A twitch in the shadows catches Morag's eye. Lord Sine has a bodyguard seated beside an aisle and nearby, Mander is standing to attention, arms tight to his sides.

Lord Sine extends a hand. 'Three years, and then we'll review our arrangement.'

For the first time Lord Vane looks weak, the junior partner. He gives the hand one vigorous shake and leaves the way he came.

Hernia flicks back the grille. 'Men,' she says. 'All that posturing!'

'What has Lord Vane delivered?' asks Morag.

'You, I assume, and a cure for our ills.'

Morag does not reply. They reposition themselves on top of the lift and return to their embarkation point. Little passes between them on the journey home. It has been an evening rich in ambiguous incident.

'Thanks for the company,' Morag says as they part. 'And the adventure.'

147 smiles. 'I'd like you to have the Long Eye – think of it as compensation for the beetles.'

Morag blushes. Even here, kindness and generosity can be found. She gives 147 a parting hug.

Back in her bare, bookless room, lying under a cold white sheet in a bed with white iron bars, she makes a mental list.

Lord Vane wants Genrich to visit his Dome – but why?

And why does Lord Sine accept?

Lord Vane has an unexplained interest in old art.

Lord Sine is biding his time.

Resources are running low, chitin and tantalum in particular.

Lord Vane is expecting a delivery, something which will resemble a mirror.

Someone wants me dead.

A multidimensional board indeed, and where between these contradictory lines might laughter, love and art be found?

Sleep is hard to come by. The memory of her body spinning and falling will not go away. Eventually the vision of starfields spilling across pure, unpolluted darkness lures her into sleep.

5

Exeat II

Morag pauses in her narrative. 'I've reached a natural break and my voice is going. Off you go, Fogg.'

Fogg looks oddly uneasy.

'What's the problem?'

'I don't add much.'

'It'll be nice and short, then.'

'It's upsetting.'

'Don't be so wet.'

'For you.'

'For *me*! How could your story upset me? What is it? Bestiality? Necrophilia? Come on, Fogg – declare your hidden vice!'

'Where do you think Lady Vane's drawings of paintings came from?'

'I'm not that dim, Fogg – from you, obviously.'

'Via your library.'

'What do you mean – *via*?'

He said nothing.

'You went to my home? How – why – with whom?'

'Cosmo Vane escorted me.'

'Cosmo!'

Morag thinks back, and remembers Cosmo taking a few days off immediately after her arrival at the Dome. It must have been then. 'All right, let's have it. No censorship, every word.'

*

Fogg knocks on the door. 'Hello-o?'

Matilda had always read Morag like a book. She would have had Fogg in her pocket in minutes. It quickly became clear to Morag that Fogg memorised words as accurately as he copied pictures. His account had the verbatim ring of truth.

She found herself reimagining the narrative from her grandmother's perspective.

Her visitor must know she is old and slow, for he does not knock again, but waits patiently.

The boy's complexion is pale; his shoulders are hunched and his head tilts like a dog expecting a blow. He is Morag's age or thereabouts, but without her poise, without *any* poise. He stands there with a battered bag in his right hand, mouthing a word he cannot complete, a study in nervous neutrality.

She smiles. 'Do come in. I'm Matilda.'

He sidles into the hall.

'I'm F-F-F-F—'

'Francis? Frederick?'

'F-F-F-F—' Spittle spangles his lower lip.

She tries a different tack. 'Foucault?'

The corners of his mouth rise. He can recognise humour, so there is hope.

'Fogg,' he splutters.

'Fogg is good, too short to ruin. At your age I got Mat, Tilly, Tilda and Till, but rarely the name my parents chose. Blessed are the Foggs, for they shall have brevity,' says Matilda with a twinkle.

Once again, his mouth flirts with a smile. 'It's about the books. I'm only here to look. I don't take anything.'

He speaks fluently enough. Only the Fs cause him difficulty, it seems, but he still sounds like a boy schooled to obey orders. He looks that way too. His clothes are drab: a long waistcoat over a collarless shirt, and trousers held up with a clutching left hand:

hand-me-downs in cheap material. He wears worn sandals. Even the Genrich pin in his waistcoat lapel is chipped.

She queries the initials. 'GSIS?'

'*The Genrich School for Idiot-Savants.*'

He must be an outlier removed from his family by Genrich, like so many others.

'I detest that word, "idiot-savants". Savants aren't idiots, for a start. It's a label invented by the ordinary to downgrade the brilliant.' She does not ask where his particular brilliance lies. Let him have the pleasure of showing her. 'How long do you have?'

'One afternoon, one night, one morning and not a minute more or I'm in trouble.'

'You'd best get started then.'

He leaves his bag in the sitting room and follows her to the library.

'Any particular books?' she asks.

'Books with pictures.'

'Any particular pictures?'

'Any of these would be good.' From his pocket he pulls a list of celebrated paintings, although few know of them now. Out of sight, out of mind.

Matilda absorbs the list before asking, 'Who sent you?'

'I know who came with me, but I don't know who sent me. The School didn't say.'

I know who came with me. Not an answer to her question, but a warning, perhaps. She returns to his list.

'We have almost all of them, and others as good in their way.' She rifles through the shelves and starts pulling out one volume after another.

He stares at each picture for no more than a few minutes, and Matilda realises he is lodging the images in his memory. *That's his brilliance: a mind like tracing paper.* Might he be part of a rebel movement dedicated to keeping art alive? Sadly, that notion feels far-fetched.

Her visitor is full of surprises. He goes through the same rigmarole, looking and remembering, painting after painting, but some engage him longer than others. He lingers over a volume on polar exploration, the old world at its most magical.

Only at the end of the day does he begin to flag.

Wanting to bestow backbone and encouragement, she assembles the best pastes and drink the Matter-Rearranger can offer, and when she returns, she discovers he has moved on to the reference books festooning the single table in the middle of the library.

'I never thought of their lives,' he says. 'Stupid of me.'

'When we're young, we see what's in front of us, and that's how it should be. It's something to be proud of. Revel in what you see. Travel light. You'll get baggage soon enough.' She pauses before taking the plunge. 'Talking of which, you can work round words beginning with F – well, unless you stub your toe.'

'Unless you're made to.'

'You can't be *made* to.'

'You can.'

'Well, not here.'

'Not with you here, maybe.'

Again, there's that demon on his shoulder. Searching for context, she asks about his parents.

His eyes go glassy. 'Lightning destroyed their chitin shield – at least, that's what they said at school. They took me aside to tell me.' His lips curl inwards. 'They said the rain is so poisonous, it was quick.'

Chitin is immune to most lightning. Matilda suspects that Fogg has either suppressed or been spared the truth. To tease out the knots, she goes back to her own early childhood and describes how it felt to move from shade into sunlight, from a sandy beach into cool water, and how these pastorales spread out across the table would sound and smell if you were there.

'How was it, the Fall?' he asks.

'The atmosphere turned toxic and corrosive, then we lost the sun. We couldn't go out. There were freak storms, with lightning like we'd never seen before. The weakened buildings collapsed, killing any survivors who had sought cleaner air in cellars and basements. The word "apocalyptic" is overused, but that's how it was.'

'How did you – how did *anyone* – survive?'

'Genrich took scans from those reported to be gifted – I was lucky enough to be one of them. They installed a chitin shield, free of charge. It bordered on the grotesque at the time, but within weeks our local town went down . . . our neighbours, the dogs and cats, the trees and flowers, every living thing. Imagine a shipwright turning up and building an ark for Noah and only Noah, for no obvious reason. That's how it was. We were blessed.'

He notices a single butterfly in a small glass case hanging on the wall. It is pinned to a white card.

'Did you ever see those?' he asks.

'Oh yes, all sorts, sizes and colours.'

'It's beautiful.'

'They called it a white admiral, *Limenitis camilla*. I fear it died for its looks.'

'Better, I suppose, than dying for nothing.'

By the time they retire to bed, Matilda feels quite revived by Fogg's company. She hopes his path might cross with Morag's. Overnight, while he sleeps in her granddaughter's bed, she tightens the waistband of his trousers and hunts out one of her son's woollen shirts from an attic drawer.

In the morning they restore the books to their harbours. Miraculously, Fogg doesn't need a single prompt: he knows exactly where every volume goes. He packs his bag, including the shirt, and as noon approaches, they gather in the front room.

'Do you have pen and paper?' Fogg asks Matilda. She hands him one precious sheet and her son's drawing pen. The pen darts across the surface like a conjuror's wand. A spreading tree dominates a modest hill, while below, a patchwork of fields stretches far away, perfect squares alternating between light and shade, each divided by hedges or streams.

'It's an outsized rural chessboard from an old-world book,' he explains. 'The moment I saw it, I thought, life turns on which square you start on. Now I'm not so sure. With help, you can move a long way, can't you?'

'With courage you can move a *very* long way in a very short time.' She smiles at how he has opened up in the course of his visit. The drawing is exquisite. 'You're sure it's for me?'

'I churn out drawings like this at school,' he said diffidently. 'It's all they ever want. This one has an extra tree, just for you.'

She props the drawing on the mantlepiece above the redundant fireplace.

When the knock comes, it is a brutal strike. Fogg's face and deportment revert to the servile look of his arrival.

Matilda blocks his way to the door. 'Owner's privilege,' she says gently.

The young man who barges in wears an outlier's casual clothes, but in contrast to Fogg's, they are finely tailored of leather and velvet.

'You'd better be done, Fogg. I've been cooling my arse in that tin can for more than a day. And I trust you got the subject I specifically mentioned?'

Matilda's voice turns to steel. 'This is *my* house. You say who you are, and you ask my permission to enter.'

The intruder spins round. In contrast to the strong build, a delicate nose and full mouth give him a sensual baby-face appearance, accentuated by the shock of black hair and pale complexion.

'What did you say?' he hisses, feigning shock at her impertinence.

'You heard,' replies Matilda.

'I doubt it matters, but the name is Cosmo Vane.' He turns to

Fogg. 'I hope you've been practising: *Frederick favours fragrant ferrets for festivals.* Say it!'

'F-F-F-F . . .'

'F-f-failed,' crows Cosmo. 'Get into the Scurrier, Fogg, and be quick about it.'

With a mumbled, 'Thanks for everything,' Fogg shuffles out, but he waits in the airlock. He wants to hear what he can, for her sake.

'What's he thanking you for?' asks Cosmo.

'I'd say respite, wouldn't you?' replies Matilda gently. She looks into his eyes, because he is gazing into hers. Some dark gift lurks there.

'I bet you can't do it anymore, whatever your saving paltry gift was. You're too old, past it.'

He strolls around her living room, running his fingers along the furniture like a cleaner checking for dust. 'An ant can lift ten times its own weight. True or false?'

'True.'

'Why?'

She hates his urge to disconcert and dominate. Aware that after a promising start, she is losing ground, she decides she will not be dismissed as ignorant. 'Its strength comes from chitin – well, strictly, chitin and sclerotin combined.'

Cosmo awards her a grudging nod as he completes his circuit. He grips the door handle and smiles. 'On the subject of exoskeletons, I've news. Chitin supplies are running low. There have been thefts, too. Necessary measures have been taken. I wouldn't want them to come as a surprise.'

And he is gone.

She hears the Scurrier depart. Taking Fogg's present from the mantlepiece, she sits in the rocking chair and eyes his world of square meadows, light and dark, stretching far and wide. *Pray God Morag finds the moves to avoid this man*, she mumbles before, wearied by hours of unfamiliar company, she drifts into sleep.

*

The exterior of Lord Vane's private craft is sleek, its interior luxurious. The seats are plush; the dials encircled with highly polished brass; gleaming silver flasks sit in silver holders; the thick, soft carpet is a rich dark maroon; the lighting is recessed and warm. It is another world. Even so, Fogg is relegated to a back seat. They soon flash past a slow, squat Genrich craft with a claw-like crane attached.

'What does that do?'

Cosmo's smile has a predatory edge.

'It's a harvester.'

'That doesn't sound very nice.'

'We reap what we sow. It harvests chitin. You should focus on what matters. You're to meet Lord Vane, so sharpen up.'

'But why?'

'Who do you think you are, F-F-F-Fogg, interrogating me? You're mighty privileged to be in this craft at all.'

And that is it, until, hours later, the full head of the Genrich Dome hoves into view. Hitherto, Fogg has seen only its crown. He gapes in wonder.

Cosmo maintains his silence until they have docked high at the rear. 'We've landed by the occipital lobe, home to our visual skills,' says Cosmo, the first civil remark he has addressed to Fogg.

They exit on to a platform.

'You go through those doors, on and right. And try not to stutter.' And with that advice given, Cosmo Vane struts off to a different exit.

The doors open on to a generous atrium where antique gargoyles and waterspouts on four tall fibreglass columns align to create an aisle to a single door. On a spike high above the door sits a weathervane with a snake entwined about the arrow which once pointed to the prevailing wind. An elderly man in black tails, salt and pepper trousers and a cream shirt with a stiff collar opens the door. His costume and a faintly unctuous stoop put Fogg in mind of a penguin.

'I am Mander, and the weathervane is his Lordship's personal rebus,' explains the penguin. He points at the words *Praemitte Tempestas* set in gold leaf above the doorway. 'And that pithy advice is the company motto: *Keep Ahead of the Weather*. In, in, Master Fogg, where refreshment awaits you.'

Flames flicker in an expansive fireplace. A man sits behind a huge pedestal desk facing the fire. There is no other furniture, save for two leather armchairs on either side of the fire, and a lamp on the desk. Floor and walls are bare, except for a luminous head like a death mask floating above a plinth in one corner.

'Master Fogg is here, your Lordship,' announces Mander.

Lord Vane rises from his chair to greet Fogg. Tall, gaunt, and of an in-between sort of age, he stands ramrod-straight. His shin-length robe, drawn tight over dark trousers, a white shirt and plain slippers, shimmers in the firelight. On the desk lie several sheets of rich cream-coloured paper, meticulously stacked beside a pen and an ink bottle.

'How was your journey?' His voice has a deep mineral quality.

'I've never travelled like that before.'

'I imagine the Genrich School is grim. Describe it for me.'

Fogg feels surprisingly at ease. 'It's some way from the Dome and mostly underground. We don't get to see the staff quarters, but, yes, our bit is grim. The flooring has decayed, so you walk from one dark island to another. The paint is peeling, the fans wheeze and the air is stale. I've got this small circular hole which passes for a window – I can just see the very top of the Genrich Dome when the murk allows. I've been there seven years now.'

'He has quite a way with words, don't you agree, Mander?'

'Indeed, he has, sir.' Mander smiles.

'But how is he with the pen? That's the question. Draw me an image you think I'd like, Master Fogg.'

Fogg is not surprised by the request. Only his modest gift could have brought him here.

'The desk is yours,' adds Lord Vane as he settles in one of the leather chairs. 'Down,' he whispers, and the flames lower.

Fogg mulls over his host's request. A peculiar room, a peculiar manservant and a peculiar craft – Lord Vane is not one for the usual. Nor, Fogg suspects, is he a patient man. He needs something simple, quick and offbeat.

The paper is so thick and rich ... Fogg shapes a spill of ink to convey the gloom in the bottom quarter of the painting and hatches above for the numinous light which dominates the remainder. A tiny dog's head, visible to the front shoulders only, peers up, as over the lip of a crater. Or is it fighting to keep its head above water or a quicksand?

Lord Vane is quick to pass judgement. 'Wonderful, wouldn't you say, Mander?'

'I would say so, my Lord.'

Fogg replays what he can recall from the commentary in Matilda's book. 'It's by a man called Francesco Goya, who painted it on his house wall. He was a lopsided person – old, deaf and desperate.'

'He was poisoned by lead,' adds Mander, delivering the promised refreshments, 'the lead in his own paint.'

'How on earth do you know that?' queries Lord Vane.

'Old memories,' replies Mander with a quizzical little bow.

'What are the colours?' Lord Vane asks Fogg.

'Dark below the dog with swirling creams and yellows above.'

'You're quite a poet, Master Fogg,' says Lord Vane, 'so you'd best avoid the ants' nest beyond that door, where little people fret over little tasks, when they should be reaching for the stars. If the ladder collapses under us in the effort, so be it.' Lord Vane raises the drawing to the lamp. 'We can make this,' he adds to nobody in particular.

'Assuredly so, your Lordship, assuredly so,' says Mander, 'although your Lordship may, of course, have other priorities.'

Fogg felt all at sea. *Make?* Was Lord Vane a painter? Did they have a machine which could translate his humble drawing into a finished piece of art, colours and all?

'The dog *is* Francesco Goya, in a manner of speaking,' Mander whispers to Fogg as Lord Vane moves on.

'What I would really like, Master Fogg, is a masterly painting of a town, one with atmosphere and style. It's your choice, but be sure to do that before you leave. We must, of course, get you back to school by Sunday night or your absence will be reported, and we can't have that, can we. So draw away, Master Fogg, until your wrists ache.'

Fed and watered by Mander, Fogg does just that. He sleeps in a bunk bed in a modest room off a passageway piled high with packing cases. A tiny, beautifully rendered golden-coloured beetle has been pinned to the wall. For a second or two he thinks he hears it hum.

By early morning, it is gone.

Over the next two days he produces a mixture of what pleases him and what he feels will please his host, almost all taken from the pictures in the old lady's library. After each session Mander secures the drawings in a large leather folder. For the town Lord Vane has ordered, he does his best with a new personal favourite, *Hunters in the Snow*, by Pieter Bruegel the Elder. Mander approves, and makes a note of the principal colours.

Mercifully, there is no sign of Cosmo Vane. Nor does Lord Vane return, but on his second afternoon a teenage girl invades the room. She has russet hair and pleasant looks, but she lacks her father's patrician air. Even her dress is modest.

'Mander says you're called Fogg,' says the girl with a smile. 'I'm Cassiopeia, Cassie for short. My brother is Cosmo, as in cosmonaut.'

Fogg visibly flinches, but she is no longer looking at him.

'What's that?' she asks, pointing at the current work in progress.

'It's a hunt in a forest.'

ANDREW CALDECOTT | 75

'What are they hunting on?'

'They're called horses,' says Fogg, because he's read about them, not because he's ever seen one.

'Cosmo would like this one. Now, draw me a little something without all these spears and swords.'

Fogg sketches at speed a small drawing from the *Looking Glass* book, a rocking horse with wings.

'My very own! You're a hero, Mr Fogg. May we meet again, come wind, come rain.' She lets fall the small square of paper, drops to her haunches to retrieve it and whispers, 'Something is afoot. I think Mander knows, but he won't say what. So be careful, won't you.'

Cassie's exuberance emboldens Fogg to ask her a question. He points at the floating death mask. 'Who's that?'

'That's my grandfather, the first Lord Vane and the first Chairman of Tempestas. He looks rather scary, doesn't he, floating in the air like that. And from all I hear, he *was* scary. But where would we be without him?' She grins. 'Father works everyone hard, but do slip in somewhere for me to live one day, will you – somewhere peaceful and isolated.'

She gives him the same smile on leaving as on arrival. This second time, it looks ever so slightly forced.

He is returned to the School in a Scurrier piloted by a Genrich employee who is even less talkative than Cosmo Vane. The staff eye him suspiciously, but no one asks about his unexpected exeat.

Fogg gives a truncated account of the trip to his one school friend, who occupies the adjacent cubicle: a curly-haired girl who has been recruited to peer at geological maps on a screen. She has a genius for detecting where pegmatite veins might lurk in granite – find them, and you may find tantalum.

He likes Niobe. He has no science; she is steeped in geology. Tantalum, she says, is a chemical element and key to the storage of electric charges. It is silvery blue-grey, hard, does not tarnish and resists chemical attack, even corrosion. Its atomic number is 73, a joining of two prime numbers. Every time you say 'ta', you utter its canonical chemical symbol. It is rare, and everyone knows it is running out. Her late father, a miner, had given her the tantalum ring she always wears. Tantalus was a king, she adds, straight-faced, and Niobe his daughter; tantalum and niobium are found together.

Niobe is just as intrigued by Fogg's ability to draw from memory. She sneaks a look whenever she can. They're fantastical, and they appear to be part of a story. She cannot conceive what interest they could hold for Genrich and Fogg is reticent about his past. 'They're better than the technical drawings they made me do when I first came,' is the most she can extract from him.

Though worlds apart in learning and talents, together they alleviate their mutual despair. He talks of perspective and the art of hatching and creating shadow; she of the beauty of rocks. The other twenty or so inmates have scientific or mathematical gifts and keep to themselves.

Even in their gloomy cubicles, Niobe's dark skin glows as much as his pallor. He finds it unifying. Hardly any black-skinned people inhabit the paintings he has memorised. There is a king who is offering a baby a golden casket, and two young men painted without fuss and therefore with their dignity. He recalls only one black-skinned woman, a maid in full dress and bonnet holding up a bouquet of flowers to her naked white mistress. He cannot understand the disparity. In his eyes, Niobe is more paintable than any of them.

She keeps herself fit and tries to keep him up to the mark, whispering of escape and how one day they will disarm their Genrich gaolers and rebuild a new world in the wilderness.

Now, she listens without interruption.

Fogg, despite his evident fatigue, is looking uplifted by his recent experience. 'All that way, and I just did drawings. What can they want them for? But something is up, something dangerous.'

'Well, you can be sure they won't tell us.'

'I'm not sure Genrich know.'

'Genrich know everything.'

'Do you think we'll survive whatever it is?'

Niobe shakes her head at such a dim question. 'Spin of a coin.' She likes using extinct old-world phrases.

'That's my natural break,' said Fogg. 'I'm so sorry about Matilda.'

'How can we know?'

'He called it a harvester, didn't he.'

'That's hardly conclusive.' *But it is suggestive*, thought Morag, and there had been talk in the Praesidium of gathering chitin from outliers' houses.

'It was the way he said it.'

'Bastard,' hissed Morag. 'I'll get him.'

'Or I will,' whispered Fogg.

'No!' she said fiercely. 'He's *mine*.'

She can see, even feel, her grandmother's end in her mind's eye.

A grumble outside and a squeaking noise wake Matilda. It is dusk. A sound like a knife on glass comes from the sides of the house and echoes down the chimney.

They are dismantling the protective shield and there is nothing she can do.

The air prickles her lungs. Later, she hears the crackle of an approaching storm. Soon the toxic rain will fall. She and her possessions, all these precious books, will be reduced to dust.

'She would want us to get on with it,' Morag added firmly. 'To my last chapter, the worst of all.'

6

Zugzwang

On the Sunday following the escapade with Hernia, a replacement uniform and shoes appear at Morag's door, but thereafter her new friend all but vanishes from view.

A young man, wearing 83 on his lapel, assumes Hernia's responsibilities at Infotainment. He breezily regales the workforce with targets:

'Two hundred pill bottles a day,' to the manufacturers.

'Ten scenes a day,' to those at the weavers.

And, as if administering a school punishment, 'Fifty lines by six o'clock sharp,' to Morag.

One evening, working late, Morag chances on Hernia emerging from the guinea-pig room with a bottle of momenticons in one hand.

'I'm not meant to be seen.' She sounds relaxed, almost wistful, and her fingers have lost their angry look.

'How long have you been in there?'

'I arrive early, and I leave late. I'm doing a double-dose trial. I spend more time *there* than I do here. I'm . . . I'm . . . really rather happy.' She pauses. 'How did you do the sea? The cliffs, the sand, the breakwaters, the sun, the creature with the tusks – they're so *realistic*.'

Morag could not resist a quote.

'The sun was shining on the sea,
Shining with all his might,
He did his very best to make
The billows smooth and bright . . .

'And I have drawings, and our library books talk about the sea, its colours and sounds. So it's easy for me to *imagine*.'

'I could spend my life walking that beach. Indeed, I hope to go back there tonight. Not that you ever quite know where you'll start or end up. It's the very opposite of life here.'

And that is it. Hernia shakes her hand, rather formally, and is gone.

Loneliness has been Morag's constant companion, but this is different, this loss of a friend, aggravated by the fact that Hernia is marooned in a world which Morag has herself in part created.

A few days later, 83 assembles the workers. On a table beside him stands an array of small bottles containing buff-coloured square pills.

'The trials are over. Today we distribute momenticons for general consumption. There's a complimentary bottle for every one of you: your passport to *Looking Glass Wonderland* and your own unique starting square. Every bottle top has a timer, to ensure we all set out at the same time and are rationed in the same way. We start tomorrow.'

83 then reads from a script quite at odds with his own spare style. 'You'll encounter objectives to realise, puzzles to solve, hazards to evade and distractions to ignore. You'll all be pieces in the great chess game.' He lowers his voice. 'And, above all, you'll say goodbye to the "difficulties" which have infected your colleagues and might otherwise infect you. That is the miracle of momenticons. They both cure *and* prevent.'

The workers raise their hands and clap in a wooden way, as puppets might. His last sentence has struck home. Their minds have been increasingly buckling under a forced diet of logic, tasks and orders.

'Take a flier and spread the word,' 83 orders. They step forward, but the script is not yet finished. 'And – *and* – there's even better to come. Tempestas, your long-term collaborators, have invited you to their Dome tomorrow evening to celebrate sixty years of co-operation. Lord Sine has accepted on your behalf and transport is arranged. Just don't forget your bottles. This will be another notable landmark in the Great Survival Project.'

Morag watches the workers watching 83. Their reservations have visibly eased at the mention of Lord Sine. Hers have not.

Before filing out, every worker, Morag included, takes a bottle.

7

The Tempestas Party

An unusual Saturday dawns. When Morag tours the Dome, she finds no chess and little sign of life. By the untenanted chessboards stand notices which list each Genrich worker's number with an assigned docking bay and individual seat for departure at 4 p.m. sharp. Morag will be sharing docking bay 3 with her colleagues in Infotainment, including Hernia.

A tap on the back halts her return journey. 'Good morning, Miss.'

Morag turns to find Mander in his usual plumage, tendering a flat cardboard box on outstretched arms. The old-world lid bears the words *Paris & London* beneath a coat of arms.

'There's a reception for outliers alongside the Genrich party. Her Ladyship thought you'd like to dress as yourself. I have made appropriate adjustments. You'll find changing facilities freely available in the Tempestas Dome. Once in your party best, head for the gatehouse with the blue-grey beams. Your invitation is also inside. *A bientôt*, and live in hope.'

Before she can thank him, Mander is gliding away towards the nearest escalator.

A gatehouse with blue-grey beams? A reception for outliers? Maybe Matilda will be there; maybe there'll be new books, too, and people whose faces *respond*. She *will* live in hope.

Morag rushes back to her room. The dress has been interleaved with white tissue paper. The words *pure silk* embroidered in gold on the label feel truthful. Laid out on her narrow bed, the dignified dark blue colour and high neck look quite plain. The hem will clear the knee, but not by much.

Once on, the dress exudes a timeless elegance. Mander has somehow managed a perfect fit. The silk kisses her skin. Beneath the dress, flat shoes, packed in green cloth drawstring bags, fit perfectly too. The ensemble matches the invitation with its old-world formal curlicue script.

She repacks the dress with mixed feelings. Will being on show compromise her independence or strengthen it? Not knowing how this expedition will end, she reserves judgement.

She packs her suitcase, not forgetting her bottle of momenticons.

At 3.45 p.m. precisely, the Dome disgorges its occupants from their rooms. They line up at the specified departure gates in numerical order, each carrying an identical backpack. Nobody questions Morag's dress-box or her old-fashioned shoulder bag. In a community conditioned to obedience and good order, her Genrich uniform is enough. They see her as being on a special mission which is not their business.

She quickly finds Hernia. 'Hi, 147,' she says with a smile. 'Can we sit together?'

'There is a board,' Hernia replies. 'We must keep to our allotted seat or, should I say, our square.' She draws Morag aside. 'Cosmo gave me a special momenticon to mark our achievement.'

'But you're going to a party – a *real* party.'

'I've already been to a party, and you were there,' she says dreamily. 'I recognised your voice. There were strange creatures too. It was magical.' Hernia checks herself. 'The other triallists are also on the mend.'

'Yes, but Lord Vane's invitation is an honour. I didn't take my momenticons, and you've taken several already. Have a break.'

'Don't worry, Cosmo's is in its own bottle and firmly sealed. Like in *Wonderland*, let's cross the river when we get to it.'

The multilevel craft is large, but the accommodation is cramped.

The manuals sit in silence. Their symptoms of angst remain visible, but there is expectation too.

An hour or so into the flight, Morag's reverie is interrupted by a *pop-pop-pop* echoing all around the cabin and immediately, everyone starts fumbling in their pockets or backpacks for Infotainment's pill bottles.

All the top seals have self-broken, including Morag's.

A familiar voice addresses them. 'This is Lord Sine. Our Infotainment department has constructed an excellent pill to meet all afflictions of the mind. Take your pill now and reap further benefits at the Tempestas Dome. I will be there to welcome you.'

They do as they're told, *of course*. Morag decides against as her neighbours subside into a strange tranquillity. Eyelids half close and flicker. Some try to rise to their feet and walk, but the travelling belts restrain them. Mouths work gently while faces flirt with new geographies; she sees the hint of a smile here, a quizzical questioning there.

The prescribed hour passes and surreal conversations break out.

'There are squares everywhere.'

'Mine had vegetation on the boundaries. But once you move, it's a new world every time.'

'Mine too.'

'How many did you get to?'

'Four.'

'And the old-world creatures!'

'I met talking flowers.'

The pills appear to work differently with different people: they have not visited the same places or met the same characters, and Morag notices that they are talking as much to themselves as each other. Much of what they say is mirroring Morag's own work. She does feel some satisfaction, but she's uneasy too; she can't forget Lord Sine's chilling philosophy: *The gift of existence must be justified by utility.* Infotainment has delivered diversion, even rescue, which should empty the Sanatorium and enhance productivity – unless the patients become lotus eaters and their utility fails.

With immaculate timing, the manuals emerge from their reverie as their imminent arrival is announced. 'We are five minutes from the Tempestas Dome. Hone your chess skills, for you will be needing them.'

This mysterious command provokes another round of speculation as the craft docks. A spacious airlock leads to a tunnel with an old board floor and a rock ceiling which glows like a luminous clock. They trudge downhill and emerge in a lost world: gnarled tree trunks twist in half-light thrown by lanterns; leaves scud along the ground; grass rustles. Strange purple flowers hang from stems which wind through the branches. A moth flutters across the path, and then another.

She has not progressed far when a familiar figure rises from a stool to greet her. Lady Vane, as ever, is a picture of elegance. She collapses the stool and carries it.

'Morag Spire, I'm so glad you came. The evening would not be the same without you.' She smiles. 'You realise they're not true moths – or true anything else.'

'True moths don't fly in straight lines.'

'You're so well informed, Morag. Such a pleasure with these dunderheads on the loose. But look closely. Aren't you impressed?'

The leaves are finely made, but when bent, they spring back on release. On closer inspection, the grass is rooted in a brown textile and the trees have a fibreglass feel. Yet huge effort has been invested in this make-believe reality. Fungi break the surface between crisscrossing roots; birds call the advent of dusk; flowers begin to close.

'Yes,' Morag says after a pause. 'Yes.'

'You hesitate.'

'It must have taken so much work – but to what end?'

'It's a penance of sorts, and a good penance requires much work.

ANDREW CALDECOTT | 85

And we will do better. There are plans afoot.' A pair of chattering manuals sidle past them. 'God, look at them.'

The visitors are marching remorselessly on. Tributes to lost flora and fauna, however finely wrought, hold no interest for them.

A village comes into view, where thatch, tile, oak and stone co-exist. A classical portico stands next to a clapperboard house, and a central square holding a stone fountain with dolphins is surrounded by a church and rows of shopfronts.

'Welcome to the Tempestas Dome and our final destination,' says Lady Vane, pointing at a distant gatehouse with blue-painted beams.

'I wasn't expecting a personal guide. Thank you.'

'We look after our own. Now, let me show you something clever. The way to the gatehouse is blocked by seven gates. Each has a one-dimensional chessboard with pieces magnetically attached and set as a problem. The first is Mate in one against any defence which, of course, they will sail through while dismissing it as an insult to their intelligence. But when they get to the fifth – mate in five – and the sixth and the seventh? It was Cosmo's idea, how to get them in the party mood! Isn't he clever?'

'That he certainly is,' replies Morag before she can check herself.

The shopfront windows in the main square are aglow, and each is different. The crafts on view match the world around them. There are shops for insects, birds, animals, false earth and rocks, grasses and flowers. Behind the displays are workbenches laden with hoops of wafer-thin wire, microtools and tiny vices, giving an overall impression of dwarven jewellers.

She halts by the insect window. There's a golden beetle sitting there, a replica of her assailants on the Genrich Dome roof, hemmed in by butterflies, dragonflies, bees and other *Coleoptera*.

A double corner shop with an arched passage linking its two wings is the only one with a sign: JINX'S EMPORIUM. As it gently swings, a mouse runs up one side, down the other and back again. Here all these artificial creatures have come alive, flexing their wings, feet, antennae and other extremities. Bees hover, a bird warbles, a caterpillar climbs a green stalk.

'We call it functionality,' says Lady Vane, tapping a beetle-like brooch on her chest.

'It's a pity Mr Jinx isn't at home. Anything in this place which isn't human moves because of him. And he's about to go up in the world, Old Master status you might say.' Lady Vane smiles again.

She's signalling change, thought Morag, *but she's not going to tell me what change or how or when.*

A generously built middle-aged woman appears in the next shop doorway. 'Your Ladyship.' She curtseys.

'Have you somewhere this pretty young thing could change?'

'It's Morag Spire, isn't it? It'd be an honour.'

'You know me?' Morag asks in surprise, as the woman ushers her through the door.

'Everyone knows you and your work. But quick, quick, love. Upstairs and use the bedroom first on the right. You don't keep Lady Vane waiting.'

The bedroom is small but homely, with the luxury of a mirror. She tosses the Genrich uniform into the waste bin. It is time to move on. *Look at me*, the dress whispers.

When she emerges, Lady Vane gives her an appraising look. 'Turn around for me.'

Morag does so.

'What a picture! And what I'd give to be your age: everything ahead and nothing meaningful behind.' She points. 'Those bloody automatons are at the fourth gate already – but now they're not finding it so easy.'

Morag has herself found the manuals exasperating, but she still finds the edge to Lady Vane's hostility unsettling.

The manuals are indeed milling around the mate-in-four chess problem, trying out moves, gesticulating, debating – their idea of a party mood. She sees Hernia in the distance, pensive and

7	3	6	4	1	2	8	5	9
1	8	2	5	9	3	4	6	7
4	5	9	8	6	7	3	1	2
5	9	1	2	8	4	7	3	6
3	2	4	6	7	9	1	8	5
6	7	8	1	3	5	9	2	4
2	4	3	9	5	1	6	7	8
8	1	5	7	4	6	2	9	3
9	6	7	3	2	8	5	4	1

367

SUDOKU

7	3	6	4	1	2	8	5	9
1	8	2	5	9	3	4	6	7
4	5	9	8	6	7	3	1	2
5	9	1	2	8	4	7	3	6
3	2	4	6	7	9	1	8	5
6	7	8	1	3	5	9	2	4
2	4	3	9	5	1	6	7	8
8	1	5	7	4	6	2	9	3
9	6	7	3	2	8	5	4	1

disconnected. She wants to wave, but she feels inhibited by Lady Vane's presence.

Instead, she slips in a hopeful question. 'Do you have any Matildas here?'

'I don't think so.'

'She might have used another name. She has white hair and all that goes with it, but she's resourceful and wise. You'd like her.'

Lady Vane gives Morag a searching look. 'A relative, perhaps?'

'A grandmother, and all I have left.'

'What about your mother?'

'Genrich took my father away, and he never came back. It destroyed her. She . . . she killed herself.'

Lady Vane physically winces. From their brief acquaintance to date, the reaction appears oddly extreme. Lady Vane gathers herself. 'I'm so sorry.' Another pause. 'So Genrich took you and left your grandmother behind?'

'Yes, and all alone.'

'Do you want candour or reassurance?'

'The truth will do.'

'Don't get your hopes up. Those bastards value chitin above people, unless it's useful people like *you*.' Lady Vane adroitly changes the subject. 'Over there, just inside the shield, you should be able to see a tower.'

It is huge and imposing, impossible to miss, once pointed out. The windows are shuttered, the stone dull.

'We call it Tiriel's Tower,' Lady Vane continues. 'It's where the weather-watchers live and work. They keep storms away, but they can conjure them too. Chitin is strong, but it can take only so much of their brand of lightning.'

Tiriel: Morag knows the poem and its memorable line, *Where does the thunder sleep?*

'It's hilarious,' crows a familiar voice. 'Hello, Mother.'

Cosmo Vane has dressed for the occasion and Morag grudgingly acknowledges that the dark velvet enhances his languid good looks.

'Why hilarious?' asks Lady Vane.

'They're discombobulated by a single board with a layout no real game could produce. White has mate in four, easy-peasy. White has two pieces; Black has a legion. But it's all about positioning.'

Cosmo darts forward to engage with the manuals, teasing, prompting and edging them towards a solution. Soon the gate opens and they surge on to the next, mate in five.

'I must find Lord Vane,' says Lady Vane. 'I've much enjoyed your company, Morag, thank you. We'll resume at the gatehouse.'

When Cosmo returns, Morag asks her burning question. 'What do you know about functionality? And golden beetles?'

'That sounds very accusatory.'

'I was attacked by a flock of them.'

'A pincer movement, no doubt!' Cosmo laughs at his own joke, but the smile fades. 'Where exactly?'

'Don't you know? On the outer skin of the Genrich Dome.'

'The *outer* skin! What an explorer you are!' His voice rises. 'Who do you think I am? I enjoy our duels. I'd be bereft without you.'

She senses she has made a false accusation against someone she strongly dislikes. His denial is not wrapped like a lie. 'What duels?'

'How about my psychotic twins against your weedy White Queen. We're fire and water, but we're joined at the hip. Anyway, if ever I do want your demise, you can be sure I'll be there to see it.'

'Thank you.'

'My pleasure. Nobody attacks a workmate of mine without permission.'

'Are you a weather-watcher?'

'No, but I cultivate them. That's what you do if you're born to rule.'

So bloody patronising.

He saunters off, but it feels like a rebuke. She has ceased to amuse.

She heads towards the gatehouse. The generous glowing first-floor windows suggest a single chamber across the full length of the building. An outside staircase on the left side leads to the upper storey. The last gate stands between the central arch of the gate-house and a large open space beyond.

A familiar figure shuffles from the shadows beneath the arch. 'Your work on our behalf has been invaluable,' says Lord Sine. 'You have such an unusual gift, with such unexpected consequences.'

Morag merely nods. She has no desire to resume relations with *bufo bufo*.

Nearby, Hernia is talking to Cosmo. Morag hurries forward to join them.

'She's meant to swallow my little present right now,' Cosmo says with a shake of the head, 'and the rude girl won't.' The single momenticon, a different colour to the others, rests in the palm of Cosmo's hand. The bottle's timer must have gone.

'Lord Vane asked me to the Tempestas reception,' Hernia explains. 'In fact, he was most insistent. We go back a long way and I have no doubt, Cosmo, your momenticons are stronger.'

'Let's say more brilliant and harder to resist.'

Morag intervenes. 'Come on, 147, party first and pill later. That way you get the best of both worlds.'

Cosmo tut-tuts. 'This is none of your business, Miss Spire. You've spent too long in uniform. You're becoming controlling.'

'All right, then let her decide for herself. She's twice our age.'

But Cosmo does not give up.

'The real point, 147, is that you'll have an advantage over everyone else. You might even be the first to solve the puzzle. Or are you just scared?'

The taunt has the desired effect. Hernia takes Cosmo's pill and retreats to lounge on the gatehouse wall.

'What have you done?' asks Morag.

'Entertained the lady. Does she look disturbed to you?'

Morag makes no further protest. Hernia is now smiling to herself, and she is herself distracted. From the open door of the gatehouse she catches – for the first time in her life – the music of multiple voices in festive mood. She abandons Hernia and walks to the staircase.

A light blue carpet flows down the stairs in a curve like cascading water. At the top, she crosses the landing into a grand chamber, which, as expected, runs the full length and width of the upper floor. Chandeliers festooned in self-energy lights hang from a high ceiling. Generous arched windows overlook the forecourt beyond the final gate, their crimson curtains held open on hooks, in contrast to those facing the village, which are drawn closed. The partygoers are exclusively from Lord Vane's world, and they're all in their party best. There is not a single Genrich uniform to be seen.

Morag deduces from the ease with which groups split and reform that everyone knows everyone else. A dusky yellow drink is thrust into her hand. It tastes delicious.

She attracts brief compliments, but they make her feel the more alone. The banter of the other guests has the ring of long acquaintance.

Then, from behind, a finger runs up her arm. Morag spins round, taken aback by the intimacy of the gesture. A tall, middle-aged man with a high forehead and shaven head faces her. His imposing dark robe is embroidered with a fist grasping a bolt of lightning. A golden wasp sits on his shoulder. He has a high but strong voice. 'This is some transformation, dull grey to a brilliant bird of passage!'

She glares at him. 'I don't think I know you.'

He looks mildly disappointed at the news. 'I'm Marcus Jaggard. I'm in charge of Tiriel's Tower.'

'You mean you're a weather-watcher?'

'The term is demeaning. It conjures old-world children lying on their backs and peering at clouds. Weather-*Master*, perhaps.' He fingers the shoulder of her dress, but she flicks his hand away and takes a firm step back. 'And real silk too. We're sheathed in the synthetic, but you are real. Imagine all those little white worms spinning their silky cocoons before dying just for you.'

For once, Morag is pleased to see Cosmo.

'Don't be morbid, Marcus. And don't pester my friend.'

Marcus does not visibly register the rebuke. 'We're close to curtain up,' he says to Morag. 'You're about to see some *real* weather.'

'Mum's the word,' interrupts Cosmo. 'A surprise is a surprise is a surprise.'

'Do you like surprises, Miss Spire?' asks Marcus.

'I don't like being mauled.'

Marcus merely grins, water off a duck's back. 'I like harmless magic tricks,' he says, dipping a hand in his pocket.

'Not now, Marcus, it's not sensible. Our time will come,' says Cosmo urgently.

'She's a guest. She must be entertained. Abracadabra.'

The room transforms. Conversation dies as insects rise from belts, bags, shoulders and even shoes. They fly around the room before settling in the rafters.

'Put them back. *Now!*'

Lord Vane, wearing a similar robe to Marcus, but more magnificent, strides across from the far side of the room.

'Whoops,' says Marcus.

'*Who?*' bellows Lord Vane.

Marcus raises his hand. 'I'm sorry, my Lord. I had a control in my pocket. I was about to do the trick of the vanishing coin for our delightful guest, when—'

'Functionality is *not* a game, and still less one for you to play with. Did Cosmo put you up to this?'

Lady Vane appears. 'Darling, we all know Mr Jaggard is a little short on manners. But nobody wants to spoil the evening for young Morag. She's the young woman wh—'

'I know very well who she is,' snaps Lord Vane.

'The atmosphere went to my head. It's not good being immured in a tower all day, every day,' whines Marcus. Previously cocksure, he now sounds oleaginous.

'I suggest you leave us,' says Lady Vane to Jaggard.

The dynamic between Lady Vane and Marcus Jaggard is one of barely veiled hostility, reminding Morag that she is a visitor to an established society comprised of individual histories and undercurrents of which she is wholly ignorant. *Listen and learn* is her only option.

'Not before putting them back where they belong,' adds Lord Vane.

'Of course, my Lord. Your slightest wish is my command.'

Marcus' hand returns to his pocket and, like a film in rewind, the insects return to their points of departure and the party resumes.

'It was a little harmless fun,' adds Cosmo.

Lord Vane turns on his son. 'If I want your opinion, I'll ask for it,' he barks.

These exchanges take place as in a play with five characters, with the audience, the rest of the room, watching on silently, their drinks untouched.

Lady Vane maintains her emollient approach. 'I know you know who Morag is, but I still think you should greet her.'

The clouds roll back. Lord Vane is suddenly charm itself. 'You're right, dear. Of course I should.' He shakes Morag's hand. 'This is your achievement. We're all in your debt, and I include Lord Sine in that.'

With a faintly conspiratorial look at Morag, Lady Vane ushers her husband away as the party resumes.

Morag tries her luck with Cosmo. 'Why was he *that* angry? Why so on edge?'

She never receives an answer, for a ripple of excitement is spreading from one window to the whole room in no time.

Cosmo hurries to the nearest viewpoint, while she goes in the opposite direction, to the now abandoned windows over the inner courtyard. She draws one of the curtains. Below her, the crowd of manuals, stretching a long way back, are fretting over the solution to the last gate, the mate in seven. The location of the pieces in the problem are passed between them. Suggestions are shouted. Pieces are moved, replaced and moved again.

She crosses to the other side, where Jaggard and Cosmo are together once more. There is much pointing from the windows.

'They're spitting images!'

'Identical.'

Morag works her way through to the front. Beneath her stands a miscellany of fictional creatures who, in appearance and dress, match the well-known illustrations of their literary counterparts with extraordinary precision: Tweedledum and Tweedledee, the Mad Hatter, the White Knight, the White Rabbit, intent on his pocket watch, and even her first subject at Infotainment, the White Queen. In their midst stands Lord Sine.

'If they're actors, they're bloody well made-up,' says the man beside her.

'We don't have any actors who look remotely like them,' says his companion firmly.

As if to confirm the diagnosis, an undersized young man emerges with a double-handed sword strapped to his back, the killer of the monstrous Jabberwock in Tenniel's famous illustration.

'Well, well, well,' says Cosmo, sidling up to Morag, 'isn't he clever!'

'Isn't who clever?'

'Lord Sine, who else? "Anything you can do, I can do better," that's his message.'

'But how could he—?'

She stops. Genetics, embryonic manipulation, brain programming and accelerated growth were the four skills Lord Sine claimed for his company. Below them is what appears to be the living proof. She is particularly drawn to the Hatter, a Cosmo creation in Momenticon world. Hyperactive, arms sawing the air and top-hatted head tilting left and right like a pendulum, he is monopolising Lord Sine.

'I rather think this makes Lord Sine worth knowing, don't you?' adds Cosmo, who has lost his default air of casual ennui, so much so that for once his voice displays a hint of self-criticism. 'To think I'd dismissed him as a common chromosome dabbler.'

Morag looks down the line of observers to Lord Vane. His expression is intense and ambiguous, suggesting both relief and unease. She concludes this detail is an unexpected development whose implications are as yet unclear.

At that moment, the seventh gate yields. Genrich citizens flood through on to the open ground beyond. In the room, silence falls. There is not a whisper of applause at the achievement, more a mute loathing. A hand restrains her progress towards the first window by the stairs. Mander, in full regalia, murmurs as if addressing his shoes while replacing her empty glass with a full one.

'Whatever you make of the evening's entertainment, Miss, it's time you made your own move. Even pawns can live in hope.'

Mander had used that the same striking phrase, *live in hope*, when handing over the box with the dress and shoes. Before she can ask him to elucidate, Mander is on the retreat, gathering empty glasses as he goes. Everyone else is hugging the front windows. The forecourt below is now well lit. The mill of manuals, bereft of puzzles to solve, wander aimlessly, until Lord Sine and his creatures appear and start circulating with bowls in their hands.

'Why are they dishing out sweets?' asks a young man beside Morag.

'They're not sweets, they're momenticons, one for each, it looks like,' replies Morag.

As the manuals swallow them without hesitation, Morag catches sight of Hernia, who looks contented, if dazed. She decides against rejoining her. As she herself had said, Hernia is twice her age and can make her own mind up.

Lord Vane, now at the front by the central window, raises a hand and clicks his fingers. The gentle light on the forecourt intensifies and the cobbles and the bare land beyond miraculously resolve into squares. It's like an exercise in reverse perspective: the squares gain size as they recede. On the edge of the chitin shield, the divisions between them acquire features, here a tree, there a bridge over a stream.

'Wow,' mutters the young man. 'I never knew we could do that.'

Beyond the shield, virtual copses, hedges and lanes gradually appear; there's even a chequerboard hill. On one side, the fields end in a beach with breaking waves.

The manuals' shuffling steps are acquiring purpose, accelerating into a stride. The impression from a distance is paradoxical. Caught in a trance, they are still competing with each other. There is only one square per person on the virtual board ahead, and each wants the best. Morag is transfixed. What they are seeing in their minds and what they see with their eyes must be merging into a single mirage.

Lord Sine is standing in a corner of the forecourt, watching with an air of detached curiosity. His *Looking Glass* replicas are mixing with the manuals and encouraging them to head for the shield.

In the distance, virtual figures have joined the scene, flitting in and out of view, more replicas from Tenniel's illustrations.

Pipes, which Morag had assumed to be plumbing, start flooding the room with organ music. The simplicity of the initial melody, an old-world nursery rhyme about a black sheep, fractures into a rich counterpoint, and then a fugue. Its opulence heightens expectation.

'What's the point of all this?' Morag asks the young man. 'They can't get out through the shield, so why tempt them?'

But to her amazement the shield is *permeable* – it merely shimmers as they pass through it. There is even a murmur of appreciation from Lord Sine, who takes a few steps forward. This is new technology, even to him.

'But – but it's lethal out there,' stammers Morag.

Nobody hears her, for Tempestas' outliers are cheering and raising their glasses, and momentarily, Morag is swept along. She has not forgotten Lady Vane's intelligence: this is poetic justice. Genrich kill for chitin, now they die for it.

Beyond the shield, the manuals stumble and fall.

Now lightning forks above the land beyond the shield, striking any unfortunate manuals who might otherwise have made it back to safety.

You're about to see some real *weather*, Marcus Jaggard had said. He's standing nearby, his smile as steely as a closing trap.

Morag finds her true self. Above the Sanatorium, she had said of the patients, *they're people*. And people they are still, people who have done her no provable harm, and they include Hernia, her one friend in the Genrich Dome.

The whole scene repels her, the festive outliers and the Genrich leadership watching their dying creatures without a flicker of sympathy.

She catches the opening words of Lord Vane's address as she hurries downstairs.

'It's time to move on. Lady Miranda and I have designed our legacy, and you will be part of it. After mere craftsmanship, we are moving on to embrace artistry.'

Once impressed by his advocacy, Morag now finds the self-aggrandisement repellent. She runs to the arch, but the gate has been closed.

She belatedly understands that Lord Sine is destroying his faulty model so his new project, whatever it is, can begin.

She stands alone, frozen by the enormity and horror of the deception. She has been lured into devising a cure which is lethal – Lord and Lady Vane must have known all along, and Cosmo, too.

Through the gate, she hears gloating voices. 'We have a clean slate.'

'You'll do better next time.'

Lord Sine's distinctive voice replies, 'I'll do *different* next time.'

As Morag hesitates at the foot of the staircase, the lightning illuminates an elderly woman emerging from the lee of a house on the main road.

'Had your fill, have you?' she croaks. She has teeth like an unkept graveyard, hennaed red hair and a stoop born of a lifetime of manual labour.

'It's horrible. Why aren't you in there cheering with the rest?'

The old woman gives her a wry look.

'Sorry, I didn't mean . . .' Morag hastily adds.

'Hilda Crike has nowt to do with any of it. I'm a menial, ain't I. I'm among the unseen and the unheard.' She grins. 'Even the undead.' She cradles a lifeless bird in her hand. 'They shouldn't be celebrating. Functionality is all over the shop. A shortage, forgive the pun, meaning there's not enough tantalum and not enough conductors. So poor Robin Redbreast flies smack into the window. Yes, Miss, we menials ain't as ignorant as we look. Hilda Crike at your service.'

'I was told to live in hope.'

'Which mad optimist told you that?'

'Lord Vane's butler.'

'He sounds menial enough to be talking sense.' She cocks her head, straining to hear Lord Vane's words. 'Art and Beauty, his Lordship says, but the Vanes confuse beauty with grandeur. You have to *work* for true beauty. Any menial will tell you that. Now, what was that advice again?'

'Live in hope.'

'The only know-how about hope sits in Pandora's Place.'

Morag revives. Hope had hidden at the bottom of Pandora's box after the world's afflictions had flown out. Mander must have been steering her here.

'Up there. Keep true to yourself, Miss.'

Crike indicates a tall, ramshackle oak-and-plaster building on the western edge of town, then moves off with a wave, poking the grass in search of more mechanical casualties. The old woman's phraseology has veered swiftly from the basic to the refined and Morag now wonders if their encounter was accidental.

The building is indeed Pandora's Place. Beneath the name, Gothic writing on a sign declares: *Counter Enquiries Only. Precision please. O.P.*

She eases open the unlocked door. A familiar must of leather and paper peppers her nostrils. *Books* – books *everywhere*, filling shelves soaring into the darkness. The library is deep and tall, with a multitude of walkways which move and intersect as she watches. A low counter sprouts lettered keys on one side and numbered keys on the other like an oversize old-world typewriter. The numbered keys are either red or white. Between them sits a huge drum, a card index of sorts. A beam of light dances along the ceiling.

'Do shut the door. This is a house of books, not a prairie.'

It takes time for the owner of voice and light to appear. He is the very cliché of a librarian. Pebble glasses hang precariously on the end of a nose with length but little symmetry; white hair flies as if electrocuted, and he sports a coal-black waistcoat, flannel trousers and a flamboyant purple shirt. High above her, he manoeuvres shelves to left and right until a stepladder appears and unwinds towards her.

His voice is reed, not strings or woodwind, and he chunters away as he descends. 'Ground, underground or air? Don't gawp, Miss, it isn't difficult. You can ask, or I can suggest.'

Unable to grasp the question's import, Morag mumbles, 'They're doing terrible things out there.'

'Well, there's a surprise. We destroy everything else, and now we destroy each other. Just like the old days.' Now at floor level, he peers at her over the counter. 'I don't know you, do I?' He pauses, peers again. 'Or do I? You've the ears and eyebrows of a Spire – and that means the genes of a book thief.' He plays the keys like a crazed organist. The drum with the card index hums as it rotates. 'Arensen on *Glaciers*, borrowed nine years ago, by Gilbert Spire. Cuttle on *The Mysteries of Arbor Spirantia*, likewise. Does kleptomania run in the family?'

Lightning is still silvering the windows, and Morag, sensing the presence of a kindred spirit, welcomes the diversion. 'Books, yes; otherwise no. I was brought up by my grandmother. She had a gift for liberal strictness.'

'You even speak like a Spire. I, by the way, am Oblivious Potts, keeper of factual reference books – now classified, alas, as fiction. I repeat my question: ground, underground or air? Ah, she looks blank. Let's take the common Eurasian wren. They want to make one or two for the orchard, but they've never seen one, never heard one, never watched one move, have no idea how it holds its tail or builds its home. What you see out there may look like a theme park, but it's a memorial. My books give the wherewithal. They do the building, and functionality does the animation. But I give authenticity, so their apology to Nature at least looks genuine.' Potts' eyes suddenly narrow. 'So *why* are you here?'

'I'm looking for hope.'

'Are you indeed? In classical myth, Pandora released famine and pestilence first. Not much for Hope to work with. Still, if you want to go looking, you can.'

'How well did you know my father?'

'Nobody knew your father through and through, but I did better than most. He was an explorer, which made him profoundly selfish and highly enterprising.'

Made. Morag havered. *Do I ask or don't I?*

'Is he alive?'

'Lord Vane funded an expedition and he never returned. Odds against, I'm afraid.'

This is not the moment for grief, Morag tells herself. *Matilda would not approve.*

'Looking for what?'

'Tantalum. I suspect he took our books with him.' Potts presses another sequence of keys and the counter unexpectedly divides to let her through. 'Off you go then. Hunt away.'

'How?'

'Camilla – that's what he told me to tell you, to be sure it is you.'

'I'm not Camilla. I'm Morag. Very much *not* a Camilla.'

'Nothing ventured, nothing gained. Best of luck.' He hands her a ball from under the counter. 'You might need this. Shake her and she shines.'

She climbs the ladder to join a maze of other ladders and sliding shelves crammed with books recording the planet's lost fauna and flora. She shakes the globe, which casts a ghostly light. Some sections house slim files with exterior buttons which trigger sound recordings. The sheer volume of data is overwhelming. She squats on her haunches and hunts for inspiration.

Camilla?

Fool! *Limenitis camilla*: the white admiral butterfly, her father's favourite and the only picture in their library. *Limen* is the Latin for threshold, so *Limenitis* translated means *Limen it is*, or *a way in*. Now what?

'Mr Potts, do you have an entry for everything?'

'From the ammonite to the frigate bird to the zebu, Miss Spire, by bay, shelf and number.'

'And what's your reference for the white admiral butterfly?'

'Your father would have liked him, a frequenter of woods. They fed on brambles and their caterpillars on honeysuckle. All gone, all gone.'

'Yes, Mr Potts, but what's the reference?'

He clacks the keys.

'Best illustration: Mason's *British Butterflies*, 1897 edition, page 203.'

All around Morag, shelves slide and shift, until she is surrounded by books on butterflies. She finds Mason, and she finds *Limenitis camilla*. Beside the gorgeous illustration, Gothic letters in pencil have been added to spell the single word *Fram*.

'And what's *Fram*?' she asks.

'*Fram* was the name of an old-world Arctic explorer's boat. She went to the South Pole too – Nansen was the explorer's name – and it's also the name of the Airlugger your father flew. Odd coincidence, I must say.'

My father was another kind of white admiral, thinks Morag. 'Could you enter *Fram* on your keyboard, please?'

Nothing happens.

She reflects. 'Nansen?'

'Last try, Miss Spire, I haven't got all day.'

As Oblivious Potts types the name, the shelves shift again and expose a narrow run of stairs which dive into the dark.

So it is a simple key: enter the two names, one after the other, and you're in. Potts must know this. But now is not the time to ask how or why.

'Thank you, Mr Potts,' she cries.

His piccolo voice echoes back. 'Arensen on *Glaciers* and Cuttle on *Arbor Spirantia*; tell him if you find him that Oblivious Potts would like them back! Mind how you go, Miss Spire. And do borrow my light.'

A subterranean passage at the foot of the stairs has rock walls and an earthen floor. The ceiling is supported by ancient timber props, like in a disused mine. As she walks, the atmosphere gets damper. Potts' globe-light catches tiny flecks of green splashing the rocks – moss, *real* moss. So all is not lost. She toys with going back to share the discovery with Potts, but the thought of the village returning from their celebration decides her against it.

The path runs straight and ends in a cavern whose centre is occupied by a pear-shaped single-pilot craft with a chitin-coated skin. It sits on three stubby legs with a ladder to a porthole-like entrance where rivets mark out the word *Hope*. She peers up and a grey circle stares back from ground level: the way out, surely.

She has never known extreme, visceral excitement until now. She is off to see her father – she is off to a new world.

Two dreams. May *Hope* deliver both of them.

8

Arrival I

Morag's craft passes through the chitin shield as smoothly as the manuals had. Its single viewing screen relays the forward view: a green fog, never thinning, never thickening, swaddling the planet in poison. There are dials for speed and turbulence which continually jiggle, but there are few mod cons and nothing decorative: this is a utilitarian craft.

Morag cannot sleep. She attributes her insomnia to an uncomfortable position, horror at the misuse of her work by Lords Vane and Sine and apprehension at what the future holds. Her father, if he is even still alive, cannot know of his wife's death, nor of his mother's possible death, and neither will be easy news to deliver. She wonders why and how he expected her to stumble on Oblivious Potts and his library. He might have foreseen Genrich's visit, but beyond that? Also, it's more than Potts: she has been assisted by a trio well past their prime: Potts, Mander and Crike. Are they in league? Might she meet them again?

Darker questions harry her too. Why has her father abandoned them? According to Potts, whom she judges reliable, Lord Vane gave him a craft for exploration, so why not take a brief detour to see his family? She is angry as well as excited. He will have some explaining to do.

Her thoughts turn to Hernia. The illness and the cure were no better than each other, but she worries that her relative solitude has hardened her. She feels a need to grieve, but whatever grief is, she cannot find it. Cosmo's role in her death is disturbing too. His momenticon had been too potent for Hernia to resist, despite the invitation to the party. Did Cosmo know of their friendship? Was he jealous? She knows the spoilt and entitled often are.

She wonders about the *Looking Glass* characters, and three in particular: the White Knight, the White Queen and the psychotic schoolboys. Lord Sine had talked of mind-loading. Has he given them characters to fit their parts? She would be intrigued to meet them – or at least the first two.

Last but not least, she reflects on Cosmo's change of attitude towards Lord Sine: a man who thinks he's God is targeted for co-operation by a man with the amorality of the Devil. The future does not look promising.

Hope slows into a descent and she leaps from her seat as the screen reveals another Dome, this one diminutive and irregular when set against those of Genrich and Tempestas, but it's nonetheless imposing.

There is no sign of welcome, or indeed, life.

Morag's expectations are blown away.

As *Hope* comes to rest, the door springs open, only to slam shut the moment Morag enters the airlock. The craft relaunches itself and swiftly vanishes back into the murk.

Globe-light in hand, she emerges from the airlock via a circular glass door. A huge rock face in front of her is stained with red ochre imprints from a human hand above a deer of some kind. This ancient tribute to Nature – Man's first painting, perhaps? – is a shaming image now, an eloquent statement of what is lost. But she is intrigued. Why bring such a huge object here?

Beyond the rock is a wide stationary escalator rising into the gloom. When her first step triggers instant movement and a flood of light, her anxieties dispel. Invisible energies are swirling around her, intoxicating in their strength and variety, unmistakably the energy of original paintings, successors to the rock at the entrance.

She has never sworn in Matilda's company, but she does now, in sheer exultation, as she goes bounding up the escalator two steps at a time. Hundreds of frames, ancient and modern, come into view, floors and floors of them. She cries out again and opens her arms. This is a magical place. Fortune at last has smiled on her.

High in the ceiling, fans activate and the air begins to freshen.

'So there you are,' concludes Morag. 'As best as I remember, and hardly your average house move. So how about yours? You arrived in *Hope*, that I know, but nothing else.' She grinned. 'You've a hard act to follow.'

Fogg took a sip of his faux champagne. 'I took a risk,' he said.

'*You?* Take a risk? What a promising start! I can't wait.'

9

Arrival II

Since his visit to the old lady, life in the Genrich School for Idiot-Savants has turned from dull to oppressive. Fogg lives increasingly in the world of his drawings.

'Are you blind?'

Niobe stands in the doorway, looking different somehow, vibrant even.

Fogg looks past her to the other cubicles. He blushes; how can he be *that* unobservant? 'Where's everyone gone?'

'The staff have scarpered to some party or other, so we're following suit.'

'How? In what? Where?'

She gestures impatiently. 'Come on, think *escape* for once. We'll use the service shuttle, of course. How else?'

Fogg is distracted by a flicker of colour above his head. A golden beetle, similar to the one he saw in Lord Vane's quarters, is sitting on a roof girder. It must be a personal message for him, and it must mean *stay*.

'All right, that's how. But what about where?'

'There are plenty of abandoned tantalum mines with shields and living quarters intact – and thanks to my job, I know where most of them are. We'll rebuild and start again.' Her eyes are sparkling: she has regained her self-respect.

Fogg flounders. 'You've thought this through,' is all he can muster.

'Of course I have! A hundred times over. Listen, I know how you like to mull, but we really do need to get a move-on.'

'I'll hold on here as a rearguard, just in case.'

'A rearguard for *what*? Stop playing the sacrificial lamb and get real. They'll be back, and you'll take the punishment, which will no doubt be terminal. And we haven't time to debate the permutations. It's now or never.'

He can't bring himself to point out the beetle. It's his special message from the Vanes, not a secret to betray, even to Niobe.

'You could do with the room. I mean, the shuttle isn't exactly spacious.'

'Don't be pathetic. There's plenty of room.'

'Anyway, I wouldn't be much use.'

'Who said anything about *use*?' She seizes his arm. 'Wake up, Fogg! Don't you understand? You're the only one I want to escape with.'

Shame burns his cheeks as he realises how his inertia must be striking her. He's a coward or a liar or both, and cold with it. 'Watch yourself,' is all he can say. 'Please.'

'I will.' She blinks away the moisture in her eyes. 'I'll leave a Rearranger for you.'

'We'll meet again—'

'I very much doubt it.' She gives him a hard, disappointed look and walks away without turning back.

Fogg sags into his cubicle chair. He hears the shuttle launch and watches the murk shift and resettle. In the far distance, blurred balls of light are circling above the Genrich Dome. Other large craft are on the move. *Something is afoot*, Cassie had said, and she might be right, but there is slender evidence and not much of an excuse for ducking the action and failing his only friend. And still the golden beetle has not moved.

Hours pass . . .

. . . until, when he is close to giving up, the beetle takes flight and hovers inches from his face.

At last: time to move.

Fogg has a surge of self-confidence. He packs his screen, his stylus and a change of clothes. He leaves the Rearranger, confident, in this new upbeat mood, that sustenance will be provided.

The beetle leads him to the airlock.

An unfamiliar craft standing on three feet has the optimistic name *Hope* in rivets above the entry door. A narrow sleeping area, no more than a strip of olive-green foam rubber, looks up at a tangle of metal beams. A stool is tucked under a small work surface. There's a crude Matter-Rearranger with two codes, for water and nutrition paste only. Yet the air is fresh. The beetle settles above the single light and its wings retract. *Job done.*

Only now does Fogg realise there are *no* controls, and when he tries the exit handle, it declines to budge.

With a vigorous lurch, the craft disengages and skims away, only feet from the surface. Fogg fights for his footing in the turbulence, catching a fleeting glimpse of the Genrich Dome in the viewing screen as *Hope* veers away. The lights are low and the circling craft have gone.

His destination is not the Genrich Dome, nor is he following Niobe.

The craft has a syncopated motion: *sway, lurch left, glide; sway, lurch right, glide*; with the same time intervals between, like a drum riff. He notices a smear of paste beside the Rearranger: the craft has not been cleaned since its last use.

He extracts one nutrition pack and the Rearranger moves to *reserve*. Two end points beckon: death or landfall.

His exuberance wanes and he ceases to care much which of the two will greet him at journey's end.

III

PLOTTING A LINE

I

A New Departure

'So here we are,' said Fogg, closing his narrative on a banal note. 'Three years is quite a time. At least we both arrived in *Hope*.'

'For God's sake, Fogg,' groaned Morag, although she welcomed an attempt at humour as better than no humour at all. 'I thought you'd be more analytical. Consider this: on the very day of our third anniversary, all our machines play up and those psychopathic twins arrive. It can't be coincidence.' She tipped the last of her faux champagne into their glasses.

'I wish I'd never drawn them,' Fogg muttered.

'You're breaking the first rule of communal living: be upbeat, never be glum . . .'

'I wonder how Lord Sine discovered them? Your encounters hardly suggest a bookish type.'

'Lord Sine was keen to impress. Asking Tempestas to help dispose of the manuals must have been humiliating.'

High up in the ceiling, a light failed, and a grinding noise grumbled in the roof.

'That's another first,' said Fogg. 'In three years I've never had a technical failure.'

Morag's cheeks registered a growing clamminess. The fans had stopped. 'Get your essentials,' she shouted at Fogg, '*now!*'

'But—'

'I said *now!*'

Only when a second light blacked out, then a third, did Fogg obey, rushing to his bedroom to pack what he could. He included the box of tricks which was AIPT and rushed back to Reception as more lights failed. Morag had vanished. He bellowed her name twice, without response.

Only a few lights remained, but more worryingly, a deep shadow was crawling across the Museum. He felt like Dum and Dee beneath the dark sweep of the wings of Morag's crow, death on the prowl. With no power, they would be immured here, without light or heat, food or drink.

'Down here,' Morag yelled from the entrance floor, and he rushed to the entrance escalator. She was standing by the airlock, waving angrily at him.

'What are you doing? We haven't a craft—'

'Do you think I'm a raving idiot? What do you think *that* bloody is?' she screamed back.

A second solid shadow was sweeping across the Dome's transparent chitin shield as the last lights extinguished, one by one. He ran down the escalator towards the ship that had been tethered beside the airlock: *truly* a ship, with a deck, a cabin and an assortment of burlap-coloured bags held on by ropes. A towering mast passed through its chitin shield.

An Airlugger!

Morag, already half up the gangway, screamed 'Hurry!' over her shoulder.

Fogg spluttered as he entered the airlock, for the air had turned acrid. Flinging his arm over his mouth, he ran on, only to trip over the bodies of the twins. Their faces had turned yellow, the skin blistered and eyes agape. Morag must have opened the outside airlock remotely, trapping them in the tunnel with an inflow of murk.

As the ever-advancing shadow passed over his head, Fogg battened down his moral outrage at their murder and squeezed himself under the closing shield with seconds to spare. He charged up a narrow gangway to find Morag standing by the wheelhouse, wrestling with an assortment of pulleys and ropes, although to little effect.

'You killed . . .' he stuttered, but his protest stalled as a violent lurch sent him sprawling. The gangway rolled up, the closing shield severed the anchor rope and the ship soared upwards at breakneck speed.

'*Shi-i-i-t—!*' yelled Morag as loose ropes went flailing through the air. A tall vertical pipe with the word *Diapason* painted on its side was attached to the wheelhouse wall; it came to violent life, emitting a series of ear-splitting shrieks.

Fogg seized the deck-rail and made his way hand over hand to the pulleys.

'They must control the sacks,' Morag shouted. 'I think we have to—'

She lost her footing as the deck heaved this way and that and the entire ship threatened to turn turtle. One bag filled with air and began to pump like a bellows. Fogg disentangled the ropes, hurried to the equivalent pulley on the cabin's other side and released the brake. Two bags were now in balance. The shrieking of the pipe abated to an ugly whistle.

'Now number three on my side,' he bellowed, 'and number six on yours; two turns on each.'

He spoke with such conviction that she obeyed, or rather, tried to. As she fumbled, unclear what she must do with number six, Fogg scurried through the wheelhouse from his side to hers and back. Inexplicably, he was in his element.

In response, a second pair of bags tilted and began to breathe and, as the ship settled a fraction more, the diapason pipe moderated to a high-pitched *thwee!*

'It's a spirit-level of sorts,' Fogg shouted out.

'I don't need a spirit-level to tell me we're at risk of capsizing, thank you!'

Fogg ignored the remark and continued to work, quite unfazed, clearly blessed with whatever the aerial equivalent of sea legs might be.

With another two bags activated and brought under control, then fine-tuned by Fogg, six of the eight were now filling and emptying in unison. The whistle dropped several octaves to a contented hum. Beyond the craft's chitin shield, murky olive-yellow vapour drifted and coiled.

'We'll leave the last two until we're fully stabilised,' said Fogg, who was now busying himself in the wheelhouse. Lights came up stern and aft, and the cabin portholes emitted a sulphurous glow.

'You've done this before?' She hardly needed to ask that; any fool could see that he had.

Fogg merely grinned and pointed out the vessel's name, *Aeolus*, over the lintel of the cabin door, with the Tempestas insignia above it.

As the vessel settled, Morag examined the craft in detail. Love had been expended on construction and maintenance. The planking had a freshly varnished patina; the deck-rails were carved; gleaming brass fittings abounded. The eight windbags, four on each side of the mast, hung on equally spaced yards. The chitin was finely rendered and, thanks to some technical trickery, channelled air which kept the windbags visible from below. The resemblance to a maritime vessel extended to a painted figurehead at the prow: the wind god himself, with convex cheeks and plumes of wind at the mouth.

With so much wood and rope, she had to be an old-world construct, adapted later to cope with the murk. Scurrier design focused on utility, and from Fogg's description, the Vanes' private craft revelled in ostentatious luxury, but the *Aeolus* exuded its own mix of charm, practicality and environmental friendliness.

'Time to try the cabin,' suggested Morag.

A disappointing scene of desperate squalor confronted them. Dum and Dee had obviously had no interest in order or hygiene.

The room stank, and detritus stained the bunks and seats. Empty bottles of *Wonderland* momenticons littered the floor.

'They were addicted and ran out of them,' Morag said, 'that's my diagnosis.'

'Mine too. "Give us our f-f-fix",' quoted Fogg.

Among its many attributes, the *Aeolus* gathered, heated and detoxified water from the atmosphere. The tank was full. The galley even had a waste chute which descended through the shield. Fogg knew where all these devices were and how they worked.

With two mops and two pails of steaming water, they embarked on a clean-up.

After an hour, the cabin looked like a cabin and was several degrees warmer. Fogg activated a fan system and the odour left by the twins soon gave way to a pleasant smell of oiled wood.

Next stop: the wheelhouse.

On a flat surface in front of an elegantly carved wheel stood twelve numbered levers, in two rows of six. One had been pulled down; the others, when they tried them, were locked in place. The wheel allowed only minor movement. Wherever they were heading, the course had been set.

'You were very switched on out there,' said Morag.

Fogg nodded modestly, ducking again the implicit question about the source of his expertise.

A desk fixed to the rear wall of the main cabin yielded a logbook. A fresh page had been pasted next to the frontispiece. Morag read it out.

Designed and built by Tempestas, the Airlugger Mark 1 was a staple of the Arctic and Antarctic surveys before the Fall and invaluable for observation work during and thereafter. It is wind-propelled, but can sustain flight for four days in a flat calm. Miniature turbines generate heat and light and its pollution coefficient is zero. Its three sister ships, Auster, Zephyr and Fram, are still in service, a tribute to their durability.

'Didn't your f-f-f-father write *F-F-Fram* in a butterfly book – alongside a white admiral?'

'He might have done,' she said, before adroitly changing the subject. 'And you have a point: we've shared stories, but we haven't analysed, and we plainly should. Let's say three observations each. You first.'

So much had happened with such urgency that time had slipped its moorings. Outside, the shimmer-light began to take hold as dusk descended.

They faced each other across the table.

Fogg had spent most of his life listening. With reticence came a gift for catching details. 'Whoever set the timer on our Dome was aware of the truce between Lord Sine and Lord Vane – or probably was. It's too much of a coincidence otherwise, both running out on the same day.'

Morag built on Fogg's idea of a guiding force. 'Whoever directed those dreadful twins here meant to give us a chance, because without them, we'd have no craft and no means of escape. I reckon they were a test.'

'A test of what?'

'Our resourcefulness.'

'Do you mind if I voice a more provocative theory?'

Morag raised an eyebrow. *How annoying can you be?*

'That depends on what the theory is. *Obviously.*'

'I don't think those beetles were meant to kill you.'

'Yes, I do mind. I was there. I *know*—'

'Suppose whoever sent them wanted to show you the storeroom and that strange object on the floor?'

'I can think of better ways. Like: "Here, Morag, let me show you my storeroom." Or am I being dim?'

'Suppose our culprit wasn't in the Dome, or couldn't risk declaring him or herself? The beetles could have pulled your fingers away before you had time to adjust, but they didn't. They had wings too, remember. They could have followed and had a second go, but they didn't. It doesn't feel right. And – and – remember there was no way into the storeroom from the inside.'

'Of course I bloody remember—' She was finding the new, in-control Fogg more irritating than the absent-minded version.

'I've still got mine.'

'Your what?'

'My beetle.'

'We've been living together for three years and I've never seen any beetle.'

Fogg grinned. 'He keeps himself to himself, but he'll be on me somewhere.' He raised his arms and spun around.

Morag, faced with an expanse of velvet, lifted the hem of the Curator's jacket and plucked the golden beetle from the small of his back. She placed it on the table suspiciously. 'How on earth did you get that?'

'I explained. *He* found *me*.'

'It's very similar to some of the ones I saw at the Tempestas party and in their functionality shops . . .'

'I've no doubt, and mine can fly too. Believe me, they could easily have finished you off.'

'You're saying my enemy is my friend?'

'Maybe. You have one too, by the way.'

'*What*—?'

'It favours your left shoulder blade.' She twisted and turned, but to no avail; the scarab had chosen Man's natural blind spot.

Fogg placed hers on the table beside his. 'Maybe he landed when Marcus did his magic trick.'

'She,' said Morag firmly, peering at her hitherto unknown companion. Why was it there? What could it do? It looked as dead as an old-world brooch. She flicked it off the table – only for the insect to spring to life and scuttle away.

'I've had enough of beetles and all these *maybes*. We must be direct and tackle the obvious questions. For one, how did those psychotic twins find us?'

They looked at each other. The logbook had offered no clues, so it was hunt the thimble time.

The benches had hinged seats with stowaways below. They rummaged through a jumble of warm clothing, a spare anchor and chain, a rope ladder with wooden rungs, an assortment of seashells and, right at the bottom, a bundle of rolled-up old-world charts. They spread the charts on the table to examine them. Some focused on major cities, long since gone, others on forestation, and a few featured obscure islands with exotic names like Hektoria, Beardmore and Jakobshavn, sitting isolated in the blue of the sea.

The names sounded like grace notes to a theme of overwhelming loss.

'They're glaciers,' observed Morag.

One map, and one only, had not been printed but was instead a crude drawing on squared paper.

'This one – it has to be,' said Fogg, unfurling it.

A jag of lightning, circled, held the centre. A cluster of near adjacent squares shaded in pencil had names scribbled in manuscript: *The Hunt*, *Winterdorf* and *The Circus*, like cards from a fortune-telling pack. Several others were blank.

A straight line ran from this central area to the southern rim, where the single word *Wonderland* had been scrawled beside the number 12.

'I bet that's Tweedle writing,' suggested Fogg, adding, 'Dum or Dee.'

Morag did not dissent. She led the way back to the deck and peered up through the chitin shield at a silver ball crowning the mast which she had taken to be an anti-lightning device.

'Suppose that's a receiver, and suppose the Museum had a trans-mitter of some kind. They didn't find the Dome; it found them.' She paused. 'I think our Dome started to transmit when the three years were up. But that doesn't explain how those terrible twins knew I might have momenticons. Someone put them up to this, and as lever twelve is still locked, I guess we're heading back whence they came.'

'One thing's for sure, this craft knows a damn sight more about what's what and where it's going than we do,' Fogg replied.

That night Morag woke to see Fogg sitting up in his bunk with an elaborate seashell held to his ear.

'You can hear the sea,' he mumbled. 'It reminds me of . . .' His voice tailed away.

A painting in the Museum of men, women and children enjoying the seaside had been among Morag's favourites. 'I think you're wondering how a species with such a gift for the gentle pleasures could end like this,' she said quietly.

He put down the shell and sidestepped the suggestion. 'It's good to be on the move,' he said. 'The sea and the wind have many affinities.'

Morag merely nodded. There was more to Fogg than met the eye. She considered asking what he could possibly know of the sea, but chose not to. Her candour about her childhood did not bind him. All the same, it was intriguing. Fogg, a mariner? How could that be?

He put down the shell and walked over to *Aeolus*' log, which troubled him for reasons he could not articulate. Another elusive truth, like so much else.

2

Landfall

For two days the *Aeolus* sailed on at a stately pace. Working the ship together eased the tetchiness of their first exchanges. In adverse conditions, Morag took the starboard pulleys and Fogg the portside. Fogg used nautical phrases for the windbags and matched them with their respective pulley numbers:

'Three turns to the mizzen, two and six.'

'Two turns to the gaffe, four and eight.'

He even invented phrases for particular combinations.

'Close the jibbo,' he called.

If they strayed out of balance, the diapason promptly shrilled in protest, but if conditions demanded a tilting deck, it did not object. The strange instrument felt like the ship's captain. Optimal balance between the various forces in play would deliver a contented hum, a musical reward to be worked for. Fogg and Morag did not return to the subject of the Fall. A *we-are-where-we-are* philosophy had taken hold of them both.

On the second afternoon, Fogg set up AIPT on deck.

'Lie down, knees to tabletop, hands entwined behind your head,' said AIPT in his usual automated voice.

'Do join me,' said Fogg. 'It's good for you.'

'No thanks, I prefer my own regime.'

At that moment AIPT reverted to the faintly patronising diction of their last hours in the Museum Dome.

'There's a qualitative difference between doing what you're asked to do and doing what *you* choose to do. In the hands of an expert like my humble self, the former is preferable.'

'Who the fuck are you?' said Morag, wagging her finger at the machine.

'Knees to tabletop,' replied AITP.

Morag succumbed, and in truth, after an hour's work out, she did feel better.

The following morning, the wind picked up to a gale, which howled around the chitin shield. The diapason increased in volume as the deck began to lean. They tightened the bags and let *Aeolus* run, her timbers joining the music, until exhilaration gave way to anxiety as the acceleration sharpened and the deck's angle steepened.

'Lean out!' cried Fogg, 'from the toprail!'

With their feet hooked in the balustrade on the deck's edge, they bent back as far as they could, with arms outstretched.

Morag could not articulate why she found their movement unnatural, until Fogg called it.

'This isn't wind – it's some other force, which is why we're circling, tighter and tighter, and . . .'

The diapason shrieked ever-higher and the timbers groaned in a basso profundo as if about to split and shatter. Fogg left the toprail and stumbled to the wheelhouse, only to find the wheel still firmly locked in place.

The tilting had been gradual, but the righting struck in an instant, as if the force driving them had abruptly lost interest. The craft plunged like a stone, shuddered to a near halt, and soared again. Their stomachs rose to their throats; their hearts dived to their feet; and calves and shins cracked against the rail.

The whole violent process was reflected in a dissonant musical accompaniment from the diapason. Then, miraculously, *Aeolus* levelled, her hectic ride slowed to a gentle drift, the diapason relaxed and – the greatest shock of all – the chitin shield retracted.

'The sky!' yelled Morag, but Fogg was already staring upwards.

The sickly yellow vapour, their perpetual companion, had vanished. Grey-keeled clouds scudded overhead, with streaks of blue between them, the lost blue of so many of the Museum Dome's paintings.

'Look!' he cried in awe.

The edge of a bank of white cloud was turning brilliant. Its puffy edges dissolved and the brilliant circle of the sun rode clear. Fogg stared at the deck, where a shadow had attached itself to his feet, and to Morag's too. The planking glowed. Their faces warmed. They had stumbled on a temperate day, a day for painting.

They had emerged into a high mountain valley whose shoulders and outcrops cast yet deeper shadows.

Morag rushed to the cabin and retrieved the Long Eye. She swept the horizon. 'There – and there! And look, another!' She pointed at three giant beacon-like structures dotting the horizon and holding the murk at bay. 'They're just like the device in the Genrich storeroom.' She handed Fogg the device.

'Spinning us around is what created the velocity to drag us through,' Fogg added as he moved from one to the other.

'Like a whirlpool,' Morag added. 'That figures.'

She stalked the deck to the wheel, and this time when she tried it, she found it liberated, although the vessel would not respond. Lever twelve had returned to its original position and frozen, and the rest remained locked. The *Aeolus* had made its decision: time for landfall.

They looked at each other. Fogg had an incipient stubble which improved his appearance. He almost looked the explorer.

'Liberated,' she said.

'A new world, for good or ill,' he agreed.

She handed him the Long Eye and he focused on the join between the lowlands and the hills. A dark line to the north had to be trees. He made an instant connection, although the shapes were indistinct at this distance. Surely *that* could not be done? He decided to say nothing: she had saved his life by sending the giant crow, so let the surprise be hers.

Below them, rocks strewed the ground like irregular paving, with grey earth zigzagging between.

Morag inhaled deeply through her nose. 'There's no scent. There are no flowers or herbs, no insects, no birds. This is no Eden, it's just us.'

'I think we're meant to explore,' replied Fogg. 'I think it's all part of the test.'

'Then I need to equip.'

Fogg noted the 'I'. Teamwork had marked their time on the *Aeolus*, but now he was apparently to be left to his own devices.

Morag returned from the cabin with a selection of objects. 'If *you're* right, there's a purpose to this place,' she replied. 'I'll take the flare pistol, you take—'

'I'm going for the boat hook. It'll do as a staff, even as a weapon, *in extremis*.'

'You can have my globe-light too.'

'You sure? Dusk can't be far off.'

'Quite sure.'

'Thank you.' He placed the small glass ball, Potts' gift to Morag, in his bag.

Preparations finished, they lowered the rope ladder and descended. Morag bent down, then trickled the grey dust through her fingers. A faint smell of toxins lingered in the earth. Nothing lived on the surface and there was nothing beneath.

She glimpsed a green-gold swathe at the end of the plain. On examination through the Long Eye, it looked oddly familiar – in fact, it was astonishingly familiar. But she kept that thought to herself, unaware that Fogg had already made the connection. She handed him the Long Eye. 'I'll take the valley. You could try the uplands. We have no Rearranger with us, so let's aim to be back by noon tomorrow.'

He offered his right hand. 'I just want to say, Morag, your grand-mother was special, really special. I owe her more than I can say.'

'Well, thank you, Fogg.'

He gave her a warm handshake. In the Museum Dome's paint-ings, men whispered to women, embraced them, admired from a distance, even ignored them, but not one work contained a hand-shake. She felt mildly insulted that he could muster nothing more after their travails together.

Morag strode off, invigorated by the spirit of adventure and the extraordinary image awaiting her. She glanced back only once, to see Fogg heading uphill. The boat hook looked faintly preposterous, as if he were wading a river. He waved to her, and she waved back before hurrying on. For the first time in more than three years, she was on her own again. In the excitement, she overlooked Fogg's retention of the Long Eye.

3

The Hunt

The air might be antiseptic, but the joy of it! A breeze toyed with Morag's cheeks and ruffled her hair. She had passed her life in surroundings subjected to human arrangement, but here the rocks beneath her feet had formed or fallen at random, and the clouds shrank and swelled in their own time.

Fogg's absence contributed to the sense of release.

The green swathe had height in the form of tall trees. Her shadow, which had been lengthening, was now beginning to fade. And here was another first: the sight and special effects of a sinking sun.

She hurried on, noticing that every tree had had its lower branches lopped. Even in the gathering gloom she could make out splashes of colour – mauve, red and blue – in among the trunks. Then she stopped and stared: the place was more than familiar, it was *exact*.

In the left foreground, bulrushes rose from a circular pond, and behind them, lifelike figures pursued a common venture: *the hunt*. On the left were riders mounted on horses, men on foot and dogs, either in attitudes of observation or on the move, every one of them looking right, while on the right, like figures faced them looking left. They had all been caught in a frozen moment.

Each tiny detail matched. Between the trunks a canal ran on a line of perspective, right to left. On the top of the canopy, the outer leaves had been kissed by gold, heralds of autumn, the season of the hunt. Felled trunks in the foreground carried an uncomfortable resemblance to human torsos. The grey mare on the right had a dressed tail, and the adjacent chestnut horse leaned back, weight on its hind legs, as his rider scanned the heavens as if in astonishment. Every costume had its due colour, each spear its proper angle. She could not fault the precision of the rendering in any respect. Even the fleeing deer were exactly placed.

Thank God Fogg wasn't here to deliver his lecture on *The Hunt in the Forest*, Uccello's last work, dating from 1470 in the old chronology, exhibit number 186 in the Museum Dome.

She ran a finger along a horse's flank, then a hunter's cheek: they felt real to the touch, but not quite real beneath. The spearpoints were razor-sharp, but the water proved to be just an illusion.

She recalled the gist of Lord Vane's address to his followers in the gatehouse: *now they would be moving on from craftsmanship to artistry,* he had said, and Mander, looking at Fogg's copy of Goya's painting, had commented, 'We can make this.' Lord Vane had also spoken of his legacy as a celebration of Man's artistry. Fogg had talked with Cassie about horses, and he had drawn this very painting for Lord Vane.

She had never fashioned a momenticon for this painting, choosing instead to give real places priority. A solitary black horse bearing two dead stags on its back stood out, heading left when everyone else faced right. Did he, like the crow, represent Death?

A twig – or rather, a synthetic brown length masquerading as a twig – cracked. In the gloom, a footman had come to life. He wore a powder-blue jacket with a red collar, red leggings, a white cap and black ankle boots, and he carried a spear. He was cleanshaven with high cheekbones, with none of the roughness you might expect in the footpad. As he quartered the ground, working his way among his static comrades-at-arms, his movements looked wholly natural.

Feeling threatened,

Morag edged deeper into the forest, using the tree trunks as cover, feeling as she imagined a stag must feel. He eyed her with the menace of a stalker.

Move or stay still? She held her position behind a tree . . .

The footsman called out, a cry half human and half owl, and his companions, both mounted and on foot, and their dogs, all jerked into instant life. Only the deer remained motionless, as if she were now the only quarry. She toyed with the idea of disabling the man in the blue jacket in the hope that halting him would halt the rest, but there were too many huntsmen and dogs blocking the way. She darted deeper into the trees, towards the wood's interior darkness, where the lines of perspective converged to a vanishing point, for she sensed an exit there, if only she could reach it before her pursuers encircled her.

She fumbled in her waistband, took out the flare pistol and fired over her head. The cherry-coloured flare burst high above the canopy, scattering streamers through the wood like shooting stars. Her pursuers halted, their heads tilted skywards.

As the horsemen resumed their focus on her, Morag reached the painting's black heart, a kernel of roiling darkness in the very centre. She stepped forward – and the mirage sucked her in, then spewed her out as if through an invisible revolving door.

Gone were the trees, gone the golden feel of an old-world autumn.

She had arrived in a shallow gulley in a freezing cold world blanketed in white beneath a starless sky. *Snow!* A momenticon had once, fleetingly, shown her its beauty, flecking the rooftops in an old-world village with a painter for company, but she had never before experienced at leisure real-life snow. She absorbed the eerily positive silence, the way the snow balled when pressed, the iciness biting through her boots and stinging her cheeks, the softening of the contours.

Etched in the slope behind her was a dark scar marking her place of entry like the mouth of a cave. She had no food, but she could not risk the huntsmen again. She buttoned her jacket and climbed in the opposite direction.

A distant beacon prompted a question: *Why invest such technology in a frozen waste?* This hostile winter landscape, such a contrast to *The Hunt*, must, she decided, have also been created for a purpose.

She clambered on, blowing into her cupped hands, until a male voice singing brought her to a sharp halt. The pitch was high, with the odd note a touch off-key: an old man's voice. A guitar joined in and she paused to catch the words.

> '*Show me the flight of the eagle,*
> *The glow of the evening star,*
> *The spirit which launched the* Beagle,
> *How we should be and who we are.*'

The singer embarked on a riff with brio. He must have a fire, she thought, to play in this cold with such fluency. When the singing resumed, she thought she half recognised the voice.

> '*Give me an acre of plenty,*
> *Where the high woods drip with clean rain,*
> *The Paradise once you sent me*
> *I despoiled, but never again.*'

She moved over the brow of a hill. Tucked into the next slope sat an old man festooned in blankets, sitting on a rudimentary bench and huddled over a device fixed in the ground, which was glowing like a fire. His face shone like a portrait; he wore his cap with a jaunty air, and the white hair, coiling out from the rim like wire, left little doubt.

'Oblivious? Mr Potts?'

He turned at the sound of her voice.

She ran down the slope. It felt like a miracle. 'Oblivious Potts! What on earth are you doing out here?'

He smiled and struggled to his feet. 'Well, if it isn't Gilbert Spire's child!' He looked ecstatic as he threw his arms akimbo and hugged her. 'I've kept a spare log for just this eventuality. Sit thyself down.'

She sat on the makeshift seat close to the device, which turned out to offer heat as well as light. On Potts' log was a wicker basket with a large book perched on top.

'Volume seventeen of the old-world *Encyclopaedia Britannica*, eleventh edition,' explained Potts. 'I get a new one every week to keep the grey cells ticking.'

She extended her hands and feet to catch the warmth, triggering a fleeting memory of Fogg executing one of AIPT's exercises.

'It's my own invention,' he said. 'Apologies, but I don't run to food. It comes in the morning, such as it is.'

'But how – but *why*?' She looked round at the fields of snow. 'Where's home?'

'Here,' he said, 'for now. But who – or what – brought you here?'

His fingers protruding from worn mittens were chapped and broken veins crisscrossed his cheeks like fractured ice, but his twinkle remained undimmed.

She knew better than to give Potts platitudes or vagueness. '*Aeolus*.'

Oblivious purred as if recapturing a long-forgotten tune. 'An Airlugger, one of the four model 1s, if I remember, carbon footprint bordering on nil.' He looked wistfully up at the sky. 'Try to imagine her in the old days, breathing like a grampus and scudding across the ice floes in search of God knows what.'

For Morag, that image connected Polar explorers, ice floes, the white admiral and *Aeolus*' sister ship, the *Fram*, her father's craft.

'Did my father write that song?'

Oblivious looked slighted. '*I* wrote the music. I *improved* the words. I made them scan.' He paused. 'But yes, the inspiration was his.'

'Did he contact you after he left?'

Again, that wounded look. 'He was an explorer. He only looked forward. I'm just one feature among the many in his past.'

'And I another,' muttered Morag before she could stop herself. She looked him up and down. 'We must get you to a warm bed.'

'That won't be possible until someone puts in a good word. I've been banished, you see. It's only my little helper who's keeping me alive.' But Potts did not sound resentful or angry, as if exile were an everyday occurrence.

'Banished for what?'

'Something I didn't do – or rather, something I did, but I wasn't responsible for. Though I'd have still done it if I had known the consequences.'

She guessed. 'You mean helping my getaway.'

Potts winked. 'A disgraceful charge. You found *Hope* all by yourself.'

'Banished from where?' asked Morag. 'By whom?'

'You'll discover soon enough, and you'll be more observant for being told less in advance. As for getting some sleep, have one of my blankets.'

Before Morag could tell Potts her news, the old man had dozed off.

Helped by the reviving warmth in her feet and hands, she quickly followed suit.

4

A Tragedienne

'She can't go in like that. She'll stand out a mile. I'll have to age, wither and cackle her.'

This statement, and the broken reed of a voice which uttered it, woke Morag from a restorative slumber beneath Potts' blanket. It was the old woman who had directed her to Pandora's Place on the day of the Tempestas party. She wore a skirt, woollen leggings, a blue jerkin, a knitted shawl, a cap which covered her ears, mittens and boots, an ensemble which gave her a distinctly medieval look. She bent forward on two sticks. The lines of her face had deepened, as had the stoop, aggravated by the large sack on her back, but she had lost neither directness nor the tendency to refer to herself in the third person.

'Oh, I don't know,' muttered Oblivious Potts.

'It's the last Friday of the month so there'll be a show at nine, and Hilda Crike will be missed if we're not there.' She hoisted the sack on to the ground and burrowed into it. 'Food for Mr Potts, Encyclopaedia J to K for Mr Potts; false nose, wig, hunchback, make-up and wardrobe for Spire's child; tot of the best for Mr Potts. Don't gawp, dear, get changing. Into your dotage you go.'

Potts turned his back as Morag changed into Crike's period wardrobe, emerging as her double, at least in terms of dress. Mrs Crike fixed the prosthetic nose, wig and the hunchback before adding make-up. 'I used to do performances, yer know. I was the last tragedienne. So take it from Mrs Crike, it's no good looking a hundred and warbling like a lark.'

'Corncrake is the one to go for,' suggested Potts.

'And do it natural-like. This isn't a panto, it's life or death.'

'Cover story?' asked Potts.

'She can be my long-lost sister: Glad, for Gladys. She was a simple woman.'

'You've come from *The Hunt in the Forest*. If you're asked, tell it as it was. No spy would come that way,' added Potts.

Mrs Crike refilled her bag with Morag's clothes and handed over one of her sticks. After a few minutes of voice rehearsals, Mrs Crike gave Potts a peck on the cheek and a final instruction. 'Do your exercises, Mr Potts, or you'll end up like me.'

'And you get along or you'll arrive right at the wrong moment. True tragediennes have impeccable timing, Mrs Crike.'

'He does like to state the bleeding obvious,' muttered Mrs Crike.

Morag's offer to carry the sack earned another rebuke.

'What a giveaway that would be! My demented sister toils on the tundra and I dump the cargo on her? Wake up, Miss Spire, this is do-or-die. And you ain't going nowhere without my say-so, Mr Potts. We keep to our traditional domestic arrangement. I've a vote, you've a vote, and I've the casting vote.'

Potts gave Morag a hug and waved them off.

'Remember, silence travels faster than cackle,' were his final words.

They set off uphill under a lightening but leaden sky, keeping to the dark scars of Mrs Crike's outward journey. 'Alongside, alongside, where I don't need to shout,' she chuntered.

At the summit of the hill, Mrs Crike delivered an expansive sweep of the arm as if introducing Elsinore. 'Winterdorf,' she said.

'Wow!' was all Morag could manage.

The town had step-gabled houses with snowbound roofs sloping close to the ground. Those on the outer rim overlooked frozen

ponds, crossable by arched stone bridges or humbler wooden structures, often no more than horizontal planks and vertical staves.
Horses and carts dotted the lanes; crows launched and landed in
leafless trees. Waterwheels stood motionless in the grip of ice.

A river, equally held in winter's iron grasp, wended through the
centre, which was dominated by a church on the nearest bend.
Willows adorned the banks.

She noted absences: no people as yet, and the remoter villages
and isolated farmhouses beyond had been sacrificed, but otherwise fidelity reigned. The two adjacent paintings on level 5 of
the Museum Dome, *Hunters in the Snow* and *Winter Landscape with
Skaters and a Bird Trap*, both by Pieter Bruegel the Elder, had been
conjoined and painstakingly brought to life.

Mrs Crike sounded moved by Morag's expression of wonder. 'As
a tragedienne,' she said, 'I have to ask. Is it fully magnificent or a
magnificent folly?'

'As an ordinary punter, I say it's wondrous.'

A solitary figure, a matchstick man at this distance, emerged with
a bundle of wood on his back. His appearance energised Mrs Crike.

'On, on,' she cried. 'He's an early bird, but if we don't beat the
chime of nine, we're toast. And stop walking like a hussy of twenty.'

Morag resumed her crouch just in time, for a guard in equally
medieval dress emerged from a lean-to beside a makeshift platform
concealed by the snow and levelled his spear at Mrs Crike's midriff.

'What do you think you're doing out here at this hour?'

'That's no way to talk to a grandmother.'

'I asked you a question.'

'I got a message that my sister had stumbled in. She's addled
upstairs, you see.'

'We don't take migrants, especially useless ones.'

'I said *upstairs*. She can clean floors and chimneys better'n a saint.'

The guard peered at Morag, who stared blankly back.

'The face that sank a thousand ships,' he scoffed.

A second guard joined them. 'That's Mrs Crike.' He peered at her companion.

'The other hag is her sister,' replied the first guard before declaring grandly, 'Relatives are allowed. And we're missing a female figure between the ponds.' He turned to Mrs Crike. 'You heard. Shut it and leg it, Crike. And take Helen of Troy with you.'

'Many a true word spoken in jest,' mumbled Mrs Crike before scuttling off with Morag. 'We ain't got time for home comforts. It's a matinee, and we're on the ponds.'

Suddenly the town was heaving with life, with everyone on the move, although not to their places of work. En route they passed a saddler's, tailor's, smithy, a bakery and a carpenter's shop, each frontage marked by the tools of their trade and each currently unoccupied.

'Quit gawping,' Mrs Crike hissed. 'I'm Big Sis and we're joined at the hip, get it?'

She led Morag to the further of the two rectangular ponds on the east side of town. Stunted synthetic willows dotted the margins. In perfect keeping with Bruegel's vision, the skaters varied from beginners to the accomplished, the former striving for balance while the latter played primitive hockey with wooden balls and curved sticks. A dog proffered its snout to his master; adults pulled children on toboggans, and in the centre, an imposing young man in a red cloak was spinning a skater around by the arm.

On the southern, nearer pond, which was separated from its neighbour by a snowy bank, curling was the game. An old woman trudged along the bridge beyond, while through the arches beneath, another dragged a rudimentary sleigh.

Mrs Crike ushered Morag into position on the bank between the two ponds, on the side nearer the town. She moved beside the man with the dog. 'Right, that's your spot: legs slightly apart and looking that way. Watch wistfully and keep away from the games. We're that decrepit. Get the picture?'

Everyone held their position, even the unfortunates prone on the ice. A horseman trotted into view on the lane to the town, the bells on his reins a-jingle. Lord Vane, conspicuous in his finery of furs dyed yellow and green, had the posture of a horseman from *The Hunt in the Forest*. He looked no less accomplished.

Still nobody moved.

The church tower chimed nine and on the last stroke, an imagined world became reality. Everyone cheered, hats flew and children jumped up and down as the painting's frozen details dissolved into a moving tableau. Lord Vane leant down to shake hands, pat heads and compliment his players as he passed, not dismounting until he reached the first pond. He strode around the perimeter, and Morag had the uneasy sensation that he was slowly but surely heading for her. She stooped to retie her boots while holding her position, thinking that was the least suspicious option.

Lord Vane paused beside her.

'I'm told under that bridge is the best spot to catch mechanical fish,' said Lord Vane.

'Me angling days are long gone,' stuttered Morag.

'Really – not even a dabble?'

Morag winced. He was playing her like a fish.

'But more importantly, we've been missing the person who stands here for some time. The omission has irked me.' He gave Morag an appraising stare. 'But I don't think I know you.'

Morag had prepared for this moment. 'Me sister 'ides me away cos I'm simple.' She looked round. Hilda Crike had disappeared. 'Gladys Crike, at yer service.'

'I'd say you're quite complex.' He called over the young man in the red cloak, who skated the few yards between them with easy elegance. 'This lady says she's Gladys Crike, Benedict.'

The young man looked into her face. 'There's only one Crike I know, and she's just shuffled off. How old are you, dear?'

'I never could count.'

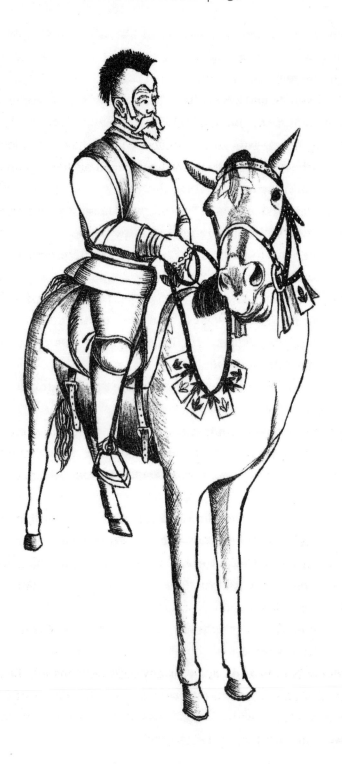

Benedict had to be a Vane. He had his father's distinctive jaw. He took her hands in his, spread out her fingers and examined the tips exposed by the mittens.

'Ageing skin looks thin and translucent. Your fingers are neither.' His voice was rich, but had yet to achieve his father's mellow depths. He lightly rubbed her fingers. 'These have the bloom of youth.' With a sudden movement he whisked off her cap and wig. '*Abracadabra!*' he cried.

'So!' exclaimed Lord Vane. 'The young woman who left my party without a word of thanks returns as a spy.'

Morag decided to be herself. She removed the prosthetic nose. 'It was a wake, not a party.'

Benedict intervened gently. 'Father, can I have a name – on the assumption it isn't Gladys?'

'Miss Spire.'

'Morag Spire,' added Morag.

'Also known as Miss Momenticon,' added Lord Vane.

'And why's that?' Benedict asked.

Morag felt sure she would have recognised him at the Tempestas party, and this question confirmed his absence. She remembered that Cassie too, Lord Vane's daughter, had kept – or been kept – away. Her analysis progressed no further, for around the pond a whisper was growing as she was recognised: *the girl with the gift.*

Lord Vane whispered to Benedict, 'This is not the place for questions and answers. Get us a room at the tavern, and hot chocolate for the three of us. Half past nine on the dot, and let Miss Spire wander.' His voice had not lost its air of command.

Lord Vane continued his meet-and-greet as Benedict sent a messenger to the tavern.

'I follow behind and check for any gaps he's missed,' Benedict informed Morag. 'Today we were a dog short. Talking of gaps, I do apologise for unveiling you, but Lord Vane would have known anyway, and with him, honesty pays.'

'Does it?' retorted Morag.

'Your elder sister knows the tavern well,' Benedict said with a wink. 'You've twenty minutes to take in the town.' He gestured to the gathering admirers. 'You appear to be part of our mythology, so you're quite safe. Do borrow my cloak if you're feeling the cold.'

He had an old-world courtesy, a virtue which nobody else, save possibly Oblivious Potts, had previously offered. He had looks too. His status she considered a negative, but so far, he had worn it lightly, a mirror opposite to Cosmo.

She declined the cloak and asked, 'Have you ever come across a boy called Fogg?'

'As Lord Vane said, best later.' With a murmured farewell, Benedict hurried off, to be replaced by Mrs Crike, who emerged from a stand of trees.

'All right, smarty pants, just because you've a pass to the top, don't go getting any airs and graces.'

'Is his horse real? Are the dogs real? Is *anything* real?'

Mrs Crike put her hands on her hips. 'We built this place from nothing and we're proud of it. The old Dome was all bits and pieces. This place has an overarching theme and something to say. It's easy to breeze in, take our hospitality and carp.'

Chastened, Morag apologised before asking, 'Who's the young man in the cloak? He has to be a Vane, surely.'

'That's how it looks, but he's not in the records. He turned up from nowhere and has been his Lordship's companion ever since. And I know what you're thinking. This Benedict fellow and Cosmo are chalk and cheese characterwise. It's a good thing Cosmo has his own place, or I'd predict fisticuffs sooner or later. Anyway, mysteries usually bring trouble, so keep your wits about you.' Crike handed Morag her original clothes. 'You can leave the octogenarian glad-rags with the barman. He makes a pretty penny out of me.'

Morag knew where to find the tavern; it dominated the left foreground of the painting.

'My hovel is over there,' added Miss Crike, pointing to a solitary house on the outskirts, 'the sticking-out bit only, should you ever need a bed, or a guide to whom to avoid.'

Fire and smoke were coiling up from the chimney and Morag could make out a man on the roof hurling water at the conflagration, just as in the painting.

'It's only for show,' reassured Miss Crike over her shoulder as she headed home, and the fire died down.

Other streets lurked behind Bruegel's façades. The craft studios from the Tempestas Dome had relocated to the narrow streets close to the church. Trades came to life as she passed. The dogs had real leads, the horses real saddles, and the men and women sported real clothes, skates and toboggans, and all these accoutrements had to be made. Workers doffed their hats or waved, and children milled around her, asking how momenticons were made and whether she'd fashioned any new ones since her days in the Genrich Dome.

Benedict emerged from the tavern door and shooed the children away. 'Never arrive on the last Friday of the month,' he said with a smile, ushering her through a maze of tables and benches to a cosy chamber at the rear where a welcoming fire had already been lit.

Morag held back her most pressing questions: *Where is Cassie? Where is Lady Vane? What about Genrich?*

'What are you burning?' she asked, for the flames were real.

'Peat from beneath our feet.'

The bricks glowed and warmed.

'You weren't in the Domes when I was there,' she said. 'Either of them, Genrich or Tempestas.'

Benedict dwelt on the observation a little too long for Morag's peace of mind.

'I was out and about.'

'Where?'

'In the tantalum mines and chitin factories.'

Morag could not summon the courage to ask whether he was a

long-lost cousin, so instead said, 'You've cleared the air. You've got water. There'll be seeds under our feet, real ones. So why devote all your time to a replica?'

Benedict stoked the fire. He was graceful for a strongly built man, and he spoke with such calm that his extrovert cry of *Abracadabra!* now felt out of character.

'Of the common flowers and vegetables, lettuce seeds last longest, but even in good conditions, six years at best.' It sounded like an entry from Potts' encyclopaedia. 'But that's not the point,' he added. 'They're fulfilled: they have their work, their rituals and a community spirit. And they're preserving something of value.'

Morag was not the person to challenge on natural history data, for she had had the benefit of growing up with several enclopaedias. 'I beg to differ. The seeds of *silene stenophylla* are viable after thirty thousand years – a slice of knowledge for which we have carbon dating and the Arctic squirrel to thank. Date palms don't do badly either. I'm talking Mother Nature; you're spouting man-made seed packets.'

A familiar voice intervened. 'You sound just like your father. He was an undying optimist who held forth with passion about the prospects for Paradise regained. He even suggested Paradise was a real place, one to be discovered and protected.' Lord Vane stood in the doorway. His mood appeared to have lightened. 'He induced me to support an expedition with that very object in mind, but he never came back. As for seed, the poisons go deep. We spent months just cleaning the peat so it burns safely. And come on, who ticks your box, Tempestas or Genrich?'

That's not the choice I'm talking about, she thought while deciding against a fight with Lord Vane. Enlightenment was her present priority. 'What happened to Genrich?' she asked instead.

'Tell her about the deal, Benedict, while I rustle up our order.'

She could see why Lord Vane was popular. He combined energy and leadership with the common touch.

Benedict stoked the fire again. 'We were all consuming too much energy. Lord Sine and my father agreed to vacate their respective Domes within six months of the cull and to seek out new technologies. It was a competition, of sorts. We invented the beacons to purify the air, although they burn energy too. So we're limited to a handful of valleys, just enough to keep our people occupied until the tantalum runs out.' He paused. 'We've not the slightest idea what Genrich have been up to. They disappeared without trace. Hopefully, for good.'

Lord Vane returned. 'You missed out the amusing bit. Lord Sine offered me a truce for three years. I mean, a truce – as if we were enemies after all we'd done for them.'

Morag bit her lower lip. Mention of Lord Sine made Winterdorf's picturesque prettiness feel horribly vulnerable. 'Lord Sine never rests, you know that. Why declare a truce if he isn't thinking of taking you over – or worse? Have you any defences against whoever – or whatever – is out there?'

Lord Vane rubbed his hands down his coat. 'My weather-watchers can lightning-strike whoever and whatever.' He spoke as if they were dragons, potent and irresistible. 'This plot of land, like all our other plots, is sub-squared: Marcus has only to set the co-ordinates. And Lord Sine has seen them at work. We sleep well in our beds.'

Lord Vane's complacency unsettled Morag. *Our time will come*, Cosmo had said to Marcus at the Tempestas party. And she had not forgotten his icy smile when the lightning had struck.

Lord Vane paused as the chocolate arrived in an earthenware jug and matching mugs with an attractive grey-yellow glaze.

'We've improved Matter-Rearrangement no end,' he continued as the landlord dispensed the dark, thick liquid. 'This is Winterdorf: science and art in perfect alignment.'

Morag, seduced by the exotic tang of the chocolate in mouth, nostrils and lungs, barely heard.

Lord Vane pounced on the dreaminess. 'There, Benedict, sits a different kind of person. We live in the present. We have made our town and now we get on with life. Miss Spire, by contrast, likes to nurse her fantasies.'

'And her old-world knowledge,' added Benedict, with that easy smile.

Lord Vane turned to Morag. 'Believe me, Miss Spire, the Arctic squirrel has no bearing on our present challenges. Nor do the extinct more generally. We're the after-the-Fall generation. We're a fresh beginning, not the closing chords of an old tune.'

Benedict poked the fire and casually redirected the conversation. 'How did you get here, Miss Spire?"

Morag took a sip, buying time. What she wouldn't give for her grandmother's counsel. How much should she reveal, how much hold back? Were the Vanes friends or enemies?

'There's a way in,' she mumbled. 'I'm sure you know of it.'

'Tell us,' said Benedict.

'No,' intervened Lord Vane, 'keep it chronological. Tell us where you went after my party.'

Morag tried not to show her relief. Here was a question which half-truths could deflect. 'I didn't *choose* to go anywhere. I chanced on a primitive craft which transported me to a Dome of sorts, a stowaway Dome for old bits and pieces.'

'All because she didn't like my party. You need to understand, Morag: Lord Sine's useless constructs were consuming vital raw materials – as were we, of course. Something had to give. Lord Sine reduced his dependents to reduce demand, and we were already working on the beacons, right under their very noses. Always best to hide in plain view.'

For once, Lord Vane sounded unconvinced by his own defence. Morag suspected he was not telling the whole truth. 'Your friend, 147, was among the dead,' she pointed out.

Lord Vane shrugged with a grimace of tentative apology. 'That really wasn't meant to happen. I very specifically asked her to the party – and only her from Genrich. I don't know what went wrong.'

'And when you got to this Dome of odds and ends, what then?' Benedict interposed gently.

'It had the bare essentials – a Matter-Rearranger, hygiene facilities and a chitin shield – so I counted my blessings and settled in.'

Lord Vane chuckled. 'You took the veil, and for three years you never went looking for company? I find that surprising.'

She had delivered a heavily edited version of the truth, but the challenge still nettled. 'The craft abandoned me once I was in, so I had no choice. Then, three years on, two identical twins dropped in, psychos with an addiction to momenticons. I managed to trap them in the airlock and commandeered their craft. After drifting for several days, your beacons sucked me in. And here I am.'

'Their craft,' asked Lord Vane, 'did it have a name?'

'*Aeolus.*'

'Well, I'm glad we were of some use. The *Aeolus* is one of ours.' He frowned. 'Not all the Genrich misfits were disposed of. Lord Sine kept some back on the sly. A pair of his more bizarre constructs made off with it. Good to know you dealt with them.'

Touché.

She had not lost a moment's sleep over the dead bodies in the airlock, and Lord Vane would no doubt say that the casualties at his party were no different, apart from 147, whom he had tried to save.

Before she could respond, Lord Vane stood up and applauded. 'You flew an Airlugger single-handed! There you are, Benedict, see what's bred in the bone! She's a chip off the old block, just as Lady Vane said.'

His choice of words and their manner of delivery had an odd, sarcastic edge, but the moment quickly passed. Lord Vane shrugged off whatever was troubling him in favour of a winning smile. 'Everyone should see snow falling before they die, Miss Spire, and in forty minutes, you will. Meantime, Benedict will give you a short tour. Never judge a town before seeing her interiors.'

And with that advice, Lord Vane turned abruptly and left the room.

'He is a good man,' said Benedict, 'who has endured a lot.'

More at ease in Lord Vane's absence, Benedict escorted her to the Town Hall, a large house on the western edge beyond the church. Stairs led to a galleried room where a middle-aged man was pointing out areas for restoration, tapping with a cane on hugely enlarged copies of the two Bruegel paintings suspended on the back wall.

'Franz and his team will refix the uprights on the bridge here – *tap* – which is beginning to sag. There are two defective crows, here and here' – *tap, tap* – 'which need recalibrating. We have reports of a leaking roof here.' *Tap.* 'The branches on three foreground trees' – *tap, tap, tap* – 'have shifted out of alignment with the master work. Such is the distorting effect of heavy snow.'

Morag surveyed the audience: rapt attention everywhere.

Next stop: the church, where a vigorous old priest with a bald crown and a halo of white hair was holding forth.

'We do encourage attendance, but it's not compulsory,' Benedict whispered, ushering her into a pew at the back. 'After the monthly show, we always have a sermon.'

'We let loose the four horsemen,' the priest boomed. 'They may be back in their stables for now, but they watch us, saddled and ready, should we mishandle our second chance. Let us remember them all.'

The congregation intoned the name of each without prompting.

'Pestilence.'

'War.'

'Famine.'

'Death.'

The priest resumed, 'Today's text concerns the second horse, the red horse. *"When He broke the second seal, I heard the second living creature saying, 'Come.' And another, a red horse, went out; and to him who sat on it, it was granted to take peace from the earth, and that men would slay one another; and a great sword was given to him."'*

The red horse.

There had been reddish horses aplenty in Uccello's wood. Morag had an unpleasant sense of approaching calamity.

The heads of the worshippers were all bowed save one. Even from behind, Morag could identify Marcus, the weather-watcher who had raised the swarm of golden insects at the gatehouse party.

'He doesn't look very respectful,' she said.

'He's the keeper of the town's defences and commands the new Tiriel's Tower.'

They did not stay long. Outside, true to Lord Vane's forecast, snowflakes were drifting down, thickening as they walked. They had a miraculous quality, as if a million artists were touching up the town.

'Is it *real*?' she asked.

'As real as you or me,' he said, in a detached, observational way.

They wandered. He introduced her as Miss Spire to those they met. He showed her the focal point of the second painting, a crude bird trap with a piece of string attached to a wooden panel, designed to crush any bird tempted by the seed beneath.

'It's for show, obviously,' he said. 'Our birds wouldn't make much of a stew.'

She considered the paintings they had selected: *The Hunters in the Snow* and *Winter Landscape with Skaters and a Bird Trap* by Bruegel the Elder, and Uccello's *The Hunt in the Forest*. Hunting and traps: had Man's predatory treatment of Nature been a root cause of the Fall?

The strain of measuring her surroundings against the paintings, the beauty of the snow and the bustle in its infinite detail, had drained her emotional reserves. She propped herself against an upright of a porch.

'You're worn out,' Benedict said. 'Three years of solitude and now us and all this? It's hardly surprising.'

Morag kicked herself for showing weakness. 'I'm fine, really.'

'The tavern has a room or two . . .'

An hour of undisturbed slumber had its appeal, but she had no intention of accepting. 'A drink or two is what taverns are for.'

They trudged back to the tavern to find its front room had come to raucous life. The Town Hall and the church had released their audience, who had had their fill of listening. A viol strained to compete with laughter and conversation. Couples took to the floor and danced, linking arms, then separating, then facing each other and slapping palms, while onlookers beat the rhythm with the soles of their boots.

'Want to try it?' said a silken voice. 'Like everything else, it's timing and rhythm.' Marcus thrust his arm through hers as if the answer were a foregone conclusion.

'Benedict?' she said, disengaging and turning her back on the weather-watcher.

'It's not my forte,' Benedict replied.

She could have throttled him. 'Then you can bloody well learn.'

She hauled him on to the floor. The steps were more intimate now, with chests touching and hands around the waist. Benedict had moved gracefully over the treacherous ice of the pond, but he had no musical ear. He and the viol were strangers.

'You have to *listen*,' she shouted in his ear.

'This is demeaning,' he said, striding from the floor.

She glared at Marcus, but to her surprise, he was gazing at Benedict as if he had never seen him before.

Then, in a single beat, music and movement stalled. The church bell was tolling, the peals exceeding any known hour.

Only Marcus reacted, darting past a young man in the doorway as he bellowed, 'Invaders!'

Morag followed the rush outside. The heights where the tavern stood gave a perfect view of the snowfield through which she and Mrs Crike had trudged a few hours earlier. The invaders had spread out in a horseshoe formation, with footmen in front and horsemen behind, their spears vertical and swords still in their scabbards. They held their position as if they themselves were imitating a painting. Every human participant in *The Hunt in the Forest* had come to town.

The bell pealed on. A blacksmith started distributing makeshift weapons from a cart, as mothers tried to usher their children through the press. Inexplicably, the intruders, despite the advantage of surprise, were allowing the town to muster a defence. Maybe the presence of the weather-watchers, Lord Vane's main line of defence, had given them pause.

That raised another troubling question. The horses and men were mechanicals, so who – or what – was controlling them?

Between the sonorous clangs from the church tower, the tiny bells on Lord Vane's bridle tinkled reassuringly as he rode out to meet the intruders. Marcus walked beside him, carrying a long metal rod. He looked to Morag like a malign sorcerer.

Benedict, who'd stayed behind, was commandeering the where-withal for a makeshift barricade.

The horseman riding the grey with the dressed tail broke away and cantered along his line of stationary troops and back. The way he patted his horse's neck struck Morag as a distinctly human gesture. Then he wheeled round and trotted towards Lord Vane.

They met a good four hundred yards from the town perimeter. A vigorous parley ensued. Though too far away to hear or see facial expressions, Morag could make out the calmness of the man on the grey, while Lord Vane was gesticulating with increasing desperation. Marcus was leaning nonchalantly on his staff some way behind. If only she had retained the Long Eye.

Below her, Benedict was shoring up his defensive line. A barricade of carts, barrels and toboggans had been hurriedly erected to keep the cavalry at bay. Men stood in a line behind, clutching staves, long-handled spades, forks, mallets and hammers.

The barricade looked pitifully short in both depth and height. She rushed back into the tavern in search of benches and tables.

Lord Vane trotted back towards the town. As he passed, he bellowed to Marcus, 'Stay at the barricade and if they come twenty places closer, teach them a lesson.'

But Marcus just stood there motionless, allowing the man on the grey to walk up to him. They exchanged words.

The weather-watcher isn't meant to be doing this, thought Morag. *He should be reducing a hunter or two to wreckage.*

Belatedly, Marcus appeared to remember his orders. He opened his arms, raised his metal staff and rammed it into the ground. A brilliant bolt of lightning zigzagged from the pebble-grey sky – but not at the invaders. It struck the church belfry with an explosive roar as the hunters charged from trot to canter to gallop in moments.

'Hold the line,' cried Lord Vane.

'Behind the barricades!' bellowed Benedict.

But Winterdorf's citizens were realists, not soldiers. They wavered, broke ranks and ran, a trickle fast becoming a flood. They would take their chance in their own homes and the narrow back streets, where horses could not manoeuvre.

'No!' Benedict yelled at Lord Vane, who had dismounted to rally his forces.

The riders, lances now levelled, poured towards the defenceless town, the footmen following at a run behind. There were no more than thirty attackers, and only thirteen of them were mounted, but they looked terrifying enough to the villagers. Morag yelled to anyone within earshot to gather stones and hold fast.

To her dismay, Benedict was running too, leaving Lord Vane isolated by the barricades, where he flailed around with a sword. He immobilised a foot soldier, who stood twitching as if gripped by a seizure, but in minutes, the horsemen had surrounded him. They ignored everyone else and, with the man on the grey pointing at the nearest pond, they jabbed Lord Vane in that direction with the tips of their spears. Bereft of support, he staggered on to the ice.

Morag rushed down the slope towards the mêlée, only to realise there was nothing she could do.

'How can you?' yelled Lord Vane as the spears stabbed at his legs and the ice around him. 'My own son—'

'This is the kinder way,' said the man on the grey.

Lord Vane was now engulfed by the attacking horsemen. Blood oozed, dripping from his cloak and breeches. His footing failed as the fractured ice around him began to heave. Even as he slid thrashing into the water, the mechanical horsemen continued to strike.

The man on the grey, lifted his sword, tipped the golden band Lord Vane was wearing from his head and raised it high. The humdrum business of death he left to his automated army, a murder done in silence.

The second Lord Vane raised his right arm one last time and disappeared beneath the ice.

Marcus strode over to the pond.

The man on the grey, the diadem of the kingdom in hand, swivelled round to face the weather-watcher. 'Lower the temperature, there's a good man. He's best frozen in. We don't want a trade in relics, do we?'

Morag stood speechless in horror, shaking her head. She had seen violence in paintings; she had seen Lord Sine's creations suffocate and die; she herself had destroyed the psychopathic twins in the Museum's airlock; but this casual, unprovoked slaughter had a brutality all of its own.

Worse still, the rider of the grey was Cosmo Vane.

My own son.

Marcus twirled his staff once more. The snow thickened and the temperature dropped. The hunters on foot had cornered a huddle of citizens against a house wall.

Cosmo trotted over, beaming. 'As of now, you're my town criers. Tell everyone that the third Lord Vane has come. We will take the world in time, but we have enemies to deal with first. If you find any of these individuals, bring them to me now. There will be rewards.'

He handed a small scroll to the fittest-looking man.

Instinctively, Morag felt herself in danger. Directly below the tavern she could see the second Lord Vane's horse idling through the snow, the bridle looped around the saddle's pommel. A convenient stand of trees masked the mechanical from the ponds. She had a chance.

She sprinted down the hill. She had never mounted a horse before, but emergency makes a quick learner. She had the wit to raise the stirrups, but the horse remained a picture of nonchalance despite vigorous kicks and yanks on the bridle. She could see Cosmo and Marcus issuing further instructions to a populace whose allegiance had instantly transferred. Some were pointing up at the tavern. Morag had little doubt that she would be on his list.

Did the horse only run for Lord Vane?

Her question was quickly answered. Benedict leapt on behind her, seized the bridle and pressed a finger into the horse's left flank.

'He doesn't know your voice, but he knows mine,' he said. 'Change of owner, Cirrus.' The horse broke into a trot. 'Go straight, go fast.'

The horse instantly accelerated into a gallop, flinging Morag forward. She clung to the pommel as Benedict wrapped an arm around her waist.

'There's a way out,' she stammered.

'I know,' said Benedict. 'There's no pursuit, and anyway, our horse is better than theirs.'

For a man who minutes earlier had lost his benefactor, this emotionless display was almost as horrific as the killing itself.

'You should have fought for him,' she cried.

'And what good would that have done?' he whispered in her ear, as coolly as if life were an arithmetical sum.

As they cantered through a landscape where sky and earth blended, she reappraised her criticism. Maybe he was right. Maybe intervention would have achieved nothing. Those distinctive Vane features would have signed Benedict's death warrant too.

'There,' she said, pointing at a glowing light in a circle of bare ground. 'Stop there.'

They dismounted. Potts' heating device, still exuding warmth, lay on its back like a dead beetle. Other belongings, including his hat, had been trampled into the snow in a swirl of hooves.

'He's called Oblivious Potts and he lives out here,' Morag explained, but Benedict was showing more interest in the device than its owner's history.

She retrieved the hat and followed the prints towards the entrance to *The Hunt in the Forest*. Flecks of blood stained the snow, but not enough for a mortal blow. There was no sign of a body, and from her reading of the tracks, Cosmo's hunters had not bothered to pursue Potts to the mouth of the cave. There she found Volume J to K from the *Encyclopaedia Britannica*, eleventh edition, lying at the mouth. Pages had been torn out and fragments of learning scattered across the hillside. A spear had gouged out its centre. Potts' devotion to old-world knowledge appeared to have saved him.

She replayed the scene in her head. Potts must have seen his attackers before they saw him, otherwise the old man would have stood no chance.

'Would they attack without instructions?'

'Mechanicals only do violence on command.'

She turned her attention to Benedict. 'What happened back there? That was shocking,' she said. 'Horrible. I mean, father and son – the lack of mercy, the brutality . . .'

'Wholly in character,' replied Benedict tersely.

'Do you have any claim to the title?'

'I do, but it's based on a lie.'

'How do you mean?'

'I'm Lord Vane's son.'

The answer disorientated Morag. She had no difficulty with the notion that Cosmo would never mention a fraternal rival, but Lord and Lady Vane had introduced her to their children without any mention of Benedict. Hernia had also described Cosmo as the heir. Yet the fleck of amethyst in his eyes, the set of his cheekbones, even his manner of speaking, resembled Lady Vane's as closely as other features resembled Lord Vane's.

'Anyone can see you're a Vane.'

'So they say.' For the first time in their short acquaintance, he was looking uneasy.

'What's the lie, then? You're a son and you're older.' Her anger at his inaction resurfaced. 'And you've just let yourself be disinherited without a fight.'

He gave his answer without emotion or side. 'I am not older. He was born first. Please don't ask why.'

And then Morag knew who he was and *how* he was, and why Marcus had gazed at him as if he were a stranger. At the Praesidium meeting, Lord Sine had promised Lord Vane a delivery that would be like looking in a mirror. Genrich had made Benedict. He was the son of parents, not a test-tube; he could seize a hat and cry

'Abracadabra!' – but emotion, feeling and warmth had been compromised. She felt a surge of biting hopelessness. The first man she had found appealing was one of Lord Sine's constructs, even if fashioned from the genes of his putative parents.

'We'd best go through,' she said.

On the other side of the entrance, the hounds and the deer remained in their frozen attitudes. One malfunctioning huntsman remained, twitching and jerking, until Benedict found the control and put him out of his misery. Of Oblivious Potts, there was no sign.

'I shall wait until dusk,' said Benedict. 'Meanwhile, we can recruit allies, half for me and half for you. Sixteen hounds makes eight each. All we need is their name or names.'

'What are you talking about – *I shall wait until dusk?*'

He ignored the question. 'My money's on one name for all. They're so alike, it wouldn't work otherwise.'

Cosmo was an unlikely dog lover, but he would want to embroider his legend. 'Try Argos,' she suggested.

Benedict did, to no effect.

'Cerberus?'

Likewise, no response.

Morag was running out of grandiose candidates. She ransacked her memory. 'Cavall?'

Dog heads twitched; dog ears pricked.

Cavall it was.

'Who?' queried Benedict.

'King Arthur's dog.'

'I don't know him.'

She could not resist a tease. 'The dog or the King?'

'Neither.'

'That's good. It would be horrible to know everything.'

She followed him from hound to hound, watching as he found the point in their flanks and whispered into their ears, one by one, 'Change of owner, Cavall. Now you follow this voice.'

She followed his example: eight for him and eight for her.

'So,' she said, 'what now?' She had misgivings about taking him to the *Aeolus*. There were two cabins, but the shared space was intimate and she did not want that kind of problem. It had been difficult enough with Fogg.

'I'm going back to town.'

She felt blindsided. In her mind she had branded him a coward. 'You're mad.'

'I need to know what he's about – I need to know his secrets, and who his allies are. I need to form a resistance. He has never seen me before, and I know my way around. There are a few I can trust.' He looked through the trees to the hillside beyond. 'This place isn't Cosmo's home. That must be elsewhere. Lord Vane gave him several beacons. Maybe you can find them for us.' He smiled. 'When the cat's away . . .'

She could not work him out at all. He had idiom, reason in spades and even humour. Only emotion was missing.

'Benedict, you're dead conspicuous. You're a Vane through and through – even I can tell that, and I'm not from these parts. You'll last five minutes.'

'I have every confidence in Miss Crike.'

'She's ancient and bonkers.'

'She's experienced, savvy and has a safe house.'

'Be careful, then.'

'I am, as you observed before.'

Morag's frustration prompted an impulsive gesture. She rummaged in her bag and pulled out a bottle. 'Before you go, take one of these. It may do you good.'

She rattled her bottle of favourite momenticons from her pocket, fruit of her long sojourn in the Museum Dome. She wanted to test the effect of her handiwork. She chose the same artist who had loosened Fogg, but a younger version.

'This one, I think.' She handed him the pill. 'Take it,' she added, 'now.'

'You're an apothecary, no less,' he said.

'It's my one and only talent. Trust me.'

She read a certain desperation in his face, the look of a man in search of an anchorage. *That's why he'll accept*, she thought, and he did. He sat down, rested his back against the nearest tree and swallowed the pill, while his eight hounds milled around his feet.

His eyes half closed, and the lids flickered. He had left her for the old world and for Paris.

5

The Affliction of Benedict Vane

He knew his mind differed from everyone else's. Every image, name, smell or snatch of music unleashed a wealth of data, which he could sort in the blink of an eye. As information on one subject would invariably trigger a deluge of secondary data, this ability to discard was critical. Others had loaded these voluminous facts in his brain, but the prioritising gift was his own.

The novelty of this scene all but overwhelmed him.

Place: The Gare Saint-Lazare, Paris.

Function: A transport hub.

Dominant character: A locomotive, propelled by steam which belches from a single funnel with a noise like a giant clearing his throat. You create steam to drive a piston in a cylinder, simplicity itself.

Time: old-world chronology, 1877.

Journey: the locomotive and the carriages it pulls have just arrived from Deauville, a seaside town in Normandy. It is mid-afternoon.

Benedict panics. His loaded memories surely cannot extend to such minutiae – then he realises he is inhabiting two minds, his own, and that of the true observer of this scene, the bearded young man seated behind an easel. It is he who knows the train's place of departure.

Easel: an upright support used by painters to hold a canvas while they work.

Morag knows what he is seeing, of course, as it is her experience he is sharing.

An engineer in a blue uniform ushers in the train like a docking ship. The smoke is beautiful, but rich in soot. The artist rests his brush and watches the train disgorging its human cargo. The panoply of a summer excursion spills on to the platform: sailor hats, shrimping nets and parasols, women in brilliant colours, and children with faces in a spectrum from pink to the colour of chocolate.

In his eyes she catches the moment when the scene abruptly fractures like a shattered jigsaw.

Benedict shook his head. 'So that's why they're after you,' he said. 'That wasn't make-believe, was it? It was real: Claude Monet on the platform when the train from Deauville gets in. How could you capture both the scene and his thoughts? I know nothing of this phenomenon.'

'I'm a freak.'

'*Seriously*.' The normally calm Benedict for once sounded almost angry.

'A great artist's creative energy leaves a trace in his or her original work. I connect with it. Then one of Lord Sine's weavers enabled me to preserve the moment in a pill. But nobody knows how or where or why I made these momenticons.'

'Doesn't Lord Sine know you're different?'

'That much he knows, but he sees only utility. I've given him his cull. He has no interest in me now.'

Benedict looked more disconsolate than in the moments after his father's killing.

'Why did you come with me?' she added.

'You're pursued, which suggests you may be worth saving.'

'Thanks a bunch.'

'There were families on the platform,' he said.

'If I hadn't been there, Benedict, there would be no momenticon. You don't need to describe it.'

'Why did they have all that pointless baggage? What's the point of plastic spades and flimsy nets? What can they learn with them?'

The remark again betrayed that emotional deficit. If she was right, Benedict Vane was as freakish as she was: he alone in the wide world had had no childhood.

'How did you arrive here?' she asked with gentle ambiguity.

He replied in the same spirit. 'I was delivered,' he said, 'long after Cosmo.'

She didn't need any more confirmation, and allowed him to change the subject by patting the nearest dog on the head.

'They'll do whatever you tell them. Just keep the language simple.'

'And what about the beacons? How many are there? Who has them?'

'I wasn't around at the distribution, but I understand Lord and Lady Vane had three each, Cosmo and Cassie two each, and various singles were dished out to advisers and favourites. The beacons vary widely. Some, like here, are large enough to clear a substantial area; others cater for much more intimate spaces.'

'So you missed out?'

'No worry there. I'm one of Nature's wanderers.' Without warning, he clasped her hands in his. 'Good luck,' he said. 'I do hope we meet again.'

Morag did not want this parting, but Benedict's curious mix of the fragile and the certain disarmed her.

'Screw good luck,' she replied, kissing him on one cheek. 'Just be on your guard. I met Cosmo three years ago. He was vicious then and he's more vicious now.'

'Come,' said Benedict to his dogs. He gave her a wave and disappeared back through the vanishing point.

She left the wood, which had lost its menace in daylight. Only the stags remained, fixed in an attitude of escape. She could see no sign of Fogg, but in the distance hung the silhouette of the tethered *Aeolus*. Hopefully, he was already on board and waiting.

All this thinking about childhood conjured a snippet of her

father's advice, as so often, delivered in simple rhyme. 'That way you'll remember it,' he had said.

> *Air and feather, or earth and bone,*
> *The furthest fastest traveller,*
> *Is the one who travels alone.*

In that spirit she ambled her way back to the craft.

'Fogg!' she shouted several times without response. 'Useless bloody man,' she muttered to herself, then, 'Thanks, Cavall, thanks, all,' she said to the dogs, flicking their ears by way of farewell.

To her astonishment, they followed her up the rope ladder on toes with the prehensile qualities of a sloth. They settled on deck, ideal companions: no hygiene needs, no call for feed or water, no answering back, and obedient to a fault.

Only when she walked into the cabin did she realise that in the chaos of Cosmo's attack she had left her bag in the tavern, with the larger jar of momenticons and its guide to their respective symbols.

She swore out loud, before shrugging off the misfortune.

Where was Fogg? This side of the murk, the hillside above was bare, with no sign of a body, but the agreed deadline for their return had passed, and Fogg had always been punctilious about time.

She shrugged and went to the wheelhouse. She had a theory to test.

Anything to keep Benedict out of mind.

6

A Coronation of Sorts

Winterdorf's notables had assembled in the tavern's main room. The naïve populace, hitherto unschooled in realpolitik, kept to the rear walls and adjacent rooms. Cosmo sat facing the hoi polloi on the most magisterial chair available. Marcus Jaggard stood beside him, lightning rod in hand.

Only the Town Clerk had the gumption to step forward and ask *the* question. 'Might we ask why his Lordship had to die?'

Cosmo toyed with telling them the truth – *the second Lord Vane was a milksop blocking my way* – only for Marcus to field the question.

'If I may, your Lordship . . .' The weather-watcher did not wait for permission. 'The late Lord Vane betrayed his principles, and he would have betrayed you.'

'To whom?' asked the Town Clerk.

'Lord Sine.'

Heads jerked up at the mere mention of *that name*.

'For experiments,' Jaggard added, following this disturbing news with a restorative tonic, 'Rest assured, life here will continue as normal. In the new Lord Vane's absence, my weather-watchers will protect you as the Constitution demands.'

Cosmo's toes scrabbled in his boots in irritation. To coin a phrase, Marcus had stolen his thunder. *Never expect favour or fealty from those you promote.* He had cultivated the Weather-Master as one would the head of the armed forces, only to discover that he would now have to watch his back as well as his front. Marcus might have the advantage in years, experience and local standing, but he, Cosmo, had more exceptional virtues: a self-fulfilling born-to-rule voice and presence, reinforced by a far superior intellect.

He rose to his feet, gesturing Marcus to silence with a nonchalant flick of the hand. 'I have every confidence in Mr Jaggard and his weather-watchers and, more importantly, in *you*. I have other forces at my command, forces you could barely guess at, should Lord Sine dare to send his perversions of nature here.'

From the corner of his eye Cosmo saw Marcus blink. *What force?*

Cosmo sailed on, confident they had forgotten his predecessor already, 'And I am not a man to rest on my laurels. Tonight, I shall travel far to unearth the roots of this conspiracy. The Spire girl is in league with Lord Sine, which is why she fled with her accomplice. She is, like her disgraced father, a chancer. Any information on these traitors will be well rewarded. Meanwhile, I have a solemn oath to take, as have you, and Mr Jaggard on behalf of Tiriel's Tower. I solemnly swear on my life and my soul—'

He gestured to his subjects to follow. Oaths bind like nothing else.

'We solemnly swear on our lives and our souls,' they intoned, eyes now fixed on him, 'to protect and obey Lord Cosmo Vane in all things, even to death.'

The mumbo jumbo done, he invited the Town Clerk, not Marcus, to place the diadem, the symbol of rule, on his brow.

Seconds later, Cosmo learned that unlike chess, Luck plays the tables of history as well as logic.

The tavern keeper stepped forward. 'Before you go, your Lordship, the Spire girl left this.' He handed a light travelling bag to Cosmo.

'I am a man of my word. I govern, but I also reward. My predecessor liked to pore over his baubles. I'll see you get one from his collection. Come back in an hour, all of you, and the tavern will serve at my expense.'

They cheered, and Cosmo bowed. He remained standing like a statue as they dispersed.

'You ticked the boxes,' said Marcus.

'All I need to know is whether my subjects are loyal or pursuing their own agendas. There can be no middle ground.'

Marcus hovered, which was rare for him. 'Who tells your mother she's a widow? I wondered if I might.'

'She dislikes you, Marcus. You've said so often enough.'

'That's why I'd break the news well. There'll be no emotional displays. Just tell me where she is, and I'll happily—'

Cosmo cut him short. 'My mother is not your province. I'm off soon, and according to this Constitution you like so much, you've plenty to be getting on with yourself.' He shook the jar of momenticons in his hand. The pills had a different coding to the *Wonderland* momenticons, which meant the Spire girl must have sorted her personal supply into their various scenes. Or had she created a new game?

He fumbled through her bag, which yielded a list of mostly dull old-world paintings with appended symbols which matched the coding of the pills. He remembered her insolent grandmother and the art books. The Spire girl must have used them to construct art lessons of some kind, using a scanner and weaver to reduce them to momenticons. What a dull, conventional waste of time. He tossed the jar and the list back into the bag, which he gave to an underling.

'Take it to my office in Acheron,' he said. 'You never know.'

And he meant it. The Spire girl had a talent for appearing at inconvenient times and then disappearing. He decided the reward for her arrest should err on the generous side.

7

Genesis

Fogg scrambled up the hill, deploying the boat hook as a staff. At the brow, the familiar murk swirled along the cliffs where the beacon's benign influence failed.

Retreat seemed inevitable, but as he turned, a circular shape in the rocks caught his eye. Beneath a stone lid, a shaft ran at an angle into the hill. He crouched and waved Morag's globe-light. The sloping sides looked man-made and intact. He squeezed through and slid down until the shaft levelled out. The air had a cloying, acrid smell.

He walked on into a more generous tunnel which ended in another opening with iron rungs set in the wall. He stowed the light and climbed down, and once back on solid ground, shook the light once more to wake it. He had reached a large cavern. Near the centre was a wheeled trolley with straps for ankle and waist and a hand brake, resting against a set of buffers. He wiped a brass plate on the bodywork to reveal a familiar command: *Praemitte Tempestas*. Away from the line, a jumble of broken crates and rusty tins suggested activity here had ceased long ago.

After checking over the trolley, he decided to risk the rail. He fastened the straps, gripped the globe-light between his knees, clasped his backpack and the boat hook and released the brake.

The acceleration, though gentle, was remorseless, and soon he was hurtling through the darkness, the globe-light flickering along the walls like old film.

The trolley did not slacken speed. Hunger and thirst began to bite, limbs to cramp, lips and eyes to parch. In wide-awake moments, Fogg wondered why *Tempestas*, with its preoccupation with weather, would have invested in a subterranean railway. The mining equipment brought Niobe's gift to mind. Controlling lightning would require high electrical resistance – was this a tantalum mine, maybe?

Journey's end, a large gateway set in the rock face, brought good news – the gates were open – but bad news too: they had recently been forced. An ugly crowbar-like tool lay abandoned amid a scuffle of footprints from bare feet. The intruders had clearly been no respecters of property. The hinges had held, but the right-hand gate had been twisted so badly out of shape that it left a generous opening.

Fogg clambered through into a huge storage bay. Iron racks and mine carts, all empty, lined the walls, and more bare footprints crisscrossed the floor. The unpleasant smell intensified. Irregular metallic sounds echoed far away and deeper still.

These phenomena prompted him to reject a second broken door in favour of a narrow, steeply ascending windowless stairwell, where the air felt fresher and the dust lay undisturbed. Up and up he climbed, like a corkscrew, praying the globe-light would last.

The stairs delivered him to a small landing where stone yielded to marble. A familiar sigil, a fist grasping a bolt of lightning, adorned the centre of a fine oak door. He lifted the brass latch and swung the door open.

Gone were the dust, the footprints and the desolation; here, a magnificent staircase rose from a marble-clad hall flanked by Ionic columns. Chitin panes protected the windows. The clasped lightning motif adorned the beams in the high stone roof. Opulent lanterns shed a warm, subdued light.

The staircase led to broad landings with doorways to right and left, all marked with imposing signs: Chamber of Maps, Chamber of Warnings, Chamber of Cities, Chamber of Records. The first three were locked, but the last door was ajar.

The ornate key showed not a trace of dust, suggesting someone had been here recently. He tiptoed in to find, unsurprisingly, the Chamber of Records resembled an abandoned library. There were numbered wall-to-wall shelves and two rectangular tables with attendant chairs. Ladders on wheels gave access to the higher shelves. The leather volumes, mostly heavy and all imposing, had been organised by subject into sections with their descriptions painted.

Two adjacent sections caught Fogg's eye: *The Saved* and *The Damned*. Another central stack was sealed behind heavy glass. A wooden scroll on the top declared in gilt letters: *Tiriel's Tower*.

Opting for good cheer, Fogg chose *The Saved*. His first shock came on the title page of the introductory *Volume I: Editors*: Oblivious Potts (Nature), Peregrine Mander (Art) and Hilda Crike (Literature). Volumes XI to XII concerned art's masterpieces. They had no illustrations, merely the letters PC, a number and a detailed description. Remarkably, each number matched the exhibit number in the Museum Dome, and the descriptions matched those in the Museum's database which Fogg had so assiduously studied. In addition, each work contained a reference to an old-world Museum and entries recording date of visit by day, month and year in the old chronology. Fogg ran through the exhibits. They too matched, save for one of the two totem-poles, which bore the uninformative marking 'Potts, obscure'.

A loose, faded black and white photograph showed three young men and two young women, arms around each other's waists, exuding camaraderie. The one on the right had to be Mander. That distinctive look of avian alertness marked him out even in youth. He could have been no more than thirty at the Fall. Pinned to it was a second photograph, a jungle scene whose two human figures, a local native Indian and an elderly white man in shorts standing side by side, were dwarfed by surrounding trees. The air looked thick with moisture, and the sky dull but cloudless. A closer look revealed one of the trunks to be a totem-pole identical to the smaller of the two in the Museum Dome: mystery solved.

The literary section listed works by author and title. Some had a resumé of plots and character; others did not.

Potts' lengthy natural history section also contained exhibit numbers and detailed commentary on all the main species.

So much organisation troubled Fogg. The Fall had been a sequence of random natural disasters brought on by Man's negligence, hadn't it? Yet these steps by Tempestas to save the best added a disturbing layer of calculation. He pocketed the photographs, withdrew and closed the door behind him.

Another thirty steps up, the staircase divided. In a deep niche a head floated above a plinth, unmistakably the first Lord Vane in his prime, quite unlike the gaunt death mask in the study in the Genrich Dome.

Both wings of the staircase met in a huge circular space which rose in a cone to a high steeple-like summit. Open-plan chambers with glass walls and a multitude of chairs and screens clung to the sides, fed by lifts. Several hundred people must have worked here once, but no longer. Coils of wire spiralled up in partitions between the rooms to meet in a writhing nest at the apex of the steeple. A huge desk dominated the ground floor level; there was a spotlit throne in the centre and humbler chairs in shadow at the sides. A miscellany of brass switches and handles had been set in the desk's surface.

The throne was occupied.

At first sight, the motionless man looked dead. His bald head, at odds with bushy eyebrows and a luxuriant white beard, tilted back. His right arm was tucked around a metal rod and his eyes were closed as if listening intently. His free arm suddenly rose, his face jerked forward, his index finger extended and cold grey eyes fixed on Fogg.

'Hear the bastards?'

The voice had an unexpected American twang and a growling quality, as if from a throat full of pebbles. He wore a suit and an overcoat, but no tie. His face had the crumpled furrows of great age, but a jutting chin exuded defiance. He gesticulated with his rod.

'Hear who?' asked Fogg.

'Lord Sine's minions, stripping us bare.' His eyes were somehow both cold and warm at the same take. He struggled to his feet. 'You have good timing, Mr . . . Mr—?

'F-F-Fogg.'

'Do you work for us? Have you orders? You don't sound very experienced.'

'I'm an outsider. I rather stumbled into this extraordinary place.'

'*Extraordinary!* Ah, you wouldn't use such a paltry word if you'd been here at the Fall.' He slapped the arms of the chair. 'The Judgment Seat.' The rod swept around the massive chamber. 'The Hall of Zeus,' he announced and, pointing at the apex of the spire, 'The Rod of Punishment.'

He's mad, thought Fogg, *but there's history here to unravel.* 'I'm afraid I wasn't alive at the Fall.'

The old man cocked his head. 'So you weren't. Your voice has the tinkle of youth.' His eyes squinted again, and Fogg realised the man was nearly blind.

He offered a hand and Fogg shook it.

'Haha! Your skin isn't papery like mine, or decayed like theirs, and you breathe without a sound despite the climb. *Youth!*' He delved into his pocket, produced a pair of spectacles with thick, heavy lenses and peered through them at Fogg. He looked reassured by what he saw.

'What are you doing here?' asked Fogg.

'I'm drawing to a close. But I'll take those slithy toves with me.' He leant forward and flicked one of the many switches set in the table. A single screen behind him came to life. It displayed a map with little red dots moving upwards. 'We've still got time – look, they've three more doors to force. I am Mr Venbar, weather-watcher and one-time lieutenant to the first Lord Vane. Before you condemn me . . .' Mr Venbar checked, as if regretting his own choice of words.

'Condemn you for what?'

A memory stirred as Fogg stumbled on what had troubled him about the *Aeolus*' logbook. Why record praise for observation work *during* the Fall? A horrifying possibility struck him as he recalled Lord Sine's comment when Lord Vane had agreed to destroy Genrich's creations: '*like father, like son*'.

'Good heavens, he doesn't know.' The old man laughed. 'Don't tell me *nobody* knows?' He flicked another handle before walking over to the keyboard and lowering his face to within a few inches from the keys.

He began to type. 'We warned them every which way,' he said, opening his hands like a conjuror releasing a dove.

The room came to life, the space above Fogg's head teeming with virtual headlines and commentating heads. *TEMPESTAS WARN* was the unifying leitmotif: warnings of flood, drought, fire, famine, storm, oceans awash with refuse, pestilence, toxic air and almost every biblical curse you could conjure, including apocalypse. The first Lord Vane dominated the spoken pronouncements, always forceful and always armed with an array of statistics.

Mr Venbar played the keys again and loosed the counter-punchers with their own leitmotifs: *PROPHETS OF DOOM*, *ADJUSTED TARGETS* and *WE WILL NOT BE DICTATED TO* delivered in a hundred different ways by men and women who sounded bombastic and no less convinced of their cause.

'We even invaded their government buildings,' declared Mr Venbar. 'With Triv.' The images cleared and a hologram of an attractive young woman shimmied in at the opposite entrance. Despite the transparency, she had the gift of speech.

'I'm Triv. Give me any month in any year in the second millennium.'

Fogg gawped.

'Get on with it,' said Mr Venbar, rapping the desk with his knuckles.

'November 2003?' said Fogg, for no particular reason.

Triv simpered like a sixth-former who knows a poem by heart.

'As the Arctic ice-shelf fractures by a further eight per cent and the last whiskered warbler dies in a New York Zoo, educated minds focus on the following questions: why did Hugh Hefner buy the vault next to Marilyn Monroe? How many cyber-surfers will tune in to watch supermodel Heidi Klum wear an eleven-million-dollar bra encrusted with two thousand eight hundred and nine white diamonds, sapphires and amethysts? As the Hawaiian crow is declared extinct outside captivity, J-Lo and Ben Affleck—'

'She does go on rather,' said Mr Venbar, stabbing a key to return Triv to the aether, 'but we can agree her point is clear. They were told over and over again.'

'*They?*'

'The outside world: the leaders, the politicos, the aristos of industry, the voters, the educators, the movers and the shakers, the whole kit and caboodle. So don't expect me to go confessing like a sinner.'

Fogg peered up to the tip of the cone where the wires and cables converged.

'The Rod of Punishment?'

'It would have happened anyway,' Mr Venbar said firmly. 'Our way was quick and clean.'

Fogg could barely grasp the enormity of the admission. 'Tempestas harnessed the weather?'

'We harnessed the poison to the weather.'

'You killed almost everything—!'

'As I said, quick and clean, like chopping the neck of a rabbit. Man was bent on destroying the world by slow torture anyway;

only a sudden, near-total loss would teach them.' He paused for breath. 'Some more respectful organism will have a turn, unless you can find a way.'

'*Me?*'

'My screens include eyes in the sky, Mr Fogg. Two Genrich identicals were after you. You came back, and they didn't. That's a start.' Another key-tap. The *Aeolus* appeared on the screen, still held by its mooring rope. 'The new Tempestas is pathetic. The second Lord Vane is pathetic. Clockwork birds and animals don't restore *anything*.'

Fogg forced himself to focus on the present. 'You said the red dots are Lord Sine's minions?'

'The alternative to you and me, doctored people, the forces of Genrich.'

'Why are they here now?'

'Everything's happening now, Mr Fogg. That ridiculous three-year truce is up, so it's them or us or oblivion. As to the details, Genrich wants our tantalum and our chitin. And who's here to defend them? Just li'l old me.'

'They're awfully close.'

'So they are.' He paused. 'Time to plan an extinction, just like the old days.' He caressed the iron rod. 'The big kazoo is long gone, but I've a few charges left, and a white rabbit to round things off. You must draw them in. Take the lift to the second-floor balcony and make yourself conspicuous, then scarper, double-quick. There's a door at the rear. Follow the passage to the outside, where there should be a way out. There are others in the game and I may be flipping you from the frying pan into the fire. But we are where we are, and it's the best I can do.'

Fogg looked at the red dots. The odds appeared overwhelming. 'Come with me, Mr Venbar,' he pleaded.

'I'm old, slow and blind, and my time has come.' He flicked another switch. 'But I can still hear and speak. This is your last chance to learn. I *lived* it. Any question you want.'

'Mr Venbar, *please*—'

'Ask away, Mr Fogg.'

Not a man for compromise, Fogg decided. 'Are there other survivors here?'

'Somewhere deep in this mountain range are the Northerners. The Vanes used them as their builders. They're craftsmen par excellence, but they burrow deep and keep themselves to themselves. Maybe, who knows, they'll be our best hope. By some miracle the air around the mountain stays clean. No doubt that's why Lord Vane chose it as his stronghold.'

Mr Venbar had such self-belief that Fogg accepted all he said on trust.

'Ask on,' the old man cried with increasing urgency, even as his voice lost strength for lack of practise.

'Have you ever heard of Gilbert Spire?'

For the first time, Mr Venbar shed his decisiveness, sounding as if conflicted. 'I fear that's too big a story for the time we have now. You'll have to work it out for yourself, if it matters – and it might.' He paused. 'In the absence of a priest, would you absolve me, in case we were wrong?'

Fogg did not dither. 'I absolve you.'

The old man smiled. 'Thank you.'

The red dots were multiplying and closing. Mr Venbar's strength of purpose returned. 'Whatever you do, don't freeze: they're foul but fast. If you're lucky, Cheshire will turn up.'

'Cheshire?'

Mr Venbar shook his hand impatiently. 'He's a stealth device and a passable guard. Now cut the cackle and up you go. First balcony, second floor, escape at the rear when you've done your bit. But don't linger.'

Fogg made it to the second-floor balcony just in time. As he took up position, gibbering shrieks echoed through the marble halls. The invaders had broken into the main building.

Mr Venbar left his original seat and took up position on the throne. He sat up ramrod-straight in a self-consciously military posture.

To Fogg's amazement, only a single man entered the chamber, dressed unmistakably as the Mad Hatter. He looked like him too, with long hair, buck teeth and oversized eyes. He carried the trademark top hat and an orange umbrella.

I've drawn you, thought Fogg.

'Well, well, who have we here?' the Hatter enquired.

'Trespassers will be persecuted,' replied Mr Venbar.

'You mean *electrocuted*,' the Hatter countered. He had the quick-fire delivery of a stand-up comic. 'Question is: *who's* the trespasser here?'

The transparent walls, floor and ceiling allowed Fogg to watch the scene unfold, but he had no time to analyse. He waved his arms to distract the Hatter, but the man had eyes only for Mr Venbar.

Venbar pointed his rod. Lightning lanced from the tip at the intruder, but the Hatter had already unfurled his orange umbrella. *Chitin.* The blast hurled him backwards, but the bolts bounced off and ricocheted into rooms higher up. Walls shattered in an explosive flash, showering shards of glass on to the floors below.

'Bring on the toves,' bellowed the Hatter, blood streaming from his nose.

Fogg cut an incongruous figure, clasping his boat hook and bag. He froze as into the Hall loped barefoot humans, of a sort, dressed in ragged shirts and trousers. With all visible skin blotched and suppurating, they looked like plague victims or lepers.

They fanned out around Mr Venbar, who waved frantically back at Fogg and growled, 'Be gone, you fool! Save yourself!'

But Fogg had an overwhelming urge to contribute. 'Leave him alone,' he cried. 'It's me you want.'

'I *said*—' screamed Mr Venbar to Fogg, but their fleeting exchange had bought a few seconds, for as the Hatter was glaring up at the newcomer, the toves held back, waiting for orders.

Mr Venbar seized his chance and ran his rod across the room, sending lightning jagging this way and that once again.

'Shred them both,' shrieked the Hatter, raising his umbrella as several toves fell dead to the ground. The nauseating smell of charred flesh reached Fogg on the balcony.

Mr Venbar conjured one more close-range strike before the toves engulfed him. Others defied gravity, running up the vertical walls like so many monkeys towards Fogg.

This time Fogg obeyed Mr Venbar. He hurtled back from the balcony and through a large room crowded with work benches, into a passage. A crash of breaking screens told him the toves were close behind. A door of solid oak confronted him, but he was in luck: not only were the heavy bolts at top and bottom unlocked, but they were replicated on the other side. As a posse of toves emerged into the passage, he darted through and slammed the bolts shut.

Fogg glimpsed living quarters branching off to left and right, but he kept to a straight course in search of Mr Venbar's promised rear exit. Behind him, the toves had launched a violent assault on the door. At the end of a second passage, another door opened on to a balcony with a view over the valley below and the curtain of murk in the far distance. *Where is this exit?* He shrugged off a wave of vertigo and returned to the passage, but all the rooms off it were windowless dormitories. The toves would sniff him out in minutes. The oak door shook and heaved with every blow, dust puffing from its loosening hinges.

Fogg retreated to the balcony arch and planted the boat hook. Perhaps they would see a staff like Mr Venbar's and keep their distance . . .

He blinked in disbelief as a feline-looking creature with a long striped tail appeared from nowhere on the balcony rail.

'Where do you want to go?' Its English was immaculate.

'Not that way,' replied Fogg, nodding towards the door whose hinges were about to give.

'Then you're fine where you are.'

'I need to get down from this balcony – now!' he gulped.

'Now, that's clearer. Speaking in negatives rarely gets you where you want to go. Jump or slide. You'll reach your end quicker if you jump. But a dead end is most likely.'

Fogg shook his head in panic.

'Definitely slide.' The cat merely smiled.

'Can we be quick about this?' he begged.

'The heavier you are, the quicker you go,' the cat said helpfully. 'Pull the ring in the floor.'

'What about you?'

'Now you see me, now you don't.'

The cat miraculously vanished just as the bottom hinge on one door gave way.

The slithy toves, aptly named by Mr Venbar, wormed their way through, but kept their distance, hissing and spitting. Blood stained their faces.

'Wait for me!' cried the Hatter from behind the door. 'I want to watch!'

Fogg backed on to the balcony and, there, set into the floor dead centre, was a hexagonal shape like a bee's cell with an iron ring in the middle. Thank God for the boat hook! He levered open the stone hatch, revealing a silvery slide like a child's winding down into an empty space. Contorting himself, he managed to pull the hatch over his head by a ring on the other side. With his bag and boat hook firmly his grasp, he hurtled downwards.

The exterior of Tempestas' old headquarters was badly decayed. Where several once proud balconies had collapsed into a scumble of concrete boulders at ground level were bent iron stanchions, caked in rust, protruding from the main wall. The slide rattled and shook as his prone body twisted and turned, but its supports held.

An outer bend yielded a fine view of the original Tiriel's Tower: colossal in scale and even more imposing from outside.

He leant over the slide's rim and looked down. A reddish-brown lid in the courtyard floor appeared to be journey's end, but in the blink of an eye, the tower's walls were seething with shrieking, baying toves. Worse, just above ground level, he could see two of them were struggling for ownership of Mr Venbar's staff.

The gradient eased and the slide slowed.

Fogg replayed his encounter with the old man. How many charges had Mr Venbar claimed to have, and how many had he used? *One to go*, Fogg reckoned ruefully, and he was right.

The strike, misdirected by the two toves wrenching the rod in different directions, narrowly missed the slide as Fogg rounded the last bend. Bolts of silver-blue flame zigzagged across the courtyard, hurling the nearest toves into the air like disorganised acrobats, but Fogg was spared.

Thick rubber encased the chute's supports at ground level and provided a protective sheath. Lightning must have long been an occupational hazard. But more toves, at least thirty, were closing from all directions. He braced himself for a fight with impossible odds, only find himself slipping through the reddish-brown chitin like a ghost. He should have remembered Morag's story: the new chitin is permeable.

On and on went the slide, now meandering through subterranean passages and carved-out chambers. On one rocky outcrop, the cat reappeared, grinned and disappeared.

The slide finally ran out feet above a strip of land, a mix of dark silt and gravel, beside a river which gurgled and bubbled off into the dark. The air felt fresh and the water clean and he could hear no sound of pursuit, just the water: *real* water, another first.

He extricated Morag's globe-light from his bag and shook it to reveal a multicoloured mosaic covering the upper walls and ceiling of the cavern. But no, not a mosaic, on second glance. The colours did not glow and the surface looked flat. He peered ahead. The dark strip meandered on like a towpath. In the gloom the higher surfaces maintained their colours. A clutch of green-black reeds looked excitingly real, and were no less real to the touch.

He could hardly go back, so he had to go on.

At intervals along the path makeshift ladders rested against the cavern walls, and curiosity soon got the better of him. He climbed one of the less precarious to discover that the coloured effect was created by thousands upon thousands of postcards, carefully fixed to the upper walls and ceiling. Old-world towns, men and women in fields, seasonal greetings, vehicles, ships, piers, famous paintings, maps, kings and queens, trees and plants, birds and animals all peered down at him, and much, much more besides. Man's last will and testament, perhaps. Effort had been invested in the arrangement, for thematic links abounded: birds beside their habitats, rulers beside their cities, camels adjacent to dunes, the garish kept apart from the subtle.

'Deltiology,' said a familiar voice.

Fogg wobbled in surprise and would have fallen, had his companion not firmly grasped the ladder. 'The study of . . . of rivers?' he stammered, thinking of deltas.

'The collection of postcards, one of the world's vanished pastimes. I'm considering a rehang.'

Fogg twisted himself round.

The wizened man below raised his own light-ball, which captured the upturned face like a portrait by Georges de La Tour, number 87 in the Museum Dome. Fogg saw a white shirt, black tie and tails. The voice did not lie. It was Mander, Lord Vane's butler.

A few missing pieces slid into place. PC in *The Saved* meant a postcard. And that mysterious change in AIPT's voice: *Maybe, sir, it's time to explore* – that had been Mander's voice. Peregrine Mander!

As an earlier suspicion hardened, new puzzles surfaced. To judge from his encounter, the second Lord Vane had known nothing of the Museum Dome, which suggested the first Lord Vane had not known either. Had Mander gone rogue? Had he been asked to make a record of the best of Art and exceeded his brief by *preserving* the best? How had he funded such a venture? Had old-world governments paid handsomely for storage? If Mander had done this for Art, what about Potts and Nature?

Fearing that a direct question might break the spell, he played along in the hope of learning more.

'Is Lord Vane down here?'

'An unlikely scenario, if I may say so, sir.'

'But you're in uniform.'

'I'm in retirement. Call it a habit.'

'You do remember me?'

'A butler of quality never forgets the rude, the kind or the talented, in case revolution comes and one's advice is needed. As I recall, you fulfilled the latter two criteria.' Mander smiled. 'Goya's dog. I can see it now.'

'You knew all about that painting. You said the dog was Goya, and in a way you were right.'

'Never say I'm right about Art, sir, or indeed, anyone else. We know next to nothing and I like it that way. When you think you know everything, mystery fades, and love with it.'

Insecurity seized Fogg. If toves could descend the sides of a vertical tower, they could surely penetrate this domain with ease.

'There are Genrich creatures up there and they're distinctly unfriendly.'

'Worse, sir, they're a mess. We should not play God.'

'You've seen them?'

'I get reports.' For a butler, Mander had a commanding presence. 'You're quite safe here. Cheshire unnerves them.' Mander picked up Fogg's bag. 'Now, follow me, sir. It's cocktail time.'

8

Blue Lagoon

The postcards remained a constant decoration, but the journey was short. Ten minutes at most brought them to a wooden bridge and a small island. An antique sideboard held a Matter-Rearranger, glasses, cutlery, plates and bowls, meticulously ordered by size and purpose. Nearby, two mahogany chairs faced each other across a circular table. Close to the water's edge were several old-fashioned trunks. The only one open was full to the brim with postcards.

By the bridge a flat-bottomed boat, moored by a chain, pitched gently in the stream.

The dead black fingers of a solitary tree stretched out from the island like a blind man feeling his way. A hammock slumped between its lower branches. Tiny lights threaded through the branches came to life as Mander ushered Fogg over the bridge to the island.

He laid the table with mannered precision and an equally mannered commentary. 'Ladder 4 has a card on the subject. You lay from the outside in order of use: forks on the left, knives and spoons on the right, knife blades facing the plate and forks with their prongs aerial, the water glasses immediately above, with glasses for more bohemian drinking beyond. Although this last question is open to respectable debate, one should never require one's guests to *reach*.'

Mander spat out the word *reach* as if it were the equivalent of vomit or extreme flatulence. To Fogg, such refinements meant nothing, but the retired butler's preoccupation with etiquette made it easier to broach more delicate subjects.

'I met a Mr Venbar.'

Mander crossed himself as he adjusted the water glasses with minute exactness. 'You live by the sword . . .'

He did not complete the phrase, but Fogg wondered how Mander could know already. The cat, perhaps?

'He alleged . . . that the first Lord Vane . . .'

Mander waved the allegation aside before the charge could even be laid. 'We are where we are.' He placed napkins beside the place settings. '*On recule pour mieux sauter*,' he added in immaculate French.

Fogg tried a different tack. 'You must have been there.'

'I was an apprentice no older than you when Tempestas recruited me. Callow, sir, callow. I was part of a company team sent to preserve a record of mankind's qualities. I hit on postcards among other *objets d'art* as transportable, evocative, universal and retrospective in reach, from Saxon swords to Byzantine jewellery.' This time he made 'reach' sound like the ultimate compliment. 'I naturally focused on the cards' pictorial side.'

'What about the objects themselves?'

'What indeed! That's a different story. But learn this, sir. People insult by every other form of communication, but not with postcards. In that medium we are universally kind and thoughtful. And the stamps, sir – ah, the stamps. That project was my only adult chapter without the tails of office. I treasure it, as I hope you do your early excursions, however they turn out. Such memories sit deep, like a first outing to the circus.' Mander blew out his cheeks and changed the subject. 'Matter-Rearrangement should be more than codes and numbers. The true connoisseur experiments. I tender a Blue Lagoon. It is not, of course, blue curaçao or real vodka, but it kicks like a mule all the same.'

This speech, while engaging, struck Fogg as a prepared move in a longer game. It had also conspicuously sidestepped the question he'd asked. Mander *was* behind the Museum Dome, he now felt sure of it.

The Blue Lagoon lived up to the review, but it had no effect on Mander's defences. Fogg tried twice more to discuss the Fall, but his host neatly deflected both attempts, despite being forthcoming on other subjects.

'Cheshire was made by the first Lord Vane to guard his headquarters. The second Lord Vane made adjustments as a diversionary toy for the precocious young Cosmo.' Mander shook his head. 'Such a complex child. By the way, it's not only the disappearing act which scares the mutants, it's that smile – the thought he finds them amusing.'

Lunch was paste from the Rearranger, but Mander achieved variations of texture and taste to which Fogg had never come close in three years of enforced practise.

'How is Mr Spire's child?' asked Mander. 'Alive, I trust?'

'She insisted on going her own way.'

'What's bred in the bone,' replied Mander wistfully. 'If Chance plays fair, she'll have passed through *The Hunt in the Forest* to Winterdorf, where she can recuperate.'

Fogg had recognised *The Hunt in the Forest* through the Long Eye, especially those distinctive leaves edged in gold on the equally distinctive trees. But Winterdorf?

Mander appeared to read his expression. 'Give her the pleasure of describing it, sir.'

Fogg nodded, and asked his next question as casually as he could. 'Tell me about Mr Spire?'

'Cross the bridge and ascend ladder 9. His ilk is there. Just be sure to replace them exactly.'

Fogg accepted the cue and ascended the ladder while Mander cleared the table, dipping each plate in the river to wash it.

Ladder 9 led to cards of great trees, jungles, mountains and unfamiliar animals, all fanning out from a small group of men.

Most wore outlandish costumes and looked more than a little mad. Fogg held up the light-ball to read the names on the reverse: George Bass, Percy Fawcett, Gaspar Corte-Real, Sir John Franklin, Francis Crozier. He memorised the names and replaced the cards with curatorial precision.

A cup of coffee awaited his return. 'They're all explorers,' said Fogg confidently.

'All explorers who *disappeared*,' Mander expanded, 'without trace. If I had a card of Mr Spire, he would be up there with the best.'

'What was he looking for?'

'His brief was tantalum, but he had a personal grail. For others it was a pole or the northwest passage or El Dorado. For him it was Paradise.'

'Paradise – I thought that was the next world?'

'He never divulged what he meant by it.'

Fogg suspected Mander of being a connoisseur of the white lie as well as the Blue Lagoon. Intuition told him Spire might not have divulged his mission, but that the old retainer did now know what it was.

'Do you think I'd make an explorer?' he asked.

'Maybe you are already, without knowing it,' replied Mander gently.

'What's the difference between an explorer and a butler?'

Fogg jumped. The silky voice came from high in the tree. Cheshire had returned. He sat on a branch with his tail curled back to his head.

'One waits and the other does not.'

'He grins at his own wit,' said Mander, shaking his head, 'which is deplorable.'

'I'd grin at yours if you had any,' replied the cat.

'What should I do now?' Fogg asked his hosts.

'Move, unless you want a mouth full of moss,' said the cat.

'I shall ferry you to the Confluence, where you must choose your own way.'

'I do grin when he's wise,' added the cat, grinning.

Mander, declining all offers of assistance, proved as skilful with a punt pole as with ladders. His tails flapped as he stooped and rose like an aged dancer who, for all his stiffness, had not lost rhythm. Fogg sat in the stern, while Cheshire alternated between the prow, the path, until it ran out, an occasional rocky outcrop and nowhere at all. The postcards disappeared with the path. Mander's light-ball, set in a recess in the prow, lit their ghostly way.

Fogg sat up with a start. The punt was not only green, but that *particular* oily man-made green. It had five protruding inward-facing slats on each side, with a ribbed white-painted floor. It mirrored exactly the punt in painting 1012 on level 25, a boat occupied by a loner in a scene otherwise fraught with summertime social bustle: *Boulter's Lock, Sunday Afternoon.*

He could not resist the urge to share his hard-earned knowledge and facts tumbled out. 'I say, Mr Mander, how's this for a coincidence! Your punt is the very twin of the punt in a famous painting which graced boxes of chocolates and biscuits and jigsaws for a generation. It took the artist, one Edward John Gregory, born in—'

'—1850, died in 1909,' interjected Mander. 'It's all on the postcard.'

Fogg cursed silently. Morag interrupted. Tweedledum and Tweedledee interrupted. Even *Mander* interrupted. Would nobody ever hear him out?

He tried not to sound testy. 'What you won't know is that it took him more than ten years to complete, and it's a social record as much as a . . .'

Stoop and rise; stoop and rise.

Mander was showing not a smidgen of interest, and Cheshire had disappeared. Ahead, the sound of threshing water had risen to a roar, drowning out what remained of Fogg's potted history of Mr Gregory, *Boulter's Lock* and the Victorian weekend excursion.

Mander bent down and shouted in Fogg's left ear, 'Grab your bag, sir, and that boat hook. The wheel of Fortune spins once more.'

The punt accelerated into turbulence; the scene was enhanced by a bloom of phosphorescence. Five streams joined theirs in a large cavern with a bare mound of rock in the centre. 'Avoid the island,' Mander commanded, 'for once on it, you'll never get off. And too near it, you'll just go around and around like a stopwatch. Keep to the side and take any tunnel you can get.'

An unpleasant truth dawned as the punt heaved and spun into the race. He could see neither jetty nor towpath, and if the island was off-limits too . . .

It was deftly done. As Fogg lurched forward and the prow spun round, Mander flicked him overboard with a gentle but well directed shove.

Handicapped by the bag in one hand and the boat hook in the other, Fogg spluttered and floundered in the icy water. The punt surged forward, Mander poling hard to keep it clear of the island.

Every possible escape route required progress against a raging current.

This is the end, thought Fogg. '*Explorer-Curator vanishes under water underground.*' *And I've not even made it as a postcard.*

A vicious tug drove him into the mouth of the third tunnel. When his right boot scraped a smooth surface below, he drove the boat hook down, where it lodged in what felt like a build-up of silt. He swung his legs in and his knees found the bottom, but rock curved above him, making it impossible to stand. He freed the boat hook and prodded upstream. The bank of sand continued below the water line, but once away from the edge it shelved steeply.

Drenched and bruised, teeth chattering like castanets, Fogg hauled himself along, knee-step by knee-step, into pitch darkness. The water had immobilised the globe-light. He could still hear the threshing of the Confluence behind him, but otherwise there was silence.

Fogg paused and took stock on his knees like a man in prayer. He could stumble on blind, or he could return to the central chamber and try another tunnel in the hope that he might be able to stand. *Think like an explorer*, he chided himself. Posing the question prompted an idea. He extricated the Long Eye from the sodden bag and opened the caps at either end. Remarkably, the lenses were quite dry. He peered into the darkness and saw nothing.

'Idiot!' he cried, sliding the catch on the side.

Darkness drained away, opening the tunnel to view. Initial signs were unpromising, no shoreline on either side, still less a path, until twisting the tube near the end magnified the view, enabling a more methodical survey. Some seventy yards away on the opposite side, a stairwell had been cut into the stone, with an iron mooring ring set in the wall alongside. On his present course, without the Long Eye's assistance, he would have missed it.

Getting there remained a challenge, perhaps the very challenge Mander had had in mind for a trainee explorer. Swim across too early and he would be swept past and never get back. He must allow a generous margin for error. He resealed the telescope's caps and continued his painful, back-breaking progress for another hour.

After one more scan with the Long Eye, he readied himself and launched.

The current in midstream was even stronger. His greatest fear was losing his bearings and heading back the way he had come, but long-suppressed muscle memory came to his aid. He swam well, but even so, he made the ring with only a few feet to spare. The stone floor in the recess was level and firm, offering instant relief. He sat on the first step, shuddering, as physical effort, the dark, Venbar's murder, a double rescue and the shock of the freezing water all demanded release.

Fogg held his head in his cupped hands and let himself go. 'Thank you, thank you,' he muttered to his guardian angel and to poor dead 147, inventor of the Long Eye. He had had luck on his side. The vanished explorers, he guessed, had run out of luck rather than skill.

A sack lying on the second step dried off the globe-light and restored full luminosity. He squeezed as much water from his clothes as he could before setting off.

The gentle gradient, fresh air and the long climb reassured him that he was heading for a new world with its own beacon, a spin of Fortune's wheel, as Mander had predicted.

He sneezed, once, twice, three times, rubbed his nose with a wet sleeve and marched on. In musical terms, he thought, his life had lurched from maestoso and andante to a sudden frantic allegro. What next?

The climb ended in surprise: no door, just a hole in the ground. He hauled himself up through a vicious tangle of dead brambles, head-height and more, to emerge beside a sheer rock face. No wonder the way had looked unused. Mountains hemmed in the valley on all sides.

Fogg vented his anger on the barbed brown canes, thrashing a path through with the boat hook. On a distant peak, a single beacon was blazing away.

He walked on until a lantern stuttered into life ten yards away.

'Hey, you, *freeze*.'

'I am f-f-freezing,' stuttered Fogg.

'Hands where I can see them.'

Fogg released his bag and the boat hook, but hung on to the globe-light.

A huge, rough-looking middle-aged man with a head like an egg, pointed-side-up, levelled a small crossbow at Fogg's midriff. It looked like a toy in such giant hands. A pleasant face, what Fogg could see of it, suggested the man's bark might be worse than his bite.

'Who the fuck are you?'

'F-F-F-Fogg.'

'And where are you fucking from, F-F-F-Fogg?'

Fogg improvised. 'The *Aeolus*.'

'Pull the other one. She went missing yonks ago.'

'The name is inscribed on this boat hook,' said Fogg.

'No arty-farty moves, Fogg. My little bolts 'ere do three hundred feet per second. They'd go straight through ya.' The man bent down and brought his lantern to bear. 'My grandma says the tallest stories are often the truest. Not my experience to date, mind, but . . .' The man quickly abandoned his dalliance with fine language. 'Where the fuck are the rest of the crew?'

'I was dropped off.'

'I didn't see nuffin.'

'I landed in the thorns.'

He tendered his ripped trousers as corroboration.

'Why was you dropped off?'

Fogg sneezed.

'And why are you sopping wet?'

'It's a long story.'

'My grandma says the longest stories tell the biggest lies.'

'I would say that's fact-sensitive.'

'Don't come the fancy Dan with me. Fact-sensitive, what the fuck does that mean?'

Fogg had had enough. 'I think I need to meet your' – he was about to say superiors, but speedily reconsidered – 'your boss.'

'You do, do you?'

'I do.'

'Right.'

'Yes.'

'That's that, then.'

'May I carry my things?'

'Three hundred feet per second. That's fucking lightning, that is.'

He gestured, and Fogg tramped off with his guard behind him, crossbow in one hand and the boat hook in the other.

Fogg decided diplomacy was called for. 'Might I have a name? I do appreciate your vigilance and courtesy.'

After a long pause, he won a grudging but emollient reply. 'The name is Lomax, as in hummocks with an X.'

Fogg gambled on the Tempestas Dome and the craft shops, as Morag had described them. 'I knew a Lomax once, talented fellow, worked for Tempestas . . .'

He struck lucky. A Lomax uncle had specialised in making fruit.

Slowly, but surely, a primitive rapport developed, Lomax's language softening as he delivered dark news. 'They say Lord Vane is dead, murdered by his own.'

'Where? *How?*'

'In Winterdorf, in one of them frozen ponds. My grandma says bad news is usually true. Lord Vane was a bit of all right. Work *and* play. You've not been here before, but you'll see.'

Anxiety seized Fogg, for Mander had expected Morag to be in Winterdorf. 'What about Winterdorf itself?'

'Locked down, they say. I'd keep well away, me.'

'You're very well informed.'

'I'm Security, that's to be expected. Now head left here, Mr Fogg.'

Lomax's manner had quite transformed, thanks to the apple-making uncle.

A settlement sprawled across a dip in the land with its back to the rock face. The houses rose like a child's brick tower, unevenly spread box-shapes with walkways between. Yellow ochre earth had been packed between mostly vertical beams of un-planed wood to make the walls. Dark slates covered the roofs. The place had been built in a shawl of tall dead trees, each dwelling's shape and layout dictated by its particular tree; some high and congested, others low and spreading. With lights at the windows, the edifice reminded Fogg of a candelabra.

Lomax broke his soliloquy. 'Right, Mr Fogg, it's question time. I wouldn't disassemble if I were you. She ain't like the rest of us, Mr Fogg. Nothing escapes Miss Baldwin.'

Miss Baldwin. Morag had mentioned a Miss Baldwin, Cassie's tutor, whom Cosmo had predictably mocked.

Fogg was ushered through a door so low that Lomax had to bend double to enter. At a single desk sat a single woman in grey, lit by a single gaslight glowing blue. She had papers in front of her. The silver hair and the furrowed face spoke of age, but the green-amber eyes were vital and penetrating.

'Who's this?'

Lomax spared Fogg his stutter.

'Mr Fogg came from the *Aeolus*, Miss Baldwin.'

'You mean he says he did.'

She smiled, and Fogg knew that look. After hours on hours of dull ritual, his arrival had refreshed her day. She rose slowly to her feet.

'His boat hook says so,' stammered Lomax, apparently in awe.

She gave the object no more than a glance. Her gaze returned straight to him. 'So it does.'

She dismissed Lomax with a flick of the finger and drummed her clasped hands against her chin, as if Fogg were a puzzle to be solved.

'Apologies for dripping,' said Fogg to break the ice.

'You look abject. Through that door and down the passage straight ahead, you'll find a towel and a splash of lukewarm water. Then first left for a selection of costumes. That's what they specialise in around here. Don't get adventurous, or they'll think you're something you're not. Ten minutes, no more.'

She delivered these precise directions in a pleasing, unobtrusive voice, as you might expect from a tutor. Mander's intelligence presented as circuitous; Miss Baldwin's was direct. No wonder Cassie had liked her.

The cramped washroom had a rudimentary shower, and after the freezing river, the water's mild warmth was restorative. The large room on the left held rows of costumes on racks ranging from the multicoloured and outrageous to the monochrome and simple, with all sizes catered for. He decided on a dignified ensemble of blue-black jacket, matching trousers and a cream shirt, although he ignored the accompanying crimson neck scarf as too garish. Pegs held top hats, cravats and a variety of outré headpieces and wigs; from others hung hoops and baskets of gaily coloured balls and, bizarrely, plates.

He returned to the front office to find the contents of his bag arranged in front of Miss Baldwin. A large card index had also appeared and, unnervingly, a dead crow.

'You've never visited the Tempestas Dome,' she said, more question than fact.

'No.'

'That makes you a curiosity. Either Genrich brought you in or Lord Vane's household did, and whichever, you must have a rare talent.'

She gazed into his eyes. It was not an easy stare to lie to.

'I wouldn't call it that.'

'I'm all for modesty, but could you demonstrate?'

'If you have pen and paper.'

Both appeared instantly.

Fogg, still on his guard, thought quickly. A painting from the Dome or Matilda's library would only beg more questions, and he had no idea who ruled here or what their objectives might be. He kept to what many already knew and sketched the Red King in his nightcap asleep beneath a tree.

'Ah, the Infotainment project. You worked with the Spire girl and Cosmo Vane.'

'I did not work with Cosmo Vane,' said Fogg hastily.

Miss Baldwin smiled. 'I'm pleased to hear it. I worked with his sister, who is a very different kettle of fish. By the way, the origins of that expression are sadly lost in the mists of time, as is so much else.' Miss Baldwin furrowed her brow. 'I can forgive child victims of cruelty for turning cruel, but to forgive the spoiled child is asking a lot.'

'Where is Cassie?'

'In hiding, I should imagine.'

'What threat is she?'

Miss Baldwin raised an eyebrow as if the answer were too obvious to need stating. 'I gather Lomax told you the terrible news,' she added. Out of loyalty to the gentle giant, Fogg did his best to look vacant. 'He has this notion you don't betray secrets if you tell one person at a time.'

'Murdered by his own, he said,' confessed Fogg.

'Speared to death by his son's mechanicals in a frozen pond.' She patted the dead bird. 'Clockwork crow post.' She paused. 'Lord Vane was a thoughtful employer. I liked him. Strong on the outside, but sensitive beneath. A lover of art, too.' She paused. 'And now Cosmo is hunting for Spire's child.'

'Why?'

'Like him, she can create momenticons. She absconds for three years, then mysteriously reappears. Maybe he sees her as a threat. Maybe he's curious about where she's been. Maybe it's something more.'

'But how a threat? Momenticons are entertainment.' He stopped to ponder his own question. 'Aren't they?'

Miss Baldwin lowered her voice. 'There's a rumour that if an object has sufficient creative energy, a person with the gift can mind-travel to the very moment of creation. That means a different place at a different time. Such a skill could be developed to work in other ways, good and bad. It's also said you can bottle these moments as momenticons for future use. It may sound far-fetched, but I wouldn't put anything past Master Vane. Or should I say, Lord Vane the Third. If he can do this, maybe she can too.'

Anxiously Fogg asked, 'Are there places where Morag could hide in Winterdorf?'

'Winterdorf does have her share of nooks and crannies. We can but hope.' Miss Baldwin placed two postcards side by side on the table: *Hunters in the Snow* and the *Bird Trap*. 'Not only does it look just like that, they dress just like that, and once a month, they even place themselves just like that in a living tableau.'

Fogg gasped. 'But I drew those for Lord Vane.'

Miss Baldwin showed no surprise. 'For future reference, our best agent lives here.' She pointed at a remote house with a chimney on fire in the background of *Hunters in the Snow*. 'She's even older than me and hides in plain sight. Mrs Crike is her name, and that's how she looks and sounds. Crikey! But she's razor-sharp underneath. Still, I'd avoid Winterdorf for the present. There's a small valley to the east of it, hard to find, but a useful sanctuary if you're in trouble.'

'But what can I contribute, unless there's a sudden demand for accurate copying?'

'Look after Spire's child when you can. Keep yourself alive when you can't.'

'That's it?'

Miss Baldwin stood up. 'Go where the wind takes you. The future is otherwise bleak. The beacons have only so much energy and chitin degenerates over time. Lord Sine and Genrich are out there somewhere, designing their own brave new worlds. To survive, we need a new direction, but where will we end up with Cosmo in the lead? It needs someone unusual to shift the gears, someone with youth on their side. Here, I'm afraid, they live only for display, as you'll discover tomorrow.'

Fogg sidestepped what sounded like an appeal. 'I don't like to add to the gloom, but there are vicious mutants out and about.'

'They're designed by Lord Sine to survive the murk, but mercifully, they don't live long; and nobody has Scurriers or other forms of mass transport any more. So we should be safe enough here. Talking of which, you can stay in my spare room.'

The interview had ended.

Miss Baldwin's slim house had squeezed itself between two bulkier dwellings at the edge of town. 'Guests climb,' she said, indicating the staircase, 'after food, of course.'

She lacked Mander's magic touch with the Rearranger, but the fare and the drink were wholesome.

After supper Miss Baldwin opened up. 'Nobody says it, but Nature is, of course, the biggest loss. *Mankind alone is created in God's image*, we liked to say, but what bilge! I'd give anything to hear a real bird sing instead of our puny imitations.'

He tried to draw out Miss Baldwin on the Fall. 'I saw a death mask of the first Lord Vane and he looked dead scary.'

'By all accounts the man had a vile temper. But he did his bit warning the world.'

'I gather he did more than that . . .'

'And how would you know?'

'I visited the Chamber of Records and the original Tiriel's Tower, where I met a Mr Venbar.'

'You'd best remember that discussing the Fall is illegal in our valleys, including this one. It's bad for morale, and we are where we are. Now, tell me all about the underground river and its ferryman.'

He did, and she listened.

Fogg's description of Mander's punting motion revealed a second Miss Baldwin behind the world-weariness and years of service. She chuckled, shook her head and dabbed her eyes. 'In his tails? You mean like Jeremy Fisher? There you are, Mr Fogg. We carry our favourite children's books to the grave. And the ones with good pictures we hold the closest.'

His simply furnished but cosy first-floor bedroom looked out on the rock face at the rear. Books with their titles removed crammed the walls on makeshift shelves. Many had art as their subject matter. Fogg declined the temptation to browse through old, familiar pastures: a new world had opened up and he must move on and adapt.

He lay on the bed ruminating on his allotted task, the protection of Morag, in the sure knowledge that she for one would not welcome it. Even his pleasure at contributing to the creation of Winterdorf had been fleeting, overshadowed as it was by Lord Vane's death and Cosmo's resurgence.

Physical exhaustion quickly overwhelmed these anxieties.

For once in his life, Fogg overslept. He dressed in his new clothes and descended to the living room to find his hostess gone. Sunlight streamed through the windows as in an old-world morning. He wandered in and out of the luminous shafts, in awe of the dancing motes of dust.

Miss Baldwin had left a terse note on the Matter-Rearranger in her elegant manuscript hand:

1. Codes on the table.
2. Get your act together (for tonight).

My act? The memory of the costumes flooded back with Miss Baldwin's warning: *Don't get adventurous or they'll think you're something you're not.* A dull, rhythmic thud reverberated through the house. He turned the note over. The reverse read:

PS Not playing cards. I do cards.

He opened the front door. The air was crisp, but sunlight bathed his face like warm wax. An array of stepladders surrounded a widely spread circle of poles and Lomax was moving from one upright post to the next, striking each with a huge mallet, while others fixed guy-ropes. Carts crammed with rolls of coloured canvas stood nearby. Within the circle of poles, banks of wooden benches were taking shape. Simply dressed men, women and children beavered away, all chatter and laughter, bustle and movement.

The Circus had come to town – or did it live here?

He was quickly noticed, and in minutes he was surrounded by people of all ages.

'Hi, Mister, how did you get here?' asked a tall, imposing man with a voice which carried.

'You could say I dropped in – a flying visit.'

'He's got a pasty face,' added a striking young girl with short jet-black hair and freckles.

'Thanks,' replied Fogg politely. Looking round, he could see her point. They had burnished, healthy complexions, all of them.

'Subterranean, if you ask me,' added a ferret-like woman.

'That's enough of that.' Every head turned as Miss Baldwin strode towards them. The throng parted. 'I can vouch for him. He's on our side, and his name is Fogg.'

The first man nodded respectfully. 'All right, but if you're staying, mate, you've got to contribute. And that means *tonight* at the White Circus you're gonna deliver a première.'

'But I don't have a party piece.'

'Well, you'd better find one double-quick.'

'Everyone has a trick or two up their sleeve,' added the dark-haired girl before performing a series of immaculate cartwheels.

'Back to work, everyone,' ordered the imposing man, 'or you'll be hammering your fingers in the dark.'

They drifted away, but the knowing backwards glances made clear their expectation that the pasty-faced outsider would be performing.

'Tell them a story,' Miss Baldwin suggested. 'Nobody has ever done that. And take the child's wise advice: get some colour in those cheeks.'

Fogg found a bench well away from the working party and watched the Big Top rise. Its dominant colours – orange, brown and yellow over white – were familiar, but as unease about his act rose to panic, he could not make the connection. At lunchtime, Miss Baldwin brought him a plate of paste and a large glass of water, but pointedly said nothing. The young girl with the dark hair joined her. Cards appeared from Miss Baldwin's pocket as the incongruous couple walked away. At distance, the girl picked a card, Miss Baldwin shuffled, then they both gestured towards an imaginary audience, working at the pos-sibilities. The message was unmistakable: if they could rehearse, so could he. But they had an act, and he did not.

As dusk fell, the carts and the workers packed up and, their job done, withdrew. The tent lit up from inside, its coloured stripes glowing. Woodwind instruments rehearsed in the gloom, notes swirling high and low, bassoon to flute. At last Fogg made the connection: *The Circus* by Georges Seurat, another of his Museum paintings, had been brought to life.

Fogg was flirting with escape when Miss Baldwin reappeared in a Victorian dress lavishly embroidered with sequins. She flicked and fanned cards in each hand like a born croupier as she talked. 'You do realise,' she said, 'you're wearing a knife-thrower's kit. I'm not sure what best suits a raconteur, but a little more mystery wouldn't go amiss. Think props – think *performance.*'

Miss Baldwin, it appeared, had a gift for provoking decisions in others. This final prompt decided Fogg. He had nothing else to offer, so a story it must be. He chose another Museum painting, one very different to *The Circus*. He would strip out the religion – well, almost – and take it from there.

'I shall need a table.'

'You're welcome to use mine.'

'Just bare wood.'

'They follow keep-the-best-wine-to-last principle, and you're the surprise package, so expect to be on late. You can have the table from my act.'

'And a coin or two?' asked Fogg, the story now firmly in his head.

'We don't need currency here, but the props boxes have plenty. Get a move on, Mr Fogg. Get the feel of the place. Sample the electricity.' Miss Baldwin's expression turned serious. 'Premonitions are the spinster's virginal gift.' Hands on hips, she added, 'We'll need courage before the evening's out.'

'I believe you,' said Fogg.

'Twenty minutes, Miss Baldwin,' said the young girl with the jet-black hair.

'This is my accomplice, Tamasin,' added Miss Baldwin.

'Ah yes,' said Fogg, 'the one with a trick up her sleeve.'

'You look better already,' replied Tamasin with a grin. 'Bordering on normal.'

'One last piece of advice: we have guests tonight. Give them a wide berth.'

Miss Baldwin strode off towards the tent, her accomplice skipping along to keep up.

Fogg jogged slowly to the costume rooms, conscious that a breathless raconteur would not do. He would have to be in period to convince. He found tight white leggings, a jacket with pied sleeves which buttoned down the front to the waist, black shoes and an épée in its scabbard on a belt. He also found the coins he needed.

Outside, two wooden flying craft bearing more than a passing resemblance to Leonardo da Vinci's gyrocopters, had parked nearby: presumably the guests Miss Baldwin had warned against.

'Performers this way,' said an acrobat, gently nudging him away from the two covered tunnels through which the audience were now streaming. Most of the women wore hats; all wore dresses with yellow as the dominant hue. The men were divided between suits and tailcoats.

A white horse, as in the painting, trotted by.

'It's not real, Mr Fogg.' Tamasin grinned at him. 'But we always start with *them*.'

An attractive young woman in a yellow performer's dress and yellow tights and a man in a bodysuit of the same colour with orange-brown hair quiffed to a spike walked behind the horse, just as Georges Seurat had painted them in the Cirque Médrano in Paris at the corner of the rue des Martyrs, close by his studio. It had been the year of his death, and his very last work. Fogg flirted briefly with telling that story instead – he could do a good hour on the subject – only to rebuke himself. *Dull facts*, Morag would say. *Get on with the present*.

Performers had a box to themselves, he discovered. They left their props on a large table beside the ring entrance, placed in the order of their acts. Miss Baldwin's cards were there, along with a miscellany of hoops, daggers, plates and the like.

His neighbour, coincidence or not, was Lomax.

'Shuffle along after each act finishes,' said the gentle giant helpfully, bulging out of a leopard-skin leotard, 'meaning, you and me come at the death.' He looked Fogg up and down. 'So what's your turn, Mr Fogg? Fighting against yourself?'

'I'm telling a story.'

'Blimey.'

An attendant added an empty chair beyond his and placed a card on the seat. The elaborate gothic script read:

Visitor: The Dark Circus

'It's tradition. When the Dark Circus visits, *they* close the show. Likewise, when we visit them. Otherwise you'd be the closing star.'

'Small mercies,' whispered Fogg.

In an adjacent box, the woodwind players, a consort of seven, were playing complex harmonies without a slip.

Lomax put a hand to his lips as the consort upped tempo and volume to launch proceedings.

The tall, imposing man who had questioned Fogg that morning emerged as the ringmaster. He strutted, cracked his whip and played to the audience.

The horse and the two acrobats were dazzling, although the audience reserved its more ecstatic reactions for new moves.

'New! Bravo!' bellowed Lomax.

This craving for novelty and the high standards on display rekindled Fogg's apprehension, as did the one fragment which clashed with Georges Seurat's vision of his local circus. Three men and two women were sitting together at ground level in prime position, like visiting royalty. Cadaverous but young, they wore dark leather coats embossed with pins and studs. Each carried a cane. The one in the centre wore an elaborate mask. They watched like a row of jewelled ravens.

The opening, the horse and acrobats, matched Seurat's scene exactly. Thereafter, act followed act: plate-spinners, trapeze artists, youthful acrobats, ageing clowns more skilful than funny, a knife-thrower, a contortionist, a tightrope-walker, a cluster of unicyclists who interchanged cycles, remarkable manoeuvres with hoops, a magician with mechanical doves, a duel on stilts, and then came Miss Baldwin, her elfin assistant and the table with the white cloth.

Miss Baldwin drew no opening applause, just an expectant hush.

She strode to centre stage, confident and unrushed. One moment her hands were empty, the next, playing cards rolled from fingers to table to hand like an accordion playing. She flipped, tossed and shuffled. She spun round and pointed.

'You, Madam, are wearing . . .'

Ever faster ran the cards.

'Tell me when?' Tamasin asked the chosen woman.

'When? What do you mean?' cried the woman in high excitement.

'*When?*' repeated Tamasin.

'Now!' shrilled the woman.

'Two diamonds,' said Miss Baldwin, pouncing on a card in the flowing pack. 'One in each ear.'

'Ooh, I say,' cooed the woman.

'You have one . . .' Same procedure with an elderly man. 'One heart!' The ace.

'New! New!' crowed Lomax, clapping his hands in ecstasy.

Miss Baldwin followed up with a single narrative sentence as Tamasin cartwheeled around the front row.

'A *king* met a *queen* who lost her *heart* to a *jack*-of-all trades she met in a *club*.'

The critical cards emerged from the ears, pockets and décolletages of the audience.

'So utterly, bombastically new!' enthused Lomax.

The audience signalled their agreement with a round of deafening applause.

Miss Baldwin hushed them. She rearranged the cards and placed one, seemingly at random, in the centre.

'You, sir, black or red?'

'Red.'

'That leaves black. You, Madam, eight to the ace or one to the seven.'

This was not new, and Fogg grasped the trick quickly enough. So had the audience. She was marking time.

'Old hat!' muttered Lomax with a shake of the head.

'One to seven,' replied the woman without much enthusiasm.

'Spades or clubs?'

And so it went on, selecting what suited the card in the middle and rejecting what did not. It garnered a flutter of polite clapping but nothing more.

Miss Baldwin summoned assistants, who removed the table-cloth.

'For our last trick, the highest card will find its true owner. The ace of spades is the card of death, a wicked card. *Pique* is French for pike, a killing blade with just that shape, and a spade will dig our graves. The ace tops a king, even a good king. Even a good Lord, I imagine. We need to know the owner's whereabouts to keep our distance.'

Silence.

This was twenty-four-carat new.

Tamasin cartwheeled around the ring to the five dark visitors. One swung his cane violently at her, but she evaded it with a flourish and plucked the ace of spades from the sleeve of the masked man in the middle before flamboyantly displaying the card to the audience, whose response melded wild applause with a pantomime hiss.

The ravens showed no visible reaction.

Fogg read the subtext. The visitors had come from Cosmo's kingdom and this was Miss Baldwin's rebuke for Lord Vane's death, the good Lord killed by a pike.

A quartet of clowns came next.

As they combined in a final mêlée, Lomax leant over. 'Fucking watch me, Mr Fogg.'

His bluff cheeriness overlaid a sharp wit. He commenced with a twig, which he strained theatrically to snap, then a wand, then a wooden pole, then a steel pole. The stronger they became, the easier he made the burden look. The white horse returned. He lifted it, belly up, earning an appreciative whinny. And he was done.

'Just a reminder, you're next, Mr Fogg,' whispered Tamasin, resuming her seat.

'He'll not disappoint,' added Miss Baldwin.

'I give you,' intoned the ringmaster melodromatically, while, cracking his whip like a tap dancer, 'a table and . . .'

Fogg rushed down.

'The one and only Mr Fogg!' cried the ringmaster.

Fogg stumbled into the amphitheatre to bewildered silence. The ravens mustered a smirk.

Cut and run or perform?

Years of no visitors kicked in. At last he had a chance to shine – and to *share*.

'I'm here to tell you a story,' he said.

Heads turned to each other in disbelief.

A story! At a Circus!

'We're in an old-world counting house. And what do they count? Money, ladies and gentlemen, money.' He spilled the coins on the table. 'In the old world, money was God. It bought your clothes, your food, your house, and land with it if you were lucky. The rich ruled and the poor went begging. This counting house has a single window, its only source of natural light. Friends gather – well, not really friends; let's call them collaborators with an occupying power. They are tax collectors, dull money men, living the greyest of lives.'

The Circus had always meant physical action. Plainspoken words which played on the mind were a new experience. He could see Lomax, tugging his chin.

'I am the youngest present in that counting house. I'm not poisoned by monotony like the older men. Take the oldest, who sits opposite. He boasts a russet beard and a fine face, but it is drained by lack of joy and love.'

Fogg could see his audience were intrigued, but still at sea. Minds attuned to Matter-Rearrangement, household chores and acrobats had lost the ability to travel to fictional realms.

'Then ... *then* ... as they talk money, and as the man with the beard watches another musty day in his life ebb away, the light from the window retreats and a door opens. Is it a physical door – the kind we know – or is it a door of *opportunity*? A new, oddly numinous light invades as two men in dingy rags walk in. One has an aura.'

He pauses, then sweeps his hand around the ring. 'Our ringmaster has an aura, and so does young Lomax, but not like this.'

'New, new,' boomed Lomax's stage whisper.

Fogg slowed, turned more theatrical. 'The intruder says nothing, but he points at the man with the beard as he turns to leave. The gesture is loaded with meaning and brooks no argument. *Follow me.*'

'And he does. And the old man is never the same again. Some follow others from fear. Such followers are fickle and may, even should, turn on their masters.' Fogg stared at the ravens. 'Others follow for love, and that path can lead to the strangest places. As I'll tell you next week.'

'More!' cried a member of the audience.

'Yes, more,' echoed others.

A moment of madness seized Fogg, who felt the climax of the scene had fallen short by an inch or two.

'And I'll show you the place,' he cried, 'just as it was. Bring me paper, pen and ink.'

The ringmaster cracked his whip. 'We're agog with Fogg! Bring him the needful!'

The pen had a good nib and balance. The paper, a generous square, also had quality. He sat at the table, quite unaware that his intensity and speed of hand carried their own fascination. The audience craned forward as Caravaggio's *The Calling of St Matthew* came alive on the page.

The ringmaster, fearing a dwindling attention span, called out, 'Music for Mr Fogg! Tumblers for Mr Fogg!'

The sight of Fogg working feverishly amid a blur of acrobats was itself a magnetic image.

Lomax leant over to Miss Baldwin. 'Fogg's a fucking – sorry – star!' he mumbled.

'He's a fucking fool,' hissed Miss Baldwin.

'A likeable fucking fool,' added Tamasin.

'The wise orphan speaks,' added Miss Baldwin, 'but he's in peril. Watch out for him after the show—'

Miss Baldwin stopped as a young female figure in black, still hooded, took the vacant reserved seat next to Fogg's. The visitor from the Dark Circus did not acknowledge the presence of her neighbours but sat ramrod-straight, looking like the Angel of Death.

Fogg finished, an oil painting reduced to an Old Master sketch.

'He needs an assistant,' said Tamasin, darting down the stairs.

The Angel of Death stared straight ahead, remorseless.

Tamasin rushed into the ring, seized the sketch and presented it to the audience, cartwheeling and vaulting from row to row, eliciting *oohs*, *aaghs* and nodding heads. A ripple of applause rose to a wave. As Fogg bowed low in acknowledgment, the man in black, from whose sleeve Tamasin had plucked the ace of spades, stood up and pointed at Fogg.

The gesture brooked no argument: *You follow me.*

'Shit,' muttered Miss Baldwin.

Fogg ignored the invitation and with Tamasin, hurried back to his seat to cheers from the audience, the young woman in black, who now entered for the final act.

She strode centre-ring and began to juggle. Other jugglers had preceded her and impressed, but her five iron candle-shaped torches spun so high they almost reached the canvas ceiling.

'Have you ever heard of light and bushels?' Miss Baldwin hissed at Fogg with a face like thunder.

'Did I go too far?' he asked. 'I mean the drawing bit.'

She nodded at the ravens. 'They come twice a year to choose one of our performers for their Circus. They give tantalum in return. They've chosen you, and one of them is familiar.'

'They never bloody choose me,' replied Lomax grumpily.

'Count your lucky stars,' added Miss Baldwin.

'He'll come back,' said Lomax jovially.

Tamasin whipped upright, eyes wet, hands shaking. 'My parents never did.'

Below them, the spinning torches ignited. Outside, dusk was deepening. Down, up, down went many hundreds of eyes, as if the spinning balls of fire held them by a string.

Miss Baldwin sensed the danger before anyone else. 'With me!' she shouted, pointing at the exits.

She was too late. The torches speared the canvas, one after the other, and held. Channels of fire spread out from each like spokes on a wheel, as the fire-juggler turned fire-breather. She spun round and belched a gout of fire at the posts supporting the performers' box. The flame had a viscous, corrosive quality. The posts fractured and collapsed, spilling the occupants into the sawdust of the ring. The audience screamed and rushed for the exits as the fire in the roof spread and blazing fragments of canvas fell into the decorative materials below, which instantly caught fire.

In the smoke and chaos, only the ravens had purpose. Two of them seized Fogg as he tumbled into the ring. The ringmaster tried to intervene, only to be felled by a bolt from a miniature crossbow plucked from under her cloak by the fire-breather. By ill luck, Lomax, snared by smouldering canvas, could not free himself in time to intervene.

The man who had pointed at Fogg threw off his mask and strode into the ring as if he owned it. He brushed aside the falling embers with regal contempt.

For a moment, Fogg dragged to his feet, stood face to face with his summoner.

Three years had passed, but Fogg had no doubt that his old torturer, Cosmo Vane, had come to claim him.

9

The Cottage

Morag watched her new canine friends through the window. On deck they lolled, rolled and slept. They even twitched in their sleep as if dreaming.

Without Fogg's distracting presence, she surveyed the controls with a fresh eye.

She already knew the basics: the diapason reported balance or imbalance, the pulleys controlled the air sacks, and the wheel allowed short-term steering to avoid such perils as a brooding thundercloud, but no more. She had first thought this a fault, but upon reflection, she reckoned the wheel had no role in long-distance navigation. But who, or what, had set the levers which chose their destinations?

She checked the twelve levers again. Number twelve had brought them here and was now locked, and so were nine others. But why locked? Did they set journeys which were too far away or too dangerous? Forbidden by authority? Or was she not considered ready for them yet?

The network of neighbouring valleys provided a sound provisional answer, but she had no idea how many valleys there might be beyond the two she had visited, although Fogg's disappearance suggested at least one other.

Irritated by the thought of the ship directing her travels, she searched high and low for a clue as to what the remaining numbers might signify, but to no avail, until she tapped the wooden panel above the wheelhouse window. A hollow sound echoed back. She pressed the panel, which fell open from a concealed hinge. Inside the cavity, a fixed compass, framed in brass, had an adjustable needle overlying the directional hand and, below it, a keypad with numbers from nought to nine, for longitude and latitude, presumably. Beside it was another smaller lever that would not move. She entered a random entry without response. Release the lever, she reasoned, and the navigator could enter his or her own course.

She stamped a foot in frustration. A dog looked up, then rolled back. *Don't waste your energy*, the gesture seemed to say. *Just go where we take you.*

That left a choice of two. She pulled up the anchor and pressed lever five.

Aeolus responded instantly, drifting on the breeze towards the mountain ridge as the chitin shield enveloped her, topmast to keel. Morag ran from side to side, activating each air bag in turn and trusting to luck. She doubted a single aeronaut could cope with extreme turbulence, but to her relief the diapason hummed contentedly and *Aeolus* gathered speed. The dogs strolled the deck, raising their snouts to the air. The cross-currents which had so plagued their arrival kept away.

Morag sat by the prow and reflected on what might drive a man to kill his own father. Benedict's arrival, perhaps, if Cosmo knew who he was and how he came to be: it would have been a devastating statement of no confidence in his fitness to rule. But she wasn't convinced. Benedict had appeared to be a stranger to Marcus, who was close to Cosmo, and the attackers had focused their ire on Lord Vane alone. That left impatience and a crude ambition to rule.

Six hours or so into the journey, *Aeolus* once again displayed a mind of its own. It veered away from its previous course and banked in ever tighter circles, slow, lazy and as methodical as a hawk in a thermal.

Is it searching? Morag clasped the anchor chain. Their destination must be small, very small, and she would have to be quick.

A new world exploded into view like a blindfold ripped from a prisoner's face as murk one moment yielded to a glorious early summer evening the next. The chitin shield swung open and she hurled the anchor over the side.

It snagged in a stand of trees.

A beacon glowed above the treeline, a miniature when compared to those in Winterdorf and *The Hunt in the Forest*. She instantly recognised Constable's *Cottage in a Cornfield*. The whitewashed front wall contrasted sharply with the natural muddy colour of the side and rear walls. The cornfield swayed in a light wind, green in shade and golden in sunlight. Lightly bruised clouds sulked close to the horizon, but overhead the sky was clear. What other work could better illustrate what Mankind had lost?

She commanded the dogs to stay on board and lowered the ladder through the treetops. She had never climbed a tree before, real or artificial, and she enjoyed the process of mapping a route to the ground, stepping from branch to branch, testing the alternatives, old-world child's play.

She walked from the wood to a gate by the field, and there he was, the donkey with the red noseband, just as Constable had painted him. Two butterflies played in the evening sunshine, but they, like the trees, the corn and the donkey, were Tempestas work – finely wrought, but imitations.

She walked through the field to the front door and knocked. A movement through the window was followed by another voice from the past. 'What a treat this is! The one and only Miss Spire . . .'

Doors can open a multitude of ways: the suspicious inch or two, the slow ritual swing, or the generous brio of true welcome. This was emphatically the latter.

Morag blinked. 'Cassandra Vane?'

'Cassie – always Cassie, *please.*'

Morag had expected a homely interior in keeping with the painter's vision. Instead, the generous front room abounded with copper piping, circular tanks, test-tubes and a work bench with racks of instruments. Glass chemical jars filled the wall shelves. A large leather basket had been filled to the brim with black earth.

'Apologies,' added Cassie. 'I like to work facing the trees. The open field induces lethargy, somehow. Do follow me.'

The next room met Morag's expectations: it was furnished with old-world chairs, an attractive faded rug and – *yes*, an array of *books* on open shelves.

'Dear Oblivious,' Cassie said. 'Where would we be without him?'

Morag hesitated. Cassie was not the type to use the royal *we*, but how could she know that Morag and Potts had met?

Cassie picked up a jug and a glass from the table. 'I have a treat for you, Miss Spire.'

'If you're Cassie, I'm Morag – none of this *Miss Spire* business.'

Cassandra Vane, even to Morag, who disliked such concepts, was more *jolie-laide*, than beautiful like her mother. She lacked the fierceness and also perhaps the perfect symmetry. She wore a simple blue smocked dress and practical shoes. Long hair fell loose.

'Morag, I offer real water from deep beneath the mountains.' She poured from a jug.

Morag sipped the chill, refreshing liquid. *No added chemicals. No staleness. Just a rich mineral taste.*

Above the fireplace, the hearth laid with peat bricks, hung two small black and white drawings: a rocking horse with wings, and this very cottage scene, reduced to pen and ink.

'I know the artist,' Morag stammered.

'You mean the copyist? How is Master Fogg?'

This was not a casual question; Cassie *minded.*

Morag rejected her first thoughts – all facts and no soul, better in an Airlugger – as revealing too much, but also as too uncharitable.

'Fine,' she replied.

'How was he before the lightning struck? *Fine*. How did he appear the night the world ended? *Fine*. Don't give me that word. Is he alive? Is he still drawing?'

Morag adjusted her bearings. *Cassie is a Vane. Don't evade.* 'Both of those when last I saw him a couple of days ago. Sorry, I didn't mean to sound dismissive.'

'Good people are rare, and good gifted people even rarer.'

'That depends on what you mean by "good".'

Cassie smiled.

'When the sun fails, there's quite a chill here.' She picked up a device from the mantlepiece; one click and the fire ignited.

Morag had been seduced by the easy warmth of the welcome, but an ordeal had been looming since her arrival. She took a swig of water.

'I've ugly news, I'm afraid.'

Cassie the charming morphed instantly. The shoulders hunched. The eyes narrowed. '*Ugly?*' She uttered the word as if it disfigured all she stood for.

'Your father is dead.'

Cassie turned her back and blew on the glowing peat. 'You're sure?' she stammered into the fire.

'I was there. I still don't know what I could have done to prevent it. I'm so sorry.'

'How did this happen?'

'Cosmo's mechanicals killed him – several horsemen with spears.'

Cassie twisted to look at her. 'I need to know if my brother was there, and if he gave the orders.'

Morag could only nod.

'So Cosmo kills Lord Vane to be Lord Vane.' Cassie shook her head and clenched her fists. 'And that bastard Marcus Jaggard?'

'Yes, he was part of it too.'

Cassie sank to her haunches and stayed there for what felt like an eternity, before wiping her eyes with an arm and rising to her feet. 'I need to go outside.'

A wash of orange misted the sinking sun. Cassie threw Morag a shawl and wrapped a plum-purple scarf around her own neck: old-world garments, and stylish with it. 'Mother's hand-me-downs,' she added.

'I hated having to do that,' Morag said when Cassie stopped in the middle of the field.

'On the surface, my father was strong. But underneath ... he liked paintings and gentle perfection.' She flicked a stalk of corn with her finger. 'One moment we were all content in the Tempestas village, building our tribute to what we once were. Potts had his library; Mander his collection of postcards. We had my brilliant tutor, Miss Baldwin, and 147. Then everything turned on its head.'

Morag kept her peace. So many questions had been triggered by so few words, but now was not the time.

'We discovered the truth about the Fall, or rather, Marcus Jaggard did. He found the old records in the original Tiriel's Tower, so of course, he told Cosmo, which started the rot. Then my parents moved to the Genrich Dome.'

'What truth?' Morag asked quietly.

Cassie sighed. 'My grandfather was a despot: if you ignored his warnings, you had to pay. The devastation was all deliberate: city by city, continent by continent. Of course, he didn't mean to destroy *everything*, but even the cleverest people make mistakes. Then destruction became the norm.' She slumped. 'Storm systems running amok somehow became acceptable to those equipped to survive.'

Morag stared into the fire. Shock gave way to anger, then incredulity at her own naïvety. Genrich had put up their shield only days before the murk came. They knew when and where in advance – of course, they did. The concentration of survivors in the twin organisations Tempestas and Genrich now made sense. Thinking of Genrich brought her lost friend to mind and she felt an urge to change the subject.

'I knew 147,' she said.

'Of course you did. She was Lord Sine's first and only ambassador to the Tempestas Dome. She was cold at first, but over time, she thawed. When her symptoms first began to show, Father insisted she run Infotainment. Needless to say, that didn't please Cosmo.'

'She's dead too, another cull by Genrich and Tempestas.'

'Yes,' said Cassie, 'I'm afraid Cosmo found her death amusing.'

'That's not surprising, as he arranged it.'

Cassie did not look surprised at the news.

Morag had never been good at holding back what she truly thought. 'So you ran away.'

'Let's say I took the veil.'

A plaintive cry sounded over their heads and they both looked up.

'That's Hector,' said Cassie, pointing at a huge grey and white bird gliding overhead. 'When we divided up into valleys, buildings and beacons, we shared out the mechanicals. I got a donkey, a shop, masses of insects and an oversized gull. The poor bird has no sea: he's lost his natural home.' She suddenly dropped to her knees in the corn, and Morag saw her shoulders were shuddering.

Morag looked away and watched the gull bank and turn to settle on the rail of the *Aeolus*.

'Talking of fathers,' Cassie said as she stood up, 'I understand yours abandoned you, and then abandoned us. They say your father could never settle. I'm sorry.'

It was an odd interjection, and momentarily, Morag lost the thread. 'You mean . . . ?'

'147 told me a minute of your father's company was worth an hour of anybody else's. She was very fond of him. I doubt she was alone.' She gave Morag's hand a squeeze. 'I don't think history is ultimately about individuals, or the way of the weather, or Nature. It's about dynasties, who are either rotten from the start or end up going that way. That's the real fault of the human condition. We so rarely get the right leaders.'

Talk, talk, talk, thought Morag. 'That's why, sooner or later, you have to take a stand and fight for what you believe in,' she said.

'And I do,' Cassie said. She pulled an old-fashioned matchbox from her pocket and rested it in her palm as if it were a living creature. She slid out the tray. A few tiny fragments of stone or earth peered back: white, grey and brown; all shapes. 'Seeds,' she said, and there was wonder in her voice. She tipped the box and a single red berry rolled into view, strident as a rude joke.

'Where did you get them?'

'From Potts. He gathered them in the outside world before the Fall. I can't imagine him young, can you? By the way, Potts' father, Jago Potts, was a founder of Tempestas. But they say he was forever on his travels, a naturalist more than a manager.'

Cassie walked, almost skipped, back to the cottage. On the front wall a green stem wound its way up a trellis; she stroked it with the tip of her finger. The thinnest of purple lines marked the margins of the leaves, and the finest hairs rose from the stems and axils.

It was real, and it was in bud.

'*Clematis viticella,*' said Cassie. 'Seed begets seed.'

'At least the donkey won't eat it,' said Morag with a smile.

Over supper from a high-grade Rearranger, Cassie spoke more of the two ages of her childhood and the lurch from contentment into tragedy. Generosity of spirit laced her conversation, until late on, when Morag chanced her arm.

'Do you know anything about golden beetles?'

'I thought you'd never ask,' said Cassie. 'Can you keep a secret? I mean, from everyone?'

Curiosity piqued, Morag nodded. 'I swear.'

'I mastered functionality at sixteen. *Nobody* makes insects like I do.' Cassie's expression had changed. Her eyes sparkled with intense pride, and another emotion which Morag could not place.

'I was attacked by a swarm of them,' Morag said. 'On the roof of the Genrich Dome.'

'You were challenged, not attacked, and you passed the test, as I hoped you would.'

Morag recoiled in her chair. 'By the tips of my fingers! I could easily have fallen ...'

Cassie merely shrugged.

Morag's voice wavered with indignation. 'You knew I was up there – *you* were controlling them?'

'147 asked if she could show you the roof. "Of course," I said to her, "it's the only sight in the Genrich Dome worth seeing."' Cassie smiled. 'You have to understand, my beetles are guardian spirits, but you have to be worthy. Misbehave, and they'll desert you, or worse. But otherwise, they're my blessing to worthwhile people.'

'You weren't at the Tempestas party.'

'Not with that creep Jaggard there, no.'

'Well, everyone had at least one insect ...'

'Let me guess. They flew up and they flew back, like the cheap toys they are. I don't deal in them, I deal in *miracle* creatures.'

Morag lacked the will to probe further, so she let the conversation drift as Cassie reverted to her more familiar self.

Only when she retired to bed in a pleasingly cosy room did Morag register the dogs, who had not barked. Nothing had been said of Benedict or Lady Vane beyond the passing reference to the latter's plum-coloured scarf. One could be ignorance, but not the other. The truth, yes, but the *whole* truth? Something else about the conversation was nagging away, a subtlety which had troubled her at the time but which she could not now articulate. No Vane, it appeared, was ever straightforward.

They both knew Morag would not be staying. After breakfast, Cassie walked with Morag back to the wood.

They shook hands in the shadow of the *Aeolus*. 'Sod this,' said Cassie, giving Morag a close hug. 'I've told you only one lie and I don't want it round my neck. She pointed up at the *Aeolus*. '*That* is not a gull. I mean, *look at him!* Hector is an albatross. And more to the point, he's not a mechanical, he's *real*. Look after him, please, he's the last of his kind. Any old paste will do, but he needs plenty of it. Oblivious says they can circumnavigate the globe in forty-six days with their unpolluting bones and feathers.'

'How did you get it?'

'A seventeenth birthday present. Only Mander and I know it's real.'

'And Potts, surely.'

'Oh yes, obviously Potts.' Cassie's stubborn eyes watered again.

Morag wondered why she should sacrifice her only living companion other than *Clematis viticella*. As an apology for letting loose the beetles? – or was that wishful thinking? Or did it connect with where Cassie thought the Airlugger might be going? It would be churlish to ask, she decided.

Cassie helped Morag up to the lowest branch. 'Climb anticlockwise for the quickest route,' she suggested.

Morag clambered up the tree, then *Aeolus*' ladder, and weighed anchor. Hector took off and circled the cottage, returning to his new roost on the rail minutes before the chitin shield closed. He kept a respectful distance from the dogs, but they showed no interest. Their programming clearly didn't extend to a living albatross.

She waved goodbye. In the wheelhouse, lever five had now frozen. Morag cursed her stupidity: they had talked people and politics for hours, but she had not thought to ask about Cassie's immediate neighbours.

Spin the wheel.

She chose the only option. Lever eight had come free.

Moments before the murk engulfed them, she glimpsed a building in the wood, an unexpected departure from Constable's masterpiece. It was the functionality shop from the corner of the main square in the Tempestas Dome.

She had had her fill of speculation. It was time to get on with the matter in hand.

10

Shadowplay

Unmitigated chaos gripped the Big Top. Nobody weighed the probabilities; nobody thought of the common good. The useless disorder of individual panic reigned, with the one exception of Miss Baldwin.

'Get those children out *that* side,' she bellowed, judging correctly which way the tent would collapse.

'*You* again,' hissed Cosmo Vane, striding towards Miss Baldwin while brushing embers away from his face. 'Get Fogg – and bring her too!'

Tamasin tried to intervene, but the swing of a fist from the fire-breather sent her sprawling to the ground.

'She's a bloody *child*,' yelled Fogg, clambering to his feet. 'Leave her alone—'

'Foggedy-Fogg,' jeered Cosmo, gesturing.

Fogg fought as best he could, but three ravens taped his mouth, hooded his face and bound his wrists. His last sight was of Lomax bearing an unconscious Tamasin to safety, and Miss Baldwin putting up a spirited resistance.

Trussed like a chicken, Fogg found himself being pushed through a throng of screaming Circus-goers.

'Run or crawl, your choice,' said a harsh woman's voice behind him.

We're heading for their craft, Fogg reasoned, *away from the town and any hope of rescue.*

A bar snapped across his waist and a chain bit into his armpits. Nearby, one of the female ravens grunted in pain.

'She's nearly three times your age, Piety,' shouted Cosmo. 'Tape her sodding feet.'

Piety!

A rush of wind slapped Fogg's face, but the craft made no noise beyond the hum of its rotors. Minutes later, the upwards motion ceased.

'I'm bored,' cried Cosmo Vane. 'Ungag the troublesome tutor – no, I said *her*, not Fogg. Another story would send us all to sleep! But I do want him to watch.'

Piety wrenched Fogg's hood from his head. The generous deck of the *Aeolus* bore no comparison to the insecurity of this craft. Feeling horribly exposed, Fogg peered down at the burning tent, no more than a smouldering eye from this height. He would have clutched the edge of his seat, had his hands been free. Piety sat between Fogg and Miss Baldwin, and another male raven sat at the controls on Miss Baldwin's left. A second craft, crewed by the remaining ravens, hovered close by at the same height.

Cosmo, standing behind Fogg and Miss Baldwin, was displaying perfect balance and a maddening nonchalance, but Miss Baldwin too betrayed not the slightest sign of discomfort.

'Do parricides always look so pleased with themselves?' she asked calmly over her shoulder.

'Where's my sister?' Cosmo demanded. 'Where are you hiding her?'

'She has her own mind.'

'She does not. She has a pale imitation of yours, thanks to all that nonsense you crammed into her. Sugar and spice and all things nice,' he hissed.

'Something like that.'

'I can open her up,' said the raven pilot on Miss Baldwin's left with a gentle smile, flicking a knife towards the tutor's face with his free hand. 'Drench Fogg in offal.'

'Let's try again,' barked Cosmo. 'Where's the desiccated butler, Mander the monstrous?'

Some truth-tellers make good white-liars, but Miss Baldwin was not one of them. She sidestepped clumsily.

'Even if I knew, I wouldn't tell you.'

'So, the wily old bastard lives on.' Cosmo's voice hardened. 'How much have you told our good f-f-friend F-F-F-Fogg?'

'He knows nothing. He's clueless.'

'Oh dear, that's two misses. It had better be third time lucky. Where is Morag Spire?'

Miss Baldwin stared back before sidestepping again. 'I've never met her.'

'I didn't ask whether you'd *met* her. I asked for her *whereabouts* – not to the square inch, mind, just a little help.'

'How could I know? I'm marooned in my valley.'

'And yet you know of my predecessor's death. How can that be? Maybe F-F-F-Fogg isn't quite as clueless as you'd have us believe.'

'Maybe a little bird told me. Why does the Spire girl matter, anyway?'

'Come, come, Miss Baldwin. She makes momenticons.'

'So do you. Isn't one of you enough?'

For once Cosmo deigned to explain. 'We all need someone to play off. We have a double act, and I get *so* bored without her. She does innocence and I do experience.'

'What do you know about experience?' asked Miss Baldwin, as if it were a counselling session.

Fogg knew what Cosmo had done to Matilda. He desperately wanted Miss Baldwin to tone down the provocation. He shook his head in her direction.

'Ancient spinster teaches experience,' crowed Cosmo, and all the ravens sniggered except Piety, who sat silent and stock-still.

Miss Baldwin, still unflustered, continued her counterattack. 'Experience is what you learn when things don't go your way. It's why the spoilt never have any.'

'Three chances, and each of them spurned,' Cosmo intoned with mock regret. 'I try mercy, and all I get is pig-headed obstruction.' He clapped his hands in the pilot's direction. 'Over to you.'

The pilot activated a lever, and a davit-like pole attached to the rotor shaft moved upwards, tightening the chain under Miss Baldwin's arms. It lifted her out of her seat and swung her away from the craft into the open air. The ravens in the companion craft started clapping in anticipation.

Far below, Miss Baldwin's former audience and fellow performers, tiny matchstick people clustered around the tent's remains, peered up. They were too far away for him to read their faces, but Fogg could imagine their horror.

'Is this wise, your Lordship?' asked Piety quietly, twisting around to face Cosmo, but he waved her protest aside.

'Cat got your tongue?' he bellowed at Miss Baldwin. 'To the middle of the ring! Let's go for a bull's eye!'

'It's up to you now, Fogg,' cried Miss Baldwin, grimacing with pain as the chain bit into her flesh.

Cosmo jeered, 'Up to F-F-Fogg! There's a thought!'

Fogg struggled in his own chains, flailing with his legs, but to no effect.

'He wants to join her,' cried the pilot. 'A double bull!'

'No, no! How could we waste such a consummate storyteller?' Cosmo raised a hand and waved. 'But an angel should be allowed to fly. *Arrivederci*, Miss Baldwin.'

The pull of a second lever released Cassie's erstwhile tutor into space. Her dress billowed as she plummeted down, but the old lady maintained her dignity to the end. She refused the third Lord Vane the satisfaction of a scream.

A cloud of sparks rose from below.

The deed done, Cosmo looked deflated.

'Home,' he cried, resuming his seat. 'And hood the Fogg. He's had quite enough excitement for one day.'

A chitin bubble enveloped each craft. The hum of the rotors rose an octave and in concert they rose, turned, and hurtled into the murk.

11

The Hindsight Inn

Fogg had prepared himself for prison, torture or humiliation on a public stage, but not this arrival. He felt the craft land and heard Piety moving beside him. After a few muffled whispers, his chain was released, and then his arms. Only the hood remained secure as they manhandled him on to the ground. Then the hum of the rotors retreated, giving way to silence.

The knot at his throat yielded to his shaking fingers in minutes.

They had left him in a hollow in an undulating landscape covered with even, synthetic grass. Both craft had vanished. It was midnight or so, he guessed. The sky above was clear, and in the distance a giant beacon glowed. The huge valley dwarfed Miss Baldwin's domain.

Miss Baldwin!

He crossed himself in a gesture of remembrance gleaned from the Museum Dome's background notes. Matilda in her cottage, the twins in the airlock, Venbar in the old Tempestas headquarters and now Miss Baldwin. He felt like the Angel of Death.

For a minute or two he bowed his head and paid his respects. Then he snapped back to his present predicament and weighed the options.

Explore – but not the way they think I'll go.

Ahead of him were columns of light rising skywards, so he walked the other way, into the dark and over a second hillock. Beyond, at least fifty gyrocraft had been parked in tidy rows. They were all equipped with racks of crossbows and spears.

It had the appearance of an offensive fleet. Who was the enemy in Cosmo's sights?

He retraced his steps and this time continued towards the light, only to freeze as he breasted the second slope. A huge grey-coloured horizontal human torso as large as a small house ended in an artificial man's head, in scale with the body, which peered back over the right shoulder. Arms in the form of tree trunks propped up the half man, with branches protruding from their bone-coloured skin.

The innards had been hollowed out, creating a generous open space with a table and benches, where several men and women were engaging in animated conversation. A wooden ladder gave access to this grotesque tavern. Above the head fluttered two pennants, respectively embroidered *The Hindsight Inn* and *Where Life Always Looks Best*.

He did another double-take, realising he was facing the Inn from the panel for Hell in Hieronymus Bosch's triptych, *The Garden of Earthly Delights*, copied to the last detail.

'Come up 'ere, fancy pants!' cried a woman's voice.

Fogg's outré costume looked less incongruous here, for the revellers were wearing equally old-fashioned clothes.

The gathering cheered and beckoned as he succumbed and ascended the ladder. Eight of them occupied the benches; the four men and four women were all drinking an ochre-coloured liquid.

'You're a new face,' said the woman who had first called out. 'We always welcome new faces.'

'The booze won't bite you,' said the jocund man on her left, tapping his glass. 'And we don't sip in *The Hindsight*, we swig.'

By way of demonstration, the man tilted his glass.

A young woman smirked. 'He's looking for the rest of the Garden, for the naked women.'

'Sorry, mate, Cosmo hasn't got that far yet,' added her companion. 'We can't wait.'

'What's your name, stranger?' asked another.

'Plain F-F-Fogg,' replied Fogg.

'Just dropped in for a pint, then?'

'I'm here to perform in your Circus.'

'Hand-picked, eh? It must be quite an act!' croaked a skinny woman, looking him up and down.

The jocund man thrust a full beaker into Fogg's hand. 'I propose a toast. To looking back!'

Fogg stumbled to the edge of the floor, raised his glass, faced outwards to the view, took a mouthful and then, as he lowered his glass, tipped as much of the brew as he could without being seen to the ground below.

'What's your act, then? Cosmo likes the sawn-in-half trick done for real or the apple-on-the-head with the bowman taking a pace back after every shot.'

'Not a real apple, *obviously*,' added a corpulent man.

'But a *real* head,' cackled the skinny woman.

'My act will be a surprise,' said Fogg expansively.

'Have you ever heard talk of Paradise?' asked the woman casually. 'There's a reward for discovering its whereabouts, so keep your lug-holes open.'

So it is a set-up. Fogg decided to give them what they probably already knew.

'I heard some adventurer called – Wire? Myer? Spire? – went looking for it. But he never came back.' Fogg raised his glass high. 'To lost explorers!'

Another half glass disappeared on to the ground below as Fogg mimed a deep swig, then tottered back.

'You haven't told us your act yet.'

'Sorry, friends, I feel a tad woozy. It's been a long and trying day.' Fogg stumbled to the bench, put his head into his hands and feigned unconsciousness.

'He's gone!' shouted out the skinny woman.

On the other side of the inside wall, behind a concealed door in the head of the half man, Piety and Cosmo sat under a low light on ornate chairs, nursing more refined drinks in cut-crystal glasses.

'Damn,' said Piety. 'Talk about the square root of bugger all. He's as clueless as the Baldwin woman said.'

'You're not thinking it through,' said Cosmo in his usual maddeningly superior manner. 'Start with what we know. He and Morag Spire arrive as strangers in nearby places at or about the same time, which suggests they journeyed together in the Airlugger we passed on the way to Winterdorf. She must have mentioned her father, because Fogg can't have met him. And if Spire had returned to his family at any stage, she would surely have said so. So we extrapolate that Spire is either dead or found what he was looking for.'

'They have an Airlugger?'

'So it seems. When I returned, it had gone.'

'Gilbert Spire was looking for Paradise? What does that mean? And where the hell is it?'

'That's what we're going to find out.'

Piety watched her master and occasional lover. Only a short temper hampered his prodigious talents; when calm, as now, he missed nothing.

Cosmo's eyes suddenly narrowed. 'Now, why didn't my good friend Piety enjoy Miss Baldwin's maiden flight? Everybody else did. I found that surprising.'

'She was your sister's tutor. Think of the secrets you could have extracted. She was around with Spire and your father.' She paused. Criticising Cosmo required a deft touch. 'You let her provoke you.'

'She paid for the pleasure.'

'She died for her cause. I respect that.' Piety hesitated. 'You did what she wanted you to do.'

Cosmo let the barb pass; this was too good an evening to spoil. 'But what of the old bat's last words!' he said. 'She left her cause to Fogg, of all people. Why would anyone sane do that?'

'Good question,' Piety said, and meant it. 'And another is – what cause did she entrust to Fogg?'

'Then let's go fishing for answers,' he replied with a *Eureka!* grin. He flung the door open and yelled at the revellers, 'Take him to the tower, the room with the scanners and weavers!'

'Yes, your Lordship,' they replied as one, before summoning a stronger ladder.

'And then scarper.'

I 2

Mind Games

Piety liked the anti-septic, rational feel of the Weavers' Room, but she did not work there; she sifted intelligence from the various valleys selected for habitation after the closure of the Tempestas Dome. A few tiny worlds still lay undiscovered in the murk, including the one belonging to Cosmo's sister. Cosmo's aim was simple enough: unite them all under his rule, and then find and destroy Lord Sine. But Cosmo's father had delivered these smaller realms in secret and Cosmo did not know where most of them were, how many there were, or even for sure who held them and what their forces might be. Then again, he could only be in one place at one time.

She could not source his interest in this elusive Paradise, save that Cosmo had always perceived the Spires, father and daughter, as a threat. Here, she thought, his logic had for once deserted him. The father was almost certainly dead and the daughter had merely animated a few characters in her head. True, she had a strong visual imagination, but *so what?*

As for current politics, the world of the White Circus would be rudderless without Miss Baldwin, and she could not see the few remaining minor realms taking long to track down.

That left the figure slumped beneath the scanner. He had a copying gift, but nothing to worry anyone. Only his links with Morag Spire could have prompted Cosmo to indulge in this bizarre experiment.

She dozed until the undersides of the closed shutters were greying with first light, to be woken by a cry from Cosmo as he yanked the scanner from Fogg's head.

'Get me pen and pencil. Now! And lock him up—'

Piety opened the door and called for help. Two young assistants carried the comatose Fogg out.

'Coffee!' barked Cosmo. He sat a table and between pauses, scribbled like a boy struggling with an exam.

'Well?' she asked.

'Paintings – paintings *everywhere*.'

'We know that, Cosmo. He came to your parents' apartment and drew. And there'll be the paintings he saw at Morag Spire's house.'

'But every brushstroke is visible. He's lived with the real things.'

'How can that be? He's a fantasist and a frustrated artist. He copies, but he can't create. Come on!'

'There's a Museum.'

'A *what*?'

'A freestanding Dome with its own chitin shield, and it's crammed with salvaged paintings and artefacts.' Cosmo put the pad down and began to pace the room.

'Does it matter?' she asked.

He ignored the question. 'And he's been to a garden, a very particular garden.'

'He can't have done. There are no gardens, not anywhere. Your grandfather saw to that.'

'He took a momenticon – I saw him do it – then he went into the painting in front of him. I saw the whole episode as it's lodged in his memory. There were water plants in bloom, and a white curved bridge. I heard birds singing – I even saw the artist!'

Piety tried not to look as nonplussed as she felt.

'You must realise what this means,' Cosmo continued. 'I didn't make that momenticon, and *he* certainly didn't. But Morag Spire was there, which means she made it. And, if I'm right, it's different to any momenticon I've ever encountered. And thanks to the landlord at Winterdorf, I've a jar of her efforts waiting for me there. I look forward to trying them.'

What we value defines us, thought Piety. *Cosmo values his gifts and his bloodline because they make him unique. Now a commoner turns up with the same gift, maybe even a stronger one, and that rattles him.* She had a flash of insight. *Powerful men are superstitious, and Cosmo is no exception. He sees Morag Spire's story as much as Morag Spire herself as a danger.*

She resolved to inspect the images logged in the weaver for herself, but now was not the time. Cosmo was at his most dangerous when impatient.

'Anything else?' she asked.

'I had a glimpse of Lord Sine's mutants swarming over the old headquarters, looking much the worse for wear. How many did we capture?'

'They're still in the lab, and there aren't many left. Your tests are rather severe.'

'And are we *sure*?'

'It appears to be a universal weakness.'

Cosmo's stop-start pacing resumed. 'And we have the timings?'

'They're constant enough.'

'When is Lord Sine's ambassador arriving?'

'Tomorrow, first thing.'

'So just one piece is missing: the location of Paradise. We *must* find the Spire girl.'

He calls her 'the Spire girl' to diminish her, thought Piety. *She really must worry him.*

Cosmo halted again. 'The Spire girl escaped Winterdorf with a strange man in tow. Well, actually, it was the other way round.'

'In what way strange?'

Cosmo flicked his fingers. 'He looked like a Vane.'

'Do you have cousins?'

'None I know about, but you know how families are. Marcus

says he uses the name "Benedict". He must be a pretender, an opportunistic lookalike.' Cosmo kicked the chair leg. 'Marcus also said he kept my father's company.'

Morag with her gift, and an ally with the blood, or at least the appearance of it. Piety began to grasp the urgency. 'He'll stand out anywhere,' she said.

'According to Marcus, that old fool Potts allowed the Spire girl to escape from the Tempestas Dome – *and* Potts was a friend of her father's. There's a conspiracy out there, Piety, and we have to unravel it.'

'What about Fogg?'

'Tonight he performs in our Circus, and his final act will be a memorable one.'

Prolonged exposure to Cosmo's brutality had dulled Piety's moral sense. She put in no plea for the young man, although he struck her as a naïve boy wholly out of his depth. 'Isn't there someone we're forgetting?' She asked the question gently, as she was broaching delicate ground.

'Like who?'

'Your mother, Cosmo.'

Cosmo wagged a rebuking finger. 'Never presume, Piety. My plans go deep – many moves deep – and every risk is weighed.'

Piety had reconnoitred the limits of Cosmo's patience in the past, and she knew she had reached them now. 'Clearly I've work to do,' she said, before leaving the room.

Cosmo had difficulty reining in his temper in the face of so much covert, unauthorised and wasteful activity, from the construction of a museum to the assembly of an old-world art collection – what *conceivable* use were they to anyone?

And yet whenever the Spire girl surfaced, turbulence followed. He must be rational and sift his mind – or rather, *Fogg's* mind – for further clues to unravel this mystery.

One oddity stood out. Fogg's Matter-Rearranger in this Dome of paintings had gone off-script, changed its voice, produced, unasked, an antique trumpet, and mentioned a Mr Vermeer.

Cosmo had no interest in art beyond masters of the disturbing image, like Bosch and Bacon. Vermeer meant nothing to him, but that was not the starting point. He had disembowelled and reassembled Rearrangers as a child, his idea of playtime. He knew their capacities and their quirks and he had studied the scope for malfunction, accidental and contrived, the latter designed to inflict unpleasant surprises on his classmates and their parents. Advanced Rearrangers had diction, a faculty he had exploited, but no Rearranger could deliver a virtual image, let alone a perfect rendering of an antique trumpet.

This is how today's nutritious paste will look, sir, was quite simply not on the machine's menu, even though virtual technology had reached sophisticated levels in his grandfather's day, when the mini-skirted Triv, a hologram, had been sent to lambast the world's movers and shakers about the approaching Doomsday.

Now in note-taking mode, he scribbled out some conclusions, his concern mounting as their cumulative effect struck home.

1. The Rearranger in Fogg's Museum was given new parts by someone with sophisticated technical gifts.
2. So much effort had to be for a significant purpose. The trumpet meant more than a trumpet.
3. Fogg and the Spire girl, as I judged their reactions, had both been surprised. This had not therefore been a regular occurrence.

Cosmo paused and ran through his notes of the other fractured images netted from Fogg's cerebral cortex: a moored Airlugger (again, unexpected), two dead identical twins, and the advancing shadow of a closing roof.

His pen hovered before descending for the last time.

4. *Someone was laying a trail for one or both of them to follow.*

For a fleeting moment, his father struck him as the prime suspect, plotting to disinherit his only son, whom he had never loved
or even liked, but the theory imploded under the briefest scrutiny.
This Museum Dome would have taken years to build, and his father
had met neither Fogg nor the Spire girl in time. Also, would not
the strange Benedict be the obvious pretender? He could not resist
a smirk. Nobody, but nobody, would choose Fogg. Someone else
was pulling the strings.

He summoned Piety once more. 'I've a mission for you.' She
stood there, silent, not insolent, yet not quite her usual enthusi-
astic self. 'I want you to go to Miss Baldwin's house and retrieve
any art books which relate to a Mr Vermeer. Take enough troops
to quell any trouble.'

'Art books?' she queried gently.

'The Baldwin woman taught my father art before my grandfather
stopped it. People never throw away their favourite books, and
ageing teachers least of all.'

'Consider it done.'

Cosmo relished the swordplay of speech, but silence he found
harder.

Piety stood there, as if a further explanation was called for. 'We
have to find Mr Vermeer's painting with a trumpet,' he added. 'It's
the key to everything.'

13

Memories

Fogg had not been as drunk or drugged as the enemy thought, still less unconscious. When he heard the words 'scanner' and 'weavers', he had known from Morag's story what to expect, and he prepared himself as best he could. He would allow his interrogator *one* discovery and no more. He chose to focus on the Museum as of little practical use, to present his memories as those of a pedantic Curator whose meaningful knowledge of life had not extended beyond the exhibits in his care.

He recalled one slip when allowing Cosmo this virtual tour of the Museum. The momenticon had slipped unbidden into view on reaching Monet's *Water Lilies* above the Biedermeier chest and he had been unable to suppress that once-in-a-lifetime experience.

But he felt confident he had kept under lock and key Mander's whereabouts, Morag's narrative and his own discoveries in the Chamber of Records.

The effort had been exhausting. He lay sprawled beneath a single blanket on the pull-down bed which folded out from the wall of his cell. While drifting in and out of sleep, a dreadful truth dawned: the weavers had weakened the seals he had set around his remote past.

Memories were seeping through, and with them an appalling, incurable pain.

*

White – white and blue – everywhere. Surrounded by snowfields and ice, sub-Antarctic ice, the research station is no more than a cluster of prefabricated buildings. He has a camp bed in a small room at the back of his parents' hut on the outer edge of the settlement.

He was born and raised here, the station's only child. Nobody counts the years, but he must be seven or eight. The cities which posted them here – and indeed, the rest of the known world – have long vanished. This small community is happy enough in the circumstances. He recalls the naturalist who encouraged his drawing, and the woman who let him release the weather balloons.

But now the murk is coming for them too, creeping ever closer, like a great brown bear hunting them. The life in this small quarter of the ocean is ever diminishing, and now dead birds and fish clog the bay. The once pure air is polluted by the stink of putrefaction. They will starve if the poison does not get them first. Adults are poor at guarding secrets, and he overhears his parents planning his future: they will give him a pill to send him to sleep when the moment comes, and that will be any day now.

He neither wants to die inside, nor to be a burden to others, but he craves one last adventure. A tiny dot on the map marks a place with a beguiling name where he has never been: Petrel Rock.

It is January, and the temperature is at its most accommodating. He dresses up warmly and packs a water bottle and the food he has been hoarding before sneaking out the back door off his bedroom. He leaves a note on his bed:

Better this way.
Love you. xx

He takes a single open canoe and barges his way through the dead skuas and penguins. It's only freak currents and atmospherics that have allowed them to live this long, or so the grown-ups say.

He grits his teeth and paddles hard to oust thoughts of his parents and friends. Mercifully, canoes are not made for looking back.

He reaches the rocky islet just before noon. The ice is manageable, but to his disappointment, there are no birds there, alive or dead. He pulls the canoe on to the shingle beach, then looks back. Behind him, the advancing orange-yellow fog has closed the view, and the open sky above his head has almost vanished too. The station has disappeared.

His world somersaults. He should be with his father and mother, not out here by himself.

Whirr.

Whirr.

He thinks this must be the noise of death, the beating of a descending angel's wings, but it's not. An extraordinary craft, one which should surely belong on the sea, hangs above the island. A near-transparent bubble opens and a rope ladder is thrown.

A commanding voice hollers down, 'Run, boy, *fast as you can!*'

He realises the stranger is right: the air has turned sour and is burning his lungs. As he reaches the ladder, other rougher voices call down, 'Shift yourself, boy!'

The middle-aged man who first called bellows to his shipmates, 'Wind like hell!' and he grips hard as the ladder hurtles upwards to the deck, just moments before the bubble closes, encasing the mysterious ship once more.

'Welcome aboard the *Fram*, young man,' says his rescuer. 'How do you come to be out here?'

'It's my mother and f-f-f-f—'

And so his stammer is born.

Thereafter, threads of narrative assemble and disassemble, distorted and disordered by grief. The crew, a dozen or so men and women living cheek by jowl in cramped quarters and some even on the open deck, deliver robust kindness rather than explanations.

Over a journey of many months, maybe year, that he cannot remember, he learns the ropes, literally, and becomes the cabin boy.

He also redraws their maps.

His saviour, a man of vigorous action, withholds his name as too dangerous for him to know, describing himself only as an exile with secrets. He follows the crew's lead and calls him Captain.

The Captain says that Fogg has courage and luck, and that is how fortunes are made. He says Fogg's time will come. He says he has no sons and will do his best for him, as his parents would have done.

But then, one evening, he announces that for a time Fogg must enter a third home, where there will be learning but little friendship. 'You will use this peculiar drawing gift of yours,' he says. 'I'll forge you a letter of introduction.'

Fogg doesn't question the instruction, for he trusts the Captain absolutely. 'What's forging?' he asks after a moment.

'Pretending a letter from me is from someone else. You have to know the other's writing, and how he uses words.'

'Who are you pretending to be?'

'The second Lord Vane.'

'Who's the second Lord Vane?'

'He rules most of the little that's left of this planet.'

'Is forgery wrong?'

'It's like a white lie when needs must.' He adds one minute's worth of advice. 'Bury your grief and hide it away. Sharing only cheapens it. Grief can destroy you, or it can make you stronger.' The Captain claps him on the shoulder. 'And I should know.'

The craft, slow and stealthy in its approach in the interests of silence, drops him off at the School for Idiot-Savants near the Genrich Dome before first light.

The Captain hands down his travelling bag with a whisper of farewell, which ends in a surprise. 'I've included a small memento.

It's a special barometer I designed long ago to detect and resist electromagnetic disturbance. I doubt I'll be needing it any longer.'

They leave him in the airlock with his letter and move away swiftly, as if the place were cursed.

14

Of Bread and Circuses

Looking back, Fogg decided that the chronology fitted. Gilbert Spire had abandoned his home for the Genrich Dome, then abandoned the Genrich Dome in the cause of exploration. Guilt at abandoning his wife and child had driven him to the wilds.

Yet a malign question, the one to which Matilda had wanted an answer, nagged away: *Why had Gilbert Spire never returned home?*

Fogg could add another. *Why hide even his name?*

A slim panel in the door opened to deliver a fleeting slit of light, a plate with a smattering of paste and a discouraging commentary. 'You'll need this where you're going.' The light revealed a jug of water and a glass already sitting on a stool in the corner opposite the bed.

The downside to his successful resistance now dawned on him. Cosmo would have concluded that Fogg had nothing more to offer, so he was now dispensable.

His first visitor confirmed this supposition. The door opened and a gaoler, short and brawny, walked in with a costume in one hand and a bludgeon in the other.

'Not bad for a shroud,' he said cheerily, prodding Fogg in the stomach. 'Put it on now. You haven't long.'

The white all-in-one garment was freckled with gold sequins at the feet, wrists and around the neck. The feet had pads, but there were no shoes. At least he would go out in style.

Another hour crawled by before the gaoler returned. 'You'll make a great target,' he announced.

'Target for what?'

'Prisoners don't ask questions. They laugh at my jokes and do what I say. Straight ahead, left at the end and up two flights of stairs.'

The floor and walls were of bare stone, as in a dungeon from an old-world castle. Fogg followed the directions to a large oak door which led outside.

'Into the tumbril,' the gaoler snarled.

The wooden cart's canvas sides and roof, stretched over wooden hoops, hid both the outside view and the driver. The gaoler fixed manacles to Fogg's right leg and left wrist before settling down opposite him.

The gaoler's feeble attempts at gallows humour punctuated lengthy intervals of silence, until the tumbril halted beside a vaulted tunnel festooned in black crêpe de Chine. The gaoler removed the irons and ushered Fogg into the tunnel, which led to the edge of the ring. The Dark Circus resembled the White in size and layout, but the dominant blacks and mauves with occasional splashes of vermilion contrasted sharply with the gentle pastel colours of its rival. The audience wore the same mix of leather, studs and exotic make-up as the embassy to the White Circus. They greeted Fogg's arrival with raucous applause.

'Who's this?' asked a young woman dressed in gothic costume. She consulted a programme.

'He's the climax,' said the gaoler with the self-importance of a man in the know. 'The final curtain call, the last trump, the full stop.'

'We close with the black and white moth. Are you Mr Fogg?'

'*Are* you Fogg?' parroted the gaoler aggressively, elbowing his prisoner in the ribs.

Fogg had had enough. 'I'm *The Fantastic Mr Fogg* to you,' he said with as much élan as he could, not noting that his stammer had for once deserted him.

Two male assistants in black now guarded Fogg as the gaoler shuffled away.

'I like your spirit,' said the young woman to Fogg. 'There's no pleasure in lambs to the slaughter, and a bull who fights to the last is occasionally spared. At least, that's the old-world tradition, and the third Lord Vane can be traditional. You know – thumbs up for style, thumbs down for the bore. Just watch out for what comes next and do your best.'

She turned to the guards. 'Get the white moth into position. And, Fogg, I suggest you listen to the rules to give us a run for our money.'

More guards blocked every exit, so for the lack of any alternative, Fogg saved his energy.

'You do not manhandle the white moth,' he said grandly when the assistants seized him roughly by the arms. Unused to bravado from the about-to-die, they released their grip. One led Fogg and the other followed him.

Clues to his fate began to register. The sawdust in the ring was liberally spattered with blood, and every adult in the audience was brandishing a miniature crossbow and a fistful of tiny bolts.

A sycophantic cheer welcomed Cosmo Vane and Piety to their seats on a raised dais, where they were surrounded by other acolytes.

The ringmaster followed their entry. His costume mirrored his equivalent in the White Circus, but he wielded a lightning rod instead of a whip.

A cylindrical cage descended from high in the ceiling. Fogg's escorts shut him in and the cage ascended halfway up the Big Top. The audience ignored the operation, their attention now focused on the baskets, five of them arranged at regular intervals around the ring.

'*Are – you* – LOADED?' shouted the ringmaster.

The audience cheered and waved their crossbows.

'Big is *easy*, but resilient. Small is elusive, but *vulnerable*. Headshots will count double later on, remember – but no scores for this one, he's just a sighter. Only one shot each – and don't forget our little forfeit. Hit the tent and it's LIGHTNING time!'

Fogg looked up. Large cork-like circles, striped for visibility, hung from the ceiling, with small spaces in between: find the spaces and your bolt would damage the tent. The ringmaster's rod crackled like Mr Venbar's staff. The crowd *ooohed!*

Fogg detected an undercurrent of genuine unease. He suspected the forfeits would be agonising, if not terminal.

The ringmaster stooped and flipped open the lid of the first basket.

A bizarre mechanised globefish floated upwards, but its flesh and eyes looked real. It floated, then zigged, then zagged, varying its pace throughout. Fogg had expected a volley of bolts and a quick end, but fear of missing the cork longstops induced restraint. With the audience playing safe, the challenge took time. One moment the fish resembled a pin cushion, the next it exploded like a popped balloon.

'Now for the REAL GAME,' bellowed the ringmaster, stilling the hubbub.

One by one, the baskets yielded further flying constructs, each more bizarre than the last, culminating in a flight of brilliantly coloured parrots, which, when hit, tumbled down in a mix of feathers and false gore, to the wild amusement of the crowd. The last parrot led a charmed life, but with its eventual destruction, Fogg's cage surged upwards, close to the summit of the tent, and the door clicked open.

Fogg walked out on to a narrow shelf high above one side of the ring. A trapeze hung down, the bar level with his feet and in easy reach, the top secured at the centre of the top. *Go for it*, he said to himself. *I'm not waiting for orders.* The trapeze's angle, he decided, once released, was acute enough to carry to the other side.

He untethered the trapeze, seized the supporting ropes, stepped on the bar and hurtled across the Big Top to a shelf on the other side. A couple of bolts flew well behind him.

'*Hold your HORSES!*' bellowed the ringmaster.

A huge circular clock on wheels with a single hand was dragged into the ring from the mouth of the entrance tunnel. At the same time, more assistants laid a raised chequerboard landing area, where soft trampoline-like squares on springs alternated with squares of sharp vertical spikes. Fogg mustered a wry grin. His recovered memories had toughened him. He had stared death down once before. At least here he had a variety of deaths to choose from: a crossbow bolt, or one of the spikes, or maybe a lightning strike from the ringmaster's rod.

'You said we'd meet again,' said a voice behind Fogg, who almost fell with shock as the black moth stepped forward.

It was Niobe.

Her dark mask and black costume were adorned with dark purple beads, giving her an almost regal air.

Fogg moved to embrace her, but she shook her head. 'Listen,' she said, 'and listen hard, and we might just have a chance. You look fit enough.'

Thanks, AIPT, thought Fogg.

Below them, the ringmaster was delivering his introduction. 'Good games, like good kingdoms, have rules. Whenever the moths come to rest on their roosts, we give them a minute to recuperate, then they're FAIR GAME, in mid-air or not.' He flicked a hand at the giant clock. 'But not only does the third Lord Vane dislike inaccuracy, he likes his rules OBEYED. If you shoot when the clock is running, punishment will be swift and *SHOCKING*. Of course, our prizes are as special as our forfeits!'

This prompted a faintly hesitant cheer.

Niobe did not move her head, but Fogg followed her eyes up to the circular gap at the top of tent where the supporting poles almost met.

She whispered, while staring straight ahead, 'The trampoline squares are bouncy as hell and throw you extremely high. If one of us can land, feet together, from the maximum height, dead centre, and the other follows, we might just make it. If you land awkwardly or on the spikes . . .' She passed her finger across her throat. 'You're heavier, but I suspect I'm more accurate, so I go first. If I fail, go anyway. The last white moth didn't listen and ended life as a pin cushion. We'll do a pass or two to get our eye in, but, whatever you do, don't release too early.'

'If I'm going to die,' said Fogg, 'it's been worth it for seeing you again. Sorry for letting you down. I hope I get the chance to explain.'

She touched his arm, a gesture of forgiveness.

'TEN . . . NINE . . .' cried the ringmaster.

'Our chances reduce if we're both in the air at the same time,' added Niobe. 'And swing *under* the trapeze, it's faster that way.'

Everywhere Fogg looked, miniature crossbows, hundreds of them, were levelled at the space between them and the opposite shelf. The odds were not looking rosy.

Niobe, a quick learner from past experience, launched ten seconds before the second hand achieved the vertical, taking the audience by surprise. The chasing volley was wayward, and one unfortunate fired too soon.

A sliver of lightning jagged from the ringmaster's rod and the offender's body slumped forward.

'SPECIAL forfeits!' cried the ringmaster.

Niobe's early swing bought Fogg time while the audience reloaded. He joined her on the opposite shelf untouched.

'Now for the double bluff,' Niobe said in the interval allowed by the ticking clock. 'I'll go halfway and come back, and the moment I land, you go right across.'

Through the slits in her mask, Niobe's eyes gleamed with fierce concentration. Fogg sensed she was enjoying the contest, despite the likely end game.

The ploy worked. The audience fired ahead of Niobe, only for her to turn her hands in a split-second, twist her body round and return. Again, Fogg had an easy passage as the audience reloaded.

But the dynamic had changed, and the audience sensed it.

The wily black moth had cheated them before, but the white moth was visibly inexperienced, and now he had the trapeze without her to advise. The majority of the crossbows aimed at Fogg as the seconds ticked away on the giant clock.

Niobe, from the opposite shelf, mimed a pendulum motion. He must go to her and back in one movement: variation would confuse.

His flight to her went well enough, but his push back from the shelf was poor and the reverse journey too slow. To his amazement, the bolts passed perilously close – without striking him. A flash of gold caught his peripheral vision: a golden beetle, blessed with extraordinary agility, was deflecting the missiles. Jeers of frustration rose from the audience.

As he clambered to safety on the shelf, Niobe landed beside him. She pulled a bolt from her shoulder like a dart from a board and hurled it down at the crowd.

'What was *that*?' she asked.

'My guardian,' said Fogg. The beetle was now quartering the open space between them as if on the hunt, before settling into a stationary hover.

'It *knows*, Fogg,' she said, 'it knows. Change of plan. It's your beetle, so you go first. Drop *exactly* where it is. Trust me.'

Fogg looked down. From this vantage point, the spikes had more prominence than the open squares, and the clock was closing. He briefly clasped Niobe's hands. Below, the clicking of the crossbows ceased. The audience had reloaded and they sensed a kill.

'Now!' she shouted.

He swung towards the golden beetle and dropped at the moment of contact, feet down and tight together. Fearing the worst, he shut his eyes, only to find himself speeding upwards like a human cannonball. The beetle had not merely been prospecting a safe square, but the *right* safe square. He opened his eyes in time to grasp the crisscrossing ropes at the apex of the tent. The beetle had disappeared, but Niobe had memorised its position and followed suit.

They clambered quickly through the space on to the tent's exterior.

'This way,' said Fogg, pointing away from the Circus entrance. Below them, the audience had lost control and were firing bolts willy-nilly at their shadows. As Fogg and Niobe slid down, feet first, the canvas, pierced by many bolts, began to tear.

The ringmaster lost composure too, as enraged by these multiple infringements of the rules as by the escape of the prey. A jag of lightning forked through the roof of the tent, severing ropes and shattering poles. The crowd rushed for the exit, only to find the huge clock blocking the way. The high-pitched music of human hysteria matched the chaos which had ended the White Circus.

On landing, Niobe aided the collapse by releasing the nearest guy ropes. 'I've always wanted to do this!' she cried in glee, as the whole tent imploded like a collapsed lung.

'There!' cried Fogg, pointing at a triangle of unguarded gyrocopters.

Niobe had the presence of mind to seize two coats from a rack outside. 'And I've wanted to do this too!' She clambered into the central pilot's seat, with Fogg beside her. They fastened the securing belts around their waists as the rotors sprang into life and the craft sailed away.

'There are direction markings on the wheel,' Niobe said, 'WC, WD and H. Any idea which to go for?'

'WD,' said Fogg. 'That's where my friend is.' He paused. 'No, wait. H – go to H. It's nearby, and we're less likely to be seen there.'

'And which friend is that?'

Fogg ducked the question. 'How's that shoulder of yours?'

'Pinprick,' replied Niobe.

'You were terrific.'

'Nothing compared to that beetle of yours.'

He grinned. 'No credit to me; it has a mind of its own. It comes, it goes. It's why I didn't come with you at the School. It wanted me to stay. I think it came from the Vanes.'

'Nothing good comes from the Vanes,' hissed Niobe.

Seconds later the chitin shield closed over them and they sailed into darkness.

'Time to catch up?' Fogg suggested. 'Ladies first . . . ?'

Niobe removed her mask, shook her hair and glared. *I'm not a believer in 'ladies first'*, the gesture said.

'As I'm sure you've more to tell,' added Fogg.

Niobe told her story with clipped brevity. 'We found a spent tantalum mine. We had water, and the Matter-Rearrangers worked well enough. For two years or so we had a community of sorts. But a couple of seams had not been mined, and that was our undoing. Genrich sent a craft with an armed crew, and we had no chance. I don't know what they did with the others . . . hard labour, I fear, at best.' Her voice turned flinty. 'They kept *me* to entertain them, because I stand out.'

'The black moth won in the end,' was all he could say.

'The black and white moths together,' she added, the edge gone, however briefly. 'Then Lord Sine handed me over to Cosmo Vane. They make a dangerous pairing, those two. "For your amusement," he said. "I've no use for her."'

'More fool him,' replied Fogg. 'But what about the tantalum? I thought you were the expert.'

'Lord Sine is above such details, and if I'd owned up, I'd have been sent back to the school. No thanks, better the devil you don't know. Now what about you?'

He told his story as briefly as he could, excluding Morag's narrative, save where it overlapped with his own.

'A Museum with paintings!' She sounded envious. 'I bet you copied the lot.'

'One or two.'

'And this Morag watched you for three years without revealing herself? That's *seriously* strange.' She paused. 'But now you say she's your friend?'

'No more than that.' He felt a need to make the point. 'She's complicated; I'm complicated. Anything more wouldn't work.'

He introduced the redoubtable Miss Baldwin and the White Circus, describing the tutor's play with Cosmo and the ace of spades, followed by her abduction and death. He kept to himself only his exposure to the scanner and his more remote past.

'Poor woman,' Niobe said.

'Brave woman. It was self-sacrifice. She set out to provoke him.'

'Why?'

Fogg remembered Piety's rebuke. 'There was something she didn't want Cosmo to find out, and I think she doubted her ability to resist. Cosmo has machines that peer into your mind, and I think she knew that. But I've no idea what it was she wanted to hide.'

'I hope they all suffocate under that tent, suffocate and burn.' She paused as if having second thoughts about the ferocity of her remark. 'Do we get better or worse for experience?'

He reached over and clasped one of her hands. 'Innocence goes,' he replied.

The gyrocopter's control markings had not lied. The chitin shield retracted as they drifted into the valley of the Hunt. There was no sign of the *Aeolus*. They landed their much smaller craft in a depression at the edge of the valley.

They were glad of the coats, for the air, though still, carried a penetrating chill.

'This way,' said Fogg.

'Remember this moment,' said Niobe, looking up at a clear night sky. 'We are *free*.' She gave him a playful punch in the shoulder. 'And as your guardian beetle isn't here, I assume we're not in danger yet.'

They wandered into the wood as a sickle moon rose, more gold than silver.

Fogg quartered the ground, as if checking for a missing landmark.

'What's wrong?' said Niobe.

'This place is taken from an old painting, a great painting called *The Hunt in the Forest*. Everyone is searching, dogs and men. On one level, they're after these stags, but on another, they're seeking something more elusive.' He gestured around him. 'The trees are just as the artist had it, and the water, the reeds – they're all just so. And every stag is where he should be.' Fogg sounded half captivated, half unnerved. 'But the dogs are gone, and the hunters too.' He bent to examine the ground. 'And they were right here. Which means they can move.'

'Not all the hunters are gone,' said Niobe. 'Not this one.' She rested her arm on the shoulder of a single stationary huntsman.

Fogg's photographic memory kicked in. 'And he's just where he should be.'

'So let's make use of him. You can't prance around outside a Circus looking like that.' Niobe removed the huntsman's clothes. More work had been done on the face than the sexless, clothed parts of his body. The skin had a rubbery sheen and the joints beneath the clothes were more functional than realistic.

'We share,' said Fogg gallantly. 'I insist.'

'I'll take the hat and his under-tunic; you have the rest. Believe me, you'd find a mirror upsetting just at this moment.'

The white tights did indeed look absurd below the hem of the purloined coat, whereas her dark equivalent looked merely fashionable.

After changing, they walked to the heart of the wood, where the darkness seemed more profound, the air colder.

Fogg held out a restraining hand. 'Miss Baldwin warned against Winterdorf, but she did mention a small valley just east of the town. We might have a chance in our little craft. Airluggers have a mind of their own.'

'I dislike retreat,' she said, extending her hands into the void. 'We can go through, I can feel it. One more step . . .'

Fogg understood the urge. Niobe had always talked of escape. Now free, of course she wanted to explore. He had to be the restraining voice of reason. 'We're flying blind, Niobe, and the odds are, that path leads back to captivity. I trust Miss Baldwin. She was giving me a steer.'

'Come on!'

'Cosmo's fiefdoms communicate. They'll be waiting. Do you really want to live out your days in a cell?'

He had played the right card.

They wandered back to the gyrocopter.

'If it's just somewhere to hide away, I'm not staying,' she said.

'Nor me.'

'Or if it's a school,' she added.

The gyrocopter's chitin shield closed as they returned to the murk. Niobe flicked the direction lever to WD. 'Winterdorf first, then on before we're seen,' she said.

They were fortunate. The gyrocopter entered the Winterdorf valley well away from the town. Beneath them, a frozen river, grey beside the white of the snow, wended its way past outlying cottages and under wooden bridges. Here and there a window glowed in the darkness.

Niobe held the craft stationary. An eerie silence enhanced the scene. They looked in rapt wonder for several minutes, while Fogg suppressed the urge to share his knowledge of the painting.

'So that's snow?'

'Pure and simple.'

'What's it like?' she asked.

'Cold to touch, obviously, and soft at first, but you can knead it into solid shapes,' he replied.

'So you speak from experience?'

He found it impossible to lie to Niobe. 'It's a long story, which I keep to myself.' He pointed suddenly. 'We've got company. We need to go. Miss Baldwin said to the east.'

A line of black crows with an ominous, predatory look were drifting towards them, and despite the languid wingbeats, closing fast.

'I was saved by a virtual crow once, but this lot look horribly real,' muttered Fogg.

Niobe swung the craft back into the murk, but two birds followed, attacking the shield with their beaks until tiny splinter marks appeared in the chitin like ice on the point of fracture. They could smell the air turning foul. Then the craft passed into a patch of clear air, which prompted the craft's chitin shield to open, and the birds were in.

Fogg unbuckled the chain from his waist, stood up, trusted to balance and swung the chain round and round, while warding his face with the other arm. His counterattack drew the birds away from Niobe, allowing her to steer clear of the mountainside.

One bird caught a glancing blow to the head and spun away back into the murk. Fogg managed to get the chain around the neck of the second attacker. Close up, he recognised beneath the black plumage the same barley-sugar hue which had marked the lifeless crow on Miss Baldwin's desk. Its beak struck at his cheeks, but he kept it clear of his eyes. The bird quivered, twitched and went still. Fogg, taking no risks, kicked it overboard.

Niobe kept to the clear air.

'There's the beacon,' cried Fogg, pointing at a tiny affair compared to its neighbours at *The Hunt in the Forest* and Winterdorf, but in proportion to a valley which was little bigger than a large field.

'God knows why your friend sent us here,' muttered Niobe, neatly landing the craft.

The new landscape, as snowbound as Winterdorf, offered no river and no sign of life, save for a single tree with its leaves intact on the crest of a steep bank. A Tempestas tree.

Niobe gently ran a finger across Fogg's cheek.

'God, your face looks like a pincushion.'

'It feels like one.'

Cold and excitement had mitigated the pain, but now, with blood trickling down his face, his cheeks throbbed. They clambered out of the craft and headed for the tree. Below the bank, a circular bottle-green door nestled between protruding tree roots, with small circular windows on either side. A vigorous knock from Niobe produced the shuffle of slippered feet.

The door swung open.

Morag had a gift for description. The lined face, electrocuted hair, pebble glasses and the twinkling eyes left little doubt: here was the very epitome of a librarian.

'Is it – it must be Mr Potts?'

'Dear boy, it's Oblivious, and what *have* you been up to? And who is your delightful companion wearing the hat of a huntsman?'

'I'm F-F-F-Fogg, and this is Niobe.'

'Ah-ha, the one and only Niobe, daughter of Tantalus and the wife of the King of Thebes. I am truly privileged! Come in, come in. I hope you had a snowball fight. It's the greatest impromptu sport ever invented, and you don't need kit.' He studied Fogg's face. 'Or maybe best not when you're bleeding like a stuck pig. In, in.'

An extraordinary home greeted them, a bewildering mix of old and new. Globe-lights illuminated shelves which lined a warren of rooms and passages. On a small writing table lay an array of capsules for messages, sitting beside an old-fashioned Morse code machine.

'Librarians,' Potts said, 'are experts in burglary, because book-lifters are the enemy. Before the Fall, I practised the art myself. All stealth and no violence, of course, but I did stow away some booze for high days and holidays. You'll find a corkscrew on the table, glasses in the cupboard and a wine rack in the corner. Do the needful, Fogg, while I get bandages and unguents for your face and the shoulder of the Queen of Thebes. This is the large mammal room, if you feel like a browse.'

Half an hour of medical treatment, accompanied by gobbets of eccentric philosophy from Oblivious Potts and laced with the novelty of real wine, quickly restored morale.

'You'll have fetching scars, and you can embellish any story with a scar. They are the grace notes of fantasy.'

Well into the second bottle, Fogg broached the subject of a very different library. 'I blundered into the old Tempestas building,' he said casually.

'When you say "old", I take it you mean old as in "the first", as in "the original" Tempestas building?'

'I mean under the mountain.'

'So,' said Potts, 'you took the high road, and Spire's child took the low road. Who learned more, I wonder?'

'Do you have any of those books here? They seemed ever so important.'

Potts gave him a wary look. 'I have records of our work, of course, but only ours. The first Lord Vane had a dark side, which I leave well alone.'

Niobe changed tack. 'Who built your house, Mr Potts?'

Potts removed his spectacles. 'Craftsmen from Winterdorf built the shelves and the beautiful door. Lord Vane collected fine wood at the time of the Fall, and quarried stone. In his way he had an eye for the future as well as the present.'

'What about the heaving and lifting? What about the hard labour?'

Fogg felt a shift in Potts' attitude to Niobe as courtesy gave way to interest. 'I have the Northerners to thank for that. They live on the inhospitable side of the massif and are, as they wisely wish to remain, something of a forgotten people. I visit them, but few do.

They're proud and they're different. They don't need beacons, a quirk of the mountains, but their settlements are in deep gorges and dangerous to access by air.'

'How did they survive in the first place?' Fogg wondered aloud, earning in his turn an appraising look from Potts.

'As I said, the first Lord Vane had a future in mind. You can't build anything without muscle or machines, and most machines pollute. But the Northerners are all counterweights, cogs and pulleys. No excrement, you might say. So . . . that's how it was. They were the chosen labour force. Top up?'

Fogg felt the wine loosening his grip on reason. 'Do you know where Morag is?'

'According to my agent,' said Potts grandly, 'she is in Winterdorf, scouting out the ground.'

'We were warned off Winterdorf as being too dangerous.'

'May I ask by whom?'

'A Miss Baldwin.'

'Dropping the eyes, Mr Fogg, signals bad news,' Potts muttered apprehensively.

Fogg had no wish to darken the old man's warm and unexpected hospitality. 'It wouldn't go with your excellent wine.'

'She would not see it that way.'

Fogg embarked on the events at the White Circus, but, despite his encouragement to tell the tale, Potts was keen to delay the bad news.

'Tell me about her performance, dear boy?'

As soon as he had obliged, Potts followed up with, 'Bravo! And yours?'

Fogg obliged.

'Caravaggio! Ah, if only saviours walked into taverns every day of the week.' Potts shrugged and refilled his glass. He had been preparing himself.

'So Cosmo Vane was there. Tell me how it ends.'

At Miss Baldwin's death, Potts stood up, shuffled a few paces, turned his back and looked down the passage, leaning on the doorway for support. They could see the tremor in his shoulders.

Minutes passed before he turned back. 'Out and out *good* people are scarcer than tantalum, and I'm not one of them. She, however, was. She never turned a blind eye, as I sometimes did.' His voice quavered, and suddenly he looked his age. 'She and I might have . . . once, you know, but we didn't.' As if on a sudden impulse, he refilled their glasses. 'She would approve of a toast. To Miss Baldwin and her fight for the future.'

They downed their glasses.

Potts maintained conversation for a while, but his energy had drained away. 'Tomorrow's plan is breakfast's business,' he said. 'For now, follow me.'

They passed rows and rows of books, for the most part natural history, retrieved, presumably, from Pandora's place in the Tempestas Dome.

'Your rooms are at the end of that passage. We have snowmelt and minerals, and you have Rearrangers, should you feel peckish. See you at nine.' He smiled. 'You're opposite each other, by the way.'

'Thank you,' they both said.

'That's the wrong way around,' replied Potts. 'If anyone has the answer to Cosmo Vane, not to mention Lord Sine, it's youth. It's a privilege to be consulted, and to have your company. Dream long, travel far, and come down to earth in the morning.'

As they washed, they heard Potts singing a plaintive melody to his guitar.

> *'How do you find the soul of a tree?*
> *Forget June's leafy bowers*
> *And December's barren choirs;*
> *Go dig for the roots you cannot see.'*

Fogg was half asleep when Niobe slipped into his room.

'In our abandoned mine, I learned one or two things I'd like to share with you before anyone else does,' she whispered. She slipped off the coat she had taken from outside the Dark Circus and joined him. She was naked underneath.

'The black moth and the white moth,' she whispered, rubbing her skin on his.

15

Booting and Spurring

Potts picked up the threads of his evening narrative at breakfast.

'Beware the weather-watchers. The current big cheese is called Marcus and the family name is Jaggard. His father was a weather-watcher for the first Lord Vane and worked his way up. His son is as dangerous as Cosmo in his way. He's older, just as clever, doesn't lose his temper and plays a long game. It's rumoured that he has an Airlugger hidden away – one of only four built – and that he keeps in contact with Lord Sine. He plays the ascetic, but he has venal appetites and loves nobody but himself. Power is what he craves. He has taken an iron grip on Winterdorf in no time.' Potts paused to pour a second round of breakfast coffee. 'There's another thing. He *hated* Gilbert Spire – for his charm, his influence over the second Lord Vane, and for his reckless sense of adventure.'

'Morag did say her father was exiled,' commented Fogg.

'Marcus engineered it somehow: one minute, Spire was the Court favourite; the next, he was gone, and he never came back.'

Fogg could describe the cabin of the *Fram*, awash with maps and books on natural phenomena, as if it were yesterday, but that was his secret, and its associations were too painful to share. 'He went exploring,' he said, hastily adding, 'He must have done, because he never went home.'

'Only an explorer takes an Airlugger,' Potts agreed.

Fogg regretted raising Gilbert Spire, fearing his feigned ignorance of the man who had saved his life and nursed him through his grief would be exposed, so he changed the subject. 'Lady Vane has apparently disappeared.'

'Do we mind about *Lady* Vane?' asked Niobe frostily.

'We do,' said Potts, 'not because she's Lady Vane, but because she's sharp as a needle and does *nothing* without purpose. She's the kind of person you want to please, which gives her influence. Nor is she the retiring type, which makes me—'

Despite the soundproofing of the enveloping earth, a deep rumble rolled through the door.

Potts sprang to his feet. 'Tiriel speaks. Quick,' shouted Potts, 'it's as I feared. How many birds pursued you?'

'Two followed us into the murk, and we got both,' Fogg said.

'But there were five in all,' added Niobe.

Four long copper poles had appeared outside the front door.

'Take two each and follow me.'

Bizarrely, Potts placed a wedge of paste on a plate before hurrying them across the meadow, plate still in hand. Sleet swirled past in that haphazard air which precedes a storm.

'Pay attention!' Potts shouted over his shoulder. 'There's a precipitous drop ahead. In our perennial white-out, it's hard to see.'

Fogg and Niobe ran to the edge of the meadow. Below them, floating in a chasm as if in dry dock, was the *Aeolus*. A rope ladder on a windlass had been fixed to the cliff edge. Lightning flashed behind them, followed by an explosive clap of thunder. The sleet was fast thickening into snow.

'There are iron supports,' Potts said. 'Hurry, hurry – and then get well away.'

Thunder boomed around the ravines, while lightning jagged this way and that.

Niobe, sitting on Fogg's shoulders, placed the rods in their receptacles, but Oblivious did not obey his own instruction, instead standing on the edge of the drop, holding the plate above his head and whistling.

'He's a Southern Royal albatross,' he shouted. 'Watch, and be amazed.'

The bird was *huge*, and almost entirely white. It skimmed over Potts' head and took the paste.

Fogg staggered back and pointed at the giant bird.

'Now *that*, I call free,' whispered Niobe to herself.

The albatross made a second pass along the gorge, then settled in the rigging of the *Aeolus*.

'We're old friends,' said Potts. 'They lay one egg a year and live well beyond fifty. What's the lesson in that?'

The sky had turned the deepest slate. One of the conductors earthed a bolt with an ear-splitting crash.

'Back to the house,' cried Potts, as a second bolt struck the cliff opposite. A fall of rock just missed the deck of the Airlugger. 'You can't take off in conditions like this.'

A stupid question, Fogg knew, but he still had to ask it. 'Morag brought the *Aeolus* here single-handed?'

'Yes and no,' said Potts mysteriously. 'She had some unexpected company – by which I mean, not human. All will be revealed, don't you worry.'

Once back inside, Potts took Niobe in hand. 'He has boots, but you do not, and inequality of footwear is a bad thing on a long journey. Follow me.'

He rifled through a large cupboard, crammed full with several pairs of light leather boots and a miscellany of scarves, staves, coats and hats. 'It's the summer gear that was left behind in the Tempestas Dome. The hoarding gene comes from my grandmother.' He handed out gloves and socks with a wink. 'She always said, "Never forget your fingers and toes."'

'Where are we going?' asked Fogg.

'Where the Queen of Thebes has been wanting to go all this time. Winterdorf.'

Potts ushered them to his study, a windowless room in the centre of the house, where several postcards of *Hunters in the Snow* and the *Bird Trap* had been laid out.

Niobe was incredulous. 'You don't mean they built a town to resemble a picture?'

'More than *resemble*, my dear. It's a mirror image.'

'Why on earth do that?'

'Because it's beautiful, because it shows what we can do, and the place ...' Potts paused. 'It was a happy place.' He picked up a pencil. 'This cottage here belongs to my agent, Hilda Crike. She talks the hind legs off of a legion of donkeys, and she'll insist I'm *her* agent, but in between the self-flattering asides, you'll get the lowdown. She tells me there's a meeting in the Town Hall at six. That's here. I've little doubt Marcus or Cosmo or both will be there, so you'll need disguises. You'll also need one of these.' On a shelf lay several bird carcases in a row, as if awaiting a taxidermist.

Potts fiddled under the wings of a blackbird and turned to Niobe. 'When I raise my hand, say "*Turdus*".'

Niobe obliged.

He placed the bird in her pocket. 'Now he'll obey you and nobody else. In bird-speak, *Back to Oblivion* means back to me. To activate his recorder, press under the right wing. Take one of each card as a map and off you go.'

'I could do a thesis on dark stairwells,' said Fogg as he shook hands with Oblivious on the top step behind another cupboard door.

'Be sure it's in time for the Christmas rush,' responded Potts with wink. 'And here's a globe-light for each of you, in case you have an argument, which I assess as unlikely.'

'Thank you,' said Niobe, kissing Potts on the cheek. 'I'd like to visit those Northerners one day. Maybe you'll be there.'

'Maybe I will. To be overlooked in evil times is an advantage not to be sneezed at.' He turned to Fogg. 'Did Miss Baldwin say anything about premonition?'

'Yes.'

'Her own death?'

'That's how it came across.'

'She called it the spinster's eye. She told me years ago I'd follow her quickly, *unless* . . . But she never specified the *unless*.'

Niobe answered as Fogg floundered. 'She meant as long as you're tied to your books, you're predictable, easy to find and easy to destroy. Cut the moorings, Oblivious.'

'Aaah,' Potts replied, nodding sagely.

He watched his visitors go, then closed the cupboard door behind them. Not lovers before, but lovers now. *You can tell from the after-glow. The best-laid plans go a little awry and deliver more than they were designed for, but this one? God only knows.*

He returned to the clothes cupboard with a heavy heart to prepare for his own journey. He had had one warning. The *Encyclopaedia Britannica* would not save his life a second time. But what are books without the freedom to read them? The Queen of Thebes had been right. Cut the moorings. He must soon set out alone for that particular mountain where so much had been set in motion all those years ago. But for the moment, his guests, and their survival, required his attention.

16

Retribution

The ringmaster of the Dark Circus, wearing only a loincloth, had been bound to a black leafless tree not far from the Hindsight Inn. His arms were arms bent over the stubby boughs, his feet twisted behind the trunk.

'Well done, sir! You brought the house down,' crowed Cosmo, astride his horse. Various retainers stood around the tree in a semi-circle, crossbows dangling from their hands. 'You, or rather, your agony, will be immortalised, a privilege given to few.'

'Please, your Lordship, the lightning rod misconducted itself—'

Cosmo ignored the plea and continued to trot down his line of chosen executioners. 'My late father would approve of this tableau. You're Saint Sebastian, no less.'

Piety watched uneasily. The ringmaster was skilful and would be a loss. She liked him, too.

Cosmo raised an arm. 'Go for the joints only: wrists, knees, shoulders, ankles – and take your time. Then go for the five senses in the face. Then you can finish it. Anyone out of sequence joins him.'

He halted the horse. The arm came down.

17

Under the Mountains

The steps were narrow, slick and steep, and the globe-lights illuminated only the next two or three flights. Fogg and Niobe changed places every half-hour or so.

'Thank you for last night,' Niobe said after their second change-round. 'It's different with someone you really like.'

'I've much to learn.'

'You know what they say about perfection.'

Fogg felt uneasy with her directness. He could imagine the boredom in the disused mine, and the need for distraction, but he disliked the thought of their schoolmates sharing a bed with her.

He set about a diversion. 'What would be useful here is the Long Eye, but it's in Miss Baldwin's house. It's a telescope which can see in the dark.'

Niobe laughed. 'Learn from a miner's daughter: there are as many kinds of darkness as there are of light. There is coloured darkness, and darkness so deep it gives you nothing. This place is close to the second kind.'

The stairs gave way to a wide passage. Above their heads, ancient roots fractured the ceiling.

'We've come down a very long way, yet we're still level with tree roots,' observed Niobe.

Fogg reached up and twisted one, which snapped clean through. 'They're quite dead,' he said. 'Potts' house must be higher than we thought. Don't forget the gorge.'

She hugged him.

'I want to land a blow on Cosmo Vane,' she said. 'A real one, a full-on uppercut to the jaw, that kind of blow.'

'For that,' replied Fogg, 'you have to be patient and wait for an opening.'

'We're quite good together, aren't we?'

Fogg recoiled – not at the remark, but at a spill of bricks from the tunnel ceiling, which exposed a chamber above. He clambered up and thrust his globe-light through the cavity to reveal a grim scene. A table lay on its side, the chairs pushed back to the walls. Four skeletons splayed across the floor: two adults, a child and a dog.

'The Fall,' muttered Fogg, 'and close to Tempestas headquarters. They really did lose control.'

Niobe joined him. 'Look how basic the clothes are, and how simple the cellar – or maybe it's only a shelter. They must have been outliers with no chitin to protect them. Nobody cared.'

'I suppose we can't be sure. Maybe they were just unlucky.'

'You really must stop giving the powerful the benefit of the doubt when they don't deserve it.'

'You're right,' said Fogg. He had yet to share Venbar's bizarre revelations with anyone.

'We must hurry,' she said, retaking the lead.

They tramped on for hours, ignoring all deviations, as instructed by Oblivious, until confronted by another brick wall, this time straight in front of them, and intact. They swept away a shroud of dust and cobwebs, but they could see no door and no handle, ring or hinge.

Niobe pressed the most colourful brick, a striking apricot-red. It retracted, only to spring back.

'It's a simple mechanism,' said Fogg, 'five rows of five bricks over a long stone like a lintel at the bottom.'

'Why send us all this way without explaining?' asked Niobe, shaking her head.

'Bear in mind that eight numbers have more than forty thousand permutations; that's eight times seven times six times five and so on. A boy at school told me that. He said it would help me get to sleep.'

'Did it?'

'No. My point is, twenty-five is much worse.'

'Then that's not the answer,' said Niobe, kicking the wall. 'Oblivious wouldn't set us up like this. I know he wouldn't.'

'He rescued Morag, but she had to prove herself by solving a puzzle first, although I rather think her father set it. It was something to do with a butterfly's name.'

'Potts did say something odd when he gave us the gloves – something about your fingers and toes.'

Fogg looked at the bricks. Twenty-five meant nothing, but add the lintel and you had twenty-six: the number of letters in the alphabet.

'I think I've cracked it,' he said. 'I really do. It's so simple. The lintel is Z and the first brick top left is A. And the word is ten letters, as in toes and fingers, so, *Winterdorf*.'

He methodically pressed the bricks in sequence, spelling out the name of the town. The wall delivered a satisfying click and under a little pressure from Fogg's shoulder, slid a quarter open. They emerged at a crouch on to a sliver of riverbank beneath the arch of a low wooden bridge. On the Winterdorf side, the wall had been disguised with wooden slats.

A gentle sleet scudded by. The thunder had ceased.

'There's a cottage opposite,' said Niobe. She pulled the postcard from her pocket, but Fogg needed no assistance; memory was enough.

He peered over the bank. 'We're in Bruegel the Elder's *Hunters in the Snow*, middle-right background, just where we want to be, which is no coincidence, I suspect. It's where Potts' agent hangs out, and Miss Baldwin's too, if I remember rightly.'

'Do we just go up and knock?' asked Niobe, knowing she would attract instant attention.

The question was never answered, for the bridge creaked above their heads and a cracked old woman's voice attempted a song:

> 'Into the dark, into the dark,
> All the anglers go,
> Clockwork fish won't rise
> To my clockwork flies,
> Quite apart from the ice and the snow.'

The woman clambered down the bank, wicker basket and fishing rod in hand, her agility quite at odds with a decrepit appearance.

'Forget the cosy cottage. I, Hilda Crike' – she pronounced her name as if she were royalty – 'live in the shanky add-on. Quick, quick, before the sky draws the curtains and the skaters come out.'

In *Hunters in the Snow*, a man on a ladder stood on the roof to douse a chimney fire in this very cottage. Sure enough, a ladder of identical construction rested against the outside wall. Fogg and Niobe followed the old woman as she ducked beneath the main cottage window and ushered them into a long low single room, warmed by a peat fire.

After the briefest of introductions, Mrs Crike took the floor. 'Guess the time, Mr Wolf?'

'Two?' suggested Fogg.

'Three?' countered Niobe.

'Darkness plays tricks with time. Four forty-five and counting. We've little time and a lot to do.'

'I thought the meeting was at six—?'

'That's the trouble with Potts,' sighed Mrs Crike. 'His heart's in the right place, but the bonce is all askew. Do go if you want to pop straight into the poacher's sack. You're wanted, and as conspicuous as a butterfly on a sand dune. And you know nothing about this town beyond what it looks like.'

'Then why are we here?' Niobe protested with a scowl.

'You're here because I've a mission for the three of you!' Her eyes gleamed like a deranged fortune-teller.

'*Three* of us?' queried Fogg and Niobe in unison.

'Any mission worth its salt requires bait, brains and brawn,' said Mrs Crike. 'Meet Benedict Vane.' On cue, a door opened and in walked a strong-looking young man, and a Vane, beyond question. 'A long-lost cousin,' explained Mrs Crike.

Benedict shook their hands and delivered his intelligence. 'They're all going to the meeting – well, everyone who's able-bodied.'

'Thanks a bunch,' said Mrs Crike.

'Except Mrs Crike,' added Benedict.

'That's enough small talk, Master Vane.' Mrs Crike's bony fist struck the table. 'The mission! *Where?* Up that road for two miles to Tiriel's Tower. *Opposition?* Depleted, but expect a weather-watcher or two. *Objective?* Reconnaissance: we need to know what they're up to, especially Marcus Jaggard.'

'Potts warned us against him,' said Fogg.

'Well, he would, wouldn't he,' replied Mrs Crike as if she were the source of all wisdom.

Niobe had been eying Benedict Vane with suspicion. 'You're not a lord, then,' she said.

'Most definitely not,' replied Benedict Vane with easy charm.

He's almost too good to be true, thought Fogg.

'That's quite enough heraldry,' said Mrs Crike. '"Benedict" means "well said" in Latin, so we take him at his word.'

A dog entered the room, distinguished by his sad but friendly expression, a lopsided gait, one slightly discoloured eye and a tail which wagged erratically.

'This is Goya,' said Mrs Crike, 'and he's not a mechanical. He was given to the late Lord Vane by Lord Sine, and I've taken him over.'

Not only Goya by name, but Goya by origin, thought Fogg. The animal was the spitting image of the one he had drawn for Lord Vane. Once again he suppressed the urge to deliver a talk on Goya's black paintings, of which the dog had been the most famous in the old world. Goya nuzzled Mrs Crike's legs.

She patted his head with one hand, while ferreting in her pockets with the other. A generous assortment of keys on a string emerged, each labelled with a number. 'Mrs Crike filched these from the Tempestas Dome. The weather-watchers like immodest splendour, so they brought the Tower doors all the way here, so they should fit.' She chose a selection of the keys and handed them to Benedict. 'One is the outside door, two to eleven will be the interior landing doors as you make your way up.'

She moved to a large cupboard crammed with props and costumes. 'Skates, fishing rod, faggots of wood. When about mischief, declare an innocent purpose. And Herr Bruegel offers plenty of choice. But no dillying, there's a price on your pretty heads.'

Only at the door did Fogg voice his most pressing concern. 'Where's Morag?'

'At the meeting, where else?' replied Mrs Crike.

'But I thought you said—'

'She's gone as me. Talk about a plum part! And I've added the vapours, to buy her space. That girl can act.'

'Miss Spire is resourceful,' added Benedict in a calm, matter-of-fact way.

'Can we get on?' added Niobe.

'When you've muffled that face,' responded Mrs Crike.

'I don't need to be told, thank you,' replied Niobe. 'But we'll need rope. You always need rope.'

'Now that's what I like: practical suggestions.'

Mrs Crike obliged, and they left in gathering gloom.

18

The Keys to Paradise

Mrs Crike had announced the scent as *Essence of Age* before dabbing the viridian-green oil behind Morag's ears. The stale, sad aroma served well: one and all gave her a wide berth. To minimise attention and maximise the view, she placed herself on the extreme left at the very front of a packed Town Hall. An elderly tramp whose natural odour was the essence of something even nastier helpfully occupied the seat beside her.

'Long time, no see,' he barked at Morag.

'When the wind blows from the east, there's no knowing,' she replied, as coached and in keeping with Mrs Crike's deranged reputation. So far, her disguise was holding.

A sullen silence reigned: the silence of a citizenry cowed into submission and shamed by their inaction. Mechanical huntsmen on horseback and on foot crisscrossed the square outside, and the town's children were under guard in the church.

Centre stage sat Marcus, flanked by weather-watchers, clasping his lightning rod like an extended sceptre.

One of his retinue announced him in deferential tones: 'The Master Weather-Watcher Marcus will now address you.'

Marcus walked unhurriedly from his seat to the rostrum. While short on the orator's flourish, he spoke with clarity and without rushing. 'Ladies and gentlemen of Winterdorf, I do not propose to revisit recent events, save to say their roots lie in old sins long forgotten and hitherto unpunished. I am only concerned with the future – *your* future – in this admirable town at the heart of our empire. I say "empire", because our outlying valleys have been left independent for too long. Winterdorf is their natural capital. Out there somewhere, Lord Sine and his grotesque creations plan our annihilation. We have captured new monstrosities who can breathe the murk.'

This news prompted a communal intake of breath.

'They want our land, our minerals, our genetic material for their foul experiments. Even now, Genrich's mutations are plundering *our* outlying mines. We must be prepared to counterattack. I have studied the generals of the old world: passive play always loses.'

He clacked his rod on the floor before continuing, 'First, we must eradicate the enemy within. Morag Spire, Lord Sine's spy, is back. She helped Lord Sine destroy his last failed round of creatures, but she did it for *him*, not us. She is Genrich through and through, and a chancer like her corrupted father.'

Morag seethed at this, a ruler's speech: *Reality, whatever the truth, is what I say it is.*

The audience, however, were visibly lapping up this tissue of lies.

'There's a reward for her head, and for any clue that leads us there. But we must have her alive.'

'She was with Mrs Crike early doors before the horsemen came,' said one.

'That's Mrs Crike over there,' added another, pointing at Morag, who stood up as if in the grip of advanced arthritis.

'We're sorry to disappoint, but we can't tell a hawk from a handsaw. Who is this Morag?' croaked Morag.

With impeccable timing, her neighbour came to the rescue. He stood up beside her and swept the room with his arm. 'Stop bullying them what can't defend themselves. We all know Old Crikey gabbles to anyone daft enough to listen and she's eight to the dozen. Lay orf.'

'May your shadow never grow less,' Morag croaked to her neighbour as he sat down.

'In hard times the half cracked keep together,' he croaked back, but she did not like his expression. It looked as staged as her own performance.

The central door at the back of the Hall opened to admit Cosmo Vane and a clutch of retainers, none of whom Morag recognised. She felt a surge of revulsion at the parricide with that permanent cock-of-the-walk, know-it-all expression who had left her grandmother to die and killed her friend Hernia. She fought the urge to leap on stage and denounce him. She wondered, too, about Lady Vane, her absence and her kindness. Had she gone the way of her husband?

The audience stood up for Cosmo.

Cosmo sat down.

They sat down.

Cosmo had a private exchange with Marcus, and Morag caught the words 'scanner', 'Fogg' and 'paintings'. The scanner had been the device which had absorbed her thoughts before transferring them to the weavers to be individually captured and transformed into momenticons. Cosmo had been hunting through Fogg's mind for clues.

She forced herself to relegate concerns for Fogg's welfare and concentrate on the matter in hand. Fogg could irritate for mankind, but he had kept her presence from the psychotic twins and mastered the *Aeolus*. He would not have surrendered these secrets readily. But had he had a choice?

Her anxiety deepened when Cosmo produced the bottle of momenticons she had left behind in the tavern during the attack and whispered again in Marcus' ear. The Master of the Weather-Watchers returned to the rostrum and resumed his address with a marked change of tone.

'We have the unexpected pleasure of his Lordship's return, and with important news. The Spire girl, the spy for Lord Sine whom I mentioned earlier, may be in the company of two young fellow infiltrators, who have recently escaped. One you cannot miss for her black skin. The other is a slim, pasty-faced man. But let me repeat, Miss Spire in particular must be produced to us *alive*.'

Morag could not resist a fleeting smile. Hope lived on. Jaggard's pasty-faced young man had to be Fogg, but who was the black-skinned young woman? She must be resourceful, as she couldn't envisage Fogg escaping Cosmo's clutches without assistance.

'And keep your eye out for a map made of many pieces sewn together,' Marcus added, just before ending the meeting.

Morag wracked her brains, trying to work out how her list of momenticons, or the pills themselves, could have any significance. The ability to visit long-dead artists at the seat of their work might be remarkable, but its relevance to Cosmo's hard-nosed imperial game escaped her. And what was this map, whose existence, it appeared, Fogg had unwittingly disclosed?

As she hobbled along the road out of Winterdorf, she knew she needed answers, and quickly.

19

Tiriel's Tower

Fogg had used the journey to Tiriel's Tower to update his companions about his discoveries since leaving the *Aeolus*. For intangible reasons, he trusted Benedict, and from experience, he trusted Niobe. The revelation that the first Lord Vane had initiated the Fall prompted concern about the roles of Mander and Potts, but Fogg liked to believe that they, as so many others, had also been deceived.

'Then why was Mander collecting the world's great artefacts?' asked Benedict.

'If you believed these terrible storms were an accident, you'd want to preserve our finest achievements, wouldn't you? I know I would.'

'How does the world get these leaders?' asked Niobe, palpable anger in her voice.

'We vote them in, or we let them in,' said Fogg. 'It's like now. Cosmo Vane wins through because he's amoral and ruthless. Maybe we should just give up on decency.'

'Then we all go to the dogs,' said Benedict quietly.

The tower and the rock at its base blended with the mountains behind. The spire was not so tall that it broke the skyline. Even the road skirted the entrance by several hundred yards. They eyed the elaborate entrance door with the words *Praemitte Tempestas* predictably carved on the lintel.

'What now?' asked Fogg.

'I behave outrageously,' said Niobe. 'They might open the door for me, but they certainly won't for you two. So get out of sight!'

Benedict, who had remained silent during this exchange, pointed at the observation panel in the door and positioned himself on one side of the lintel. Fogg shrugged and took the other side.

Niobe hammered the knocker down, twice. The echo played through the massive tower. She knocked again, furiously. A single set of footsteps eventually came, and the observation panel flipped open.

'Who the hell are you?' said a young man's voice.

Niobe sounded operatic, measured but strident. 'I command the winds. My face is burnished by the sun. I demand an audience.'

'There's nobody here.'

'There's you for a start.'

Pause.

'What did you say you do?'

'The weather isn't all thunder and lightning, and nobody messes with me. I've an urgent message for your master. But I'm not sharing secrets with a one-eyed door and a man I can't see.'

'What's your name?'

'Auster.'

'I've never heard of you.'

'That's how I like it.'

'All right, Auster, I've strict instructions . . .'

'To let no visitors in. I'm no ordinary visitor. I'm a friend of Marcus Jaggard, with urgent news about Miss Spire. You have ten seconds, or I'm off.'

'I don't believe you.'

'Miss Spire is on a wanted list. I suggest you reflect on the consequences of *not* opening that door. Ten, nine, eight . . .'

A lock turned.

The door eased open a few inches, enough for Benedict to get purchase. He flung it wide and Niobe poleaxed the weather-watcher with a straight right to the jaw.

'The meeting will have started,' Benedict said. 'We haven't long.'

Niobe bound the guard to the staircase with Mrs Crike's rope and filled his mouth with her scarf. 'A present from the black moth,' she whispered in his ear. They hurried up the stairs, which spiralled around a central well filled with coils of wiring, towards the tower's summit.

With a little trial and error, the doors off the various landings yielded to Mrs Crike's keys. Banks of screens tracking weather patterns dominated the rooms beyond. Though modest in scale compared to Mr Venbar's great tower, all the desks were in use and every surface was spotless. Marcus' study occupied the entire seventh floor, his status apparent from the Master's ceremonial dress hanging on a rail, the quality of the furniture and a rack of lightning rods. To Fogg's surprise and amusement, the Master took trouble over his physical fitness. A space had been left on a shelf, crammed with large volumes of weather charts, for an AIPT model identical to his own in the Museum Dome.

The locks to his desk resisted all comers. On the top, paperweights secured a detailed map with mysterious diagrams. Beside it stood a pile of atlases.

'I can't help you with this,' said Benedict.

'I can,' said Niobe. 'They're largely my work.' She shuffled through the pages and consulted the paper markers in the atlases. 'At the Fall, they lost control of satellite technology. He's trying to match geology surveys with conventional maps. He's after tantalum. Most of the old mines are cleaned out now, but there is the potential for unexplored prospects.' Niobe paused. 'The odd thing is, I worked for Genrich, not Tempestas. This bastard is playing a double game.'

Fogg offered another perspective. 'Morag's father was on a mission to find tantalum when he disappeared – everyone thought it a blind, but was it? Maybe that's why they're so desperate to track him down.'

'I'm afraid I know nothing of this,' replied Benedict, as if his ignorance were a personal failing.

'We need to hurry back,' said Fogg. 'It's well past six.'

'Perhaps we could disable the lightning,' suggested Niobe.

'No time,' replied Fogg firmly.

'Then I'm taking a souvenir,' said Niobe, seizing one of the shorter lightning rods.

Benedict restored the papers on Marcus' desk to their original position and scrupulously relocked each landing door.

'Think of the guard,' he said. 'He's done nothing wrong. The less visible the intrusion, the better his chances.'

At that moment Niobe reappraised Benedict. He might not be so bad after all.

They left the guard in a state of groggy recovery and headed at speed back to Mrs Crike's house.

2 0

A Close-Run Thing

After the meeting had dispersed, Cosmo, Piety and Marcus adjourned to the private tavern room which Morag, Benedict and the late Lord Vane had occupied just a few days earlier.

'So,' said Marcus, 'fill me in.' Looking at Cosmo tossing the jar of momenticons up and down in his hand, he asked, 'Are they the key?'

'One of them is. They were left a trail they were too dim to see.'

Piety had never seen Cosmo so radiant.

The landlord knocked on the door.

'I said,' hissed Marcus, 'his Lordship is not to be disturbed.'

'Damned if you do, and damned if you don't,' replied the landlord, 'but I've a man here who insists on speaking to Lord Vane.'

Cosmo waved a lordly hand. 'As you found the momenticons, Landlord, we'll allow you one mistake. Show him in.'

'I'd hold your nose, my Lord.'

A foul-smelling tramp, Morag's neighbour at the meeting, sidled in. Incongruously, he shared with Mrs Crike an affection for the royal 'we'. 'We slum it, my Lord, and we live off scraps,' he grunted, his tongue licking his lips.

'You'll do worse than that, unless you tell me what you know.'

'Mrs Crike ain't Mrs Crike.'

'You don't speak in riddles to Lord Vane,' said Piety menacingly.

'We ain't here to be mocked,' said the tramp. 'We goes by our nose, we do. That weren't Mrs Crike at the meeting. It were a suppositor. She scarpered like Mrs Crike on the lane to 'er place, but the longer she went, the quicker she got.'

Cosmo sprang to his feet. 'After her!' he cried.

Morag had indeed gathered pace. She could not believe that Cosmo had found a solution which had eluded her. Cosmo's search for a map meant a search for a specific location. Just before his death, during their meeting in the tavern, Lord Vane had said that her father regarded Paradise as a real place to be found and protected, and he had funded her father's expedition with that very objective in mind. Suppose her father had found this place? The only connection between him and momenticons was their shared gift, but how could that reveal a map?

She returned to Fogg. He knew nothing about Paradise and nothing about her father's gift, so it had to be a remembered image which had excited Cosmo's curiosity and put him on the trail.

She replayed in her head the fateful day when the Museum Dome clock had stopped and their new mission had launched. But it wasn't only the clock that had failed. AIPT had told Fogg to explore, *and* the Matter-Rearranger had delivered a virtual antique trumpet instead of coffee.

Morag stopped dead in her tracks. *The trumpet.* And the Rearranger had mentioned an artist by name. Belatedly she realised quite how extraordinary both actions were. She had an answer, or at least half a possible answer.

Half a mile from the bridge, cries echoed behind her. Horsemen were closing fast; she could see the riders' lanterns bobbing along. She jettisoned her cap, picked up her skirts and ran, but she had no hope of escape without help.

She shouted, 'Cavall!' and whistled, and the mechanical hounds lolloped towards her from a nearby snowfield.

'Stop the horses!' she commanded them.

Without breaking step, the eight dogs turned, bounded on and attacked the mounts of her pursuers, many of them their one-time partners in the *Hunt in the Forest*.

Pandemonium broke out. She heard Cosmo's voice crying, 'Disarm them – *now!*' but the hounds evaded the riders, viciously snapping at the horses' legs as they tried to resume the pursuit, constantly switching the assault to those most likely to break free.

Morag ducked down to the riverbank and sprinted towards the bridge. She had no idea how to open the door from the Winterdorf side, so she could trust only in luck and Mrs Crike.

Iced-over mud slowed her down, but she made the arch of the bridge, where a single limping dog joined her, its skin torn and internal machinery damaged.

Above her, someone was walking the boards of the bridge.

'Quiet, Cavall, stay,' she whispered.

The passage door was ajar. She and the dog squeezed through and Benedict slammed the door shut behind them.

Mrs Crike relished long odds and the stage.

The young man's mount had torn legs, through which a moving mechanism was visible.

'Who the hell are you?' bellowed Cosmo.

'Mrs Hilda Crike, when I last checked the mirror.'

'She's not the same woman,' said his companion, a woman dressed in dark leather.

'Were you at the meeting?' asked Cosmo.

Mrs Crike shook her head vigorously and brandished her fishing rod. 'Alas, my kind of advocacy is out of fashion. It's all prose and no poetry these days.'

'Did you see a young woman?' asked Piety.

'She ran right past my fishing hole and dropped that mask on the way. A spitting image of yours truly. Bloody cheek.'

'She's heading for the tower,' suggested the young woman.

'Get back to your hovel, or I'll have you strung up,' Cosmo bellowed at Crike, turning his horse towards Tiriel's Tower.

'No worries, young sir. Even clockwork fish don't like clodhoppers over their heads.'

Crike disassembled her fishing rod and marched back to her lean-to.

Nobody looks beyond the demented. Play the White Queen. Hide in plain sight.

21

The Art of Painting

'This is Benedict,' said Fogg.

'We're already acquainted,' replied Morag.

'And this is Niobe.'

Morag shook her hand. 'Ah yes, the other escapologist. You're headline news, the pair of you. Good to see you, Fogg, but we've no time for a catch-up. Cosmo thinks he knows where Paradise can be found. He says a scanner told him. Paradise, by the way, appears to be a real place.'

Fogg lowered the globe-light, shrouding his face in shadow. 'He used a scanner on me, but thanks to your story, I was able to prepare. I did my very best to give him no more than a tour of the Museum, but he may have seen the Monet momenticon and what it did. I'm pretty sure he didn't get a glimpse of you.'

'And the conversation with the Matter-Rearranger? The antique trumpet? The name Vermeer?'

Pause.

'That could be. Towards the end I did run out of paintings.'

Niobe stamped her foot. 'Can *someone* fill in a poor miner's daughter? Who's this Vermeer?'

'Fogg knows best,' said Morag.

'Jan Vermeer was an old-world artist who lived in the city of Delft. He lived in a time of plague, war and economic collapse . . .'

'Tell her about the paintings,' interrupted Morag impatiently.

'Well, the Museum had three . . .'

'Tell her about the *Muse of History*.'

'It happens to be my favourite,' replied Fogg, irked by the inter-ruptions, 'and one of Vermeer's too. He never sold it. He painted himself painting his model dressed as Clio, the Muse of History. She holds a history book in one hand and a . . .' Fogg stopped and slowed. 'And a trumpet in the other. Just like the trumpet the Rearranger produced instead of coffee!'

'The poor miner's daughter is still lost,' said Niobe.

'And what's behind Clio?' asked Morag, now enjoying herself.

'A map – in fact, an enormous map, which takes up most of the facing wall.'

'A map! Aha!' Niobe cried, 'we're getting warmer.'

Now for the burning question, which only Fogg could answer.

'What's it a map of? I don't know, but I bet you do,' said Morag.

'The seventeen provinces of Germania Inferior, otherwise known in the old world as the Netherlands,' replied Fogg instantly.

'There's no tantalum there,' protested Niobe. 'It's all coastal sediment. That can't be Paradise. We're wasting time.'

'It's a toxic desert, to boot,' added Benedict as an array of Tempestas statistics and maps flitted through his head.

'Damn,' muttered Morag. 'Damn, damn, *damn*.'

Benedict reflected on his visit to the Paris railway station. 'When you take a momenticon and get to where the artist is, can you touch an object?'

'I could feel the bridge at Giverny,' replied Fogg, 'and I could smell the blossom – but you don't bring anything back.' He added ruefully, 'Well, apart from the memory.'

'Yes,' mused Benedict, 'you bring nothing back – but might you do something there?'

'It would break the connection,' replied Morag, only to hesitate. She had brought a tiny flower back from the hillside in the icon, hadn't she.

'*Your father had the gift too, in his own peculiar way,*' Matilda had said on their last evening together. She had also said, '*The better you get, the longer you can stay, and the more you can do.*'

So maybe . . .

Benedict continued, 'Suppose it's not the map itself, but a direction marked on the map?'

'By whom?' asked Niobe.

Morag began to mumble as potential implications burgeoned. 'By my father, because he wants me to join him, if and when I'm ready, if and when I've proved myself.'

'The only problem with that theory,' said Fogg gently, 'is how on earth your father could know you'd learn to make momenticons and end up in a museum with that exact painting – let alone that particular Matter-Rearranger to give you a steer?'

'He has the same gift, and he would know if he were in on the whole arrangement from the start,' Morag admitted. 'He could still be alive and in touch with Potts and Mander. The odder question is why you were put there with me.'

Fogg shrugged. He did not want to go *there*; not with Morag, not with anyone.

Benedict came to the rescue with a change of perspective. 'Cosmo knows Morag makes momenticons. Cosmo sees the trumpet as an intended clue. Cosmo works out that if you have the gift, so did your father, and your father was the man searching for Paradise. He decides that the map might hold the answer.'

'And I'm afraid Cosmo has my other bottle of momenticons, including the one for this particular painting. Fortunately, I also have a small reserve jar of my favourites. *The Muse of History* is one of them.'

Niobe intervened. 'If the map can be written on, it can be unwritten, and from what I know about your friend Cosmo, that's what he'll do if he gets there first.'

Niobe's words rang true.

Morag fumbled in her pocket and produced the small bottle. Fogg held the globe-light close.

'It's this one,' she said. 'I'm well practised now – I can last for quite a time. But don't touch me, whatever happens, or you'll break the spell.'

'Be careful,' said Benedict.

Niobe offered water, but Morag had already swallowed the momenticon.

Morag has never encountered such stillness in a room. Behind the curtain sits the artist, wearing red leggings, a slashed black velvet jacket over a white shirt, black sash and jaunty cap. On a table, a strange-looking box faces the model, whose dress and pose mirror the painting exactly. The black and white tiled floor, the chandelier with the double-headed eagle, the trumpet, the map – they are all, like everything else, *just so*. She is there in spirit, not in body, but if the theory is right, her father has contrived to do both.

She glides towards the map, keeping in touch with the artist's thoughts to maintain the connection: Vermeer is painting himself painting the painting. She edges to the map. It is huge, many separate pieces stitched together. The bearings are tiny, but they appear in the most accessible bottom right-hand corner. Her father has made no effort to hide them.

She memorises them before returning to the painter's work in progress, which is more advanced than on her first visit. She is mesmerised by his ferocious concentration and his facility for matching what he sees to the painted image.

As she admires, a hostile presence intrudes. A pleasant scene morphs into a haunted room. Even the artist looks round.

Cosmo has not come for enlightenment. He is here, as ever, for power and plunder.

Before she can erase the figures, the map explodes into confetti, the room heaves and fragments – but at least she has what she came for.

'Sixty-two degrees fifty-eight minutes south; sixty degrees thirty-nine minutes west,' Morag spluttered. 'But Cosmo was there too. I was just in time.'

Morag could think only of her father, and of getting to him before Cosmo Vane.

'What now?' asked Benedict. 'Mrs Crike's reconnaissance mission was also a diversion. They'll look for us round the tower first, but only for so long. We can't go back to her.'

'Where will Cosmo think we've gone?' asked Fogg.

'Potts,' said Niobe. 'They'll know two of their birds have disappeared, and they'll guess where. He's in real danger.'

Morag snapped from her reverie. 'Run!' she suggested.

'Run,' Niobe replied.

'*Turdus firstus*,' Fogg said, prompting Niobe to extract Potts' bedraggled mechanical blackbird from her pocket.

'Say that again?' asked Morag.

'I was attempting a practical joke.'

'Potts Post,' explained Fogg. 'You dictate your message and let it f-f-fly.'

'That's not a *practical* joke, Fogg,' Morag said, 'it's a *bad* joke with a practical message.'

Niobe flicked the switch and delivered the message slowly. '*Cosmo back; with you soon; Paradise possibly regained; pursuit likely; on your toes.*'

Then she uncupped her hands and said, '*Back to Oblivion.*'

The mechanical wings whirred and the bird flew off down the tunnel.

'Now we run,' said Morag, and they did so, two abreast, Niobe with Fogg and Morag with Benedict, who had slung the stricken dog over his shoulder.

'You do realise that's a machine?' Morag asked.

'Maybe that makes two of us,' he replied.

They changed the lead from time to time. Running behind them, Morag sensed an intimacy between Fogg and Niobe, but without the bite of jealousy. She was more preoccupied with Benedict. His calmness did her good, but did its origins in programmed knowledge rather than real experience matter? Predictably, he had an elegant, loping stride and breathed with the ease of a practised runner.

They completed the return journey in half the time.

Potts was there to greet them. 'Quick, quick, my children,' he urged.

'We know where Paradise is,' said Morag, and when she gave him the bearings, he looked both relieved and concerned.

'They feel right, but it's a hell of a journey, and—' He held his qualification back, saying instead, 'The *Aeolus* is provisioned and ready for boarding. Fogg, with the help of that stolen craft, I've retrieved your belongings from the White Circus. Now, off you all go.'

He hustled them through his front door. In this kinder weather, they descended the cliff edge to the deck with ease.

Benedict gently laid the twitching dog down beside the wheelhouse.

'Hurry, hurry,' repeated Potts.

Benedict and Niobe looked lost. He had not been programmed in the ways of an Airlugger, and her youth had been confined to subterranean caverns and the Genrich School for Idiot-Savants.

'Fogg's the skipper,' said Morag. 'Just do whatever he says and we'll be fine.'

Fogg lived up to his billing. 'Benedict, think of it as an old-world sailing ship. So, that's the windlass to haul up the anchor. Niobe, there are pulleys for each bag, and numbered wheels for each pulley. We have to balance the sides or we'll go up crooked and catch the side of the gorge. You take portside, that's the right, and I'll take the left. Just do exactly what I say. Now, wheels 3 and 4, two turns.'

Like Morag before her, Niobe wondered at Fogg's transformation.

'Wheel 1, just a half, so we lean away from the gorge a little. Leave the others well alone.'

The bags in question tilted almost to the vertical as Benedict wound in the anchor and the *Aeolus* rose from her mooring. The diapason hummed contentedly.

'That means you're doing splendidly,' said Fogg. 'We'll work on Morag's bearings as soon as we're clear.'

'I think I know how,' Morag replied, heading for the wheelhouse.

The ship rose without a single contact with the edges of the gorge. Fogg's intuitive grasp of a precarious exercise he had never done before was remarkable. Or was her premise wrong, Morag wondered.

As they cleared the canyon edge on an even keel, they cheered. Potts emerged from his house in a white robe with a white hood, which made him near invisible. He carried an atlas in one hand and a strange mask in the other.

'You're going to Antarctica,' he shouted up.

'Where in Antarctica?' Fogg shouted back. The very name meant only death to him.

'Deception Island,' Potts replied.

An instant later, the calm shattered: three of Cosmo's gyrocopters emerged from the murk, supported by a small flock of raven-like birds.

'Go! Go!' yelled Potts. The old man discarded his atlas in the snow and ran back up the slope towards his house as nimbly as a man half his age.

Fogg bellowed his orders. 'All ropes to three, in order, starting with number one. We head for the murk.'

On the deck lay the boat hook and Fogg's other belongings, returned by Potts. Now the pulleys were in place, Niobe seized the boat hook and attacked any bird in reach, while Benedict found a light anchor and whirled it round his head. But they had no apparent defence against the gyrocopters – until Potts, now back at his house, released a flock of birds of all sizes and colours, clearly with orders to counterattack.

Nor was the old man finished. He ran to their stolen craft, took off with ease and joined the dogfight.

The diapason screamed and Fogg swore: a crossbow bolt had pierced a sack. 'Take three and seven back to zero,' he shouted. 'We have to keep her stable.'

'What *is* Potts doing?' Morag muttered to herself as she punched the bearings into the device in the cockpit recess. The *Aeolus* responded to the instruction, but the new course was leading them right across the open line of fire, just as Potts' craft veered away from the fray towards the beacon.

'What the hell's that?' cried Niobe, as a magnificent white bird dived at high speed to shatter a crow attacking another windbag.

Only Fogg had grasped Potts' strategy. The strange mask had been the giveaway. He yelled up to Morag, 'Close the shield – there's a manual override beside the wheel.'

Morag sank to her haunches. *Override? Where?* She could only see a brass plunger, so she pulled it – and just in time. The shield closed as Potts reached the beacon and turned it off.

The murk flooded in.

Caught by surprise, the gyrocopters were engulfed before their own shields could close. Potts' craft disappeared from view.

To Morag's relief, Hector had made it back to the ship's rail.

The diapason settled into a discontented grumble.

Morag descended from the wheelhouse. 'He's called Hector,' she told Niobe. 'He's a Southern Royal albatross, and he's real. Cassie gave him to me – maybe she knew where we were heading.'

'I'm worried about Potts,' said Fogg. 'He didn't get his shield down in time – I reckon he didn't want them to guess what he was up to. He's sacrificed his home and his books for us, and himself too, unless that suit and mask did the trick.'

'We had them in the mines,' said Niobe. 'Even the basic ones give you a good hour or two, so let's keep our fingers crossed.'

The *Aeolus* was still lurching, the diapason protesting.

'Fortunately, we have a couple ourselves on board. We're hopping rather than running at the moment, so we'll have to repair that sack.'

He retrieved the necessary repair equipment from the same locker as the suits. At the stern, the shield had a tight, barely visible airlock which would enable one crew member at a time to ascend the rigging above it.

Niobe volunteered. 'I've not been much use until now,' she declared. The suits were light, almost like a second skin. 'It's a job for the black moth,' she added, pulling one on.

'And the white,' added Fogg, reaching for the second suit before anyone else could offer.

Above the shield, the murk had a hostile quality. Visibility was minimal, the air was freezing and vocal communication proved impossible.

The bolt had passed clean through the bag, leaving two opposing holes. With a bone needle and thick thread like yellow string, Fogg and Niobe set about patching the chitin-coated sack. She worked the needle one way through the resistant material and Fogg threaded it back, and somehow, between them, they managed it. Re-emerging on deck, they had the satisfaction of hearing the diapason abandon its grumble for a contented hum. The ship levelled and acceleration picked up.

'*The Crike & Potts Show*,' said Morag with a smile before addressing a trickier subject. 'There are two cabins and the bunks are well spaced. I suggest Benedict and I take the top cabin; Fogg and Niobe the lower.'

Nobody dissented.

Potts had reprovisioned the ship in their absence with warm clothing, a second Rearranger and small crossbows and bolts. Fogg's rescued belongings had been secured in a small travelling bag. To his relief, both the Long Eye and the barometer, his parting gift from the Captain, were there.

He returned the Long Eye to Morag. 'It saved my life,' he said.

For the first days, they slept late and shared highlights from their respective adventures. Niobe led an exercise regime on the foredeck and cultivated a relationship with Hector.

Benedict painstakingly restored Cavall, the last surviving dog, plying a much finer needle and thread for the skin and using a discovered set of microtools for its innards. In fact, he did more than repair: once pronounced fit, the others discovered that the mechanical now responded to a range of hand signals devised by Benedict.

At the end of the first week, they agreed to a serious review of the past in the hope of working out what might lie ahead.

'We're taking quite a risk,' Morag pointed out. 'Paradise may not exist, or the bearings may be wrong, or it could be a trap.'

'I can only say,' said Fogg, 'that Potts, Mander, Mrs Crike and Miss Baldwin didn't think it a trap. They wanted us to take this risk.'

'Imagine a tantalum mine huge enough to keep us going for centuries,' said Niobe.

'We need to start at the beginning,' said Fogg. 'Mander collected the art ages ago, in the time of the first Lord Vane. He and Mr Spire were close, and they must have seen how Cosmo was turning out. So Morag was chosen for the Museum Dome.'

Morag shook her head, but he insisted, 'Oh yes, you were. You're unsullied by the F-F-Fall and have a special talent. They hide you safely away and set a trail. You have to prove yourself to get here, and so far you have.'

'Bollocks! I'm a nobody, and so are you,' replied Morag. 'And this rosy retelling won't do. Even if my father is still around, he's a selfish bastard who ran out on his family, drove my mother to suicide and ruined *his* mother's last years. I sincerely hope this wild goose chase isn't to rescue him.'

Fogg broke an uneasy silence with an uncharacteristically emotional comment. 'Your f-f-f-father also inspires loyalty and puts himself out for his f-f-f-friends.'

Morag hammered the table with both fists. 'How the fuck can you know that?' she yelled.

'Steady on,' said Benedict calmly.

'Because he did it for me,' Fogg said gently.

Silence.

Morag stared at Fogg, pale with rage. She shook her head in disbelief. 'He did *what*?'

'My parents were scientists at the outer reaches of Antarctica. I was born at the research station. The murk came late to us, but come it did. I didn't want to be a burden, so I took a kayak and rowed to a small island – Petrel Rock, if you're interested. The *F-F-Fram* happened to be passing, nothing other than an outrageous f-f-fluke. Your f-f-father . . . well, he adopted me. He said he could never equal my parents, but that he would do his best. And he did. He never gave anyone his name. To the crew and to me he was always "the Captain", but I know it was him. It's your eyes, Morag, at certain times. Eventually, he took me to the Genrich School, and the rest is history.'

The seashell clasped to Fogg's ear in the marches of the night and his mastery of the *Aeolus*' idiosyncrasies now made sudden sense.

Niobe put an arm round his shoulder. 'That's why you're anxious going back.'

'The murk leaves nothing,' said Fogg, 'just so much dust. But, yes, I'm anxious going *anywhere* near there.'

'Why didn't you say?' asked Morag.

'Your f-f-father told me grief has to be buried. He said sharing makes the pain worse and he should know. I've f-f-found it wise advice until now.'

'Any other revelations?' said Morag, her rage spent.

'Well, yes,' said Benedict, 'as it seems to be confession time.'

'No,' said Morag, 'that's *not* necessary.'

He patted her shoulder. 'I rather think it is.' He turned to the others. 'My father ordered me from Lord Sine. I'm a genetic construct with the faults ironed out. I know more than any of you, but also so much less.'

'You mean you *are* a lord?' asked Niobe.

'Succession is for *natural* heirs, not freaks from a Genrich birthing pool.'

Another silence.

'Does Cosmo know who you are?' asked Niobe.

'He might think there's a cousin on the loose, but, whatever he thinks, he wants me dead. He wants everyone on the other side of the board dead, and a pretty checkmate too. Obviously.'

'That figures,' said Morag.

Benedict relieved the emotional siege by shifting the gears to more practical matters. 'Deception Island is in the South Shetland Archipelago. It's six miles long and four miles wide. It had the safest harbour in Antarctica.' Images played in his head. 'It's shaped like a croissant.'

'A *what*?' Niobe said, laughing.

'A croissant – an old-world pastry. It looks like a crab with his pincers out. In the old days, whales and penguins abounded. There may still be volcanoes.'

'Give us names,' said Fogg. 'Come on, Mr Know-it-all, share whatever you've got.'

Benedict smiled. He had that rare glow which camaraderie bestows. 'Fact-sprinkling, it's how you get labelled a bore,' he replied, drawing on various literary tropes.

'Names!' the others demanded in unison.

Benedict suddenly looked weary, as if this were an act he had tired of.

Morag gave him a peck on the cheek. 'Please,' she said.

'Well, if you insist. Deception Island is rich in them: Neptune's Bellows, Fumarole Bay, Sewing-Machine Needles. And for the rest, you'll have to wait. I understand one should always leave a few surprises.'

Morag felt her defences crumbling. Benedict was taking on his vast reservoir of data and seeking out humanity. She kissed him again, and his cheeks shone.

'Hector must be told,' said Niobe suddenly.

The conversation blossomed.

They would never be happier.

Jaggard sat in his study, putting into practice a lesson from legend. Offer three goddesses the prize of a golden apple for the most beautiful, and they will fight. Offer two powerful men the way to an invaluable treasure, and they will fight, only in their case, to the death. Lure Lord Sine to Deception Island with the promise of tantalum, and he and Lord Vane would, with luck, eradicate each other. He knew Spire was dead, but they did not. He was, he reflected, puffing out his chest, an unusual kind of double agent. He served three masters, but only one who mattered: himself.

He picked up his pen and began to write.

Dear Lord Sine,
I have information of mutual interest . . .

22

What's Bred in the Bone

Lord Sine had kept his side of the bargain, honouring the truce with Tempestas by abandoning the Genrich Dome for more modest quarters, if a large house with an old-world portico could be called modest.

The humbler workers toiled away in underground bunkers like ants, out of sight and out of mind, save for their end product and the half an hour a day they were allowed to enjoy the gardens. Lord Sine's new replicants shared the efficiency of their predecessors, without the anxiety flaw, but they had even less capacity for original thought. In consequence, outliers did most of the creative tasks which Lord Sine could not be bothered to address himself.

Syphax emerged from underground and made her way towards the house. A modest beacon, the technology stolen from Tempestas, kept the air clean. She caught a flash of red in a remote shrubbery, where an unfamiliar middle-aged woman was wagging her finger at a gardener. Syphax could see no cause for complaint. Foliage and flowers, all in tidy, serried rows, offered a wide variety of shape, colour and texture. True, if you peered into the throats of the blossom, you would see only a stub without style or stamen: a barren garden, for all its luxuriance, but that limitation did not bother Syphax. Indeed, the approach seemed appropriate. She had come about a flower, after all.

She eyed the stern face of the guard. He would need some persuading.

Whenever depression struck, induced by some disappointing aspect of his latest creatures, Lord Sine would retire to his new study to read the opening chapters of *Genesis*. The sixth day must have been one hell of a day: animals first, humans to follow. Having messed up on humans, no wonder He needed a rest on day seven. He had not even got his orders right. *Be fruitful and multiply*. Fine idea, if your starting couple are intelligent survivors, but where does it end as eras come and go, as the genes twist and dilute and overcrowding stifles the planet?

I shall succeed where You failed, because, unlike You, I discard my failures.

This train of thought never failed to lift Lord Sine's spirits in these darker moments.

23 sidled in. Lord Sine put down the Bible and peered through the window, noting the young woman kicking her heels on the garden path.

'Apologies, Lord Sine.'

'An apology suggests what follows isn't worth saying,' Lord Sine hissed. He half relished and half resented the ease with which he induced incoherence in his minions, and he made no attempt to fill the silence.

23 hopped from foot to foot before stammering, 'My Lord, she doesn't even merit a number.'

'She will talk only to you.'

'Who is *she*?'

'Syphax.'

'Who is Syphax?'

'She's a gene-splicer.'

'We have scores of them. What's different about this one?'

Silence, the silence of a frightened man: fear of wasting his master's time hanging in the balance against the fear of costing his master a revelation that might matter.

What's different is her persistence, you fool, thought Lord Sine, *but why waste pearls on swine.* 'Send the woman in,' he said.

She's an outlier, Lord Sine instantly concluded. She wasn't one of his – she was not uniform enough for that – but he could see qualities in her height and stealth: feline, in a word. The cat who walks by herself.

'What is this secret?' he hissed. 'You have three minutes.'

She showed no interest in the time limit, instead measuring her words with care. 'The name is Syphax. I'm here because I deserve recognition.'

Lord Sine would have had her instantly removed and eliminated, but for the restless intelligence in her eyes. Outliers could surprise him still.

'I asked, what secret?' he repeated.

'Your Lordship was interested in the Spires. You should be still.'

Outliers did show defiance from time to time. It was crude stupidity usually, but he liked to test them, just in case. 'How do you know of my interest?'

'You examine their genomes more than any other.'

'My inspections are classified.'

'The lock is easy to break.'

'And why should I renew my interest?'

'Mother, son and granddaughter share an unusual cluster of cells by the optic nerve.'

Lord Sine's visits to such data files are indeed classified and encrypted, but he shelves that point for the time being. 'That is blindingly obvious.'

'Indeed, but do you know what the cells do?' asked Syphax.

Half fuming, half intrigued, Lord Sine merely glared.

'They catch energy,' she continued.

'Really? From what?'

'Objects . . .'

'Objects!' responded Lord Sine. His incredulous expression was untypically close to outright laughter.

'Paintings. It's the optic nerve, after all.'

'Prove it,' he snapped.

'I was intrigued by Morag Spire's work at Infotainment, so I visited her room at the old Dome.'

Quite a display of initiative, decided Lord Sine, *and a brave one, entering an outlier's quarters in breach of a whole raft of rules.*

'In her bag, I found an ancient icon, and with it a pressed flower. I removed a flake of paint and a snip off one petal.' She paused for effect. 'They're not only both centuries old, they're *exact* contemporaries. And . . . that very flower appears in the icon.'

Lord Sine opened a drawer. His chubby fingers dabbled in a pile of lapel badges liberated by the purge at the Tempestas Dome. He slid one across his desk.

'50,' he said, 'and quite a promotion. You will work here, when summoned. But that will do for now.'

After the gene-splicer, suitably gratified, had departed, Lord Sine turned his attention to the closing sentences of the message from his weather-watcher mole in Tempestas.

'Despite his disgrace, Spire secured an Airlugger for his exile on the strength of an undertaking to look for tantalum. Knowing Spire as I do, if he is alive and settled on Deception Island, it will hold tantalum in abundance.'

A strategy began to form which might net both the Spires and the mineral he desperately needed. If he could destroy the Vanes too, all the better. With his secret ally, Tempestas would soon follow.

He flicked a switch on his desk. 'Get me the Hatter, and an update on the Goliaths. *Now.*'

A slight knocking noise came from a cavity beneath the floor, home to a private cabinet at least double the size of a human coffin, where he housed in near-freezing conditions batches of novel multicellular lifeforms of particular interest. Preoccupation with the relative failure of his last human models, and his creation of real, thinking *Looking Glass* characters (just to show Tempestas that he could go one better than them) had led to its neglect. These miniscule constructs mixed and matched cells from different natural organisms. Gilbert Spire had been working on one of them, Lord Sine recalled, at the time of his exile.

Another switch on his desk should have lifted the cabinet into view, but instead the mechanism juddered and stalled. He peered down. The cabinet's steel sides had buckled.

Feeling anxious now, Lord Sine called for assistance from the lobby. First, he had the cabinet's temperature lowered even further, to neutralise whatever had done this damage. Then he ordered his minions to prise open the lid.

Steam coiled from the cabinet's interior.

'Don't touch *anything*,' hissed Lord Sine.

The cabinet's interior had been destroyed, with shards of broken phials and trays littering the surface. Nothing alive was immediately visible.

'Get the thickest leather gauntlets you have and clear the debris.'

The minions, though programmed to obey Lord Sine's commands, retained their rational instinct for self-preservation and proceeded gingerly.

Only one construct emerged, having apparently destroyed or assimilated all the others. Unevenly shaped and a dark mahogany colour, the organism had grown to the size of a small fist. On its surface, small lignified filaments stood erect like hairs in an attitude of fright. The sharp drop in temperature had had no effect. Its surface pulsed faintly, like a heartbeat fluttering the skin.

'Bring our strongest reinforced coffer and seal it in – and I mean *strongest*,' Lord Sine commanded. 'Give it nothing to feed off.'

Senior assistants arrived to secure the strange object in its new home, which far exceeded its size.

Lord Sine took 13, his most reliable geneticist, to one side. 'There was brain tissue in there for the *Wonderland* creatures, and cardiac cells too, but it's absorbed them all,' said Lord Sine. 'What does it suggest to you?'

'A most unusual seed.'

'I agree,' replied Lord Sine, 'but what does it grow into, if anything?'

13 could only shrug. He had never encountered such an object. 'What shall we label it?' he asked.

'*Arbor spirantia*,' replied Lord Sine.

'Is it a known species?'

'I assume not,' he snapped. 'It's the kind of play on words that outliers find amusing. Spire worked on it.'

The man looked blank.

'An outlier who worked here once,' Lord Sine added.

'Creator?'

'An outlier called Spire.'

13 suppressed his surprise that an outlier could fashion something so outlandish.

'Where shall we put it?' he asked.

'Out on the rocks, where the murk shifts and we can see it.'

'That's likely to kill it.'

'We'll see,' said Lord Sine. 'Place a sensor inside and report any growth without fail.'

'Yes, your Lordship.'

The Hatter's imminent arrival for his diplomatic briefing prompted Lord Sine to turn his attention to more immediate threats and possibilities.

23

The Great Game

Lord Sine's ambassador walked in, placed his top hat on the table and, uninvited, sat down. He wore a red costume which ended at his knock knees, and blue-and-white-ringed socks with cross-garters.

Cosmo Vane half smiled. Lord Sine must have created this ludicrous figure with the mop hair, buck teeth and demented smile to declare his peculiar talents through those very looks: *I can do better than you, better than Infotainment. I can create body and mind. I can make imagined people real. I can bring a book to life, flesh-and-blood life.*

The resemblance between the Hatter and Tenniel's illustration of this unstable character troubled Cosmo more than his father's obsession with replicating paintings. A wiliness in the ambassador's eyes had put Cosmo on his guard.

'I know you're not as mad as you say you are,' said Cosmo jovially.

'I know I'm not as sane as I think I am,' replied the Hatter.

'I need your master's help to take an outlier stronghold code-named Paradise. Our database suggests there are scientists there, the best genetic material imaginable for your master's laboratories. My proposal is simple. He gets the people, or whatever remains of them. I get the place. It's a generous offer, as only I have the bearings.'

Cosmo tendered an envelope and offered a hand.

The Hatter ignored both.

'Lord Sine wants one of the Spires, the father or the daughter. It doesn't matter which, but the father would be nice. If they're there, he might be interested.'

Cosmo tossed his hat at Piety as if she were a lady-in-waiting, and, uninvited, sat down. 'Our intelligence suggests that if old Spire is alive, he'll be there, and the daughter is on her way in an Airlugger.'

'He wants at least one of the two *alive*. That's our condition.'

'Have you ever tried a scanner?' Cosmo asked. 'Just a single thought, of your choosing. I'd be most interested to see it.'

Cosmo hankered after a sly peep into the Hatter's mind, but his visitor was not to be fooled.

'We hatters like our heads intact, and you shouldn't patronise, Lord Vane. Your virtual frolics are nothing to me. I'm a new model. Diplomacy is my talent. Nobody means quite what they say. Nobody says quite what they mean. Then we all shake hands and make a grand announcement. Like: *Lords Sine and Vane agree to carve up Paradise.* We do it to hear the little pieces clap and the cheap cards drum their feet.'

'Is Lord Sine serious about this venture?'

'He is serious about the Spires – unless, of course, you offer up yourself instead. *Whoops!* I meant what I said! I said what I meant!'

Piety winced. The Hatter was chancing his arm, but Cosmo merely grinned.

'A Spire alive and kicking in return for the place, then,' said Cosmo.

'Both Spires, the father especially.'

'Both! For such a prize, your master will have to contribute rather more. My requirements are in the envelope. Deal?'

The Hatter opened the envelope and read its contents three times, the right way up, the wrong way up and then in a mirror produced from his pocket. 'It looks sound from all angles,' replied the Hatter. 'Paradise regained!'

He placed the envelope in his hat and offered his hand.

Cosmo disliked the handshake, and not just for the clamminess. The Hatter wore a new and eager 'mission accomplished' look.

But Lord Sine did not know what he knew.

24

Making a Perfect Storm

One down and at worst, six to go. Marcus Jaggard sat at his desk in the Winterdorf tower, weaving a black ribbon in and out of the fingers of his right hand. He had written down the six names to illustrate the enormity of the task confronting him:

Cosmo Vane
Cassie Vane
Benedict Vane
Lady Vane
Morag Spire
Lord Sine

He smiled at one absentee, the loathsome Gilbert Spire, whose disposal long ago still gave him pleasure, though it was not a crime he had any intention of revealing. Let Lord Sine expend his energies on the thought he might still be alive.

The contrasting reactions of the populace to his address and Cosmo's harangue in the tavern had convinced him that the power he craved, power over all, would not come easily. His hopes of an alliance with Lady Vane looked slim. Regrettably, she was showing no signs of forgiving him for his little lapse. Cosmo had a weakness which only he knew, but it was not yet a card to play. Benedict Vane threatened his designs, as did the Spire girl, who was not only the offspring of that bastard charmer but supported by persons unknown. Eradicating them both without Cosmo knowing would simplify his upwards path.

As for the final hurdle, that game might never be played if Lord Sine and the Vanes could be persuaded to destroy each other. After all, he had the private ear of both.

The map in front of him showed Potts' newly discovered miniature realm close to Winterdorf. He summoned his best weather-watcher.

'You know when they left, and from where. You know the winds and the barometric pressures. You know their destination. You know an Airlugger's average speed and that – by some miracle – one of them at least can fly it competently. You know how the weather systems move and how far and fast we can move them. I want a storm to end all storms, far enough out to leave no visible wreckage.'

The weather-watcher consulted his charts and marked out co-ordinates with a pencil. 'Precisely here,' he said, 'and precisely then.'

'Many birds with one stone,' replied Jaggard.

25

A Title Which Fits

Hilda Crike angrily wiped her sleeve across her cheek. Crocodile tears were a valuable part of the trade, unlike the real thing, which she considered a sign of weakness. She had acted a demented crone for so long, she had lost touch with whatever her normal self might be. True emotion had been buried deep by the stress of resisting malign forces and the demands of secrecy, but now it had surfaced, raw and exposed.

Daily communications from Potts and regular bouts of his company, his offbeat humour and fighting spirit, had been an anchorage. He had offered her love once, decades ago, and she had declined, not for lack of affection, but from the conviction that in the turmoil after the Fall, her independence mattered.

For days, she had heard nothing from him. She had seen the gyrocopters arrive in Winterdorf and forewarned him. She had seen three leave Winterdorf and not return, followed by two which had come back. Had the young ones, with all that promise, perished too? Had Cosmo Vane's forces caught the *Aeolus* at its mooring? She would totter once more into town with Goya and listen for any crumbs of intelligence.

Hidden away beneath her floorboards, she kept her database of lost literature. She did not read fiction, for fear it would soften her ability to combat the hard edge of reality, but from time to time she allowed herself to skim the titles. An old favourite stood out on this particular morning. It summed up a healthy faraway term objective and, with it, the price to be paid, and so gave comfort of a sort: *The Loneliness of the Long-Distance Runner*.

IV

COLOURING IN

I

Terra Incognita

Aeolus' passage through temperate air to biting cold occupied many days, and in this last phase, Hector came to life. As the rigging above the shield acquired silvery pennants of ice, he ran up and down the ship rail. He allowed Niobe, and only her, to stroke the nape of his neck.

They found board games in a locker and, bizarrely, quoits, two badminton rackets and a tube of shuttlecocks. Benedict would only play games of luck. Every possible chess opening, every combination in backgammon, every probability at cards he held in his head. Luck's random gifts gave more pleasure.

One morning Fogg introduced AIPT, as rescued from the Museum Dome, and relieved Niobe of the burden of running their exercise regime. Lashed to the mast at a height where it could see everyone on deck, AIPT delivered one hourly session a day (to the minute). The machine coped readily with the influx, until the end of the session, when it turned judgmental.

'Man 1, despite years of tuition, has his usual faults. Woman 1 has promise but no discipline; Woman 2 has discipline but little promise. Man 2 is perfection. Observe how the quads work with the spine, how the hamstrings are strong but never tight. Relish the symmetry.'

This repeated panegyric embarrassed Benedict and infuriated the others. A week in, Fogg disabled AIPT on the hour in the interests of crew unity.

They kept their tempers. Morag and Benedict talked and embraced like lovers, but Benedict had not pressed for anything more and something, not a lack of desire, was holding Morag back. She wanted to know the whole truth before committing, and there was a dark void at the centre of the narrative that unsettled her. Fogg's presence in the Museum Dome now made more sense than hers. Had she been manoeuvred there to help him track down the map or, God forbid, to partner her father's adopted son? She had grown fond of Fogg, but not in *that* way.

As in the Museum Dome, personal rituals eased the monotony. The conventional challenge of steering a true course did not apply here, for the wheel had locked. They were in the *Aeolus*' hands.

Every hour, Benedict would walk Cavall on a circuitous route, encouraging the dog to ascend the mast to the shield and back, while gradually expanding the range of commands. Niobe perfected her gymnastics on a rope strung between the masts. Fogg, preoccupied by the thought of Antarctica, and Morag, tantalised by her father's fate, found relaxation less easy. A book of more rarefied card games provided a measure of relief.

One night, fifteen or so days in, Niobe, lying beside Fogg, eased open the door to her own childhood. 'It's odd, Fogg, to think of you brought up in the glare of sun on snow and me in caverns underground.'

'I had my share of near perpetual night. Midsummer's day is the shortest day in Antarctica.'

She ran her finger along his clavicle. 'I inherited my nose for tantalum from my father. He was infallible, but his skill cost us dear. Genrich were forever moving us on. We never had a settled home, and our last was a sprawling, ugly mine. I was there when my father gave his verdict: "The safe seams are worked out. The one that remains should be left."'

Fogg stayed still. He sensed an unburdening.

'But of course the Genrich overseer knew better. He insisted on being escorted to the last deposit. Deeper and deeper we went. At the mouth of the last chamber, my father said to me, "You stay here, and don't move an inch." He wasn't the kind of man you disobeyed – not in a mine, anyway. The roof of the chamber had fissured like cracked ice.

'"Dead quiet, *if you would*," my father said, but the bastard overseer walked to the middle, pointed at a seam of pegmatite and yelled, *"Tantalum, tons of it!"* at the top of his voice.'

'The echo sounded like the breaking string of a huge instrument. Then came the roaring thunder of a cave-in. They didn't even try to get the bodies out. "They're well buried already," one of them said. So there my father lies, beside the imbecile who killed him. Now you know why I dislike authority.'

'Well, he'd be proud of you,' were the only words Fogg could find.

In the darkness, a musical note tinkled, sounding like a tiny bell. Fogg leapt to his feet – he had never heard that noise before, neither on the *Fram* nor the *Aeolus*.

'Where's it coming from?' asked Niobe, scrambling into her clothes. Though dulcet, the sound had an eerie, warning quality.

Fogg fumbled his way to the source: his travelling bag and, more specifically, the strange barometer. His gift from Gilbert Spire all those years ago had come to life.

'The Captain gave it to me,' he explained, holding it flat in his palm.

Niobe sniffed the air. 'It's horribly humid all of a sudden.' She held a globe-light over the instrument, which revealed the pressure needle on the main dial was descending alarmingly fast. Fogg wished now that he had examined the instrument with more care. The face had numerous smaller dials and needles.

Above them, they could hear Benedict and Morag stirring in their bunks.

The bell continued to tinkle. The chill night had turned sultry so quickly that sweat spangled their skin.

'This is unnatural,' said Niobe. She steadied herself against the bunk and tried to make sense of the instrument's complexities as the vessel began to heave and the diapason to grumble. 'Why does a barometer have an altimeter – and what are the eight small dials for?'

'Wait a minute. Spire said he designed it, so he must have had a specific reason and a purpose; and as far as I know, he only ever flew Airluggers like this one.'

'So,' exclaimed an exasperated Niobe, 'all right, we agree this weather is truly abnormal.' As if to confirm the point, a silvery flash transfigured the entire sky, but without a hint of thunder. 'Weather-watchers?' she snarled.

'And it's not a barometer,' cried Fogg in a flash of revelation, 'it's an Airlugger defence system!'

They clambered into their clothes and rushed on deck to find Benedict and Morag already there. The vessel had begun to rock and the humidity to climb as the diapason turned shrill and the barometer chimed ever faster.

'What do we do?' Morag yelled at Fogg as the *Aeolus*' creaking timbers joined the cacophony.

'We trust to your f-f-father,' Fogg bellowed back. He examined the numbers on the eight dials as they changed in response to the imminent assault. The larger altimeter dial had two needles. They had no time for theories, so he hastily explained his conclusions.

'The main dial is barometric pressure, and it hasn't stopped falling. On the medium-sized dial beside it, the moving needle shows our actual height and the stationary needle our recommended height. The eight tiny dials in two columns of four, each numbered like a clock, represent the eight windbags, left and right. As the *Aeolus* is a sister ship, we have to hope it works for us.'

He rushed through his orders:

'Morag, take the right side. One and three, four reefs; two reefs on five, and leave seven as it is.' Fogg hurriedly calculated the adjustments for the even numbers. 'Benedict, secure anything loose on deck.' A fragmentary memory came back from the distant past, from another violent storm, but this time on the *Fram*. 'Niobe, I think there's a wheel on the mast, close to the shield. Turn it if you can.'

Niobe clambered up the mast, located the small metal wheel and turned it, raising a silvery spike into the murk above the shield.

Meanwhile, Hector and Cavall had decided on shelter; Hector in Niobe's cabin and Cavall in Morag's.

As two sets of parallel bags turned vertical, the *Aeolus* rose at speed.

Benedict resumed his role as a substitute Potts. 'It's sound in principle: eagles rise above a storm by using the thermals which bring the weather,' he announced.

An extravagant bolt of lightning suddenly engulfed the craft. The spike could not earth the lightning, but it dispelled the bolt as if itself the source of power, the hand of Zeus. Seconds later, an ear-splitting explosion deafened them all.

Thunder unannounced from a distance bursts straight over your head? Come on, Fogg thought, *pull the other one*. Clasping Spire's barometer, he resorted to hand signals.

Niobe dropped back to the deck as the vessel lurched sideways.

There was another flash, another simultaneous detonating roar.

Then, as abruptly as it had begun, they rose clear of the storm like one of Benedict's old-world eagles. Beneath them the murk sporadically glowed and growled.

They cheered as the temperature fell sharply and the humidity vanished, all save Fogg, who remained glued to Spire's barometer, which was maintaining its fretful tinkle. He shook it, but to no effect.

'Wait!' he cried, before yelling out fresh instructions. 'We have to descend again – *now!*'

'Back into the storm? That's bonkers,' said Niobe.

'No eagle ever does that,' added Benedict.

Morag shivered. The fall in temperature was as unnaturally sharp as its rise had been. 'Do what he says!' she cried. 'It's a trap – the coup de grâce in case we survived the first blow!'

Fogg yelled out another set of contrasting readings to Niobe and Morag, who were manning the pulleys. Two rows of bags inverted as the first shards of hail hammered on the shield. Down *Aeolus* dived, graceless as a stricken bird. The early blows were rattling like pebbles on the shield, but in minutes, large stones of ice started flailing the vessel, which yawed and shuddered under the impact.

Rocks next, thought Fogg, *and we're lost.*

But as they descended quickly, prow dipped, the surge of cold air above weakened the thunderstorm below. The hailstones liquefied into torrential rain and the thunder and lightning did not return.

The *Aeolus* settled, Cavall and Hector emerged, the rain abated, the hail's obscuring white mantle on the shield melted away, the diapason hummed and the barometer fell silent. This time the cheer for their triumph over the elements went unchecked.

'That was *not* Cosmo,' said Morag with a firm finality.

'How can you possibly know that?' asked Niobe.

'It's not Cosmo's way. He wants me alive, and he likes to be present for his victories.'

Fogg thought back to the third Lord Vane and to Miss Baldwin. 'She's right,' he said. 'It's not his style – and he does like to watch.'

'But it is Marcus Jaggard's,' added Niobe. 'You should have heard Potts on the subject. He's stealthy, ruthless and clever.'

'He's also an arrogant lecher,' added Morag, remembering his pawing hands at the Tempestas party.

'I should have waited in the Winterdorf tower and finished him off,' muttered Niobe. 'We have three surviving rulers: Sine, Vane and Jaggard. And they're all bastards.'

Fogg remained the practical sailor. 'We must check the shield for damage and retract the conductor.' He paused and flourished the barometer. 'Morag, we owe our lives to your father.'

Morag weighed the implications, which were disquietingly familiar. *Had the gift been a mere memento, or had it been intended as a counterpoint to the weather-watchers in years to come? If the latter, had her father expected her path to cross with Fogg's?*

Wheels within wheels within wheels.

'Maybe, maybe not,' she muttered back.

2

Reunion

The storm had delivered a sharp reminder of the enemy's reach and ingenuity and the dangers they faced. They checked, cleaned and oiled the crossbows. They found and mended the hairline cracks in the chitin shield, using a device whose function had hitherto eluded them. Benedict set out to calculate their distance from Deception Island, having discovered that Spire's versatile barometer also recorded distance travelled.

On the very morning that Benedict announced that they must be close, danger returned. Niobe caught a sulphurous tang in the air moments after Fogg observed that the murk on the eastern side had acquired a darker core. Turbulence followed. Fogg ran back to his cabin to retrieve the barometer, but Benedict was quickest.

'Hard away,' he bellowed up to Morag in the wheelhouse, 'it's a volcanic plume.'

The diapason shrilled a warning.

To Morag's relief, *Aeolus* sensed the threat too: the wheel, usually unresponsive to any attempt at a drastic manoeuvre once a bearing was set, did not protest as Morag spun it as hard as she could. *Aeolus* leant like a schooner catching the wind. A chittering of tiny rocks and volcanic glass on the shield confirmed Benedict's diagnosis.

Benedict and Niobe bent back over the upward rail as the bags wheezed under the strain. They had never experienced such speed.

The altimeter needles kept together: this was not an attack they could rise above. Nor did the dials change.

Fogg, not sure whether to reduce or increase the contribution from the windbags, adopted a middle course, on the grounds that generating their own power would assist stability.

'Hold on hard,' screamed Niobe as the diapason rose a note.

Seconds later, with a violent lurch, *Aeolus* broke through into clear sky and settled into a comfortable cruising speed. The shield rose and they peered down at a brilliant blue ocean. Winterdorf had stunned each of them on first sight, but after a diet of tight claustrophobic valleys, they felt drowned in space. A few suds of high cumulus measured their shadows on the sea. The air was pleasantly warm.

Only Benedict, always analytical, looked back. How could a clean ocean be sustained, let alone held in? The answer lay in a huge, jagged ice-wall, stained ochre at the edge of the murk, but turning white on the seaward side.

Morag pointed at a small iceberg drifting sedately beneath them like a meringue. Hector settled fleetingly on the rail beside Niobe, then flew in a sweeping arc down towards the sea. His three-metre spread of feather and bone left *Aeolus* trailing in his wake.

Benedict added the Nature Notes. 'They're monogamous – they mate for life – and if they lay it's not more than a single egg every year.'

'He and his kind are made in the image of God,' murmured Niobe, 'not us.'

'I can't see any land,' added Fogg, relieved to see no sign of Petrel Rock or its neighbours.

Morag had the benefit of the Long Eye. 'Straight ahead,' she said. 'And it's Deception Island, all right.' She called Fogg up to the wheel-house and handed him the telescope. 'Do you see what I think I see?'

A glance at the horseshoe-shaped island was enough. 'There are two Airluggers moored in the bay. One is much bigger than us, with f-f-four more windbags on each side, and many more cabins. That must be an Airlugger II – only one was ever built, as I recall. The other looks like the *F-F-Fram*.'

Hector's freedom laid bare Morag's anxieties. The *Fram* had been her father's craft – would he still be alive? How would she confront him? What was the Airlugger II doing out here? Cassie's remark gnawed away too, that history is not about individuals but dynasties, which either start rotten or go rotten over time. She envied Fogg his independence of parental influence, only to detest herself for the thought. He was gripping the handrail, his mouth set. The initial wonderment had passed and now she could see in his face the hollow of inconsolable loss.

For a moment she flirted with the wholly impractical idea of turning back, only for the ghosts of dead allies to appear at her shoulder: Hernia, Miss Baldwin and, very likely, Oblivious Potts too. She gave herself an order: *I will not let the past infect the present.*

As the open arms of Deception Island came ever closer, they gathered on deck to discuss the options. Fogg alone knew that even from this distance, the landscape did not look as it should. He recalled his early days at the research station, and the community's botanist who had befriended him. Even now, in the Antarctic summer, he would expect ice and slate-grey moraine to dominate. There would be vegetation, yes, but mainly lichens and moss, liverworts and fungi, with rarities if you knew where to look. The swathes of green on the lower slopes looked altogether lusher, and nor was the air anything like as chill as it should be. He kept these thoughts to himself.

'I suggest we find a remote beach and take it from there,' said Morag.

'We're hardly inconspicuous,' said Fogg. 'It might be better to be more direct.'

He handed Niobe the Long Eye.

'Wood smoke,' she said.

'Antarctica was all forest and swamp ninety million years ago.'

'That's extremely helpful, Benedict,' Morag said frostily.

'We may not have to decide,' said Niobe. 'The smaller craft has launched.'

'It is the *F-F-Fram*,' confirmed Fogg, as his one-time home sailed towards them.

No craft is quite like another, nor are sailors mere clones of each other. Morag's father had a perfectionist's gift for maximising the wind. Nobody in his old crew had been able to match him. Fogg had little doubt he was at the helm now. Message flags ran up the rigging: the bright colours suggestive of welcome, not hostility.

Morag put the Long Eye down and moved to the prow, wondering, *How do you greet your father after your mother's abandonment and suicide?*

She would keep to her resolution: welcome first, recrimination later. *But you still had to find the words. You still had to honour your mother's memory.*

Hector was quartering the sea below. Not for the first time, she envied him.

Without warning, the *Fram* accelerated, closed and rose right above them. Down a ladder, holding a wooden tray with glasses in one hand, came Gilbert Spire.

Fogg gave an impromptu wave, but Morag could only stare. She should have realised he would come in style, eager to display his gift for bravado and surprise. Age had greyed his temples and dragged the hairline back; sun and air had burnished and lined the face, but he looked in rude health and his voice still delivered every phrase as if freshly minted.

'Fruit for the travellers,' he cried, 'from the last orchard on God's earth.'

He dropped on to the deck with a dancer's grace and placed the tray on a hatch.

He opened his arms wide. Nobody moved.

Fogg broke the uneasy silence. 'Mr Spire, it's me . . .'

'Of course, it is, the one and only Fogg, brought to me by Fate and now returned by Fate; and my one and only daughter too.'

Morag let him embrace her, and she kissed him on both cheeks, but she set her mark straight after. 'Much has happened, Father; not all of it good.'

'Yes, well, when the shadows come, we can talk about that. For the here and now . . .'

He handed out glasses as Niobe and Benedict introduced themselves, before holding his own up to the light. 'We call it the Potts Pearmain; hardy, eatable, and with juice to die for.'

He took a swig. The others had never consumed such a natural drink in their lives. The colour, the smell, the taste and the hint of fermentation were all alien, but a tentative sip became a mouthful became a swig.

Spire's salient characteristic was energy. Having introduced the cider, he turned his attention to the rigging. 'In a force three from the starboard side like today, let out two and six a half more, shorten five a fraction, and add a one and a half more to four. But you've done well, Fogg. You've remembered.'

They made the adjustments he suggested; the *Aeolus* leant a little and picked up speed. The diapason had never been so quiet.

'Carlo's in the *Fram*. He's good, but not this good,' said Spire with a smile, more amused than bragging. 'Let's take him on. You'll find pennants in the main cabin stowaway. Run up purple and yellow to challenge. We'll do the decent and give him a head-start.'

It was an inspired move. The race between the two Airluggers broke whatever ice remained. The crews waved and cheered each other on and, true to Spire's forecast, the *Aeolus* drew away.

As they closed on the island, Spire added commentary. 'Chinstrap penguins,' he cried, pointing at the flock bumbling towards the water like a bevy of town clerks heading for work.

But even Spire was not omniscient. He pointed down. 'What the *hell* is that?' he cried.

'*That* is a Southern Royal albatross,' replied Niobe.

She liked Spire. He had handed her the first glass, an unspoken gesture of equality.

'And he has a story too,' added Morag.

'*Touché,*' cried Spire good-humouredly. 'Out a notch at one and five,' he bellowed at Fogg, and now Morag understood the bond between them. Physical action, instruction and the sense of being part of the crew had helped Fogg earth his boyhood grief.

That's not a favour you forget.

Spire slowed the craft as they entered over the narrow entrance through the jaws of the bay.

'Neptune's Bellows,' said Benedict Vane.

'Are you guessing, or did you know?' commented Spire with a wink.

'I'm chock-full of useless facts,' replied Benedict.

'You look very like a Vane. Is that a fact?' asked Spire.

'It's an accurate opinion,' replied Benedict with a quizzical smile of his own.

Spire nodded, as if reserving the subject for later, and resumed the commentary on the bay. 'You're looking down at a blown magma chamber. The volcano below is probably still active, but it's a risk we take. The island is in fact the crater's rim. With the Fall, when changed temperatures dispelled the ice and reduced the glaciers, we found more than enough volcanic soil. Maple, ash and olive are the staple trees, and they provide a shelter belt for the fruit farm.'

'Where does all this seed come from?'

'That, dearest daughter, is a secret, and one best kept.'

And not only seed, eggs too. With a tinkling call, a flock of small birds rose from the trees beneath them as they anchored beside the much bulkier Airlugger II. The name *Ceres* had been elegantly carved on the prow. The goddess provided the figurehead too, flowers cascading back from her outstretched hands.

On the ground, teenagers were securing the ladder. A village of houses with dark rock walls and slate roofs were clustered around the landing site. Crops, trees and grasses decorated the lower slopes, with more severe rock and scree higher up. On a promontory, the sails of a solitary windmill gently turned.

'First things first, if I may be bold, your clothes are rank and you need a wash. I recommend the sea at the cove around the point. There's a cabin with a primitive freshwater shower, soap of a sort and a change of clothes. Yes, you were expected.' Spire slapped his thighs with mirth. 'But you've never seen the sea, and none of you can swim, so beginner's rules. There's a drag tide, so it's up to your waists only, and wade slowly. Off you go. I've other guests to meet.'

Spire's voice might lack the richness of Lord Vane's, but its dynamic insistence made it hard to disobey.

Fogg was quicker on the birds than Benedict, whose library of images could not match Fogg's real-life experience. He pointed out a South Polar skua harrying a flock of gulls. 'Skuas are great fliers, but pirates at heart. They steal the work of others.'

Morag thought the birds lucky to be free; Fogg, mindful of his first home and a bay clogged with avian bodies, thought them lucky to be alive. He greeted them like long-lost friends.

The cabin held an assortment of old-world bathing costumes and rubber-soled sandals. The chill water washed away the grime as silver fish scurried past. The penguins showed no concern at sharing the sea with humans.

They've let them be; that's good, thought Fogg.

A volcano beneath the sea had struck Morag as an apt setting for the reunion. His spirit undimmed, her father had established a human colony at one with Nature, but he had also delivered Fogg to the Genrich School for Idiot-Savants without bothering to visit his mother, wife and daughter. But *why*? He was clearly capable of honouring commitments, having apparently gone to great lengths to set a trail to bring her and Fogg to his private Paradise.

Having craved answers, she now feared them.

Niobe indulged the senses: the tang of brine, the sky, the bird calls, the movement of the clouds, the swing of the sea, but above all, the *openness*: a miner's daughter released at last. She wrestled with whether to offer comforting words to Fogg, for his parents must have worked nearby.

You can only do as you would be done by. In his position she would wish to be left alone. She said nothing.

Benedict fought against the voluminous data in his head clamouring for attention. 'Enjoy, just enjoy,' he muttered to himself.

By the time they had dried, showered and changed, the light was failing and the island had assumed a more brooding presence. Slats of dark volcanic rock on the high slopes dominated the softer greens below as the latter slipped into shadow.

Technology had not stood still, even here. A floating globe-light, spinning like a top, guided them to their assigned quarters, a small building on the edge of the village with bunk beds and hot and cold running water. A note from Spire announced the evening meal in an hour. *Moon-face* will show the way, said the postscript.

Moon-face, alias the spinning globe-light, obliged. A pavement of flat volcanic rock had been laid between the houses. The long, low single-storey communal dining room reminded Fogg of a mead hall from old legend. Everyone at the trestle tables rose from their benches and cheered their entry.

Members of the *Fram*'s old crew pointed and waved.

'Look! It's young Foggy!'

'*Old* Foggy!'

'Hoy, Froggy!'

Spire rose and called for calm. 'It's a privilege to have visitors from the Lost World, but it's beyond words when they include my long-lost daughter and our adopted cabin boy.' More cheers. 'We sit early tonight because Morag, Fogg, Miranda and I have a little business to discuss, which is best done before Master Pearmain

Potts addles our brains. Half an hour, no more. Then Niobe and Benedict can tell their tales. We've found peace, but they come from a troubled world, which means they have stories to share!'

Miranda! Anxiety seized Morag. What was Lady Vane doing here? And what was this business they had to discuss?

Spire directed Niobe to one table end and Benedict to the other before ushering Morag and Fogg back outside.

'My rooms are best,' he said.

Her father's two-room cabin was modest in furniture and fittings, offering no greater style or comfort than those of his comrades, but the uninterrupted views were exceptional, looking towards Neptune's Bellows on one side and a low-lying orchard on the other. An iron wood stove was glowing. A central lantern hung above a round table set with six chairs. Shelves with racks of files and occasional books filled the spaces between the windows.

Shocks of the unpredictable variety are one thing; those you might or even *should* have foreseen are quite another. Lady Vane emerged from the bedroom. She was wearing trousers, an open-necked shirt, a cable-stitch jersey and a scarf knotted around her hair, the familiar picture of unforced elegance. She looked very much at home.

Morag did not need the confirmation her father's greeting provided. The exchange of looks between them sufficed.

'Darling, you remember my daughter Morag?'

'How could I forget her?' Lady Vane offered a beneficent smile.

'And this is my adopted son, Master Fogg.'

'Master of Lord Vane's pictures,' she said, with another smile.

For Morag, a raft of ill-fitting pieces fell into place at last. Her father had been Lady Vane's lover, and she had followed him here. He had not betrayed his family by avoiding them; this greater betrayal had come first. Guilt, the fear of exposure and maybe an unwillingness to lie had kept him away from his true home. Morag now understood Lady Vane's equivocal reaction at the Tempestas party when she had revealed that her mother was dead, and it helped to explain her father's exile.

'This cannot be easy for you, Morag,' said Lady Vane.

'Damn right, it isn't. My mother poisoned herself, thanks to you two.'

'She did what?' asked her father quietly.

'She walked into the murk, leaving us with a hideously sentimental message: "To join him."'

'I'm terribly sorry,' said Lady Vane gently to Morag. 'But I rather assumed—'

Spire intervened. 'Morag, I didn't *choose* to leave home. Genrich commanded my attendance, and like you, I had no choice.'

'You were caged in at home. You couldn't wait to leave. All you ever read about were glaciers and volcanoes and explorers.'

'He won't deny that,' Lady Vane interrupted. 'He's an adventurer. He'll probably break my heart too, without meaning to.'

Morag glared at her father while addressing Lady Vane. 'At least *you* stayed with Lord Vane. You didn't abandon your husband.'

Lady Vane looked at Spire and then at Morag. 'I stayed for a long time, that is true, but it's complicated. I had an heir to look after.'

Morag stabbed a finger at her father. 'He gads about while women stay and women suffer.'

Spire shook his head. 'Only you, Miranda, and your mother, Morag. You have my word.'

'If he hadn't come south, I'd be a bundle of bones on Petrel Rock,' intervened Fogg, before pleading with Morag, 'Nobody is asking you to forget, but I do say *forgive*.'

Morag was in no mood for forgiveness, and certainly not before she had winkled out the whole truth. 'So Marcus found you out and Marcus gave the game away?'

Lady Vane turned sharply away.

For the first time, Spire raised his voice. 'We don't mention that name here – *ever*. "The weather-watcher" will do, if you must.'

Lady Vane stood up. Her eyes had turned glassy. 'I spent the best years of my life without your father. I know what your mother felt. That's why ...' She sat back down without completing the sentence. Even *in extremis*, she preserved her elegance.

Was this display of high emotion just an act? Morag was feeling deeply uneasy.

'My daughter should know the whole truth,' said Spire to his lover.

Lady Vane bit her lip before continuing, 'Genrich were on the rampage, seizing any chitin they could get their hands on. Outliers counted for nothing. When Cosmo devised his momenticons, I saw a way to get Genrich onside, and to bring you and your family back in. Cosmo was meant to rescue your grandmother too, but for some reason he didn't.'

'I don't get this,' replied Morag. 'How could you know I'd be of any use with momenticons? My father was long gone by then.'

Fogg, the closest to a third party in the room, felt the atmosphere thicken as the question hung unanswered.

Spire knelt down, opened a cupboard and took out a bottle and glasses. 'This is the very spirit of the earth. I save it for when courage is needed. I suggest one mouthful before, and as many as you like after.'

The apple brandy filled the room with the richness of autumn. *Season of mists and mellow fruitfulness ...*

The gesture struck Fogg as oddly timed, until Lady Vane resumed, 'There is a word which men use of women: it's cruel and unfair, but it is descriptive. It's no less cruel or true the other way around.'

Morag glanced at Fogg. He looked as though he knew what was coming, when she did not.

Lady Vane delivered the word with delicate gentleness. 'The second Lord Vane is *barren*. Your father is not.'

'No, no, no ...' stammered Morag.

Lady Vane spoke calmly. 'You share the gift with Cosmo because you share a father who also has the gift.'

'That – that can't be,' she stammered. 'Cosmo and I – we're *poles* apart. He's a *psychopath*, for a start. He had your husband killed.'

Lady Vane stood up and walked to the window. She opened it and stared silently up at the cliffs.

Fogg could see why Spire had found her irresistible.

At last, she turned back. 'Lord Vane is *dead*?' she asked.

Fogg looked at Spire. He felt sure Spire already knew, which meant Lady Vane did too, although not necessarily how.

She dabbed her eyes with a handkerchief. 'How?' she murmured.

'He was driven beneath the ice by mechanical horsemen under Cosmo's orders.'

'No, no, dear, you must be mistaken. He has his peculiar ways, does Cosmo, but he would never do *that*.'

'I was there, Lady Vane. I saw it with my own eyes. And he as good as killed my grandmother too.'

'He did *what*?' said Spire.

'Fogg was there. He saw, he heard.'

Fogg barely spoke above a whisper. 'There was a machine waiting outside when we left. He called it a harvester, and he seemed to relish the fact.'

'Even *he* could not do that . . .' stammered Spire.

'Of course not,' said Lady Vane. 'It's a misunderstanding, a coincidence.' She paused. 'Cosmo is our love-child.' There was a hint of steel in her voice. 'There's nothing to apologise for.'

Your first misstep, thought Morag. *That's hardly the remark of a grief-stricken widow just moments after hearing of her husband's violent death.*

'That young man with you – who is he?' Lady Vane asked, tucking her handkerchief neatly into her sleeve.

'He's a Vane, I believe, but distant. A cousin of some sort.'

'A throwback,' said Spire casually.

'The first Lord Vane was an only child,' Lady Vane said, a shade too quickly.

'As we know, nobody's perfect,' replied Spire.

Fogg, in despair, watched the complexities unravel and reshape. His parents had been straightforward people, loyal to each other and focused on research for the betterment of mankind. They were dead, while Spire, Cosmo and Lady Vane lived on, locked into a convoluted dance of politics and power.

Two possibilities occurred to him: Lady Vane needed an heir and had used Gilbert Spire because he had the requisite qualities of charm and leadership, or she truly loved him and Cosmo was an accidental consequence. Or maybe it was a mixture of the two. Whatever the truth, Fogg felt sure this conversation had gone far enough. Emotional exhaustion would bring its own perils.

'Forgive the analogy,' he said, 'but I believe we have cleared the air.'

Spire threw back his glass. 'Bravo, Fogg, you've not lost your touch.'

Morag had read the books: this was a Greek tragedy, playing out. Her half-brother had killed her grandmother and his stepfather, his true father's rival. Such deeds have consequences which echo deep into the future.

But that look from her father, whom at the deepest levels she still trusted, required a stay.

'Well said, Fogg. Let's drink up and join the others,' she said.

3

Loose Talk

'What interests me,' asked Niobe, 'is where all this life comes from?'

'Where it usually comes from,' replied Carlo, 'eggs, seeds, chrysalides.'

'Yes, but where do *they* come from?'

He laughed. 'I've a six-year-old son. Every answer to a "why" fosters another "why" or a "where" or a "when".'

'But I'm *interested*,' she protested.

'Let me surprise you. *We're* interested, too. We're researchers, or the children of researchers.'

Carlo had olive skin, a vigorous handlebar moustache and dark bedroom eyes. Niobe was happy to flirt. 'Your English is oddly musical.'

'Do you know about the fall of the Tower of Babel and what came after? There were so many lingos that nobody got anywhere. When Señor Squire arrived, half of us spoke English and half of us Spanish. We had a ballot and English won – by a single vote.' He leant over conspiratorially. 'I always suspected a fix, but I'm happy. English has Shakespeare, which is good enough for me.'

'You still haven't answered my question.' She nudged him playfully on the shoulder. The ring on his fourth finger said he was married, and the easy smile said that he liked women but loved his wife: the best sort and the easiest to work.

'Because there isn't an answer. An Airlugger comes and an Airlugger goes.'

'Like the Airlugger II?'

'That oversized bastard? No, Señorita. It's the *Zephyr*, big sister to the *Fram* and the *Aeolus*, and only just in. She's like the Ark, you know: two by two, the boy and the girl.'

Niobe persisted. 'Come on, Carlo, forget the transport. Where does the cargo come from?'

'One word is all I know.'

'Yes?'

He stared at his drink. This was clearly classified ground.

'I lost that in your magnificent moustache.'

'Simul,' he whispered.

'Simul?' she repeated, just as quietly.

'We have gulls and penguins, but never before a parrot,' cried Carlo, slapping Niobe on the back.

An attractive woman three places down scowled in Carlo's direction, and Niobe diplomatically turned to her neighbour.

At the opposite end of the table, Benedict was approaching celebrity status.

'All right. Who – or what – is *Euphausia superba*?'

He proved as equal to this question as to its predecessors. 'You refer to the Antarctic krill. We worry about overcrowding – but imagine thirty thousand of them to a cubic yard of seawater.'

'He's a walking library!'

An older man with a wily face tried a different tack. 'What has the name of a big cat, feeds on chocolate bars and bears arms?'

Benedict floundered. His databanks did not run to puns, jokes or teasers.

'The leopard seal,' said the man, laughing at his own cleverness. 'Get it? He eats *penguins*, which were also old-world chocolate biscuits, and seals bear arms. Rather unfair, I grant you, but that's the difference between learning by rote and out-thinking a sphinx.'

A lean, foxy-looking middle-aged woman, whose more opulent clothes marked her as a visitor from the *Ceres* and one of Lady Vane's servants, also ignored Benedict's strengths. 'What I want to know is how you got that mind and those looks?' she asked suspiciously.

Benedict reddened. 'Stumped twice in an over,' he said.

As Lady Vane and Morag entered the eating hall, Spire ushered Fogg to one side. 'Is my son Cosmo coming here?'

'We suspect he is.'

'I feared as much. How did he get the directions?'

'He scanned my memory with a machine, he guessed the right painting and used one of Morag's momenticons to get there.'

'He used a scanner on you? How charming. There's no limit to what that boy will do. He has all the bad in us and none of the good. Do me a favour, Fogg, and say nothing to Lady Vane about this, or about your time at the Museum Dome. Lives may depend on it. For now, let's disguise our worries with small talk.'

They joined the others, to find 'Lady Vane' had become simply 'Miranda'. Save for the woman who had shown interest in Benedict, her crew had remained on the *Ceres*.

The residents had been isolated since the Fall and, Spire apart, they knew little of the outside world. Perhaps for that very reason, the evening passed pleasantly enough. The company reminded Fogg of his parents' research station: inquisitive and dedicated men and women of a scientific bent. If they provided welcome novelty to the community in terms of news, the old-world food offered its own rewards in return. Flat illustrations had told them next to nothing. After lives consuming paste, the texture, taste, shape and colour of the vegetables and fruits, and the sticky opulence of the honey flooded minds and senses.

Paradise regained indeed.

Back in their cabin, nobody discussed the earlier revelations. Neither Fogg nor Morag had a mind to, and Niobe and Benedict did not ask.

4

Pillow Talk

Rooms are like books, at the whim of the beholder's inner eye. Their dark chamber with open beams and uneven floors could have been labelled crude and uncomfortable, or, no less truthfully, cosy, with rustic charm and views to die for.

'I promise I've lived like a monk.'

'No longer, I hope,' replied Lady Vane, lying on her side, head propped on her left hand so her hair spilled over the sheets. Two contrasting bodies: one beautiful, pale and opulent, the other lean, burnished and honed by exercise and the outdoor life. 'I do like my creature comforts. You can't want to live here any more, can you?'

'This place is *awash* with comforts, Miranda. You've not yet been fishing. You've not seen the view from the mountain or heard the golden oriole. Who would want to leave here?'

'The bed is hard,' she replied.

'We collect bird down, and the longer we stay, the more comfortable our mattresses will become.'

'Well, this one has a long way to go. You must come and try mine.' She tousled his hair. 'I'd miss the food, I grant you. But we could ship your good earth back home. We'll have sunshine, at least so long as the beacons last.'

'The earth belongs here. The earth *is* here.'

'What did the boy Fogg mean about your rescuing him?'

'It was a chance encounter, long ago. He was the sole survivor of a station just like this one.'

'Why does that make him special?'

'He's more resourceful than he looks.'

'The resourceful one is the other young man. Surely you noticed?'

Spire merely raised his eyebrows.

'He has my eyes – and he also has a rare fund of knowledge.'

That tinge of purple in her irises was indeed unique, and Benedict's undeniably had a hint, if you looked hard at faces, as Lady Vane invariably did.

Tread carefully.

'Nobody has your eyes, Miranda.'

'That's my point. But the set of the jaw is Lord Vane's. It's *most* disconcerting.'

'Fiction is full of prodigal cousins returning to the fold – chips off the old block and all that. He has no ambitions, that you can tell.'

'*Everyone* has ambitions. The black girl is curious too. I'd say she's a troublemaker. I don't like the way she looks at me.'

'You're used to deference. There isn't much of that there.'

'We don't seem to be agreeing about very much.'

'That's because we're open with each other.'

Lady Vane unleashed one of *those* smiles. 'Of course I'm sad about my husband. The hunters' programming must have gone awry. But it does simplify things. You and I and Cosmo, a new dynasty—'

'There is also the weather-watcher . . .'

'He will pay,' she hissed. 'One day, he will pay. And he's another reason why we can't linger here. If we do, he'll take everything.'

'Come here, Miranda. The night is young.'

'And so many monkish vows to break,' she replied.

5

The Lie of the Land

The following morning, Spire gave them a tour of the island. He wore his pride in the community's achievements lightly, always 'we' or 'they' and never 'I'. Morag found herself on the road to forgiveness. He explained, without detail, how the wherewithal for transforming the landscape had come from outside, but the community had done the hard labour.

In an orchard heavy with fruit, Benedict pointed to the nearby slopes. 'Where are the glaciers? The ice moraine?'

'He explained yesterday,' said Morag testily. 'This is a new world, with new data which you have to load from the *outside* in.' She grimaced at her giveaway blunder, for the truth about Benedict's origins threatened his very existence.

An alert Niobe sought a diversion. 'You have so many insects, Mr Spire. I want to see a moth, a real moth. Young Fogg and I have a thing about moths.'

The diversion failed.

Spire put the warning diplomatically but directly to Benedict. 'Benedict, I can see, and so will others, that you're the son Lord and Lady Vane should have had.' He pointed across the orchard, first to a stunted tree with hard, mean-looking apples, then to another, heavily laden with opulent fruit. 'Mix and match,' he said. 'You graft a fancy strain on to a tough trunk, but the best-laid plans can go awry. Just be careful. People may think you're a pretender to the throne, whatever your intentions.'

'He means,' said Niobe, 'watch your back as well as your front.'

'I don't have eyes in that direction,' said Benedict.

Morag smiled. Benedict was changing. Whether it was intentional or not, a flicker of humour was peeping through.

'That's what friends are for,' she said.

'We passed a plume of ash,' said Fogg, 'not so very far from here. Isn't that a worry?'

Spire pointed to the western side of the island's central bay and the rocky stacks outside. 'All these outcrops emerged from eruptions, one of them not that long ago. We had to blow up the lava stack blocking the harbour. The main danger here is magma beneath the seabed mixing with seawater, a recipe for violence. Of course, without these losses of temper, the ice wouldn't have melted and we wouldn't be where we are now.'

Absence had not dimmed Morag's instinct for subtext in her father's speeches. He was holding back now, but she could not see why.

They left the lowlands and climbed steadily. Slabs of rock had fashioned a high cave hidden by a rough door in dark painted wood. Spire waved them in. At his touch, a globe-light on a round table activated and rose. The walls, floor and ceiling were all unhewn rock, save for the levelled area beneath the table and chair. A simple stove with a flue occupied the centre of the rear wall.

'Morse code?' said Benedict, pointing at the small machine with a single lever and button.

'Never have visuals if you want to keep your sources secret.'

A spike on the table held a sheaf of deciphered messages.

'Potts?' asked Morag.

'Mander?' asked Fogg.

'Old friends, both. But I haven't heard from Potts in days.'

Beside the messages stood two ancient volumes shrouded in protective plastic: Arensen on *Glaciers* and Cuttle on *The Mysteries of Arbor Spirantia*.

This was not the moment to raise the question of overdue library books, Morag decided. 'His home was under attack when we left,' she said. 'He turned off his beacon to allow our escape. We're very worried about him.'

'Oblivious is as close to a wizard as the real world gets,' Spire replied. 'He vanishes without explanation and returns just when you've given up hope. Like Cosmo Vane, he is never passive. They hate each other, as you can imagine.'

'We haven't told the other two about Cosmo,' said Morag. She needed him to confess to her friends.

Spire did not hesitate. 'He's my son, more's the pity. I wasn't there for most of his upbringing, so whether it's nature or nurture, I don't know. But he is what he is, and he has to be stopped.'

To Morag's irritation, Niobe and Benedict exchanged incredulous glances.

She stamped her foot. 'Of course it's true! Cosmo makes momenticons, I make momenticons. Father could if he wanted to. It's been staring me in the face all along.'

'Thank you,' said Benedict to Spire. 'I shall keep it to myself.'

'Yes,' said Niobe, 'but you're right, Cosmo *must* be stopped. He gives no quarter, so nor can we.'

'He will come,' added Fogg, 'and soon. He has a huge fleet of gyrocopters.'

Spire shook his head. 'They wouldn't get him anywhere near here. He must have something else up his sleeve.'

'Isn't there a fourth Airlugger?' Benedict asked.

'There is, and he might have it, but I rather doubt it. All the same, my son deals in nasty surprises, so be warned.'

Courtesy of the radio waves, and long before Morag had arrived to confirm it, Cosmo's adventures had reached this far-flung horseshoe of rock at the edge of the world. Fogg imagined Spire stooped over this very table, scribbling out the story, letter by letter, translating the dots and dashes which had recorded his son's latest atrocity. It cannot have been easy.

Morag braved a different question. 'Are you Cassie's father, too?'

'No,' Spire said firmly, 'I was long gone by then.'

'Who then?' she asked, instantly regretting the question.

Pain sucked in his cheeks and puckered his eyes. 'That is not my story to tell.' He paused, letting the moment pass. 'I'm showing you this place in case anything happens to me.' He did a circuit of the room as he spoke. 'The generator switch is there. My hand-drawn map of the less obvious paths is at the back of this drawer. The old cupboard has reserves of dried food. The recess up there gathers fresh water. There are two camp beds. It's a hideout as well as an office, and it's very private. You can't see it from below, even with a telescope. Now we'd best get back. I'll show you the gentoo penguins on the way.'

They would remember the descent: he not only knew the names of the fauna but where the rarities lurked, down to the tiniest lichen, another lesson for Benedict. Data might give you names and habitat, but only fieldwork yields the rounded truth.

To Morag's relief, Spire the guide gave Benedict pleasure, not pain, and her father seemed to know it. He was investing in them.

Fogg too was changing. He had lost his pallor and had become less didactic. Niobe, Morag felt, anchored them all. She was steadfast in her constancy, and she never made the mistake, common among those distrustful of authority, of turning authoritarian herself.

Her father had shed the burdens of the previous evening. She loved him again, as she had as a child. His agility of mind and body were extraordinary. Cassie had quoted Hernia as saying ten minutes in his company was worth an age with the rest, for all his weaknesses, and Hernia had been right.

But deep down, the shadows were closing, and Lady Vane had brought them. Nobody dared say so, but they all knew.

They consumed bread and a delicious green pesto on the mountainside from Spire's capacious pockets while they watched the penguins from a respectful height.

Walking back along the shoreline, Niobe, Benedict and Fogg bounded ahead to give Morag time with her father. She had one more chapter to explore.

'Fogg says Mander collected the paintings.'

Her father nodded. 'As I understand it, at the Fall, Tempestas were awash with money from wealthy donors. They built a chitin-protected museum in the middle of nowhere and as the great galleries and museums corroded and headed for collapse, they persuaded curators and governments to surrender their best for safe-keeping.'

'Did the first Lord Vane know?'

'That's a very perspicacious question. I don't think he can have done. I suspect Mander was not beyond a little creative accounting.'

'And how did I end up there?' asked Morag.

'We made sure you were brought to the Genrich Dome when you were old enough to look after yourself.'

'And at the time of my exile, I asked Lady Vane to keep an eye on you, and it appears that she did. I didn't know then how Cosmo would turn out – nobody did. I still don't know how you reached Infotainment. That was probably Cosmo's doing. He liked to look at outliers' genetic profiles, and Lord Sine happily indulged him.'

'That figures. Lord Sine knew that you, Matilda and I shared something unique, and I suppose Cosmo realised that too.'

'I wonder if he suspected. A half-sister with common gifts would not have been a happy discovery.'

'It would never have occurred to him,' said Morag, 'the thought I might be at least half his equal.'

'That wasn't a risk we were prepared to take. Where was his claim to inherit if he was exposed as a bastard? That's why we engineered your escape.'

'Does *we* include Lady Vane?'

He shook his head.

Morag read much into that unspoken denial. *Love is not necessarily trust.*

'I went to the Museum Dome when I dropped Fogg off and left the bearings for this place in the Vermeer. Much later, Mander dropped in to make the arrangements to set you on your way when the truce between Genrich and Tempestas was up. That seemed as good a time as any.'

'You do realise the "arrangements" included two psychopathic twins aiming a drill at Fogg's eyeballs,' Morag said.

'The *Aeolus* belongs to Mander and Potts, and Mander has odd views about people *proving* themselves and making it the hard way. I suspect he sent them in the hope they would encourage you to share your history with Fogg, *Wonderland* momenticons being part of your past. I knew none of this at the time.'

'And Fogg?'

'He drew like an angel, even as a boy. I still have the maps he copied on the *Fram*. What better man to curate the Museum? He has luck too, and hidden reserves. We expected you to meet and get on.'

'Like an arranged marriage?'

'Like school friends,' he insisted defensively.

'He already has one of those,' replied Morag. She changed tack; there was so much she did not know. 'What work did you do for Lord Sine?'

'I have many regrets, and that's another.'

'You're not telling me.'

'I hope it was destroyed as I advised. But we should concentrate on present threats, for there are more than enough of them. Do call Master Fogg. I think his adventures might hold the key.'

She hailed Fogg, who ran back.

'I need to hear about your exploits, Fogg, but I don't want potted highlights. Just anything, and I mean *anything*, when the enemy let slip his intentions.'

Fogg ran through the episodes most likely to have escaped Spire's notice: Mr Venbar, the slithy toves, the Dark Circus, the scanner, even Cosmo's conversation with Piety when they thought him unconscious.

Spire showed particular interest in the last. 'Repeat, if you would, word for word, as best you can.'

'They had been experimenting on Lord Sine's creatures and the test results had pleased him.'

'These toves are just killing machines, in your experience?'

'They obey their commander. They can gather tantalum. They can survive the murk. But otherwise . . .'

'Now there's a point,' muttered Spire, more to himself than anyone else.

'I thought we were dealing with present threats?' intervened Morag.

'Getting wet is the most immediate.' Spire pointed up at an increasingly milky sky and called over the others, as if Fogg had nothing more to give. 'Telltale clouds,' he said. 'A storm is brewing.'

'We're storm experts,' Morag said.

'Weather-riders more than weather-*watchers*,' added Niobe.

'Your gift from the *Fram* saved us,' said Fogg, 'in the nick of time.'

Morag tapped her father on the shoulder. 'Let me guess. The watchers tried to destroy you too.'

'It's their favourite two-card trick: escape the lightning and the hail gets you.' Spire grinned. 'Mercifully, you can prepare for predictable assassins.'

He broke away and ambled off alone along the shoreline. Morag knew that look: he was wrestling with a conundrum, probably born of Fogg's intelligence. He paused at a cairn on the beach and fumbled among the stones, as if rebuilding it. Suddenly he opened his arms to the sky and squinted at the vanishing sun. She knew that gesture too. He had found a solution, but one with a heavy price, to judge from his sombre mood on the final stretch.

She let him be.

Supper that evening passed without mishap. Only Lady Vane appeared to have lost her natural poise. She looked apprehensive, and several times Morag caught her glancing sidelong at Benedict. She clearly knew nothing about him or his origins.

The storm pounced around midnight. Fogg called it the 'igloo effect'. When windows shook in their frames, chimneys howled and the rain beat on the roof tiles like a drum, a cosy room felt like a harbour against the elements. He lay on his back. His friends were asleep, their breathing even and untroubled. A curtain divided the two double bunks. To avoid complications, Fogg slept above Benedict, Niobe above Morag.

Fogg guessed at their dreams: Niobe would be in a mine with silvery seams which dissolved into vapour like ghosts; Benedict was fleeing from facts to freedom and wide-open spaces; and Morag, on the seventh rank, was poised to rise from humble pawn to Queen. And his own dream? To be back in the Museum Dome tendering wisdom to a bevy of attentive visitors?

Maybe, maybe not. Benedict was showing the perils of excess knowledge over experience.

He drifted and dozed until near dawn, when the light squelch of footsteps outside disturbed him by stopping, as if flirting with entry, then resuming. The rain had passed.

Minutes later, Spire, also half woken by hesitant steps outside, had the same thought, but this time the outside door shook with a vigorous knock.

Spire sat up as Lady Vane slipped out of bed and hurried to the door.

'Darling, just look at you,' she said.

'Mother, my craft went down. I don't want your sympathy, and I certainly don't want to see your paramour. I want a meeting with the inhabitants. Eight o'clock sharp.'

'Cosmo?' asked Spire, leaping from his bed. 'Is it you?' The bedraggled figure undoubtedly was Cosmo, the boy become a man. 'You were only so high when last I saw you.'

Cosmo ignored Spire as if he were not there, an irrelevance.

'I'm sorry to hear about the craft, but how are the crew?' asked Lady Vane.

'We can mount a search and rescue operation,' added Spire.

'Fuck the crew.'

Spire changed tone, sounding more assertive as he stepped closer to Cosmo. 'May I ask why you're here? We've little to offer you.'

'I'm touring my empire.'

'They've never heard of you.'

'Then it's time they did.'

Lady Vane placed an arm around Spire's shoulder. 'Gil, dearest, he's the new Lord Vane. I suggest you put on your clothes and call the muster. If you don't, I'll do it. Only the dining hall is large enough.'

Spire was sorely tempted to tell Cosmo the truth. *You're not Lord Vane. You're a good old-fashioned bastard, a love-child by a commoner.*

Instead, Spire did as his lover asked, trailing a hand across Cosmo's wet shirt as he left. Once outside, he lifted his fingers to his lips.

Fresh water.

You may be clever, but I'm not a fool, he reassured himself. *I play moves deep too, and there's one move you've yet to grasp.*

He went first to Morag's cabin. 'Cosmo is here,' he said.

Morag rose from torpor to vigilance in seconds. 'Where? With whom?'

'With his mother. He arrived alone. He says his craft went down in the storm.' Spire did not feel able to accuse him outright. The rain had been heavy, and the salt might have washed off. 'He's called a meeting in the dining hall at eight.'

'What right has this fop to call anyone to a meeting?' asked Niobe, sweeping open the curtain which divided their bunks.

'His birthright, he would say.'

Niobe spluttered in outrage.

'Cosmo is not a fool,' Morag reminded them. 'Well, obviously not, with his parents. He'll have hidden pieces to play.'

Spire had a hard look about him. 'Keep Benedict well away from the meeting, and from Cosmo. And promise you'll do whatever I say.'

There was silence.

'Morag, on behalf of everyone, *promise*.'

The word *promise*, in the mouth of her father, carried irony, but Morag nodded, and the others followed her example.

'The dining hall at eight, then,' he confirmed.

Outside, the mantle of cloud was breaking up.

'Watch yourself,' Morag warned Benedict. 'I'd find a mountain top. There's nothing like a view when rain clears.'

Benedict said nothing. He had another plan. He had consulted his databank for instances where deep knowledge with limited experience had fought the malign and won. One name surfaced from old-world literary fiction, and it had furnished a prompt. A dispassionate detective known as Sherlock Holmes had triumphed by rational deduction. He, Benedict Vane, would follow that example and investigate Cosmo Vane's reappearance.

First, Spire visited Carlo, whom he liked and trusted, and who had influence with the whole community. He was already up.

'*Mala tormenta!*' said Carlo. 'I hope your craft survived it.'

'It's survived much worse, but we have a different problem.'

'That's no surprise. Women with airs and graces always bring trouble.'

Spire gave a wry laugh. 'Men with the same affliction likewise. Her son is here.'

'I hope he's here to take her home. She's beautiful, Señor Gil, no doubt, but she's dangerous, mark my words.'

'Unfortunately, he's the new Lord Vane and heir to the Tempestas empire.'

'We're no part of that and we never were.'

'You try persuading him of that.'

'Why do I have to persuade him of anything? It's our town. We built it with our bare hands. He has no rights here whatsoever.'

'Lord Vane likes taking what isn't his. He has a very flexible sense of property.'

'Well, I like to be polite to guests, so we'll listen to what he has to say. But he's not our ruler and never will be.'

'My advice, Carlo, is to play for time.'

Carlos shook Spire's hand. 'All right, then. Let's do the rounds together.'

Apprehension furrowed every face, save for the Vanes, mother and son, who sat at the head of the table by the door wearing a countenance of entitlement. Lady Vane's servant stood behind them, stony-faced. Everybody else had to file past them. Some sat, some stood.

Morag, Fogg and Niobe kept together near the fireplace, where peat bricks were glowing. Spire stood between them and his son, a statement of neutrality, Morag thought. Carlo sat facing Cosmo. Morag fretted over Carlo's relaxed demeanour: he could have no conception of how his adversary treated even the mildest opposition.

Cosmo had said nothing to her. Indeed, he had studiously avoided even a glance at her.

Niobe found the dynamic nauseating, while Fogg could not even look at his old tormentor.

Lady Vane gave her lover a smile, half warm, half cold. *We composed this dance of death*, the smile said, *and now our son is playing it out.*

Gilbert Spire had been lonely when he and Miranda had first met. He had judged her unhappy then. Now he realised 'bored' would have been the better description. She relished action and power, unrestrained by morality. Cosmo had taken his lead from his mother. He looked at the view of the cliffs and shrugged.

You earn your rewards and you pay for your sins, and my dues will be called in soon enough.

Cosmo rose to his feet. Though much younger than most of the audience, his patrician air of command impressed. He had dressed in local clothes, but the belt, the ring on his fourth finger and the chain about his neck were all made of gold and ostentatious in style.

'You know, they call this place Paradise,' he started expansively. 'I'd say you've a fair way to go to achieve that accolade, but it's hardly your fault. My late father, the second Lord Vane and the ruler of Tempestas, neglected you. As his successor, I shall make up for this lamentable lapse. You deserve a residence fit for a ruler. You deserve recognition. You deserve our science. All this will require your labour and our materials. Loyal service will, of course, be properly rewarded.'

Carlo stood up. 'Here, Señor, we strive to be equal. I'll happily give you a tour to prove it. You'll find rough parity in the dimensions of our houses, the views from our windows, the share of the food, and indeed, the responsibilities. We rule ourselves. We always have.'

Lady Vane awarded Carlo a smile devoid of warmth. 'What is your name?' she asked. 'We always like to know.'

'Plain Carlo.'

Cosmo continued, 'The first Lord Vane was my grandfather. He and Tempestas fought to preserve the old world, but it would not listen and paid the price. I don't expect you to make the same mistake.'

Carlo did not stand up this time. 'We're settled here. We're content. We respect the good fortune which spared us. Paradise was a simple place, as I remember.'

Cosmo's temper began to fray. 'You don't know what you're missing. This place is ramshackle, crude. Have you no aspirations?'

'Not for high falutin' palaces,' said a woman on the other side of the table.

'This place has no colonial history, and we aim to keep it that way,' said another.

Cosmo's tone hardened. 'I've come from the other end of the world to improve your lot. I expect a smidgen of respect.'

Spire noticed his son checking the time. He edged towards Morag and whispered, 'He's about to leave. We must all follow, and *quickly*. But first, they must listen to me.'

'What's your world like then?' asked a young man. 'What have you got which we haven't?'

Cosmo laughed. 'Science, entertainment – all that distinguishes us from the penguins.'

'We rather revere the penguins,' said Carlo.

Niobe had had enough. She stepped forward to the edge of the table. 'Do you want to know what this Cosmo really offers with his golden chain?' She paused as every face turned towards her. 'Or rather, what he imposes: brutality, torture and misapplied science. As a footnote, he killed his father to get where he is now.'

'I was coming to those three,' snapped Cosmo. 'How do you think they come to own an Airlugger? They're thieves on the run who deal in lies.'

The point raised a murmur. Airluggers were indeed rare and precious.

'They make no demands, and they're friends of Mr Spire, which is good enough for us,' replied Carlo calmly.

'*Friends of Mr Spire*,' repeated Cosmo, as if weighing the implications.

A middle-aged woman who had been sitting near Benedict the previous evening made the decisive intervention. 'And you're forgetting the fourth, the one who looks like you *physically*. He's quicker on the uptake, better-looking and he talks to us as equals.'

Cosmo's face turned the colour of ash as this hot needle drove through the tiny gaps in his armour. His mother had not mentioned the presence of the pretender. As for superior looks and intelligence . . .

'Where is he?' Cosmo demanded, clenching his fists.

The woman shrugged her shoulders and smirked.

'I said, *where is he?*' bellowed Cosmo.

'He isn't here, love,' she said.

'Prepare to learn, *you*,' hissed Cosmo, before marching out with Lady Vane.

Start with the interloper, Benedict decided. The damp flat rocks shone like mirrors as the sun broke through. He noted two oddities about the *Ceres*. Her rope ladder was down, and a chain extended from its prow to the stern of the *Aeolus*. The former could be explained by Lady Vane's servant descending to join the meeting, but the latter could only be to prevent their escape.

The ladder on the *Aeolus* was usually rolled up and secured beneath a tarpaulin in a storm. The ladder had not been down the previous evening, and he assumed the same regime would have applied to the *Ceres* until the servant's descent. Even the thickest cords rot over time.

The rope was sodden, which implied that the ladder had been unrolled for hours. *So Cosmo had arrived in his mother's craft*, he reasoned. *Nothing ventured, nothing gained.*

He climbed the ladder and heaved himself over the gunwale on to the stern deck. The craft had cabins fore and aft, lavish in size and decoration compared to those on the smaller *Aeolus*. On tiptoe, he edged his way to the wheelhouse, where a map of Deception Island marked with land and undersea contours was lying across the captain's chair. A tide table had been propped on the front ledge.

Before he could analyse the implications, a huge man in chest armour emerged from a prow cabin. He was twirling two long-bladed daggers between his fingers with disturbing finesse.

Benedict shuffled back towards the stern.

'Who's there?' shouted a rough voice. 'Show yourself!'

The guard strode towards him with balletic grace, blades still spinning like a circus performer's.

Benedict could find no better weapon than a long broom propped against the handrail. He snapped off the brush end, summoning moves from the bamboo kendo school as he did so. His programming allowed him to translate image to action with surprising ease. He started twirling the shaft like a drum major's baton. The giant paused, fleetingly baffled, then bowed deep: courtesy, even in battle. Benedict followed suit in a ritual move which nearly cost him his life. As his head rose, he caught a flash of steel and shimmied to the side. The knife point impaled the mast beside him.

Kendo will not do. He switched to the javelin. With elbow high and feet tight together, he hurled the broom handle like a Greek hoplite. Caught flush on the forehead, the man staggered back, but then, roaring like a goaded bull, he quickly recovered his poise.

Benedict, now weaponless, unlinked the chain tethering the *Aeolus*, jumped on to the handrail and launched himself towards the Airlugger. He caught her anchor chain as he passed.

The guard raised a crossbow and now too high to drop, Benedict could only swing from side to side to make himself a more difficult target.

But no bolt came, for the guard turned away as a strange booming noise echoed across the sound.

It was the warning call of a thousand penguins.

As Lady and Cosmo Vane hurried from the room, Spire strode forward and hammered the table. 'Listen, and listen carefully. If I'm right, we're about to be invaded, with no quarter given. They'll have no interest in your possessions, only in snuffing every one of you out. You can't win a straight fight, so don't waste time looking for weapons. Your best chance is to outrun them. Grab your children and head for the mountains – take the back ways, the steeper, the better. Unattached young men and women should take the more conspicuous paths. Go! *Now—!'*

Carlo leapt to his feet, echoing his instructions. 'Do what he says! *Go—!'*

Community spirit took over as they followed their orders to the letter, leaving the shadowy, less obvious defiles to the weaker and more vulnerable.

Within minutes, only Spire, Morag, Fogg and Niobe remained in the dining hall. Spire turned to Morag. 'Get to the *Fram*. You're on air rescue duty if they need it high up. But keep away from the shoreline and the bay.'

'What about the *Aeolus*?'

He pointed through the window. 'Your friend Benedict is there already. Niobe and Fogg, you draw them uphill. If you get to my lair, let Crike, Potts and Mander know that Cosmo and his mother are here. There's a code book if you need it.'

At that moment a strange boom, as if from a huge, agitated crowd, shivered the windowpanes.

'Penguins in shock,' said Spire, without elaborating.

This was her father of old: dynamic, decisive and fearless bordering on the impetuous. 'And where are you going, Father?' Morag asked.

'I have a little stratagem,' he replied. '*Now hurry!*'

Fogg and Niobe ran along the beach and took the most direct trail to Spire's mountain retreat. Other young men and women, many in pairs, had also commenced their ascent, hurrying through the lower fields and orchards, only slowing as they picked their way through the clumps of volcanic rock.

At the top of the first crest they looked back to see a bullet-nosed shape rising on the inland side of Neptune's Bellows. Close to the surface, it resembled a whale, but once clear, the shape was unmistakable: a submersible craft. All along the shoreline, penguins were hustling urgently to the sea. The craft halted as close to the shore as its bulbous green-black hull would allow.

Benedict, now on board the *Aeolus*, also saw the submersible rise. He weighed anchor. Nearby, Lady Vane and Cosmo were ascending the ladder of the *Ceres*. Meanwhile, Lady Vane's servant scaled the mooring cable of the *Fram* with surprising alacrity and detached her from her mistress' vessel.

Morag raced from the village towards the *Fram*, but she was too late: the anchor rose and the Vanes now controlled two of the three aerial craft.

Morag cursed. The Vanes had abandoned her father as if he counted for nothing. She swept the scene with the Long Eye. Fleeing men, women and children dotted the hillside, and panning along the bay, she found her father, running away from the settlement along the shore; he'd gone too far to catch.

She turned her attention to the deck of the submersible in time to see two hatches opening simultaneously. From the stern emerged an incongruous figure dressed as the Mad Hatter, clasping a lightning rod. He fitted exactly Fogg's narrative of the assault on the old Tempestas headquarters, as did the ragged army of Lord Sine's half-humans, who were spewing from the front hatch and launching themselves into the sea with manic ferocity.

Alerted by a scream from Morag, Benedict, who'd been transfixed by the scene below, looked up to see a grappling iron lodging in the handrail by the prow, and the *Ceres* bearing down on the *Aeolus* with a long thick spike emerging from her prow.

The giant guard held the wheel, while Cosmo was gesticulating at a clutch of armed men readying a boarding device.

Benedict struggled for a strategy. He could not free the grappling iron *and* manage the craft – but to his astonishment, Cavall, unbidden, seized the rope and severed it with his razor-sharp teeth, leaving Benedict to activate the pulleys.

Although slower in a straight line, and therefore vulnerable to ramming, the *Aeolus* had the advantage of nimbleness, as well as a tighter turning circle. Running from side to side, replicating Fogg's know-how as best he could, Benedict banked sharply round and lowered the rope ladder, which Morag grasped minutes before Sine's toves swept ashore.

'Keep her turning,' shouted Morag, but Benedict did not need the advice. The *Aeolus* quickly outmanoeuvred the *Ceres*.

Morag clambered up the swinging ladder as fast as she could, hauling it up behind her to prevent pursuit.

On the deck of the *Ceres*, Cosmo was fulminating, first at the *Aeolus*' escape and then at developments below. 'The bastards! Why aren't they fighting?'

Lady Vane rested a hand on his shoulders. 'I've warned you many times, Cosmo, Gil is no fool.'

'But our strategy turns on it.'

'No need to panic. They're gaining by the minute – and you forget, I have my own best men in reserve. They're armed, and this rabble is defenceless.'

The toves had waded ashore and now, ignoring the village, they swarmed up the mountainside, bent only on killing. Any stragglers were quickly engulfed and torn to pieces.

'This is horrific,' cried Morag, as she swung herself over the rail. 'What do we do?'

Working in tandem, they brought *Aeolus* up to speed. Benedict's manoeuvring had left the heavily laden *Ceres* wallowing in their wake, while the *Fram* was merely drifting.

'Let's get those children.' Benedict pointed. 'We'll do for them what your father did for Fogg.'

'Back down the ladder,' cried Morag, with one eye on her father, a tiny figure still running along the lower cliffs close to the shoreline.

'Get up, get up!' she shouted in his direction, willing him to obey his own injunction and take the high road. But she could tell his 'little strategy', whatever it was, was dictating a different course.

On the mountainside, Fogg shouted at Niobe, 'It's a massacre.'

'Not yet, not yet—'

'It soon bloody will be. We have to go back – we have to help.'

'That's what they want you to do. I've a hunch as to what Cosmo is up to, and your father too. Just keep going.'

A group of seven or eight slithy toves were only a hundred yards below them and closing fast. Arms swinging from side to side, they clambered up, often on all fours, baying like hounds on the scent. Rocks lacerated their bare feet and legs, but a frenzied hatred for ordinary humans drove them on.

'They're catching them,' cried Cosmo, cheering like a spoiled child at every falling victim.

'But not for much longer, if your fresh air experiments are accurate,' said Lady Vane quietly as she consulted a gold watch on a chain. 'Maybe my men will have to finish them off.'

Cosmo watched, his joy at double-crossing Lord Sine tempered by the thought that his strategy might not succeed in killing off all the villagers. He could not believe that Spire had had the guile to order them to flee to the high ground. So far, the majority still survived, stretched far and wide over the mountain.

Niobe and Fogg knew they would be caught some way from Spire's retreat, so they stopped and started hurling rocks at their pursuers, fighting side by side, determined to go down together – until a triple miracle intervened.

Fogg's golden beetle made an appearance, buzzing at the eyes of the toves, and Hector joined it, diving in from nowhere and knocking the nearest to the ground.

Then came the coup de grâce.

'Look!' cried Niobe.

It could not have been the beetle's work, but the toves were staggering back, clasping their throats instead of protecting their eyes. Their baying gave way to a strangled, gurgling noise – and the same phenomenon was repeating itself all over the hillside.

The mutants were recoiling and falling, lying still where they lay.

'Clean air!' Niobe hugged Fogg. 'It's the clean air – they were bred to survive the murk. Spire sent us up here to stretch them, to make them breathe deep. Bloody brilliant.'

Fogg remembered the conversation between Cosmo and Piety in the weavers' room. Cosmo must have been testing the toves' endurance, planning for them to do the dirty work by killing the villagers, only to die themselves, leaving him in sole command of Paradise.

He hesitated. Was Lord Sine truly that gullible?

'Do we stay, or get back down and reoccupy the village?'

Niobe pointed at the *Ceres*. 'Look up at the deck. Lady Vane has soldiers, and they look heavily armed.'

Lady Vane was reassuring her son. 'They'll be easy pickings now. They've no weapons, they've lost a fair number and we have the village. They can starve on the mountainside if they want. Superior force always wins.'

'He's still standing,' observed Cosmo, pointing at the Mad Hatter, whose unruffled pose had an ominous look. *All according to plan*, it implied.

'Shit,' cried Cosmo suddenly. 'Telescope!' he yelled.

Out of the submersible's hatch climbed four giant men. They were naked, their skin glowing like brass, without visible sexual organs, but festooned with weapons.

A second hatch opened and a huge ballista emerged, manned by normal-sized men and women.

It looked like Lord Sine had out-thought Cosmo Vane.

'Head for the murk!' screamed Lady Vane.

'And don't fly straight,' cried Cosmo.

Spire had taken the most inaccessible route across the bay and now he descended, zigzagging all the way, to the cairn on the beach. He hurriedly removed the stones and picked up the small but heavy box beneath. There had been several, kept to clear rocks blocking the harbour, but only this one remained after the last eruption before the Fall. He had attached floats to the sides to ensure it would not drag him down.

He carried the box to the sea, floated it, and waded in.

There was a remnant of the old undersea glacier remaining on this side of the bay. Beneath its icy shelf lay a magma chamber. Any encounter between seawater and magma at two thousand degrees Fahrenheit would cause an explosion, and a lethal outburst of steam at surface level. However, the chamber was small, and the inhabitants should now be high enough up the mountainside to survive. Any risk was surely better than torture and death under Cosmo's rule, or experimentation in Lord Sine's laboratories.

As the sea reached his neck, he could see the *Aeolus* heading for the murk, and the *Ceres* attempting to escape in a different direction. He grimaced as a huge bolt from the ballista narrowly missed the hull of the *Ceres*. He had been fearful of killing his lover and son, while equally fearing the consequences of their survival. Now he would let Fate decide. His remaining anxiety had been for the penguins, but Lord Sine's ugly craft had mercifully driven them well out to sea.

His beloved *Fram* lumbered over the bay. Clearly an amateur was at the helm.

He swam on his back, which was slow work with such a heavy cargo in tow. Although he was still some distance from the submersible, he could see the monolithic constructs on the hull. He knew Lord Sine of old: he was not a man who was easily taken in.

He armed the device, set the timer and removed the floats. Lord Sine might have planned one move deeper than Cosmo, but even he had overlooked the ultimate surprise move: self-sacrifice.

Spire did not attempt to make it back to shore. He had no chance. Instead, he bathed his face in the sun. *You earn your rewards and you pay for your sins, and posterity better remembers explorers who die in their prime.*

Morag looked back from the stern of the *Aeolus*. Through the Long Eye, she watched the unfolding tragedy as if in a theatre. Her father, swimming on his back, was towing a crate out to sea. Everything fell into place: his silence during Cosmo's address, his pause by the cairn the previous evening, his instructions to keep to high ground.

She handed Benedict the Long Eye and looked away. 'I'll man the craft,' she said. Tears ran down her cheeks as she grappled with the ropes. She did not want or need to see. Imagining was bad enough.

The explosion had a primal violence. A huge plume of orange fire rose from the bay, which was bubbling and steaming like a kettle on the boil. Lord Sine's submersible burst into flames and his myrmidons melted.

The *Fram*, under the inexpert control of Lady Vane's servant, lurched sideways under the blast and careered into the mountainside.

Carlo had watched Spire's journey. As a geologist, he knew what he was planning. His people barely needed telling, but he gestured up the slopes anyway. They would all have to sit this out.

He clasped his hands, bowed his head and crossed himself. His friend had chosen martyrdom over shame.

*

Fogg and Niobe clambered into Spire's retreat in a state of shock.

With laborious slowness, Fogg tapped out a message on the Morse machine, an odd mix of brevity and sadness.

At Deception Island. Vane takeover and attack by Sine foiled by Spire at cost of his life. Aeolus flies on. Vanes escape too – probably. Hector alive and well.

By the time he had finished, Niobe had vanished. He looked outside. The fiery plume had disappeared, but the bay lay shrouded in steam. The cries of survivors echoed across the mountainside.

He went back inside and explored the deeper recesses of the cave. A well-hidden trapdoor had been opened in the floor. A wooden ladder ran down into the dark. Far below, he could make out a faint glow. Spire had said his retreat held a few secrets.

Here we go again, he said to himself as he followed a sequence of ladders, each resting on a shelf of rock like a landing. They ended in a huge cavern.

Niobe stood stock-still, the globe-light hovering above her head.

He walked over and kissed her on the cheek.

'Tantalum,' she whispered. 'Tons of it.'

V

SIGNING OFF

I

The Burial Party

Lord Sine peered through the visor of his chitin suit at the old-fashioned harvester closing in on what remained of the fortified coffer, which had somehow survived the murk. The claw drove into the ground and lifted the wreckage with difficulty. Tendrils from the box had spread deep into the ground, but they did not push resistance to the point of self-injury. *Arbor spirantia* abruptly released its grip as the harvester's mechanical claw growled under the strain. It was the action of a sentient, intelligent organism. The coffer appeared to suck in the murk as it rose, reducing it to mere ribbons of vapour.

Lord Sine's communicator crackled into life. 'Perhaps we could make use of it,' suggested Syphax. 'It appears to feed on toxicity.'

Gilbert Spire!

Lord Sine prayed that the Hatter would bring him back from Deception Island to explain his creation. Spire the outlier had refused to work on Lord Sine's human models, dabbling in Nature instead. During his time at Genrich, he had stumbled on an aborted project of the first Lord Sine's. The origins were obscure, but the idea had been sound enough. Old-world trees fashioned wood from carbon dioxide, releasing oxygen in the process – so why not fashion a tree to process the murk? For reasons unknown, Lord Sine's father, whose research knew few frontiers, scientific or moral, had abandoned it.

At the time of his exile, Spire had left behind – in a high-security steel box – a tiny organism, no bigger than a pea, labelled *Arbor Spirantia* (seed 1), with his own warning note to leave well alone.

'It feeds on *everything*,' replied Lord Sine. 'Get a craft and take it as far away from here as you can, bury it deep and seal it in with rubble. Deprive it of air.'

Lord Sine watched the harvester moving ponderously away on what he trusted would be a long journey. He dismissed the thought that study might be preferable to banishment. What he could not control, he must destroy. It was that simple.

2

Of Cards and Books

Benedict wrestled over whether to speak or not. For the lack of any real-life guidance, he consulted the literature in his databank: in some books, victims of grief never stopped talking; in others, they endured agonised silence. He decided it was Morag's decision to make.

They drifted for two days with barely a word between them. Morag wore a grim expression. He slept alone in the second cabin.

Morag could not find closure. She felt cheated by her father's death. She had not seen him for decades, only for him to choose the path of self-sacrifice just as their reunion was blossoming into a healing process. Worse, he had kept this choice to himself. She should have challenged him during their final walk on the beach when, kneeling by the cairn, he had reached a resolution. Had he known then that Lady Vane would betray him? Had that been part of his reasoning?

Release came on the third morning, from an unexpected source. For lack of anything else to do, she checked the hidden device in the wheelhouse where they had entered the directions for Deception Island. A scroll of paper had been taped to the glass. Her father's distinctive handwriting delivered a final message:

Show me the edge of the wind,
Where the sky's an open road
And the angels who have sinned
May rise to lighten their load.

Find me the eye of the storm,
Where the stillness hangs like dew
Where past deeds do not inform,
And we dream of pastures new.

Her questions dissolved in the face of this simplest of answers. He had needed atonement and release. A gesture would not have sufficed, and he had devised the only possible winning strategy. They would never have defeated Lord Sine's new breed in ordinary combat. He had not sought her advice, because that might have weakened his resolve. He had left the fate of his son and his lover to the whims of chance.

He had played a perfect last hand.

She wiped her eyes on her sleeve and went down on deck, determined to be her usual forthright self. She would carry her grief privately, just as her father had instructed Fogg.

'Fogg went through this,' she said to herself.

Benedict sensed the change and took the plunge. *Be positive.* 'Your father would not have left us rudderless like this.'

Morag gestured to the craft. 'She's in one of her moods. She won't accept directions. She won't go back to Winterdorf, or to Paradise. She won't go bloody *anywhere*. We're going to sit here until the Rearranger runs out or old age takes us.'

'It's unlike you to give up.'

'I'm not giving up, I'm being practical,' she snapped.

Benedict put on his fictional cape and deerstalker before rummaging through the tangled narratives he had carefully memorised. 'There were two books,' he said.

'What bloody books?'

'The ones your father borrowed from Oblivious Potts and never returned. They were in his retreat, remember? Arensen on *Glaciers* and . . .'

Morag was engaged, but her mind had lost its sharpness. 'Remind me.'

'Cuttle on *Arbor Spirantia*.'

'The breathing tree. So . . . ?' She paused. *A pun on Spire?*

'I think it indicates a place, or an object which tells of a place, just as Arensen's book points to glaciers and Deception Island,' suggested Benedict.

'A place with no directions isn't much use.'

Benedict gave her a very odd look.

'Benedict, what are you thinking?'

'Er . . .'

'Come on, you can't look at me like that and not say.'

Benedict could not dissemble. He did not know how to. 'I was remembering how the great Dr Watson brought out the best in the great detective.'

'Benedict, do you have any idea how fucking *patronising* that is?'

'One is abnormal and a loner, the other normal and gregarious. Together they *spark*.'

'Normal! Thanks a bunch.'

Benedict looked puzzled. Wasn't 'normal' a compliment?

Morag shook her head and grinned. 'So, Sherlock, what's the solution?'

'An antique trumpet brought us to Deception Island,' he prompted.

Morag sifted the past for answers. On that fateful last day in the Museum Dome, Fogg's Rearranger had conjured a virtual trumpet, a vital clue, as later events had shown. Her Rearranger had conjured playing cards, ten of them, equally divided into two hands of five. Did that matter too?

An image flashed into her head: Paul Cézanne's *Card Players*. Fogg had droned on about Cézanne's three versions of the same theme, although the Museum had only one. Two peasants in contrasting hats, jackets and trousers face each other across a table. The one on the left, his cards visible, holds a hand of . . . *five*.

Cézanne had painted them in his studio, and she had been there with him. That painting had been one of her favourites.

'Give me five minutes,' she said.

Morag went to her cabin, found the momenticon in her jar of favourites and swallowed it.

The sitters were there, just as before, the one on the left drawing on his white clay pipe as he studied the deal. The artist looked intently at his subjects as he painted. They were his friends. He knew them beneath the skin too.

She sidled up behind the pipe-smoker. The directions had been neatly inscribed in pencil in her father's hand on the three of diamonds.

She returned on deck and called Benedict to the wheelhouse, where the lever had freed up once more. She entered the bearings.

Aeolus banked to starboard in acknowledgement of an order recognised and accepted.

'Onwards and upwards,' she said.

The story will conclude in

SIMUL

Acknowledgements

First and foremost, I thank Jo Fletcher for believing in a plot, which, when first outlined in a bar at St Pancras Station, must have sounded preposterous. Her guidance and support have been invaluable ever since, as has the encouragement of my agent, Ed Wilson.

My eldest and youngest children provided penetrating insights at an early stage when I was struggling to fix the parameters of this new world. I raise a glass too to Sharona Selby, the proof-reader with a third eye for any plot detail which is slightly out of true. She would make a good detective. And I must also thank Nicola Howell Hawley for her illustrations, including the splendid map which adorns the endpapers. My outline idea for the cover has been brilliantly brought to detailed life by Leo Nickolls in a way which far exceeds my expectations.

Last, but in truth, first, my thanks to Ros for everything, and not least putting up with a man who scribbles in his spare time. Gratitude is too slight a word.

TELEFON
BAY

PORT FOSTER

mount
achala

FUMAROLE
BAY

mount
kinkwood